PLANET PORTUM

RETICERE SERIES BOOK TWO

LAUREN LOGAN

CONTENTS

PLANET PORTUM

RETICERE SERIES - BOOK TWO

PLANET PORTUM

LAUREN LOGAN

Cover Art by Zack Simpson
@Zachariah.C.Sampson

COPYRIGHT

Artwork: Zack Simpson Instagram @Zachariah.C.Sampson
Front Cover Design: Allen Wahlström Instagram @Bafacoach.W
www.asenzathletic.myportfolio.com
Editor: Christine Pearcey Chrispearcey@hotmail.com
Translation: Amanda Fox

For those who hurt.

CONTENT WARNING

Trigger and content warnings for Planet Portum are listed on www.authorlaurenlogan.com.

Planet Portum is strictly for mature readers of 18+.

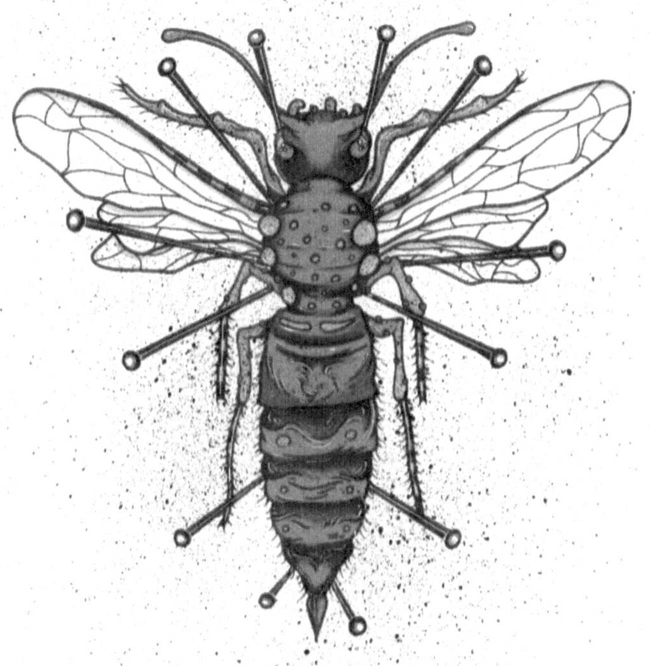

PROLOGUE

"*Tune certum ea est mortuua? Ambae mortui sunt?*" Are you sure she is dead? Both are dead? she asked. There was a short pause before the person on the other end of the phone responded. The female with greying, blonde hair continued, "*Eōrum favcium occidit? Vidisne accidit? Agnosco, non habear pradeicit eventum.*" He cut their throats? Did you see it happen? I must admit, I could not have predicted that outcome, she said into her communicator before hanging up.

She set the sleek, grey metal communication device down on her long, gleaming glass desk with a soft ting that echoed through her glass office. She hated the old Emperor's office and never once set foot in it when visiting. That was before she had her glass office built. Everything about her was based on transparency, like the light of a bright star.

She peered up and through her glass ceiling at the distant star whose gases were slowly being pulled toward the black hole. The teardrop shape would stretch to a tendril of gases until, eventually, it would become a string of single atoms and be devoured by the black hole. She hoped one of her children would see it in their lifetime.

Outside of her window, the camps for additional soldiers were in the process of being erected, and faint construction sounds permeated her office. She walked over and slammed the window shade shut, blocking out the expanse of red-toned land outside. She wondered if obnoxious noises would ever stop enraging her.

She swirled the amber liquor in her glass and said to herself, "*Ille multo extrahēns puellam eam, eam mulierculam bellam, Ariel.*" So much for extracting that girl, that pretty young woman, Ariel. The poor little human female didn't have a chance against those ruthless insects.

She had tried to pull her out of that awful forest. The best field team lost three quality recon people to those damn carnivorous jade trees. After the one failed attempt to pull the woman out, she refused to send more soldiers. She wasn't sending anyone back in there again.

Even if it was for a brilliant, young, human woman.

It was hard when she learned that the olive-skinned pest had tracked the young woman down and had his way with her, against her will. He repeated his sexual crimes several times before him and the woman's ultimate demise at the hands of that other red brute.

Those primitive villagers finally got the message and sent that red bug off to the jade woods to kill the woman and that olive monster. The retrieval teams had taken a fourth of the people from the village before the residents figured it out.

Most of those that were removed were still being held under the northern base, only because she didn't have any buyers yet. It was a good thing that they didn't eat much and could survive in a cell alone for years at a time. Only something with low intelligence, like a roach, could withstand such treatment and then, post confinement, function in a conventional manner.

They made such perfect servants, and she never had to worry about them saying anything because none of them had enough brains to speak. She had giant, colorful parrots on her ship that could communicate better than these lowly creatures. With their level of intellect, it amazed her that they could even be trained to be servants at all.

She refocused her thoughts on the young, human woman. Finally! A human who had intelligence.

She always hated that slimy green one with black hair, and she was glad he was dead.

How had the pretty young woman ended up in the jade woods all the way from one of their sacred planets? It had been easy to detect a signal from the tablet she dropped and locate where she was from.

They needed to send a ship to visit the woman's origin planet soon and perform a progress check on the populations there. If this human species was close to discovering a space propulsion method, she would have to send the first-contact team to find out more information.

The last time this happened, the Emperor waited too long. The species they were tracking were on the way to the slave planet, Sclavus Six, before they were intercepted. If that group, the Genil, had landed there, the galactic legion would have had to silence all of them. The Empire officially taught cadets that the Genil had landed on Novum Donum, which was much further away from their home planet and locked by a several light years-round pocket of gas.

It would have been a shame to lose so many brilliant beings. Some of them were her ancestors. The Genil had all been assimilated into her own culture years ago when the ecosystem on Novum Donum began to fail.

She blinked away those thoughts and refocused on the current task of planning soldiers' death benefits for all the lost recruits. There would be losses in the thousands for the legions.

Neither she nor her predecessors would ever admit it, but silence was the costliest expense for the Empire.

If her first plan doesn't work, she will have to take more drastic measures. Thankfully, a thousand more soldiers had just been relocated to Sclavus Three and a thousand more to Sclavus Six. This means that the situation here would be resolved soon, and she wouldn't receive any more calls about random beings showing up out of thin air.

Thank the Gods that it wasn't someone from that pesky shipwreck a few years ago. She stamped them out with one last air raid a little over two years ago. She still has no idea how those damn rebels found their way to this planet, Sclavus Three, The United Trusts and Colonies (UTC) most protected secret. She wasn't letting anything near this planet. This planet held information that could damage their diamond-strong hold over all the space-faring planets in the galaxy - information that could hold a prism up to the clear light that emitted from her Empire of transparency.

With so much happening elsewhere, she was ready to get on her way. There was discord brewing within the UTC, and she needed to wash it out. It was only a matter of time before another revolt began building steam. She was going to hit it harder than ever this time.

At her age? She couldn't tolerate any question of her authority, and if she needed to make her position bright and clear once again, that's what she would do. If that required painting the streets of the withered planets with all the colors of their people's blood, then so be it.

The base operations commander entered and said, *"Imperatrix, navis principalis est exspectāns. Locī ab meliorem includus erit ad rationem navigationem."* Empress, the imperial ship is ready and waiting. Coordinates to Melior have been locked into the navigation system.

"Gratias tibi, Dux Dolior." Thank you, Commander Dolion. She stopped before walking out of the luxurious office and without turning round said, *"Licet ut habebam barbarī calceōs sed aliquid ultra? Capetē. Pauca monumenta hoc occasio, Dux."* Let the barbarians have shoes, but anything further? Take them. Only a few souvenirs this time, Commander.

1

Rising from the soft, damp ground, Oz and Jael looked around and found the buckets of clean water that August had hidden under the trees for them. They each wet a fresh cloth to clean the ink and hardened tree sap off their chest and necks.

The blue and red octopus ink that Oz had saved turned out to be quite useful as faux blood for their ruse. Jael had molded and fashioned the tree sap around their necks and set it with a blazing, red hot jade-wood stick. She had painstakingly created a pouch inside for the ink so that when August slit their throats, it would pour out like blood and look realistic on the satellites' images.

Jael hoped her simple plan with the tree sap and ink worked. It looked genuine enough that in person, she could see the pain in August's eyes as he drew the knife across her neck. It was important he had the memories in case the elders were waiting for him at the edge of the village. August had warned that they may want proof.

Only a few intervals of sleep after August arrived, she was lying on the deck during a clear night, and she noticed the tiny flash of light in the sky. After spotting a few more, the source was unmistakable.

They were seeing the signature flashes of satellites as light bounced off them. Whoever was taking their people was watching from above.

With August involved in their brainstorming, they formed a plan to, hopefully, find out who their enemy was and where they were taking their people. At the same time, they planned to quietly build a resistance under their enemy's watchful eyes and ears.

Jael and Oz would head as far north on the peninsula as they could. They would camp out and watch until they discovered who the enemy was and possibly even find out how their people were being taken.

Meanwhile, August would go to the village and spread language and progress like a virus to his people, who had been oppressed by fear for millennia.

In preparation for their journey, the three of them spent several weeks making tactical clothing from the clothes that August had brought with him. He had multiple sets of dark, cedar-colored silk cloth and bed rolls. They painted thin layers of tree sap onto the dark cloth and added a protective board to the other side to prevent bleeding. They then hardened it with heat. Once they finished the stiffening process, they constructed pants. Even the starched jeans of the cowboys in Texas weren't as stiff as the sets of pants they had made, Jael thought.

They needed to break in each pair of pants, which was quite humorous, but necessary. According to Jael, Oz looked like a cornered cat as he forced his legs into his pants. He disagreed, even though he had never seen a cat before.

Jael had to ram a stick down into her pants in order to pull her the legs far enough apart to put them on. They weren't sure how August got his pair on, but it sounded like he was fighting a beast in the living room.

Eventually, they broke in every pair enough to be wearable, then they folded and packed them all away.

Oz sewed multiple pockets and added little wooden buttons to keep the small flaps closed. He reinforced the top waistband to hold up the utility belts that August had designed. After breaking in the pants, they discovered a need for reinforced fabric in the knees, so Oz added more layers.

The boots had been Jael's idea, and Oz designed the soles. They seemed to be working perfectly. They had each molded the inside layer to their feet, and then Oz sewed them together with thick layers of sap-stiffened silk. He dipped the bottoms of the boots into sap and slowly made tread by repeatedly pressing them to a heated mold until he had the shape he wanted.

Jael was entranced as she watched Oz work to create their finely crafted boots. He braided long strips of silk for laces, then dipped and rolled them by the hearth to harden them.

The laces were a little stiff, but besides that, the boots looked like they came from a sporting goods catalog, right down to the stitching. They were incredibly comfortable, and the movement they allowed was better than she had ever experienced from boots on Earth. Jael thought back to the pretentious sporting goods store in her home town and wondered if they were still trying to send her the magazine that she didn't want. She didn't miss her life on Earth much.

Once she finished dressing in the tactical clothes from her pack, Jael turned and had to cover her mouth to keep from making a sound. Oz was standing behind her, wearing a fitted, dark cedar-brown, long-sleeved shirt tucked into dark brown tactical pants, and had already put on his lace-up boots.

The definition of his chest and shoulders filled out his shirt like a glove. His pants and boots gave him a modern look that she hadn't thought she would ever see on him. Except for his olive skin and tail, she bet he would fit right in on the cover of those sporting goods' magazines. His hair had grown almost three inches since the tree had eaten him and was just long enough to sweep in front of his eyes. He was quite literally the hottest thing she had ever seen, and she was having a difficult time remaining silent. He gave her a shit-eating grin before he leaned over into his pack to grab his belt.

The first part of the plan was to trek through the deadly woods and cross over into what Oz and August decided to refer to as, the wilds. The wilds were the only place that was worse than the woods where they had made their home --the home and life they would have to leave for a long while, maybe permanently.

Doing her best to hold back the emotions brought up by these thoughts, Jael knew deep down her home would always be with Oz. Wherever he was, she would also be.

After crossing the wilds, they had to pass through the misty peninsula. They weren't sure what would come next. Oz's people had never ventured that far north, and they didn't dare cross into the water. According to him, there were octopi and other creatures the size of high-rise buildings lurking in the deeper waters.

During one of their long talks, he shared a memory with her about an enormous octopus that had landed on his treehouse during a tidal wave. She nearly vomited from the intensity of the memory. He had been slung around like a toy while he sliced at the snapping creature with his claws.

After a long battle of wills, the octopus finally relented and dropped him in the water, allowing him the chance to swim up and crawl inside the treehouse from underneath. He had to wait days for the octopus to finally die so he could begin the grotesque dissection and removal process.

The octopus supplied him with enough black ink to fill a bucket, so he considered it a win. He obtained red and blue inks from much smaller octopi after they found themselves washed up on his deck during the nearly thirty tidal waves he had endured in his treehouse.

Oz and Jael would remain as silent and unseen as possible so the satellites, hopefully, wouldn't catch sight of them, and they could maintain the element of surprise. They knew the satellites had something to do with how these unknown beings were stealing Oz's. There wasn't any other way the abductors would know who to take.

They also suspected the enemy had to be overpowering their people using some type of chemical or technological device. Whatever it was could render a large being unconscious quickly enough to not to be able to fight back.

The idea quickly formed that Oz would share the knowledge that Jael had passed on to him with August. August would then spread the gift to the people of the village. Oz only passed on the academic knowledge and filtered out any of Jael's personal thoughts or information. He wanted to be respectful of her privacy, and he believed her thoughts should remain her own. However, he did include those kinky, alien novels. He loved to tease Jael about them.

He thoroughly enjoyed beginning their mind connections by reading some of the spicier passages to her. Jael's skin would heat, and she became visibly bothered, which he loved to see regularly.

Regarding the mission, Oz suspected that August would run into some opposition and hoped his friend could pull off such a feat of political persuasion. August was going to have to mobilize their people without setting off a warning that they were doing anything out of the ordinary. Some of the elderly in the village were known for being whistle-blowers and exposing anything that could get someone taken.

Not surprisingly, the villagers had a public vote naming August as the one to hunt down Oz. August never had any intention of killing him and had always planned to fake his death, but he would need proof he did what was required.

It was partially August's father's idea to fake Oz's death. In distress, he followed August into the woods and acted out the scene.

August had always been close to his father, but after this display of compassion for his old friend Oz, August decided that his father was also Oz's. August knew his father thought the same.

This was something Oz took to heart.

They needed it to look like August succeeded in killing Jael and Oz for causing the disappearances of the villagers. And then? He would just return to the village for life as usual, while secretly beginning to form a resistance.

The plan was simple, but both parts were equally a long shot. Through the odds, they all maintained hope they could give their enemy a face and name. Eventually, they hoped they would be able to liberate their people from a millennium of forced silence.

Once Jael's knowledge had been passed to August, they quickly discovered that all of Oz's people were likely as brilliant as Oz. August adapted to the new language within moments of Oz giving it to him. The look on August's face as the knowledge sunk in, and he was able to begin processing was something Jael and Oz would never forget.

It was truly a gift to watch.

Once August was speaking, he connected with Jael and made it clear to her that Oz had always been exceptionally creative. August expressed that he was confident that if anyone could find out who was stealing their people, it was Oz.

That conversation with August had been a significant test of her mental shields. She and Oz had, thankfully, been practicing. She didn't tell August, but his voice in the connection sounded like a small child. It had taken everything within her not to laugh.

As Jael laced up her boots and slid on her belt, she thought about what an experience it had been watching Oz learn and grow his mind.

With every completed project or goal, Jael became more enamored with his brilliant mind. She could sit and listen to him speak about the scientific knowledge he had learned from her memories for hours. She remembered pieces of what he spoke about from college, but he explained things in such a simple way that it was astounding.

Jael especially loved Oz's explanations of mental conditions and his views on genetically linked diseases. He believed that environmental triggers could cause disease to develop, but your own set of genetics likely dictated your specific set of symptoms.

He considered that profound mental health differences between beings might be thought of in a similar way - maybe traumatic stressors could easily cause a plethora of predisposed mental health conditions depending on each individual's genes. Jael had never taken a psychology class and had no idea if he was correct or not, but it all sounded logical.

Oz was exceptionally kind to Jael about her personal struggles and made sure she understood she wasn't alone. He had plenty of his own struggles, not just being alone for all those years or all the people he had lost. He always explained it to her the same way. He had done something so wrong to her that he still struggled to cope with it. He wouldn't elaborate much, but she understood.

His trauma was her screams.

To give her what she wanted.

For him to speak.

But Jael couldn't accept that he was wrong because nothing about that felt right. The moment she heard his voice in her head, every bit of fear over what he did to get them to that point was erased. She couldn't have been more delighted when she finally heard him speak to her. What he had done was worth it. Sure, she had been more than terrified, but he had a damn good reason, and she wouldn't change it for the world.

She finally got what she had always wanted from him.

Although she could hear his voice in her mind, Jael still wanted to hear Oz's voice aloud, and this mission might lead to just that. As he quietly lifted his pack onto his back, he slid his eyes to Jael and grinned when she looked up after tying her boots. He helped her to her feet then lifted the pack. Once she had it on her back, he helped her adjust its straps to fit her petite frame. He handed her one of the filled water sacks and slipped his onto his belt while she did the same with hers.

Once they finished preparing, they both took one last look back at their home then quietly turned to head north.

2

The delicious scent of the flatbread on the breeze was enough to make August keep walking even though he was mere yards from Mercy's vine-riddled old house. The house was easily five to six hundred Earth years old, one of the first ever built in this village.

He had to resist the strong urge to pass by her quaint little house and knock on the neighbor's door and ask for a fresh flatbread. He was starving for an authentic meal.

He had no idea how Oz had lived off only fruit and nuts all this time. He reigned in his raging appetite and approached her door. Just as he lifted his hand to knock, she swung the door open, and with a yelp, she slammed the door in fright. Dust, sticks, and leaves fell from her roof and landed all over him and the ground around her home. He raised an eyebrow as he listened. A creaking noise and a loud snap meant something had broken in the back of the house.

Once it dawned on her who stood outside, Mercy quickly reopened the wooden door with a smile and her golden eyes shining bright. Leaping out and onto him, she swung her arms around him, and he slowly slid his arms around her.

With his head resting on hers, he breathed in deeply. He had missed the delicate scent of roses in her hair. He had missed her long shiny brown hair and her golden tan skin. He had especially missed her goofy antics and was happy to see she was still her wild self.

In her excitement, Mercy pulled him inside and slammed the door, causing her tiny wooden home to shake. If he wasn't mistaken, she was bouncing, and he looked down to find that she was, in fact, bouncing on the tips of her toes.

Suddenly remembering why he'd had to go on his journey in the first place, she shot her hand up to connect with August and find out what happened.

Had he followed through and killed his best friend?

The worry marring her face reminded him of exactly why he was so happy to see her. She had the biggest heart of anyone he knew.

But no matter how happy he was to see her, the memories of Mazarin surfaced to remind him of what he had lost.

Who he had lost.

Guilt ate at him because he was still here, and she wasn't. He tried his best to hold back his feelings and act happy to see Mercy. But this thing with Mercy? He felt like it was all wrong.

Even after thousands of moons without his beautiful blue Mazarin.

Mazarin would have wanted him to move on, but he wasn't ready and couldn't even consider that yet.

Bringing August back to the present, Mercy squealed with delight when Rew popped her head around his shoulder. He leaned over and let the shiny black, long-haired tarantula down inside her home to explore, sending Mercy into a fit of flailing hands. Mercy gave Rew a sweet little pat as she passed by and received a small chirp of thanks from the spider.

Once Rew was headed toward the living room, Mercy was again looking into August's bright orange eyes. He reluctantly lifted his hand to hers, and their hands met between them.

After the connection was made, August shared memories of Oz and Jael. He began with the time they spent inside Oz's treehouse and then shared a few of Oz's memories of when he first found Jael. Mercy was shocked at seeing an alien in her first glimpse but expressed an incredible desire to know everything about Jael, the little brown, curly-haired alien Oz found in the woods.

August knew at that moment Mercy was ready to receive the gift.

He began grinning and motioned for her to sit down. She furrowed her brow but did as he requested. Clearly, she was confused about why he was so happy, especially after everything she believed he had had to do. August sent her feelings of joy as they slid against the wood walls and onto the floor together, their right hands facing each other.

After they were seated on the wood floor in her foyer, August passed Jael's knowledge on to Mercy through the connection and grinned as he watched her eyes light up with understanding. The information passed through, and she absorbed it right away, just as August had.

With her full lips, Mercy seemed to form a silent, "What?"

The imprint of language settled in, and the knowledge began crashing and exploding in her head like a wave slamming against the rocks of a shoreline. She released a soft gasp and gently pulled away from the connection as she sat back against the wall behind her. August continued to grin as she sat and processed the magnitude of the information he had given her.

He considered it a gift to be able to watch her bright golden eyes as her mind broke free from its brittle glass cage. Within moments, Mercy developed the ability to speak and process information with symbols instead of only images and abstract thoughts.

Diving into Jael's knowledge, Mercy took one of her long brown braids into her hand and began twirling it absently as she gathered her new thoughts. They sat in the small foyer for a long while before August rose to rummage through her kitchen, as he often did.

He reached a hand out for her, and her eyes moved slowly to meet his. She looked as though she had been through a mental hurricane as she took his hand and rose to follow him into her kitchen. He never had any food at his house and had come to rely on her for many things, such as dinner.

She grabbed his thick arm, and he turned his broad body carefully to look at her. He guessed she must have reached a point where she was ready to speak because she shot her hand up to connect.

Once connected, she said into his mind, "This is the most profound gift anyone has ever given to me. How can I ever repay you?"

A smile spread across his face, and he chuckled as he replied, "I hope you don't mind. I named you Mercy. Jael named me August, and I thought it was fitting. She said where she lived on Earth, August was in the summer and that the sweltering month in Texas was my type of red, whatever that means."

Overwhelmed with emotion at her own name, she said, "I love it. I am honored to have such a beautiful name. And I think August suits you perfectly. So, Oz found an alien woman in the jade woods?"

"He showed me the same thing I showed you. Other than that, Oz only sent me her knowledge and was guarded and careful not to reveal much about her. He explained that one day, after we find out who is stealing our people, we will be able to all openly speak. We can ask Jael then. Can you imagine? Speaking like they do on Jael's world? Can you imagine how much our people could accomplish with this information? And our ability to process it all so quickly?" August asked intently.

She answered, "Is that the plan then? They will track down the enemy and we will spread knowledge?"

He grinned as he said into Mercy's mind, "Not quite. Our job is much more fun than that. Oz and I talked about the caves and how we could make a soundproof place there, a base." He continued, "You and I get to go lava tube mapping. I decided on the way here that afterward we must find out if any of the houses in town are located in the right place to possibly dig an entry point. It might be a long shot but it's worth looking into.

"At the same time, we need to be rounding up friends that we know will be receptive to the gift and the plan. The older villagers will think we're committing blasphemy and try to have our throats slit in the streets, so we need to keep things generally quiet until we hear from Oz and Jael."

Mercy's mouth gaped open and she replied, "Are they going to the north to the rumored peninsula? It could take a thousand moons or more for them to return. We must do all of this carefully, so the satellites circling above won't see us, right?" She continued, "But what if we block the cave opening with something? Do you think we could speak out loud if we made sure it was sealed? If we could speak out loud, we could progress a small group of us from a basic starter civilization to technologically advanced in a few hundred moons. I know we have massive veins of metallic ores lining all the lava tubes and caverns. Jael has basic knowledge of so many fields. I know we could expand on what she knows with the right tools, especially her kind's apparel."

Feeling her exhilaration, August chuckled and said into her mind, "You are raising my heart rate with your excitement. I think one of the metals you're imagining is copper. I think it blocks electromagnetic waves or something like that."

She laughed and broke the connection before throwing her arms around him. She rose to her toes and kissed him on the cheek when she passed by and then tossed him a flatbread before she headed to the hearth to heat a bucket of water.

He looked back at her and grinned as it occurred to him that she needed indoor plumbing. After one hot shower at Oz's treehouse, he knew that he needed to find time to build one for Mercy's house.

As if she somehow knew he was thinking about her, Mercy slid her eyes over to him. He laughed at her wanting grin and the swing of her hips at him. After he rested, he knew he would be heading out to the woods to get started on her new heated shower.

August tried not to feel guilty as she beamed and headed

to her room. They had everything except true intimacy. August still loved Mazarin, and Mercy would never pressure him into moving on. He didn't know how far she would go to seduce him -- probably pretty far -- but she would never make him feel obligated to do anything. He loved that about her. Mercy was patient and understanding beyond anything he could ever be.

It had been thousands of moons, and he still held on to Mazarin, but not in the hope of seeing her again. It was because once he crossed that line with Mercy, Mazarin would truly be gone. Mercy would likely wait as long as August needed, but as time passed, she began to seem discouraged.

August hoped this gift of knowledge, and his gift of Rew, would appease her long enough for him to figure out what to do with her. He wanted her more than anything, but it felt too soon.

He started wondering when Oz and Jael would return. Maybe once their enemy had a face and a name, he might be able to come to terms with Mazarin's disappearance. She was the first to go from the village in a long while. Usually, people in intimate pairs were taken together or had significant others taken before the single people. Occasionally their young were taken but never before the age of ten.

Forty-five were missing after just two thousand moons, but none had gone missing since August left the village to travel to kill Oz.

When Mercy grabbed his bag and started on his clothes, he released a breath of relief. He had been dreading it. The rain had made the trip muddy, and some of the clothes were rolled up with mud splatter still caked on them. He watched her intently as she pulled his dirty clothes out of his bag and sorted everything. She always insisted on doing his washing because she knew he was careless with it. He didn't care nearly as much about his appearance as she seemed to.

Since Oz was sent away, August had spent most of his time with Mercy and his other best friend. He needed to visit his friend's home right away and get him and his partner to pick names after giving them both this gift of knowledge. He wondered if "partner" was the term they would prefer. He needed to ask first.

That might be what he eventually wanted Mercy to be to him, his partner. It just seemed like a fitting way to explain their relationship. August tapped on the wall, and she popped her head out of her room, clearly undressed with the door open.

He suppressed a shudder as he signaled to her that he was leaving, and she excitedly waved before popping back into her room and shutting the door.

He took a deep breath and turned to leave, stopping for a moment and looking back at her bedroom door, wishing he could force himself to go into her room. He knew she wanted him to, but he couldn't.

Not yet.

It wasn't fair to Mercy.

August left and walked down the stone path toward his own home. He wanted to bathe and get himself ready for his second stop since returning.

3

As Oz and Jael approached a clearing, Oz climbed halfway up a tree and plotted a course around the bare ground with patches of thick grass. While he was in the tree, she looked at all the flowers in the clearing.

There were some that were bright yellow and looked like trumpets with odd bulges at the base of the petals. Others were orange and reminded her of hibiscus flowers, but the pistons were enormous and had a large, round, pink dusty ball at the top. She noticed some vibrant red roses and thought about her neighbor's yard with the tiny half-dead roses under their window. She didn't think her old neighbor ever watered them.

Looking up, she wondered how long Oz would be in the tree. The clearing wasn't large enough to branch off, or so it seemed from her angle. They didn't want to be spotted by the circling satellites and had to stay out of sight until they reached the wilds. Once there, no one would be looking for anything, and they wouldn't have to be so cautious. That is what they hoped, anyway. All their guesses were blind, and Jael felt waves of anxiety rumble in her gut about their plan.

Sometimes Jael wondered what the hell she had gotten herself into, and she wished they could just go back home and hide. But something was calling out to her. Something said this was right and to keep going, no matter what.

She was beginning to believe his crazy idea that his people could be truly free one day.

Oz's people never came anywhere near the wilds because of the constant mist, not to mention the massive and cunning black and red-belly orb spiders. The spiders collected there because of the vast forests with calm seas and the abundant wildlife. Orb spiders usually didn't find their way into the jade woods because of the immature trees. Carnivorous plants didn't reach too far north, beyond the reach of the tidal wave. They remained within the boundary of the saline soils. The massive oak, pine, and pecan trees that surrounded the village and the wilds grew so fast that the jade trees didn't even get a chance to take root. The beastly spiders and scorpions had been hunted in the woods around the village until they were no longer found there.

The only place that the creatures thrived is the wilds, and that was between where she and Oz were now and the peninsula where they were headed.

Jael recalled the spiders Oz told her about. They looked like giant versions of a spider from Earth, called a black widow. He didn't need to tell her they were deadly, and she hoped they could avoid them, but he had given her an unsure look at that thought. She hated the idea of giant spiders.

This planet was beginning to seem prehistoric.

Peering around from his perch, Oz couldn't help but be

thankful that Jael was in much better shape now than she was a few months ago. They would be able to make it many miles before they would have to find a cave.

He was trying to hide his nervousness about stopping. Oz would need to muffle Jael's snoring somehow and was still unsure of how he was going to pull it off. He was not sure they would be able to remain covert with her loud gurgling and snoring. It had lessened over time, and she slept more peacefully with him every night, but he didn't think that was nearly enough.

He had secretly wanted to grasp her tongue and hold it out of her mouth while she slept to see if it freed her airway, but he had not been brave enough to try that yet.

He continued to wonder if the airway in her throat was constricted and if two rolled pieces of silk stuffed between her teeth would help. Wishing in the next moment that he had some sap to mold, he sighed with irritation that he didn't pack a small jar of the versatile substance.

She noticed his irritation and pumped her legs to catch up, then tapped him on his arm to get his attention. He stopped and looked at her expectantly, so she put her hands up to ask what was wrong. He pointed to a tree, then quickly mimicked the action of collecting sap.

Jael understood perfectly. He was just irritated he didn't bring a container for some tree sap. She thought for a moment and held her hand up before swinging her pack off her back. From it, she pulled a small, empty wood jar with a fitted lid.

Oz grinned and snatched the jar from her open hand then walked over to a tree while retrieving his knife. He slammed the knife into the tree and made a wedge for the sap to flow into the jar. Jael had no idea why he wanted some sap, but she was glad she had packed the empty wooden jar.

He walked over and handed her the filled jar, then kissed her deeply. Slipping his tongue past her teeth, he growled as he grabbed her hips. He gave her a sly smile and then slapped her rear before grabbing his pack.

They continued until all the moons had passed overhead, and she was beginning to tire. She spotted a rocky ledge and snapped her fingers to get his attention. He looked to where she pointed and nodded yes, grinning at her for the quick spotting. They approached and found a small opening. He nodded that the coast was clear after a quick sniff of the damp air for predators.

They quickly slipped through the opening and found the cavern to be enormous. He pulled out one of the jade tree sticks and held it between his knees as he struck it with his flint to light the silk wrapped end. Once he got it lit, he lifted the bright firelight into the misty air and illuminated a pathway to a deeper part of the cave.

There were stalagmites and stalactites everywhere, with massive crystals jutting from the ground. Water dripped and flowed somewhere in the cave, but they couldn't see any water other than that dribbling from the cave ceiling, creating the mystifying, coned mineral structures.

Leaning side to side to avoid face-planting into a crystal or one of the hundreds of stalagmites, Jael and Oz carefully traveled down a narrowing pathway of level dirt. They scaled down some giant crystals and rocks before entering a second large chamber.

After some searching, he finally found a dry, flat area where they could set up camp for her to sleep and him to get some rest. Unrolling their stuffed bed mat, he looked up when he noticed her stomach growling. He stopped and handed her some dried fruits and nuts.

Back at their treehouse, he had explained to her that he didn't need to consume nearly as much food as she did. He had stored so much recently because he had been eating when she did, but he hadn't at all needed it. After a lot of explaining, she finally understood that he could forgo eating for nearly a month and a half, and that stopped her protesting about it.

She just felt that watching him go over a month without eating would be difficult. His biology was vastly different from hers, and she had to learn as she went. He said if he continued to eat heavily, he would eventually put on weight. She would have to see that to believe it.

He would also be able to reduce his water intake to almost a quarter of his usual amount, saving much more for her during their travels. She didn't like that much either but was thankful when he always seemed to have a full water pouch for her.

Although she didn't like it, she conceded and ate without him.

After her meal, they lay down, and Oz wrapped his right arm around her and held up his palm to see if she would talk with him before she fell asleep. Still just as giddy about their ability to connect as she was in the beginning, she quickly wiggled around and held her palm up over her hip for him to connect with her.

Once the connection was made, Oz said into Jael's mind, "I need to make a mouthpiece for you to help with your snoring. I'm afraid I won't be able to muffle it any other way without waking you."

She looked up to him with her mouth agape and then

cocked her head to the side, replying, "Oh, Dr. Ozias, I also have an ache between my legs. Do you want to check that out for me too?"

He laughed and kissed her softly on her lips and whispered in her mind, "Why don't I take care of that ache first?"

She bit her lip as he broke their connection and began kissing her down the column of her neck, his short black hair brushing her jaw as he traveled down to her chest. He lifted her shirt and pulled up the new sports bra he made for her changing form. She had finally developed some healthy curves and he was in heaven with her body. He took a peak into his mouth and twirled his tongue as he began working on pulling down her pants, only tugging them to the middle of her thighs and then sliding her belt from her belt loops. Turning her on her side, he kissed softly down her right side to her bare hip. He then swung her legs up and took her hands, guiding them to hold her own calves. Taking the belt, he wrapped it around her forearms and legs, latching it through the buckle and pulling it tight.

Shuddering with need, Jael let out a soft squeak as Oz descended on her entrance with his mouth. Knowing she couldn't make a noise, she bit her tongue as he took her bud in between his teeth and rolled it back and forth while he flicked the tip with his tongue.

While he gripped her with one hand, he snaked his other hand over to her chest and rubbed a thumb over her peak, pulling her closer to bliss. His tail twitched behind him as if saying it wanted in on the action too. It uncurled and found its way to her entrance, and she let out a soft squeak when she felt it push inside. Her body shivered with the unexpected intrusion, and he leaned over and added his tongue into the mix, flicking her bud in a quick rhythm. As he slid his tail in and out, he gripped her hips, and her breath quickened when he spun the tip of his tongue around her most sensitive place.

Moments later, Jael trembled and then curled inward with her shattering release. Her bound arms and legs shook as he licked her feverishly until her waves slowed. He released the belt and then eased her legs down. He reached into his pack and pulled out a small cloth and wet it so he could clean her up.

Not caring in the slightest about cleaning herself, she quickly tossed the damp towel on her pack and didn't bother pulling her shirt down as she shoved him back onto the mat. Without pause, she began unbuckling his pants, causing a rough sigh to exhale from him. The heat in Oz's gaze was enough to set her off again as his length sprung free from his pants. She descended on him with her mouth and both hands, but after just a few passes, he'd had enough. Leaning his head back and clicking deep in his throat just twice, he grabbed Jael's hips and flipped her around in front of him. He quickly seated Jael at the end of his length and sunk himself deep within her. Leaning over on her, he grabbed her around her waist and kissed her shoulder as he pumped in and out.

Hitting that perfect place, she reached out to grab his hips behind her and rocked and shifted her hips as she remained fully seated on his length. He tightly gripped her hips as she moved on him and then matching her rhythm, they moved together. A bead of sweat rolled down Jael's back as she felt his hand at her bud, pressing as he thrust deep.

The building wave became unbearable, and he set his forehead against Jael's back as they both shattered together.

Leaning back with Oz as he sat up, Jael was out of breath as she unsuccessfully tried to roll her bra and shirt back down. Assisting her from the back, he helped finish pulling down her clothes as she rocked forward to pull herself off his length.

Finding the damp cloth, she cleaned herself and then passed it to Oz for him to do the same. He tossed the small material into the cave's darkness and then buckled his pants as she lay down to get some sleep. She was floating on a cloud of joy as her head lay on the soft covers.

Reaching over to tap her, he looked at her with his eyebrows raised, and she suddenly remembered the second thing they needed to do. Make her a mouthguard.

Taking her face in his hands, he studied her mouth and throat, then had her open her mouth while he moved her jaw. He seemed satisfied and raised his hand to ask for the small round jar from earlier. After fishing it out of her pack, she handed it to him and watched as he took some out and rolled it into a sticky ball.

He held the ball of sap over the flame to warm it then kneaded it until it was long and round. He tapped Jael on the edge of her jaw, asking her to open her mouth, and she complied. He set the sap on her bottom teeth and then pressed it down. She noticed he set her jaw forward slightly, and it felt like her airways were already clearer. After he was satisfied that he had a decent imprint, he carefully lifted it out of her mouth.

She wiped the spit from her chin and thought about how she and Oz had discussed the sap having many properties that were similar to silicone. He believed the jade trees evolved the sap's unique chemistry to protect the forest from burning during lightning storms.

Thinking about the lightning storms brought back memories of when he was temporarily deaf from the blasts of thunder. Brushing off the bad memory, she returned to thinking about the biology of the trees.

The jade trees took a hundred Earth years to reach their full height, so it would make sense that they would want to resist burning. The thick succulent leaves of the jade trees were filled with a sap that was corrosive during its immature stage, but when matured, displayed strikingly different properties.

Jael hoped August had made it through the jade woods and back to the village safely. They hoped August would be hard at work spreading her knowledge to his friends, and that he didn't run into too much resistance.

While Oz heated and set Jael's new mouthpiece, he thought about August showing him which friends remained in the village. He was happy to see one of their closest friends, a black-haired man with brown skin, had found a love interest that he recognized but didn't say much about. He made sure Jael got the impression he didn't want to talk about the man's companion, and she left that one alone. According to August, they were doing well, and he was happy about it.

Their close friend's new love interest was a man that had a brilliant blue color like Oz's sister, but his was darker blue rather than a brighter blue like her. No matter the shade, the color blue always made him think of his sister.

When Oz saw August's memories of the rest of his old friends and how they'd changed and grown, it brought bittersweet feelings. That missed time would be over once they finished the mission to find out who their enemy was.

He finished heating the mouthpiece and handed it to a yawning Jael. She quickly slipped it into her already open mouth and bit down. He was pleased with it, and she rolled over to fall asleep as he finished cleaning up their campsite.

Once he had cleaned up, he joined Jael on the mat, and within a few deep breaths, she was asleep. He watched and braced himself for the wretched rattling sound, but it never came. He threw his hands up and nearly woke her with his excitement. Pulling his hands back to avoid waking her, he noticed she was breathing normally and not snoring a bit.

He looked toward the sky and thanked the creator as he lay back and got comfortable on their bedding. He still had hundreds of books to read from her memories and couldn't wait to start on the research behind her EmDrive -- the device that brought her to his planet and to him.

He roughly knew how she was transported, but he wanted to understand how it worked before he arrived back in his village. If they were going to go up against highly advanced beings, Oz's people would need to level the playing field.

4

After bathing and dressing in clean clothes, August felt much more like himself. Since Mercy was so receptive to the knowledge, he hoped his best friend and his best friend's partner would be as well.

He was becoming annoyed with them for not having names, so he began calling his best friend Smarty Pants and the partner Mr. Picky. He would never tell them these silly nick names, so it didn't matter what he picked. Right?

He noticed the fragrant scent of roses on the breeze as he walked through the village, waving at several of his neighbors and friends of his mother. Their verdant yards and short, solid wood fences with foliage and vines spilling over made him jealous. His house didn't have anything growing in the yard. He had killed everything he tried to grow and eventually gave up.

Not all of his people had the same skills, he reminded himself.

He approached the door and nervously knocked, hoping they were home. Mr. Picky answered the door with no shirt on and plenty of his blue skin on display. He never had *all* his clothes on, not that anyone really minded. Clothes had always been somewhat optional for their people.

Mr. Picky motioned his arm in a half circle for August to come inside, then hugged August in a genuinely kind embrace, concerned about the task he was sent to complete. August pulled back and gave a wide grin to reassure him that all was well.

Just to be safe, August hadn't told anyone except his father about the plan to fake Oz's death.

Mr. Picky looked unsure but reached over and tapped the wall twice, causing Smarty Pants to emerge from the back. August grinned at his black-haired friend, and he held his hand up to connect. Smarty looked at him inquisitively, his light-tan eyes deeply focused. After the odd scrutinization, he slowly met August's hand with his own.

August passed his friend a few memories with just Oz in them, and Smarty smiled sadly. August knew to take it slow, because his friend was certainly the skeptic of the group.

When August felt like it was the right time, he transferred the memories from his time with Oz and the little alien woman. Smarty Pants' mouth dropped open, and his pale tan eyes went wide with shock. He shot his eyes to his blue-haired companion in surprise before sliding his big tan eyes back to August. August simply grinned and nodded his head, then signaled to his dumbfounded friend to sit down for the next part.

His friend smiled and gladly sat down on the wood floor before August transferred Jael's knowledge through their connection. This alien language was a gift that August was delighted to bestow upon his silenced people.

As the information rolled around in his mind, Mr.

Smarty Pants grinned at August, and through the connection, his first words were, "This is one hell of a gift."

August chuckled and said, "The name Jael chose for me is August. Pick a name, then give your partner this gift and have him pick one too."

August's friend contemplated for a moment and replied, "I like the name Jacob, and I guess partner is accurate. I will be delighted to share this knowledge with him. I am curious how this transfer of knowledge works. I assume we need to keep this a secret? I don't want to get my throat slit by some old woman while I'm trying to trade for avocados on the street."

"Yes, it's a secret. I think we should let the stubborn elders find out on their own after it's too late. We don't want it to get out to everyone yet. Mercy and I will search the lava tubes in the area and help make some plans for the next step, building a soundproof room where we can work. There are satellites watching from above. Jael said something about bugs being planted all over the town, but I'm still unsure what that means. We have lots of bugs, and I don't know how these planted bugs are any different. The unknown beings who steal our people are being sought out by Oz and Jael. They're putting a face to our enemy, and hopefully, they will return with valuable information. It could take them less than a thousand moons, and we cannot delay preparing. Will you help us?" August nearly pleaded into Jacob's mind.

Without hesitation, Jacob replied, "We will both do anything required. I don't need to ask my love to know he will feel the same. I'm not sure what he will do for the project besides distract me, but we'll see."

Chuckling, August said, "I think that's a you problem not a him problem."

"Yes, I think I prefer Jacob to Smarty Pants," Jacob said with his eyes narrowed.

Laughing, August's face heated with embarrassment. He must have accidentally sent him the nick names with the gift.

He ended their connection, and they both rose from the floor. Jacob smiled back at his curious blue-eyed partner as he led August to the front door. August walked toward the door, careful not to knock off the rack of drying herbs hanging in the hallway.

After he finished with his friends, August headed down the rock path to Mercy's house and knocked on her door. Beaming with excitement, she swung open her door with a pack slung over her back, already ready to go. Rew was behind Mercy with her face in a bowl, tipping it from side to side as she greedily ate, likely munching on overripe fruit.

He released a sigh as he thought about the long walk. Giving Mercy a half smile, they headed into the forest and toward the nearest lava tube's entrance, just like they had done so many times before.

A few thousand moons ago, right after Mazarin was taken, Mercy would drag August out to the lava tubes and caves to explore and help him cope with his loss.

As they neared the entrance of the cave, August had Mercy climb onto his back so he could jump down into the hole left by the collapsed ceiling of the lava tube. With the new boots on, he easily landed, and he was able to grip the damp, slick rock below without slipping.

Mercy slowly climbed off August's back, and her tail brushed against the underside of his, sending a shiver down his spine. Wide-eyed at what she had just done, her face heated with embarrassment.

Smirking at her embarrassed expression, August turned and started walking in the direction of the village. The lava tube grew darker the further they traveled from the entrance, so Mercy stopped and lit a small torch made from the exceptionally dense jade wood that August had brought back. It burst to life, and she put her flint away then caught up with August.

Once she reached his side, he moved more quickly, and they traveled in a relatively straight line down the extensive lava tube. They passed jutting boulders and crystals coming out of the walls and floor. The ceiling was free of moisture, so there were no stalagmites or stalactites, leaving the cave ceiling barren, save a few bugs.

They entered a massive open chamber with a whistling breeze singing through multiple tubes branching off to the left and right. The floor was relatively free of boulders and crystals and was dry.

Straight ahead of them, the cavern narrowed into a small slip space, and they both had to tuck their tails between their legs to squeeze through sideways. Once they emerged on the other side, they found another path that led straight in the direction of the village. They weren't sure how far they would need to walk, but he and Mercy knew they still had a long way to go to explore the whole cave system.

They continued, and she suddenly grabbed August by the arm and gestured at the wall to their right. He approached the wall and lifted his light to see what she was pointing at. In front of them was a massive wall of solid quartz with thick veins of the signature blue green of oxidized copper.

He grinned back at Mercy, who was so excited she could hardly contain herself. He wanted to continue, so they made their way around the large quartz deposits jutting from the floor and continued along the narrow space.

He noticed they were no longer heading in the right direction, and they needed to turn around. August signaled to Mercy that they needed to turn back, but Mercy shook her head in disagreement and pointed forward. He reached his hand up to connect with her, and she agreed, meeting him halfway.

August spoke first saying, "Mercy, this narrow cavern is drifting too far off course. We need to turn back and find another way toward the town."

She replied, "I've been exploring these caverns and lava tubes since I was a child. I didn't start when I brought you here the first time. This narrow cavern travels back toward the village, and it leads to a large chamber. You have to see it. It will be perfect for building something soundproof so we can speak. I remember exactly where it is."

Stunned, he replied through the connection, "This entire time, I thought I was leading us, but you have known where to go from the start?"

"You seemed like you knew where to go, so I had no reason to stop you unless you started going in the wrong direction," she said as she shrugged her shoulders.

In a sharp tone, he said, "Oh, well, OK then. You lead."

August broke the connection abruptly and stuck his muscled arm out, motioning for her to lead. Mercy reluctantly went ahead, suddenly unsure whether or not she had said something to upset him. She moved quickly and headed directly to the large cavern a short distance ahead of them.

She remembered finding this place as a child. August was

standing back, so she waved him over. He slowly approached her, and she held out her hand to connect. When his hand met hers, she dropped the light and put out the flame by rolling the handle into the dry dirt with her foot.

He spoke in an irritated tone, "Why did we need to connect again?"

Feeling his irritation through their connection, she quietly said, "Because it's pitch black in here, and I'm uncomfortable, OK?"

Shaking his head, he sighed and said, "Just stay quiet, and maybe we can hear something."

Mercy stood silent along with August, but the only thing the two could hear was utter silence in the black cavern. Not even the hint of a trickle of water was audible.

She said, "I think this cavern is completely sealed, but we should see if there is any water dripping, or air flows toward the back of the chamber."

"Sure, that's fine," August said sharply.

She quickly pulled her hand away and took out her flints to light her small torch again. He was already staring at her with his big orange eyes when the torch lit, causing her breath to catch. She turned away and began climbing up the rocks to get to the end of the chamber.

She proficiently scaled the small rock wall, and he couldn't tear his eyes away from her graceful, full figure as she ascended the slope. He needed to get the hell out of this dark cave with this gorgeous woman in it -- right away, August thought. He took a steadying breath and followed behind her.

Being with her around other people was one thing, but here they were completely alone. Thankfully he was wearing his usual loose pants and tunic so he could hide his not-so-unexpected, but unwanted, excitement. Stopping to adjust himself, he wondered if this trip could get any worse.

She reached the top long before he was even halfway up the rocks. After approaching the cave wall, she spotted a drip of water coming from above and trailed it to a crack in the cave ceiling. She thought this area might be near the surface but not close enough for sound to pass through. When August finally finished scaling the rocks, she showed him the water, and he nodded.

Knowing they were finished for now, he reached out and tapped her shoulder, signaling they should head back. She nodded, and they started on their way.

5

As Jael and Oz reached the edge of the jade woods, the number of jade trees began to slowly be replaced by oak and pine trees of an equally giant size. The tall oak trees were a massive version of the trees she remembered from back home, Jael thought as she picked up an oak tree leaf that was easily a foot wide.

As she continued on, she noticed the pine trees had a slightly different scent from the pine she remembered on Earth. It was mixed with a hint of something sweet, like maple or brown sugar. She deeply inhaled the lighter and more appealing scents of the woods. There were fewer carnivorous plants excreting the smell of death to attract unsuspecting bugs.

Signaling to her that he wanted to stop, she watched as Oz slung his pack off his shoulder then walked over to help her with hers. They took a quick break while each put on a long-sleeved shirt to help combat the growing chill, then they started back on their journey.

He hated the cold, and she knew he would be stopping

them again soon for another layer. She felt a chilly breeze of increasing strength and wondered if they were approaching a storm. She hated the thought of being exposed to the elements, but she knew they were beginning to get low on water so the rain would be a blessing.

Spotting an immature jade tree, Oz shot his arm out and stopped Jael with a fright. With a shaking breath, he turned back to her and grabbed her hand to connect.

"There is a small jade tree a few yards away, follow me and watch the ground. The roots protruding up around this area won't be as noticeable because of the sticky black dirt. Keep to the flat ground until I signal you," he said, then he broke the connection, not waiting for her to respond.

Grabbing her hand tightly, he led them directly away from the tree and then turned, making a large circle around it. They both let out a sigh of relief when they stopped and turned to see the tree was far enough away. Smiling at her, he waved that they were safe.

The pair continued toward the river in the distance. Realization sinking in, she turned to Oz and held her left arm out. He quickly met her left wrist with his right hand and formed the connection.

With her brows lifted, she asked, "How are we going to cross the river without getting everything soaked? Plus, isn't that current too strong to swim in?"

He just stared at her with a smirk and smugly said, "Are you serious? Have you not screamed in terror during my long leaps?"

Rolling her eyes, she replied, "I was hoping you weren't going to suggest that."

"It's not about getting everything wet. Have I never told you about the rivers? Besides the strong current, it's home to some of the most disturbing creatures I've ever seen. The pond back home was fed from a closed-off natural spring, so it doesn't have any creatures like the rivers have." He just shrugged and grinned at her as he broke the connection.

Jael hated it when he leaped with her on his back. Holding in her scream would take strength that she didn't know if she had. Her chaotic thoughts took over, and she began thinking this entire plan was insane. Her cascading thoughts made her doubt that they were going to find out anything -- if they ever made it to the north peninsula at all, that is. These mystery beings were probably thousands of years more advanced than Oz's people, or even hundreds of thousands of years. Who knows what kind of technology they would have?

As she approached the grassy edge of the river, she began to get nervous about him jumping with all the extra weight. Clearly, he was nervous too, as he surveyed the area trees for a jumping point. She decided that she was just going to close her eyes and pretend that she wasn't on Oz's back, sailing over a churning river filled with monsters.

He took off his pack and organized it so that all the supplies were wrapped inside the bed mat within the bag. Grabbing her pack, Oz did the same with hers and then cinched them both up. He picked up his bag first and then looked closely at the other side of the river.

Was he going to throw his bag? Jael's gawked when he did just that, his pack landing with a plop on the other side of the river. It sat upright and didn't move after the exceptional landing, almost mocking her with its perfection. She slid her gaze to Oz as he scouted a spot to leap from, then he picked up her bag and launched it into the air. It landed a little too perfectly next to his. She thought she might be sick for a moment, so she sat on the ground.

He tapped twice on the tree, and she looked up at him with fear in her eyes. He helped her up, and they headed over to the tree he had chosen. After a long loving embrace and a quick kiss to her full lips, she nodded to him that she was finally ready. Crouching down, he tapped his back and waited for her to climb on. She just stood there. Could she physically make herself climb on his back?

He slowly turned his head and slighted his eyes at her. She let out a quiet huff and slid on his thick muscled back. She locked her legs around his waist and held on around his neck. Shooting up the tree like Jael weighed nothing, he found footing on the lower branches and quickly made his way up.

Halfway up, he chose a branch that stuck partially out over the river and began walking out to the edge. Already sick to her stomach, she buried her face in Oz's back as he neared the edge. The branch began to bow, and he bounced once. Before she could take a breath, they were soaring over the river. She snapped her eyes shut and prayed she didn't scream or, worse, lose her meal on Oz's back. Clamping her mouth shut and gritting her teeth, she desperately tried to ignore the flying feeling in the pit of her stomach.

He landed on his feet across the river like some kind of gold medal gymnast and tilted his head back with his eyebrows raised. He tapped her arm as if to say, "I told you I could do it."

She rolled her eyes as he knelt to let her off his back.

Wow! How did I end up with the one man in the universe who can be such a smug prick without ever speaking a word?

Walking toward the river's edge, he waved to Jael to come closer and stand on a tall rock by the river. As she warily approached, he leaned down and picked up three small sticks. Ripping up a few tall pieces of grass, he wrapped them around the sticks and tied the grass in a knot.

Turning to look up at her, he pointed to the water a few feet away from them and then tapped near his eye. With her watching the water, he tossed the sticks into the shallow edge, and the bundle sat on the surface a moment before she noticed movement from deeper under the water.

From underneath the silty riverbed came what looked like thick, long white earthworms. They wriggled free of the muck and began swimming toward the stick.

Bile bubbled in Jael's stomach as the worms grew closer to the surface, and she realized they were much worse than just worms. They reminded her of lampreys, but these were over three feet long and solid white with segmented bodies. Their round, tunneled mouths were filled with rows of flesh-boring sharp teeth that seemed to rotate inward toward their throats. The grotesque creatures seemed to be highly intelligent and, upon noticing the object was a stick, retreated. As they swam back, two began fighting, and she watched as one bored into the other, causing it to flail back and forth. The worm's blood swirled in the water around them like a blue cloud.

Not wanting to watch anymore, she signaled for Oz to help her off the tall rock. She was disgusted enough for one day. She was just glad he hadn't told her about them before their jump.

She would have probably marched her happy, un-blood-sucked ass right back home to the treehouse.

Shivers rocked her as he slid her pack on, and she did her best not to think about the river monsters.

Once she and Oz had their packs on, they continued into the forest, heading straight for the wilds. As the fallen dead leaves crunched under her boots, she thought about the frightening place they were walking into, and the alarm slowly took root.

With every step, apprehension spread through her like dark tendrils of oily dread.

6

Giving the gift of knowledge and language to his friends and family was never going to get old, August thought as he watched his father's bright orange eyes light up with delight. His mother had gone first and was currently standing at the living room window and staring into the forest, deep in thought. Her brown hair shone in the light from the window, and she seemed at peace.

This gift of knowledge was like taking a breath of life and truth. To simply upload years of education in mere seconds into another being's brain? It was amazing.

August found it all slightly ironic. Their specialized nerve connection had evolved due to millennia of conditioned silence. The beings who silenced them had inadvertently led their people to evolve the very biological mechanism that may end up becoming their path to freedom.

August's father grinned and spoke through the connection, "My son, was this gift repayment for the compassion you showed by saving your friend? Or was this freely given to you by this alien woman?"

With a smile, August replied, "Father, choose a name, then we can discuss everything."

His father sighed and said, "I will need to consult with your mother before I do anything."

August laughed and broke their connection. His father grinned and embraced him in a firm hug, smashing August's face into the red fishtail braids that lay over his shoulder. He rubbed his face as he followed his father to the front door.

Avoiding Mercy wasn't going to solve anything, but August knew that he didn't want to go straight to her house every day. She was waiting for him to get himself straightened out before they could begin anything. His heart and mind weren't anywhere close to where he wanted them to be, but she was so tempting, he almost couldn't bear it.

He didn't have a choice, though. August knew he needed to see her. There was no one else as creative as she who was willing to help him as much. None of his part of the plan would happen without her help, and he knew it. He just didn't want to rush things and regret it.

When he held his arm up to knock, he heard the sweet sound of her laugh from inside her house. After knocking, he heard her jump to the floor and run for the door. She swung it open, revealing her bright shining self. August's breath caught when she turned around, and he saw that she was wearing a freshly sewn, dark brown pair of leggings. Her perfect curvy body was on full display, and he gulped as he watched her walk. How was he going to get anything done with her wearing pants like that?

Obviously, Mercy had been reviewing the clothing and working on what she knew she could get away with. August was conflicted. She was strikingly beautiful, but he had always had Mazarin, and he never really thought about anyone else. He had always seen Mercy as the beautiful person she was, but he had never thought of her in a deeper way.

But he was thinking about her now, and he had been unable to get her off his mind for some time. He watched her beautiful behind walk all the way into the kitchen where she kept the fresh flatbread from her neighbors, and he nearly drooled down his chin. She pulled the flatbread out and slid the wrapped stack over to him. Holding up a finger, August waited, and she emerged with a small wooden jar. She pried the lid from the jar and showed him her version of jam with cooked smashed fruit and honey.

He grinned, took the jar to smell the jam, and followed Mercy to sit on the padded bench and share a meal with her. When she sat, he made sure to give himself enough room. If he so much as touched any of her skin right now, he might lose his mind.

Once they finished their meal, he reached his right hand out to connect, and she met him halfway. After the connection was made, he passed over his memories of sharing language with his parents.

She was delighted at his father's reaction and said, "Thank you for sharing this with me."

With a grin, he said, "I thought you would enjoy seeing my parents' reaction. I see you made yourself a pair of the leggings from Jael's memories."

"Do they look alright? I like them! I think climbing will be much easier with these on."

He stared at her and tried his best not to think about her flawless round behind in those leggings, scaling a rock wall.

Adjusting his position on the bench, he scooted away from her slightly.

After an audible gulp and a strange look from her, August said, "Since Jacob and Callum are already in the cavern, we should get ready and go meet them there."

She nodded, broke the connection, grabbed her sack, and signaled that she was ready to go. The pair headed away from her home and traveled behind the village toward the entrance to the lava tubes. Weaving through the trees, they heard the rumble of rain, so they ran the rest of the way.

Once they arrived, Mercy climbed on August's back to jump into the lava tube below. He did his best to swallow down his thoughts about her body wrapped around him.

They reached the cavern where they had found the copper veins inside the wall of crystal. There, they saw Jacob and Callum hard at work chipping away at the wall of crystal and putting the more significant-sized pieces of copper into buckets.

Luckily, Jacob and Callum lived in the woods at the edge of the village and could easily walk out of the front door of their home and straight to the lava tube's entrance without ever leaving the cover of the trees. The pair had already mined six buckets of copper by the time August and Mercy arrived. Mercy reached into a bucket and pulled out the ore, studying it. Remembering other large veins of metals in other caverns, she signaled to August to connect.

August approached and gave her his hand.

She said into his mind, "I can lead you to several other places where we can mine different types of metals."

August nodded and broke the connection. She headed toward the last chamber, where the other lava tubes branched off to the left and right.

Mercy took the tube to the right. There was a short drop, and they came upon a smaller but still considerably vast chamber that was a quick walk from the last. She walked over to the cave wall with her torch and held it up, showing him the veins with different metals. The light from the torch sent a cascade of glitter around the cavern as it bounced against the sparkle of the thick bands of gold and thinner pockets of silver. A thrill shot through August as he looked at this grand wall of opportunity. These were some of the metals they needed to build electronic devices.

Nothing had been named except for a handful of people, and August realized they would eventually need to start naming things too. Everything would receive a name if it didn't have one, he decided. He let out a deep sigh and thought that what they were doing was more like a military operation than anything else. So, the lava tubes and caves would be their base of operation, the base. It was a good start.

August signaled to Mercy to connect, and she held her hand up.

"We need to make these caverns and lava tubes into a base with a lab so that when Oz and Jael return, we can have somewhere to speak out loud. Maybe we can even begin developing electronics and technology? We need to progress as fast as possible. I need you to evaluate everyone we recruit and choose a job and position for them. I also need you to come up with some kind of basic hierarchy, with positions that we can all vote on," August said while squinting at Mercy through the torchlight.

She nodded and said, "After we have the lab sound-proofed, let's work on electric lights before we do anything else. I can't see anything by firelight."

Nodding, August ended the connection, and they headed back toward Jacob and Callum to find a good place to build their lab.

Jacob and Callum had an enormous amount of copper. They had discovered that the surface of the copper vein only revealed a tiny portion of the large amount just behind the quartz wall. They would have plenty of the copper ore to line their lab and prevent any signals from passing through. Jacob waved to Callum when he saw August and Mercy approaching.

Signaling to Jacob to connect, August raised his hand.

August said into Jacob's mind, "We need to build the lab now that we have a source of copper. Mercy and I are going to her house to begin the plans for lights from Jael's memories of basic electronics. Hopefully, we can use some of the jade tree sap and the copper you've mined to make some wire.

"Take some of that copper ore to the village smith and have him refine it into small bricks. After you're finished with that, fell some oak trees on the other side of the village and pretend to build onto your home. Then you'll be able to bring the cut wood into the cavern undetected and begin building the lab in this chamber."

Jacob nodded and broke the connection, heading toward Callum to share their tasks as August signaled to Mercy that he was ready to go.

The two hiked back to the cave entrance, and August jumped up first. They headed toward the village as the rain slowed. Big drops of cold water dripped onto her head from the trees. Her bare scalp between the braids was exposed and cold now, something she hated. She guessed they all hated being cold.

She turned to meet August's gaze and tipped her head toward the village. Nodding, he understood and started running behind her when she took off at a swift pace.

Once back in the village, they went straight to Mercy's house. When she opened the door, Rew leaped from the floor and into her arms and began purring and hugging her shoulder. August chuckled and then stroked the sweet spider's fur.

Mercy handed her off to him and went to the kitchen to prepare a meal for them. After setting the excited tarantula down, August met her in the kitchen, intending to help.

Not noticing that he was behind her, Mercy turned around and slammed into him hard enough that she let out a grunt. He grabbed her around the waist to catch his balance, and his eyes widened in shock as she became all too aware of his desire pressing against her. *Those damn leggings,* August thought, as he felt his heart pounding inside his body.

Stunned, she still had her hands up and elbows tucked into her sides in fright. Rew, between their feet, was furiously scarfing down the piece of mango Mercy had been cutting up. Not knowing what to do, August stood there, staring into Mercy's beautiful golden eyes. Unable to tear himself away, August wasn't sure Mercy had taken a breath yet.

Reality hit him like a rock. He couldn't keep doing this. Mercy was so bright and beautiful, and he had strung her along. Guilt slammed into him as he pulled away from her. He wasn't ready for this yet. She didn't deserve to be led on. He had to leave.

Turning around, he started for the door when he felt her hand softly slip into his. Whipping around, he found her shining golden eyes filled with concern.

Now scowling, August had to say something. Or do something? This pursuit of hers had to end, or he had to back away. Something had to give, and he didn't know what it was going to be.

Further furrowing his brow, August abruptly held up his hand to ask why she was stopping him. Mercy's eyes were already filled with devastation, and she began to quickly back away from him down the hall. Her eyes darted around, trying not to look at him, anything but look at him. Turning, her loose braids fanned out behind her from the motion, and she quickly ran for her bedroom and swiftly shut the door.

Sinking his head and leaning on her foyer wall, the guilt of hurting her made his breath catch. He thought back to all the times he caught her looking at him when they were children.

Was that where this all started?

When they were children, August was always so close to Mazarin because she was Oz's sister, and they just always knew they would end up together. Mercy could have anyone, he thought. Why him? He was clearly an asshole.

Mazarin had been gone for thousands of moons, he had a breathtakingly beautiful woman who wanted him, and he had just hurt that woman. Guilt filled him, and he willed himself to head to the bedroom instead of home, where he wanted to run. With August's boots tapping as he walked, he knew she would hear him coming. He could hear her take in a sharp breath as he approached her door. Unable to find his words, he stood at her door and tried to gather his wits.

Slowly opening the door to her dark room, Mercy looked out at August. His guilt was magnified when he saw the sparkle of moisture in her eyes. Had he brought her to tears with his rejection of her advances? Overwhelmed with grief for hurting her so intensely, he took Mercy and brought her to him. He wrapped his arms around her and held her head to him as he desperately tried to think of something to say. He could feel her sharp breaths calm, and maybe she would be OK if he just embraced her.

No, he thought, he had to face this. Above everything, Mercy was his friend, and she deserved an explanation. After he took a deep breath, he led Mercy to sit on her padded bench, and he followed behind, sitting next to her. This time they were closer to each other.

Mercy initiated the connection and spoke first, "I have had eyes for you since we were young. When we were adolescents, I thought I loved you, even if it was from afar. I know you noticed. I can't help how I feel. If you don't feel the same way, then I think it would be best if you found someone else to work with you directly. I thought I could keep being your friend, but I don't think it's possible."

Speechless, August just lowered his eyes and nodded. He felt a brief moment of her overwhelming anguish as she severed the connection and swiftly padded back to her room, scooping up Rew as she went.

He swallowed his guilt and left Mercy's home. As he was walking away, he looked back and saw her watching him from her open bedroom window. Rain pelted his head and began soaking through his clothes.

Lowering his head, he headed straight for his mother. He needed the advice of a woman, a wise woman.

7

Standing by the last jade tree, Oz was hesitant to continue. The trees were less dense, and he could see the sky through the canopy. He turned to Jael and pointed up to the spot where he saw the large gap in the leaves. She nodded and then pointed to another way around. He nodded in reply, and they continued around.

After walking several more miles, Oz looked up and froze. He grabbed her shoulder firmly and pointed up. Hanging above them was the first sign that they were in the giant orb spider's territory. It had taken a long time to get to this point, and they were officially in the wilds. A chill ran through him. He took off his pack, set it down next to her, and signaled to her to stay with the bags.

Without sparing a second, he leaped onto a low branch and scaled the tree. He pulled down the clump of silk from the branch high above them and inspected it. He was down the tree in seconds and next to her, where he stood as close to her as he could. He took in the scent of the silk webbing and then smelled the air. Thankfully, the beast was not close.

Not yet anyway. It was, without a doubt, a red belly's territorial marker, which meant that Oz needed to keep his eyes and ears trained on their surroundings. It took both of them wrapping the long scrap of web around the trunk of a tree to get the sticky substance unstuck from Oz's hand. They needed the additional grip of the tree bark to pry it free.

The childhood memory of his mother showing him what spiders can do was as fresh in his mind as the day she shared it with him.

The enormous spiders set sticky snares to capture unsuspecting creatures in their webs in the trees. When they returned to find a creature dangling, they would bite them, injecting a potent venom. The spider then waited for the prey's insides to dissolve so she could suck out the liquified bodily juices.

Oz kept his eyes trained on the ground for anything suspicious, but all he could see were leaves.

Noticing the change in his composure, Jael brought herself in closer and handed Oz her wrist. Without looking down, he brought his hand up and held hers as he made the connection.

He said, "She's hungry and might even have a nest. I can tell by the smell of her web. Jael, I don't like that you are with me for this. I wish there had been a way for you to go to the village."

Thinking back to her time in the local library office, she remembered the letter opener she had thrown at a corkboard thousands of times, out of boredom. She pushed away her fear and took a calming breath of confidence.

With her eyes focused on Oz, Jael responded, "I've been practicing throwing knives for months. You know I'm good. I'm in great shape. We don't have a choice at this point.

We've gone way too far to turn around. Your people have been through enough. We have to do this. I'm scared out of my mind, but the idea that we could save your people... it's all worth it."

After slighting his eyes at her for a moment, he broke the connection and grabbed her face, meeting her lips for a sensual kiss. Smirking at a wide-eyed Jael, he pulled away, and they continued on their way. He darted his head around and back to the ground as they walked. Oz stayed alert, checking in all directions for any type of sound or movement.

After a while, he began to relax but didn't take his attention from the area. Out of nowhere, Jael had a disturbed feeling crawl over her and threw her arm out in front of Oz, halting him in his tracks. She licked her dry, cracked lips and put her hand on the knife tucked into her utility belt. He followed suit but was still unaware of why she had stopped.

She drew her short knife and held it in her closed hand with her thumb resting over the end of the hilt. Oz narrowed his eyes at her and quickly darted his head around, sniffing the air. It struck her then that she was sensing something which neither of them had visually picked up yet.

Taking a deep breath first, Jael lowered herself to a crouch and lifted a round stone from the forest floor. She stood up and peered at Oz before she darted her eyes forward. Looking down at the round stone that fit like a baseball in her hand, she slid her eyes around the clearing, then softly tossed the stone into the leaves a few feet in front of them.

In a flurry of chaos, the leaves on the ground shot upward, and the snare bounced into the air above them. Grabbing Jael around her waist, Oz held her to his body while he leaped backward several feet and shoved her behind him. Flipping around, she stayed at Oz's back, looking in all directions for the spider. He halted as still as death and tapped her ankle with the heel of his boot.

Turning her head to see where he was looking, Jael's eyes met the most horrid creature she had ever seen in her life. Multiple glossy black eyes stared at them while eight polished black legs twitched, and a bulbous round body slowly moved up and down. Hints of the signature red underbelly were visible as she moved her abdomen.

She was barely three yards away, and her body was as tall as Jael. The beast was enormous compared to the scorpion that she had watched Oz battle on the treehouse deck.

Her beady eyes were focused on them as her spindly legs began to stalk forward.

Looks like the spider was going to take her chance.

Oz shoved Jael back and pointed to a tree behind them before turning around to face the spider. Fear coursed through his veins like lava, burning him inside and igniting his instincts.

Backing away as fast as she could, Jael ran, hiding a short distance away behind a tree. She watched as Oz sized up the creature and readied himself, leaning over and shifting his balance on his feet, preparing to leap.

The giant black orb spider moved straight for Oz like the wind whistling between the trees. Jael gasped in terror as she watched him leap over the spider and reach for a branch in the oak tree above. The tree branch bowed down as he grasped his hands around it. After smoothly swinging himself up and onto the branch with one arm, he slid his knife between his teeth, then broke a small branch to grab the widow's attention.

Watching intently, Jael noted the spider's poor vision. She knew that she needed to stay aware in case she needed to help Oz.

The massive spider followed the noise, as Oz had intended, and just as it drew near, he leaped onto its flat thorax. The spider began bucking like a bull when he landed, and its ten-foot-long, needle-like legs shot out in all directions.

During the spider's moment of panic, Jael was able to get a full glimpse of the fire-red hourglass on the beast's underbelly. She released a shaking breath as she reigned in her focus and watched Oz battle the deadly creature. The only thoughts keeping her from panic were that she had seen Oz kill the scorpion and that he had killed one of the giant red bellied orb spiders on his own before.

This one was three times the size of the other spider, and it seemed like it was filled with rage instead of fear, unlike the one from Oz's memories.

Oz had nothing to grab onto and slid down behind its first set of legs to grip either side of it with his thighs. He needed to anchor himself if he was going to slay this beast. While he was trying to find his grip, the orb spider wildly bucked and spun, trying to get Oz off its back.

Keeping as still as a statue so not to draw attention, Jael kept her eyes trained on the creature in case she needed to swing herself around the tree.

The beast slammed against the rough trunk of a tree across from where Jael was hiding. The force of the impact caused Oz to swing forward and go face to face with the furious spider. He popped back up just before it caught his face with her pedipalps. Oz could hear the snapping of fangs as he quickly pulled away in fright from that sinister mouth.

Regaining his wits, he pulled the knife from between his teeth and slammed it into the middle of the spider's horrid face. The massive beast screeched as it crashed and rolled face first, crushing Oz underneath its enormous plump body.

Terrified, Jael sprinted from behind the tree and found Oz's upper body sticking out from under the creature's round abdomen. The spider's legs twitched as Jael peered around at him, and she found him with an ear-to-ear grin of triumph. She nearly fell over with relief.

His face lost its smile and a ghostly presence fell over Oz. Jael felt a chill roll down her spine. As her heart began racing, she slowly turned her head and looked behind her.

Small round black forms began crawling down the trees. They were dropping down from the branches on thin sparkling threads of silk. The trill of insects was ringing in Jael's ears as the black forms grew closer, revealing long-legged, large and small-bodied red bellied orb spiders. They were the size of full-grown cats. A mass of them were now slowly approaching and Jael whipped her head back to Oz, but he simply shrugged before he pulled his knives from his belt.

The spider that Oz had just killed, was a mother with a freshly hatched brood that hadn't dispersed yet.

Jael turned her head around and found that one of the foot-and-a-half wide round orb spiders, a female by the look of it, was less than a yard away. She gulped and Oz grunted along with the sickly sound of cutting flesh.

Turning her head to catch a glimpse of him, she saw he had his own approaching horde of menacing arachnids. He had just skewered one and threw it off into the woods. Still trapped under the large body of the massive black orb spider, he thankfully had a tree at his back -- likely the only blessing either one of them had.

When she turned her head back around, Jael found that several now surrounded her. Her stomach sank when one creeped forward, and she knew it was the last moment before she would have to fight for her life.

Jael swung her body forward and sliced at the closest spider, opening its back. It fell and another crawled over it. She did the same thing again, stabbing the spider before bouncing back. Fear was coursing through her as she took a second knife from her belt and began slicing the spiders. The density of the creatures increased, and Jael could hear Oz loudly grunting behind her as he diced through the juvenile beasts.

The spiders kept coming, and Jael and Oz kept slicing and stabbing. She was becoming more frantic by the second as the spiders began running, instead of creeping forward. Oz made a hiss behind her, and she begged the creator that he had not been bitten.

Jael moved backward a step, and something bounced on her back. She turned swiftly to find an orb spider suspended on a silk thread trying to grab her with its long, needle-like legs. She swung her knife out and tried to slice through the spider before turning back and founding another at her feet. Jael kicked the spider, and it snatched her leg, eliciting a soft, high-pitched screech out of her. She sunk the knife into its thorax, and it fell to the ground and pulled its legs into its body.

She felt a spider land on her back, and she slapped her hand over her mouth as it sunk its teeth into her shoulder. Praying she would hit her mark, Jael swung the knife under her arm, toward her back, and felt it slice into the back end of the spider. It slid down her knife and fell to the ground as she shook with fright and reached for her shoulder. It was a small bite, and she hoped it didn't inject her with too much venom. She realized she didn't have time to think about it and quickly shook her head to rid herself of the distraction.

She whipped around and found five orb spiders circling her, three males and two females. Jael blew out a shaky breath and jumped for the closest male, sinking her knife into it as she aimed her other knife at the female next to it. By the time she had pulled her knives free, the other three were at her feet. She stomped a male, then sunk her knife into one female and then the other.

Her shoulder was becoming sore, but she felt OK otherwise. She desperately hoped males weren't as venomous as females.

Jael scanned the area and found she had killed all that she could see. She ran around the tree to find Oz had a killed all except a few that were still advancing on him. He had a small welt forming on his forearm. Without hesitation, Jael leaped toward him to kill one of the last four. She swiftly stabbed two more as Oz wearily took out the last one. He tossed it to the other side of the beast crushing his legs, as he had most of the others.

She slid to her knees and stuck out her hand for him to connect with her.

He said into her head, "I got a nip from female, but she didn't do much except break the skin. I'll be fine. Would you mind gutting this beast so I can free my legs? They're unharmed, just pinned. Her body is too heavy for me to move in this position, plus there is a large tree branch under my right leg. I don't want to risk shredding my thigh if I don't need to."

He continued, "We need to hurry and get out of her nest's range, but not too far out of her territory, so we can both get some rest. Did you get bit anywhere?"

With bile rising in Jael's throat, she wearily nodded and said, "I think a male bit my shoulder, but it doesn't hurt too bad."

He nodded and she broke the connection to stand back, peel off her two shirts and pull her long knife free from her utility belt. She handed Oz her shirts, and he winked at her standing there in just her bra. She refrained from rolling her eyes but did shoot him a salty glare.

Oz knew this next task would be repulsive, and he would likely tease her endlessly if she vomited, so she steeled herself before plunging the knife into the thick belly of the beast.

Breathing over her shoulder to get fresh air, Jael sawed her way through the tough, waxy exoskeleton, and the incision gushed blue blood onto the ground. As she continued down the red hourglass, splitting the glossy abdomen, a gelatinous yellow organ emerged and protruded out of the cut. Jael did her best but began to gag as several white parasitic worms slithered their way out and wriggled in the air as they emerged from the putrid yellow organ spilling out of the beast's gut.

She was thankful she'd had enough sense to remove her shirts first, as her arms were saturated with blue blood. She stood back as she finished slicing the beast all the way to the tip of its silk spinner. She dropped the bile-covered knife and walked around to signal to Oz that the gruesome deed was complete.

Obviously not hiding her disgust, Jael watched as Oz threw his hands to his face to keep from laughing out loud. Rolling her eyes, Jael plopped on the ground uphill from the grotesque guts and watched as Oz pushed the shiny abdomen off his legs. The spider's insides squeezed out like a thick cyst being drained. Holding back a gag at the sound and smell of the spider guts slapping onto the ground, Jael was relieved to see Oz easily pull his legs free from under the partially deflated thorax. She did her best not to look at the spider's organs as white parasites crawled free from inside the muck and wriggled around, appearing to be wailing in sorrow at the death of their host.

Jael gagged again at the thought of the black parasitic worms which had crawled from the organs of the scorpion corpse. She quickly swallowed, trying to keep down the bile rising in her throat. The worms must come in different colors, which is something she could have gone without knowing.

After quickly stretching his legs and retrieving his knife from the creature's face with a wet scraping sound, Oz handed Jael a cloth dampened with clean water so she could wash her hands and arms before putting her shirts back on. While Jael was cleaning her arms, he knelt down and gently kissed her sweaty forehead.

He helped her up after she was clean, and she quickly redressed before they put their packs on and headed in the direction of the peninsula.

Wondering how in the hell Oz always knew which way to go, Jael held her pointer fingers in all directions and then shrugged her shoulders. Understanding her question, he simply tapped his head and raised his shoulders in answer. She guessed that meant he had a natural sense of direction.

A cold wind blew by them, and Oz shot Jael a concerned look. Hopefully, they had enough layers and cloaks to stay warm. Everything north of the peninsula was covered in ice.

Once you get to the end of the peninsula, you reach the dark mountains. August told them all of this before he left to return to the village. He said the memories came from his mother, and she was probably right, according to Oz.

Jael loved that they passed memories like stories. She wondered how old that memory was.

It could have been hundreds of years old.

A rumble in the distance warned them it would storm soon, and they would be able to set up their rain catcher and refill their water sacks. Jael wondered if the storm would have lightning and shivered, remembering the lightning storm that made Oz temporarily deaf. It was time to stop for a rest anyway. They heard the thunder crack in the distance.

He dropped his bag and set up their bucket and rain collector in a small, clear area. He hoped they wouldn't need to worry about being spotted by the satellites this far north. The trees were much thinner.

It was much colder here than at the treehouse, and the storm rolling in was from the north, meaning more chilled air. He pulled out the dried fruit and nuts for Jael and then started setting up camp. They weren't too far from the slain black widow and her brood, so Oz wanted to enjoy one peaceful rest before they crossed into a different spider's territory.

As they set up camp, Jael spread the large dark brown waterproof cloak over herself and sat against a tree with her pack sealed up behind her. Using the heated jade tree sap to harden and waterproof the silk was genius, and Jael had Oz to thank for it. The water collector was made the same way and worked exceptionally well during their time in the woods.

Holding the sides of the rain collector, he stood in his

cloak and filled the bucket. Once it was filled, he filled their water sacks, and she guzzled the rest of the water in the bucket.

After she finished drinking her fill, Oz set the bucket back out in the rain and put the collector funnel back in the bag. Jael moved her cloak, and Oz sat next to her in the dry spot on the soft leaves. He pulled Jael onto his lap and leaned back against the tree.

Jael covered his legs with her cloak, and they sat under the tree together long enough for Jael to begin to twitch with the first signs of sleep. Oz had to reach behind himself to reach her bag and find her makeshift mouthguard before she started snoring. He found it right as her first snorts and heavy breathing started.

As Jael slept, he held her while the rain fell. Oz felt like he could live in this moment forever. The serenity of the woods and the warmth of this beautiful woman were all he needed. Oz closed his eyes, resting with his ears alert until Jael finally stirred from her deep sleep many hours later.

The rain continued long enough that the bucket was filled again by the time she woke up. It was still raining, but they needed to continue on their way.

After Jael and Oz drank their fill of the rainwater, they each took a quick cloth bath then packed up to leave.

8

"You are a dim-witted fool. How could you spend so much intimate time with that sweet young woman and then deny her advances? Why would you do such a cruel thing? You know how she feels about you," August's mother, Sarah, pursed her full brown lips at him while they spoke through the connection.

Full regret for asking his mother's advice was settling in as she continued to fry him like her flatbread.

She usually served it crispy and burned.

August's mother asked sharply, "So, do you or do you not have feelings for the woman?"

Sighing, August replied, "Yes, of course I do, but…"

Cutting him off, August's mother, Sarah, sharply said, "*But* nothing! You will march your crimson hide over to Mercy's home and explain yourself, whatever your excuse is. You'll do it before I visit her *myself.*"

With that, Sarah cut the connection with her son and swiftly pranced off. She headed straight into her garden in the backyard to finish weeding with his father. The two never did one thing apart, and August wondered how they had stayed together so long without strangling each other. They were always mad at each other, but they never let it interrupt their relationship. The two always found a way to make it work. August shuddered as he watched his mother rip a vine up from the ground and toss it into the brush behind their home. She hadn't been this angry since he had broken a hole in a wall in their house.

He needed to fix this mess. He needed to visit Mercy. It had been too long, and he had to face this. He needed Mercy in his life, and in more than one way. Everything he should have been doing had stopped since he upset her.

He briskly walked in the direction of her home but nervously detoured and took a stroll past the silk farms. Great lengths of the forest were filled with tree tarantulas that made the silk for the town to use and trade with. They weren't as friendly as Rew, and they were gigantic creatures. Rew was less than twenty years old and was just a baby for her kind. Many of the villages' spiders were over one-hundred-and-fifty years old and colossal.

After walking back around the village and passing by Mercy's stone path three times, August prepared himself to tell her the truth. Finally, he approached her door. he knocked twice and then waited.

Leaning against the house, he was beginning to think Mercy wasn't home.

The door opened partially with a creak and a whoosh, golden eyes already glaring. Mercy furrowed her brow and swung open the door, wearing nothing but her bath towel with dripping wet, unbraided hair. Crossing her arms and narrowing her eyes, she glared at August with fire in her gaze, and he thoroughly regretted waiting so long.

Mercy was pissed.

She backed up to the wall behind her and shot her arm out in irritation toward the inside of her house. As August walked by, Mercy's eyes didn't leave his until she turned to slam the front door shut. Not expecting the slam, August took a sharp breath and headed for the light-brown padded bench in her living room. With her arms crossed, Mercy padded over and plopped down next to him.

She crossed her leg toward August, and he couldn't hold back his eyes as her towel slid off her left thigh. He could see the crease of her soft hip peeking out. Trailing his eyes back up, he found Mercy still glaring and intensely unamused at his ogling. Closing his eyes briefly, August roughly exhaled and then put his hand out to connect. Reluctantly, she met his hand, and he initiated the connection.

Mercy spoke first, "What do you want?"

He met her eyes and said, "Mercy, I should have told you the truth. Not many of my actions recently have had much to do with you."

He paused, thinking of something to say, when she said, "Oz's sister?"

Eyes wide with her spot-on guess, August quietly said into her mind, "Yes, I named her Mazarin. I'm sorry, Mercy. If I move on, then I must accept she's not ever coming back. That she's gone forever."

Quickly adjusting her towel to cover herself again, Mercy severed the connection and walked to her front door and opened it. Taking that as her answer, August walked over to face her before leaving. She pointed straight out of her front door, and he waited a moment before her, trying to decide what to do. She didn't budge, so he solemnly walked out.

The moment his boot left the doorway, she quietly shut the door behind him.

August had *really* fucked it up this time. Maybe starting with his feelings for her would have been a better idea. He had never been great at this when he was with Mazarin either. With Mercy, he was doing nothing but annihilating her feelings with every word and action.

Callum would know what to do, and he hopefully wouldn't be as irritated as his mother, August thought as he sulked down the path.

Going directly to Jacob and Callum's home at the edge of the village, August found them both just returning from the smith with a thick sack of what looked to be brick-shaped pieces. August realized then that he had two reasons to speak to them, but he needed to clear up this mess with Mercy first.

He walked up to Callum, tapped his shoulder, then pointed to their front door. Callum nodded and tilted his head to the side to give August a concerned look. Once inside, Callum sat on their living room bench, and August joined him. They held their hands up and connected.

August spoke first and said, "I need some advice."

"Let me guess. Your giant red ass fucked up again, didn't you? You pissed off Mercy, and she isn't accepting your half-attempt at an apology? Or did you just make it worse some-how? Oh, red belly spider, you made it worse, didn't you," Callum said as he glared at August.

"I made it worse," August admitted as he nodded and then shifted his eyes to the floor.

Callum started again and in a kind tone said, "I am going to say something, and you are *not* going to like it. Oz's sister is gone, and she is not coming back."

Pain laced through August's gut at Callum's words, knowing they were true but not ready to face them yet. He had made every excuse. He made up reasons that didn't truly make sense to justify his inability to let go.

Callum cringed as he felt a hint of August's pain through the connection.

Grief lacing every word, August said, "I don't know how to give Mercy a chance without feeling like I am somehow giving up on Mazarin."

Blinking rapidly, Callum slowly asked, "You named your missing girlfriend? August, please tell me you didn't *tell* Mercy you named your missing girlfriend. She has been gone for thousands of moons. It's fine to give her a name, but don't tell Mercy until you have worked this out with her."

August sighed, closing his eyes, and said, "I probably should not have started with that."

Aghast, Callum shook his head and said in his typical cool demeanor, "Sarah was right. You are a dim-witted fool."

Eyes flying open and in absolute shock, August said, "You somehow managed to speak to my mother about this already?!"

Callum raised his dark blue eyebrows and pursed his full lips, then said, "Oh come on now. You know your mother is the rumor mill. She sees everything from that hill your parents live on. I think she has the best vision in the village."

Staring at Callum in disbelief, August said, "What do I do about Mercy?"

Callum smiled and said, "It's simple. You grovel with gifts until she accepts your apology, and then you *fuck* her brains out. I do love this language thing. It's so colorful."

With disbelief at Callum's answer, August shook his

head and changed the subject, asking, "What happened with the copper refining? Was the smith able to remove the impurities?"

Callum looked at Jacob and signaled for him to bring the bag of metal bricks over. After Jacob set the bag between them on the bench, August reached in and pulled out a perfect copper brick. Callum opened the bag more and revealed bars of platinum, gold, and a silver.

"While you have been at home sulking, wallowing in your own filth and wasting precious time, we have been hard at work building the lab. The frame is up, and we will be finishing it soon. Jacob already figured out the lights and is just waiting on us to finish the wire. Lucky for you, that means we need more sap, so you and Mercy get to go on a little trip together."

August's heart began pounding in his body, so Callum severed the connection and waved his hand goodbye in front of August before abruptly standing up and guiding August out of his front door. Callum hated being on the receiving end of other people's emotional overloads.

For the second time in a short while, August found himself on the outside of an abruptly shut front door. He needed to go home and rest to think. Then he would go back to Mercy's and grovel, he thought as he rubbed his face.

9

Lying on his back in the middle of his dusty wood floor, deep in thought about Mercy, August thought about how he was going to stop being an idiot. He had to let Mazarin go. She was gone. She had been gone for so long. No one had ever come back. Just because he'd found Oz alive the jade woods didn't mean Mazarin would be found. He had held this desperate thought that, if Oz had survived, then maybe Mazarin had a chance wherever she was.

Snapping him out of his thought-spinning rest, a knock sounded at August's door, and he leaped up to answer it, sending dust billowing into the air. He headed to the door and swung it open to find Mercy standing in front of him. Her eyes roamed his body, and he wondered if he should have at least put a shirt on before he answered the door.

With a hand on her hip and her beautiful face holding a scowl, Mercy was leaning on a staff with two stacked wooden buckets next to her. Wearing something new from Jael's memories of fashion, Mercy was very clearly doing her best to torture August with a revealing, loose, tan cropped shirt and dark brown leggings that rose to right above her hips.

This was going to be a long journey, August thought as he turned away from her.

He held up his hand for her to wait for him and went to put on his boots. After lacing his boots up and selecting a long knife, he went into his spare room and collected his staff and buckets.

Once he was ready, he headed outside, and Mercy took off, briskly walking toward the jade forest. August leaned his head up toward the colorful sky and reminded himself that he deserved this.

Mercy was not nearly as tall as August, but right now he was having trouble keeping up with her without running. Nearly having to jog to catch up, he tapped her on the shoulder, and she whipped around to glare at him with her bright gold eyes. August dropped his staff and buckets to grab her arm, but she shook him off, sprinting away. He had to run to catch up after collecting his staff and buckets.

The swinging lids to August's buckets clanked against the sides as he ran. She didn't look back once as she continued through the oak trees that surrounded the village. He wondered how long she would give him the cold shoulder and what he would have to do to prove he was sorry, that he was *ready*.

Exhaling roughly, he finally caught up to Mercy and couldn't tear his eyes from her perfectly round behind in those leggings as she powered forward in front of him. They moved toward the jade forest with the same quick pace the entire way.

Mercy didn't slow until she spotted a tall jade tree ahead

of them. After darting her head around to look for imma-ture trees, she slowed down but still hadn't turned around. August was dripping with sweat when he reached the tree, heaving to catch his breath.

He didn't wait and stabbed the knife into the tree. Working it down to open a wider seam, he began filling his bucket with the thick sap that poured out. She stood behind him, prepared to fill her bucket after he was finished.

Once his bucket was filled, he turned and held his right hand out to take Mercy's bucket and fill it for her. Eyeing him narrowly, Mercy reluctantly handed over her bucket. August swapped it out with his, then Mercy took the filled bucket from his left hand. After all four of the buckets were filled, they covered them with fitted wooden lids, then tied them with silk strips to their staffs to carry them back to the village.

August stopping her before she took off with her buckets was not on her agenda, and Mercy muscled by him before he could finish tying his buckets to his staff. He was trying to ignore her game, but he was tired and drenched in sweat. His tunic wasn't helping, so before he took off after Mercy, he took it off and slung it over his staff.

Mercy nearly jogged the entire way back to the village with her buckets of jade sap swinging behind her. August thought he might die if he was forced to look at her magnifi-cent backside any longer. Sweat dripped into his eyes and he used his shirt to wipe them, but the sting persisted. He couldn't help thinking that this entire journey to the jade woods for sap was just to punish him. It was probably Callum's idea.

Once the village was in view, August followed Mercy back to her home, and she surprisingly let him inside. She emerged from the back of her home with a light brown damp towel for each of them.

She refused to look at him as they toweled the sweat off their faces and bodies. Having enough, August threw his towel down and waited for her to look up. She slowly raised her eyes, and he stalked forward, pinning her against the wall. He held her shoulder with his left hand and then raised his right hand to connect with her.

Reluctantly raising her hand, Mercy initiated the connection.

Leaning his head over, August softly ran his lips along Mercy's jaw, heat spreading into her from the touch.

He said softly into her mind, "I need you to understand. I *want* this, Mercy. I want you. I just need more time. *Please* give me more time."

With a shaking breath, Mercy slowly slid her right hand up August's side and leaned her hips into him. He closed his eyes and broke the connection to slide his right hand around her head and held her to his thick chest. He pulled her head back and kissed her under her jaw once softly and then pulled away, exhaling roughly. Mercy looked at him with longing eyes, but also with forgiveness, and nodded her head.

He knew this was his last chance, and he would not screw it up this time. He needed his brain back for what would happen next with their plans. He had to sort out this mess he'd made with her so he could think straight. He needed this because he cared for this golden-eyed woman, and when his people were free, he wanted her with him.

Their people were on the precipice of an intellectual and technological revolution. Knowing his skills as well as

Mercy's, would be essential, they needed to work together. Neither of them had time for unsorted emotions.

Now that she wasn't acting like she wanted to bite him and draw blood, he felt he could move on and talk about their plans. August knew Jacob wanted Mercy to start making boots as a cover for their sap needs. He reached down and tapped his boot and then pointed to Mercy.

The old way of communicating was cumbersome and suddenly seemed so primitive. Only a short time with this incredible gift, and so much had already changed.

There was no going back now.

Oz was right. Jael's language and knowledge were like a key opening his locked mind. Maybe this is more than just a revolution. He thought as he could see Mercy's brilliant mind spinning with ideas about how she would create the boots. She was the only person he knew who was as crafty and creative as Oz. If anyone could replicate Oz's excellent work, it was Mercy.

Mercy pointed to his boot and signaled that she needed him to take it off and hand it to her. He sat on her bench and complied. After looking at the boot, she pointed to the other one, so he removed it and handed it over as well.

Looking back and tilting her head, Mercy inspected both boots carefully, then took a bucket of sap to her back room. She returned for a candle but held her hand up for August to stay put.

She had a long, wooden craft table with every tool and gadget his people could have imagined without outside knowledge. Mercy loved fashion and always had. She had been making her own clothes since she was young, and the outfits would often become the next fad. With fewer than two hundred people in the village, there weren't many for a fad, but Mercy seemed to constantly defy the boundaries of her limited world.

The village was never big enough for her.

Mercy's parents were among a larger group that were taken long ago for progressing too far. Despite this, her convictions for this undertaking were possibly just as strong as August's. She made that clear when she got to work right away, pulling dark brown silk from one of her multi-colored piles. Rew was on a tan hammock rooting around in the corner with several newly spun silk sheets suspended around her.

The spider purred when August looked in her direction, and she stretched before she leaped from her perch and into his arms. Landing gracefully, Rew then sat on his arm with a plop. She wiggled her furry legs under his arm and snuggled up to him as he watched Mercy.

August couldn't do the things that she and Oz could. He was not cut from the same cloth. He was more like his mother and needed to stick his hands in everything.

The villagers sometimes labeled his mother "the gossip." But in reality? She was the village leader, and everyone knew it, especially his father. He wished he had some kind of skill, but he didn't have much of anything except his physical abilities, which were above average for his people.

Paying attention to Mercy again, August watched as she worked. Then it hit him; he needed to check on Jacob and Callum. It had been several moons' cycles since he had seen them.

After collecting her paintbrushes, Mercy took her cut fabric pieces and headed to the hearth. Rew crawled from August's large arms and headed back to her perch. When Rew crawled off, August followed Mercy into the living room. He approached her from behind as she crouched by the fire, tapped her shoulder and signaled that he needed to go.

Slowly standing up in front of him, Mercy waited to see what August would do. He exhaled roughly and then took her face into his hands and rubbed across her cheek with his thumb. He wasn't ready yet, but he wouldn't keep stringing her along.

This might be slow, but he would try for her.

Carefully, August pulled away, and Mercy hinted at a smile before he turned to leave.

Peering down at his feet, he wiggled his toes and headed to the door. He would have to go barefoot until she was finished making her first pair of boots, but he didn't mind. He had never worn shoes before and didn't think he would notice having to go without them for a while.

Upon leaving Mercy's house, August headed for the lava tubes where Jacob and Callum were working. The trees rustled with a gentle breeze, and August was glad to see the weather was better.

Reaching the cavern entrance, he expected to hear light clinks and hints of construction, but he heard nothing. Wondering if he should go back to Jacob and Callum's house to see if they were there, he decided to check out the progress before he left. Making his way through the cavern, he saw the construction ahead and shone his light to see better.

As he walked up to the lab, August was astonished at how fast they were moving. They had already built a solid room where they could precut and assemble pieces of wood instead of solely using the fake room at their house. He opened the heavy door, shocked at the weight, and then let it shut slowly, holding the torch at his side because of the light already in the room. The thick wooden door sealed behind him, and he found Jacob with his hammer raised. He was dripping with sweat, hovering over a hammered sheet of copper. He leaned up and held the copper sheet to the wall to check the fit.

Astonished, August stood there and stared at Jacob working, unaware that Callum was approaching quietly from behind.

"Hey! Have you fucked Mercy yet, or what?" Callum asked aloud, startling the stars out of August.

Jumping out of his skin, August whipped around, his two braids swinging behind him, and he gasped in horror at Callum speaking out loud.

Callum threw his head back and laughed, then said, "You are too much. Stop being ridiculous. We can talk in here."

August slid his gaze to Jacob, who promptly rolled his bright tan eyes and immediately returned to work. Clearing his throat, August squeaked in an attempt to speak and then slapped a hand to his open mouth.

Callum chuckled, and August cleared his throat again and said slowly, "This is harder than I thought."

His voice was still high pitched, and he cleared his throat a few more times.

Jacob and Callum laughed. August scowled with his dark red brows and, in a deeper tone, said more quickly, "You both can fuck off."

Callum let out a howl of a laugh, and said, "You sounded like a little child every time we connected."

Jacob chuckled in agreement and Callum shot him a broad, affectionate smile.

August just rolled his eyes and cleared his throat one more time before saying, "I don't know how to change my voice when I connect. I hate you both."

"Callum, you are with me. We need to make sure none of the areas we are building are too close to the surface," August continued.

Finally breathing normally again after his laugh, Callum nodded then grabbed his torch. He swung his head back toward August as he passed by and made a zipper motion over his lips before striding to the door. Before opening the large door, he blew Jacob a kiss with a wink, then swung it open, allowing August through first.

Pulling a rolled silk from his bag, Callum handed it to August, and he unrolled it to reveal a map of the lava tubes. It showed all the large and small chambers, and even the direction of the town. Callum pointed to the last large chamber, then to a lava tube which was closer to the thickly wooded area behind his home.

By the look of it, Mercy had made the map. He could see tiny details where she had drawn any cave formations they would have to walk around. August was constantly awestruck by her and her creative talent.

Callum and August traveled back toward the large chamber that was closer to their way out. August made a mental note to have the slip space widened into a hallway once they sealed off the caves and made them soundproof. He hated squeezing his large body through the small space.

Soundproofing just to simply speak to one another made August boil inside. The idea that they, whoever they were, had been watching his people fanned the searing, furious fire bubbling deep inside of him. He wondered how long ago his people would have developed a more advanced civilization, then he thought about all the missing people. Since he had been born, more than a hundred villagers had gone missing. He wasn't sure of the exact number, but he knew it was too many.

A town in the mountains had been blessed with the fewest abductions. There were three villages on the other side of the continent, and one had lost more people than the other two. August's mother had traveled as a child, and she told him all the differences between the villages and towns. Some of the villages across the mountain were much more reclusive and secretive than his own.

His strategic mind ran through what he knew, and he agreed with Oz that the anonymous beings must be coming by ground from the peninsula. He wondered if Oz and Jael had found anything yet, or if they were even alive. If anyone could succeed, it was Oz, but he still wasn't convinced that even Oz could pull this off. No one had ever laid eyes on their enemy and made it back to talk about it.

When they reached the spot on the map that Callum had pointed out, August set several lit torches around to see better. Seeing nothing of interest, he took one of the torches, while Callum rubbed the rest into the dirt to put them out. There is no reason to waste oxygen in the cave.

There was no sign of dripping water, but August knew that the lava tube they were exploring had dipped in elevation from the larger chamber. He would trust Mercy's judgment, and they would carefully begin digging. She had specified a place that sometimes had steam. That's where they needed to build a geothermal generator, and Jacob had already designed the machine. The spot they were exploring was perfect for it.

Next, they would need to put up soundproof walls in

the lava tube so they could work on other projects inside the other chambers of the massive cave.

Eventually, there would be at least fifty people working in the base. A thrill shot up his spine like lightning at the thought of all the people in his village speaking to one another openly.

They needed to recruit more people, and August sighed, knowing this was his responsibility. He knew the right people, but it had been a while since he had seen them.

His mother would be able to convince them. With her help, August knew that they would want in.

10

Out of nowhere, Oz shot his right arm out in front of Jael, stopping her dead in her tracks. Warily peering over at Oz, Jael took his ice-cold hand and held her left wrist up so he could connect with her. He stood frozen, eyes focused out into the suffocating fog. All was quiet as he breathed deep, slow breaths through his nose, scenting the air.

They could only see a few yards at best, so Jael guessed he could smell something ahead. The air was thick, with a chilled rolling breeze high in the pine trees, and she watched as Oz's breath became a cloud, entangling with the freezing mists.

They each had on multiple layers to keep out the stinging air, but the bitter cold found its way in and chilled them to the bone. Shivering, Jael wasn't sure all the clothing they had would be enough to keep out this cold for much longer. She was thankful there was no night on this planet. If there had been, the ground would be below zero after dark.

This far from the equator, it remained frigid. For at least

a week, Jael's face had ached from the air, and her trembling only stopped when she had Oz's body heat to keep her warm.

Inside her mind, Oz said, "I can smell a campfire. It's just north of here. We should both approach silently until I give you a signal, then I can get close to the camp. Maybe I can smell the creatures through the fog. They may have some of our people with them. I want you to stay back and wait."

He continued, "If I am caught and don't return, head south until you find my old village. Hopefully, some of them will know who you are by the time you get there. Try to stay out of view of the satellites. I love you."

"Please be careful and you better come back to me. I love you, too." Jael nodded her head, and Oz pulled his hand away, breaking the connection.

She did her best to hold her thoughts because, if he didn't return? She wasn't going south. She would turn into something she was afraid of. Jael would set aside her morality and do whatever it took to get Oz back -- at *any* cost.

After he took his boots off and pulled his knife free, Oz turned to Jael and kissed her without warning. The steamy kiss promised more later, and Jael melted at his affection. How could he expect her to just leave him if he were caught? She would rather lose her life trying to free him.

Breaking the kiss, Oz silently walked off into the fog, stalking toward the camp. Jael felt inept without any decent hearing or sense of smell, so she sat down where she was. She didn't think Oz would object. He wouldn't *force* her to stay back, but he wanted her to for a reason, and she was not questioning him.

Jael pulled one of her knives from her belt and flipped it

in her hand a few times as she balanced her rear end on her pack. Smiling to herself, she felt relieved she'd had time to brush up on her old letter-opener-throwing skills from her high school job at the Sumner Public Library.

With absolute silence, Oz stalked through the massive pine trees, unable to see, but he had intense senses of smell and hearing. He could build his surroundings spatially from his senses, cutting straight through the dense fog.

As he approached, Oz thought something with his scent had to be wrong. He was tilting his head to the side and thinking hard about what he was smelling. Maybe he just hit his head at some point when he was battling the deadly orb spiders? That would be better than the alternative, and what he believed he could smell in the air. Yes, Oz thought definitively, that is more than a familiar type of scent. He didn't want to accept it yet. He had to see with his own eyes. A slithering fear began clawing its way up his spine as he crept toward the camp.

He clearly smelled his people as well, but no one he recognized. Once he was close enough, Oz could hear words being spoken, but he didn't recognize them. He could hear several different voices, and he smelled at least three of his people. His heart sank as he had to accept what his powerful nose was screaming at him. Having enough information to go on, Oz silently returned to Jael and their packs.

Oz found Jael shivering in the cold, sitting on her pack. Her knife was embedded deep in a tree, and he walked over to retrieve it to hand it back to her. Taking a deep breath and sighing, he was thankful this part of their journey was almost over.

He sat next to her and pulled her into his lap, wrapping

his cloak around them both. Once her chill settled, Oz took her wrist in his hand and connected with her.

With a scowl on his stern face, he said into her mind, "There are three of my kind. I'm sorry for what I have to tell you. There are several other creatures in the camp that smell, well, a lot like *your* kind."

"Are you saying there are my people, human people, and some of your people with them?" Jael quietly asked into the connection.

Feeling her anguish, Oz flinched and replied, "I'm so sorry. I know the beings are human in that camp. I think *humans* might be the creatures who have been taking my kind."

"Humans on Earth haven't reached the stars yet. I was probably the first person to ever leave my planet and land somewhere life-sustaining. Are you sure you could smell humans in that camp? It wasn't some kind of a trick?" she asked in desperation.

"I'm sorry. They smell too much like you, but there are subtle differences. There are several of them, and they are all similar to you. It's unmistakable. Most are likely male or at least have male hormones. There was only one female scent. I can even tell she's currently bleeding."

Jael said, "I still want to help you save your people. This changes nothing for me. The people must eventually sleep if they're human, which means they will probably take shifts. It's not likely more than one at a time will be asleep, but we might get lucky. I just had some excellent sleep and rest thanks to you and the rain, so I will be good for a while if I need to be."

Oz looked concerned, "I don't want you to be in any kind of danger at all. I would rather go in alone, free my people, and possibly take out the humans as well. We need to find out everything we can about them."

Looking at him in earnest, she said, "You are not going in alone! I am not the weak girl you first found dying in the woods. If you recall, I wrestled, caught, and brought you a giant pill bug all on my own. I can throw knives like a pro. I have more than proved I can help in a fight if I need to."

Shaking his head, with fear snaking down his spine he said, "I will not tell you no, but I don't like this at all."

Jael broke the connection and took Oz's face in her hands. She kissed him and slipped her tongue between his teeth, accidentally catching one of his fangs and wincing. Oz broke the kiss when he tasted her blood and looked at her, concerned. She smiled at him, her teeth stained with her bright red blood, and he scoffed at her terrifying look. If she was trying to make a point, then the point was taken. He quickly reached into his bag and handed her his water pouch.

Red blood was much more alarming than blue, Oz thought. It was like a warning and a promise.

Once Jael's tongue finally stopped bleeding and the thick fog swirling in the breeze began to dissipate slightly, they stood up. Oz pulled the meticulously crafted knives that August had given them out of their small bag. Jael and Oz both strapped all the knives to their belts.

Shel removed her boots and set them beside their bags. Thankful for their socks, they quietly walked through the pine trees, and Oz signaled to her to go around while he continued on his path forward.

Jael nodded and began walking around toward his people, hoping to free them if she could, but she wasn't entirely sure how. She would have to figure it out as she went. One thing she was not doing was wholly shifting her attention away from Oz. If he found himself in danger, she would be intervening. No matter what it cost.

Remaining silent, Oz slowly neared the closest tent. Hiding behind a tree, he peered around at the campfire. Only two humans were sitting by the fire. At least one must be in the tent. Oz roughly exhaled and readied himself as he saw Jael begin to approach the northernmost tent.

Quickly and silently, he ran to the back of the tent and lay on the ground at the bottom seam. Slowly and painstakingly careful, he stuck his razor-sharp knife into it and sliced a small hole in the bottom. He peered inside and found two men asleep. One was breathing heavily, while the other was twitching slightly. He kept his eyes on them as he slowly sliced down the bottom edge of the tent. The knife went through the canvas material like it was fresh sap, not making a sound.

Once it was large enough, Oz slipped through the hole and crouched, leaning back on his heels. He sat up and rolled his shoulders back before pulling a second knife from his belt. Moving toward the center of the tent, Oz knelt on one knee in between the two cots. Looking to either side of him and then closing his eyes, Oz said a prayer to the creator that he was doing the right thing.

In one swift motion, Oz slit both men's throats, then brought the knives down to wipe them on the men's chests before placing them back into his belt. Both gurgled as they reached up to their throats, dying within seconds. As their blood began dripping from the edge of their cots, Oz stood up and swiftly walked to the door. He could see the silhouettes of the two people at the fire. He knew he only had seconds before he needed to move, but he couldn't see if they had guns.

Oz didn't have time to wait because it endangered Jael's life. So, he quietly walked through the tent opening and toward the two people sitting at the fire. The man moved at the last moment, and Oz was forced to go for the petite woman. She complied instantly with his knife pressed at her throat, and they stood up with the fire behind them. The man rolled away and quickly righted himself, pulling a gun from his belt and holding it up to Oz. He looked confused and terrified to see Oz in modern clothing.

The man said, "*Quid id est?*" What is this?

Jael walked up from the darkness between the tents and shook her head. She wasn't able to free his people. Oz looked back at the man. When the light-skinned man finally saw Jael, his eyes widened in shock.

Saying, "*Reverti! Reverti!*" Get back! Get back! to Jael, the blonde-haired man waved his hand frantically.

A deep growl left Oz's snarling lips, and the man shot his fearful green eyes back to Oz. Oz firmly held the squirming brown-haired woman to him with his knife as the man trained his eye on the target of his gun. Letting out a shaking breath, Oz realized the man was going to take the shot, and he steeled himself. Just as he prepared to duck behind the woman, Oz saw something twinkle behind the blonde man's head. In confusion and shaking his laser-focused attention, Oz furrowed his brow.

Something glinted in the firelight, and a knife slammed into the man's neck.

Blood poured from his lips and neck as the gun fell from his limp hand. The blonde man spat blood from his mouth before his eyes rolled back, and he fell face first onto the damp ground.

The woman, who Oz still held, yelled out, "*Non!*" No!

As the man's body twitched one last time on the ground, Oz held the woman firmly in his grasp, then slid his hand around her throat. He held tight until she slumped in his arms. He laid the woman on the ground and slid his eyes over to Jael, who still stood in the same place a few yards away. The moment Jael's gaze met Oz's yellow eyes, she doubled over and spewed vomit all over the ground.

After he disarmed and restrained the woman, he searched their camp for water and found a tall canister in front of the fire. Jael was still kneeling on the ground with her hand on her face when Oz approached with the canister.

She guzzled the water, then Oz helped her to her feet and pulled her to him. Wrapping his arms around her, he held her tight. Remaining silent, tears poured from Jael's eyes. Oz kissed her on the head, and she took several deep breaths trying to calm herself.

After a few long moments, Jael wiped her face before she looked up at Oz and tilted her head for him to follow her to the north tent. When he walked in, he found three of his people bound and gagged, all unconscious on rounded, – oval-shaped metal cots.

These cots were different from those the humans slept on. These looked like pods with some kind of electronic panel at one end. They were held up by four thin legs that looked as if they retracted.

After unsuccessfully trying to rouse them, Jael began searching the black bags in the corner of the tent. Oz walked to the grey bins by the door and popped the first one open.

It contained dried foods of all kinds in packages, so he sealed it, setting it in a pile in the middle of camp.

Looking in the biggest duffle bag first, Jael discovered a small white plastic box with a small syringe symbol in red on the top. She popped it open to find three, large pre-filled syringes with "somnum" on the label.

Is that Latin? Jael wondered. If it is, does that mean sleep? Why the hell would they be carrying these syringes? Looking over at the sleeping people, she wondered if they needed to have the substance administered in intervals because it wears off.

Jael looked down at the three vials and the three unconscious people, their tails stretched between their legs in an uncomfortable looking position. There were exactly three cots and that was all. Nausea bubbled inside as Jael realized this was all preplanned, right down to how many people would be taken. She leaped up after setting the white box down, then went to find Oz.

Jael found him crouched and quietly staring at the now wide-awake brown-haired woman. Jael slowly approached and glared at the woman. When she reached Oz's side, she held her left arm out and he wrapped his right hand around hers and connected with her.

The woman sat clueless as to what they were doing. Oz and Jael kept their eyes on her.

Jael spoke first into the connection, "I will hold her down and you force a connection with her. There is no sense in interrogating her. We don't speak the same language. They speak Latin, a long dead language on Earth. I know some Latin because it is the language of science, but I don't know nearly enough to communicate."

Oz slowly brought his eyes to Jael and removed the

connection. He stood and then took her face in his hands and kissed her passionately, leaning her back and kissing down her neck. He slowly pulled away and Jael grinned at him before he released her and walked over to a dumb-founded and bound human woman. Her reaction to their kiss told Jael everything she needed to know about how well their relationship would be accepted if they ever beat their enemy.

When they beat them, she corrected herself.

The woman began to shake her head no as Oz approached and he brought his tail over his shoulder in threat. The tip of his stinger began poking out of the end of his tail, and he hissed as he showed her his sharp teeth. The woman cowered and stopped moving. Oz pulled her by her feet and made her lie down on her side on the ground. While Jael held her legs, Oz wrapped a gag around her mouth and then pushed her face into the dirt while he put his index finger in just the right place at the back of her neck.

When the spine entered her neck, she let out a sharp scream through her gag and thrashed against Oz and Jael. Jael narrowly missed a sharp kick to the shin but managed to grab the woman's leg before it made contact. Once the connection was made, the woman stilled. Oz nodded to Jael, and she released the woman's legs. He would be able to keep her paralyzed as he looked for the information he needed.

As Oz reviewed her mind, his brow continued to furrow, and he became more furious by the moment. Jael noticed Oz's face going from concerned to enraged in seconds. Without warning, the woman's body began shaking, and Oz pressed her head into the dirt with excessive force.

Oz was draining her in his fury.

Jael knew he wouldn't be doing this without a reason,

and she made no attempt to stop him. The sight was appalling, and she turned away as the woman shook and vomited past her gag into the dirt. Urine began pooling around the woman as she lost control of her bladder.

When the brown-haired woman eventually stopped breathing, Oz pulled his hand away and sat back on the ground. He slid his hands over his face as he gathered his composure. Jael was stunned, but she was fully aware Oz had just discovered something terrible enough to make him drain the woman.

Draining any creature was supposed to be unacceptable to him. Without having to do much soul-searching, Jael didn't feel like this was wrong. She felt worse for the pill bug who had faced the same fate. It suddenly felt a lot more humane than slitting her throat for whatever heinous crimes she had committed.

One thing was clear. Oz would never have killed her without a great cause. Jael slid over to him and put her hands on his knees. He slid his hands from his face to reveal brightly glowing yellow eyes. They were beautiful and heart-broken, with glittering tears threatening to slide free. Holding out her wrist to him to find out what happened, Jael was desperate to be there for him in his moment of despair.

Foregoing her wrist, he pulled her into his lap and held her tightly for a long while. The sounds of the fire crackled as Oz held Jael to him, rocking back and forth ever so slightly.

Once he calmed, he tipped his head back to the tent and signaled he wanted to wake his people first. Jael climbed from his lap and went to the humans' tent. She found a spare, solid black jacket and put it on. She was freezing, and the clothes they brought were not nearly enough.

This must be a semi-permanent camp, she thought. There were enough supplies here to last for months. After collecting some supplies for their soon-to-be travel companions, she headed out to find Oz.

She met Oz in the north tent and found him looking at a box of syringes, one Jael had not seen yet. He went to the duffle bag and pulled out a long band and a bag of gauze, then unbound the blue woman's arms. After taking her left arm, he took the bottle and a bit of gauze and cleaned the vein in the crook of her elbow. Then, he took the first syringe and injected it directly into her vein, emptying a third of the vial.

Oz repeated the process with the second woman and the man using the other two syringes. He replaced the three, half-used syringes back into the white box and handed it to Jael, then pointed outside to the crate he had already dragged out. She walked out and put the syringes inside the crate which held the supplies they were taking with them. Oz untied the rest of his people's bindings and waited for the administered medication to wake them. While they waited for them to rouse, Oz and Jael went around the camp and collected any usable gear.

11

Spinning through her home, Mercy's new heavy boots clunked on the wood floor, as she went up and down the hall, twirling and twisting around. She pushed her bench out of the way and began prancing around, moving her body to the music in her mind. Mercy was always dancing when she was by herself. She didn't dare do it out in the open, but in her home, she was safe, and she could dance all she wanted.

Lost in thoughts about clothes and shoes, Mercy realized that her new items were so much better than the old tunics and wide pants. She hated the flowing loose pants and other traditional village clothing. Cropped tops were her new best friend, and she was currently wearing a tan pair of workout shorts with pockets that she had just made.

On Earth, Jael's people were so free and open with their fashion. Mercy loved it. This stood in stark opposition to her own people.

As she spun around once more, she saw a blur of red and stopped. Heart in her throat, Mercy quickly darted her head toward her foyer and found August, slack-mouthed and eyes glittering, daring to laugh.

Mercy howled with laughter at getting caught dancing, and August chuckled while he signaled to her with a roll of his hand that she could certainly continue. She spun around once more toward August and kissed him on the cheek before she skipped to the kitchen to toss him some of her neighbor's flatbread. The flatbread smacked August in the chest, and he threw his arms up to catch it. He sat down on her bench to eat the warm bread.

They had set plans to work at the base, and Mercy must have forgotten. August could hardly pull his simmering eyes away from her as she bounced around her home, getting ready. Now that she was paying attention, Mercy realized how loud she was. Between the boots and the old wooden floorboards, she was making a racket. No wonder she didn't hear August at the door.

Emerging from her bedroom, she had only changed her shorts for longer leggings. Glancing at August, she wondered why he looked as if he were ill.

She walked over and stood in front of him, close enough so that when he looked up at her. He saw the underside of her full breast under her cropped top. His eyes began to bulge, and his blood pressure skyrocketed. August swallowed audibly and swiftly grabbed her hand to make her sit down next to him. If he had to keep looking at the underside of her breast peeking out, he would do something about his desire too soon, something he would regret.

Seated, Mercy took his hand and initiated a connection with him, then asked, "August, are you doing, OK? Do you feel alright?"

A cough and a rough throat clearing later, August

smirked and said through the connection, "I will be. Let's get going. Jacob and Callum have done a lot of work on the lab."

Mercy leaped up, breaking the connection, and nearly succeeded in pulling August off her padded bench as she did it. He shifted forward and his wild dark red fishtail braids spilled over his shoulders. August sighed and thanked the creator he was much taller than Mercy. Her choice of clothing was downright killing him today.

Bolting to the door, Mercy nearly forgot the boots she made for Jacob and Callum. She ran back to her spare room, grabbed them, and put them into her big silk bag before heading out with August.

As he waited for her at the door, he stared out into the open woods on the other side of the stone path. Mercy remembered August's father doing the same thing during storms. She was flooded by memories of times when she would look out her open bedroom window and see August's dad deep in thought, looking into the woods like they were going to reveal a secret.

She missed living next door to August's parents. August's mother was one of Mercy's favorite people. She had hardly seen the parents who raised her and didn't feel a bond with them like she did with August's mother. She understood Mercy in a different way. Something told Mercy that his mother saw a little of herself in Mercy. If she could be half the woman August's mother was, Mercy decided she would feel accomplished in her life. Thoughts of speaking to his mother in this new language sent Mercy's heart pounding, and she filled with excitement over what words she might say. To express herself with these symbols in such detail sent her mind out into the universe, beyond the auras in their sky.

As they walked, Mercy stayed ahead of August, continuing her excited prance down the stone path in her new boots all the way to Jacob and Callum's house. When they arrived, they both presented the new boots to their friends as the door opened.

Callum grinned as Mercy handed him the boots, then sat down right where he was to try them on. They fit perfectly, and he stepped out of his door and hugged her in thanks. After he walked back inside, Callum tapped on the wall twice for Jacob who met them in the foyer. August handed him his new boots and Callum grinned, tapping his chest to say thank you.

Once they were ready to head to the cave, they exited the home through the back, under the cover of the trees. Mercy twirled and spun through the woods, her wild, golden-brown braids flying around her head in a halo. Not having to think about where she stepped and trying to avoid a twig or rock was much more freeing than she had anticipated. It was absolute bliss and Mercy was going to soak up every moment, every single step.

After dancing the entire way to the mouth of the cave, Mercy wasn't tired in the slightest and sprung from the edge, heading inside. She landed on her feet with hardly a sound, then Callum, Jacob, and August followed.

Mercy was excited to see that Jacob had already set traps. The only reason she knew this was that she smelled the slight scent of a spider's silk which was slightly different from Rew's. Jacob walked by and stepped over the silk line to show where it was located, and the rest of the group followed. Mercy was curious about what would happen when someone tripped the line but would wait to ask until they were able to talk.

Before they arrived at the first large chamber, Jacob took his torch and held it up, showing Mercy the camouflaged entryway that they had just finished. It looked as though the wall was solid with rock and stone. The concrete mixture must have been developed from Jael's memory. The wall matched the cave surroundings so well that if she had not already been here before, she would have never suspected there could be a door there.

Grinning and proud of himself, Jacob walked up to the door and simply pushed in a leaver that was hidden by a false rock. The mechanism clicked, releasing the door handle. Jacob easily slid open the door, and they all heard a suction sound as the seal was broken. After the door was propped open, they entered a small dark room. Once inside, the camouflaged door was shut behind them. Jacob pulled a finger-length piece of metal from his belt and slid it into a hole in the smooth, dark wall. He turned it to the left once, and it clicked, opening the door.

After removing the key, he guided everyone into the large cavern and shut the door behind him, sealing it with a large bar. Jacob and Callum continued on while she stared at the wall. Mercy was stunned. The entire thick wooden wall was covered in a thin layer of copper.

She silently gasped as August came up behind her and slid his arms under hers. Wrapping his arms around her, he tried to think of what he would say first.

August leaned in with his lips close to her ear and whispered, "I can't wait to hear your voice."

Frozen and unsure about herself, Mercy cleared her throat and squeaked. August chuckled in her ear, and she squirmed to get out of his arms so she could try again. August released her so that she could focus, and she cleared her throat.

This time Mercy was able to speak, and she said, "Can we just live down here? I can go get Rew. She will love it."

Smiling, August said, "No, but eventually we are going to make sure we can all speak wherever we want. I know Oz and Jael are going to return. If Oz can survive fifteen earth years among those jade trees in the dead woods, he can find out who is taking our people. We can do this. I know we can."

Mercy threw her arms around him and softly said, "This is the best day of my life."

After he kissed her on the head, August said, "Let's get to work so we can make sure we're ready when Oz and Jael arrive. They will need to remain hidden, which means they will need a place to stay. You will be helping Callum design the living areas of the base."

"I would love to! I was worried you were going to make me haul dirt," Mercy said with her eyes wide.

"Really? I would never make you haul dirt," he said and smiled.

Mercy leaned back to narrow her eyes at him as she flatly said, "Oh, I must be confused since you have treated me like dirt for so long."

With that, Mercy spun out of August's arms and skipped away toward Callum. With that kick to the gut August sighed and shook his head before trying to think about their next step.

The northern lava tube would serve as the general housing area, and the main chamber would be for operations. The small cavern behind the main chamber would be for command and have the command's housing. Oz and Jael would stay there until enough of their people could be recruited, and they could hold a vote.

They would need to set up military and government structures. August's mother was the best strategist he knew. That woman could figure out how to shift people around to do her bidding without them ever having a clue. August needed an expert if he was going to pull this off. He just had no idea how he would convince her.

Suddenly, it struck August. He didn't need to convince her. August could get *Mercy* to do it.

Mercy was the child of two parents who had been missing since she was too young to remember. August's mother told her she could often hear Mercy's mother singing softly to herself, and her father often painted symbols he should not have used.

Symbols that represented ideas.

Mercy knew now that the memories that were passed to her meant language was developing, which was forbidden. Mercy was given to August's neighbors, but she was far more attached to August's mother than she was to her adoptive parents.

They were quiet and did their best with Mercy, but she was a blazing ray of rainbows and sparkles. As a child, she had so much energy that her parents had to build her a swing inside her bedroom. Rainy days meant Mercy would tear through the house like a storm, so they quickly learned how to keep her entertained. The swing went in the year after they were picked to be her parents.

Mercy looked at Callum as he grinned and held up the prototype for the lights they had been designing. Light-emitting diodes (LEDs) were the easiest to experiment with, according to Jacob, who had ultimately ended up completing the project. Although her mind should have been on LEDs, it was back on August and the nonsense he kept pulling, putting his arms around her with no intention of doing anything more.

August has the emotional availability of a swarming shit fly, Mercy thought. If he thought he had heard the end of this, he was out of his mind. If he didn't want to be with her, that was one thing. But he did, so Mercy would drag August, kicking and screaming, out of his shell if she had to. She was tired of watching him live in a mostly empty home and never challenged himself to do better.

Mercy refocused on her job and took a good look at the new lights. They were identical to the ones from Jael's memories. She knew Jacob was intelligent, but she was a little blown away that he had already developed lights. When she sat down to help, all she could do was laugh and think about the beautiful dress pattern she had left sitting on her craft table.

Forgetting she could talk freely now, a thrill of excitement shot through her as she asked Callum, "How did Jacob make these lights so quickly?"

Thinking for a moment, Callum responded, "Jacob is having trouble picking up the speaking part, but he seems to have found his calling while experimenting with electronics and chemistry. He loves engineering. I think when we get all of this going, he wants to lead the engineering area."

Mercy grinned and said, "He found his place so quickly. I hope I can find my passion that fast. The speaking part is much more complicated than I thought, but I practiced with just my mouth after August first gave me the knowledge. I think that's the easiest way to pick it up. The muscle memory is there, it just needs to be exercised. I can't believe even muscle memory can be passed through the connection. If I stopped thinking about my words, they would be jumbled and confusing. This requires a lot of attention."

"Do you think, once everything is over, that we will keep using the connection that we've used for so long? It's a part of us, but it's also a reminder of our forced silence," Callum explained.

Mercy thought a moment and said, "I don't know. We might want to keep using it just to preserve our culture. It's invasive, but it's unique to us. Don't forget it can also help us heal if we are ever severely injured."

"Yuck, don't remind me," Callum said as he cringed and shivered.

Mercy laughed as she said, "I hate it too, I ripped the skin along my arm once as a kid, and my mom made me drain a small scorpion she found in the garden. It was awful, but my arm healed quickly. It had been a gaping wound from falling on a sharp rock."

Callum stared at her disgusted and scowling and said, "Can we talk about something that's not repulsive, please?"

Mercy giggled and said, "Sure. Where are we going to hang these lights? And did Jacob find a way to power everything?"

Narrowing his eyes, Callum said, "I didn't pay attention to how it works, but Jacob already made rolls of wire and said to hang the LED lights wherever we want. He has some contraption built over one of the hot springs that August dug up in the back of the south lava tube. It's unnerving to be around, it hums, and you can feel your hair stand on end."

"Jacob already found a source of electricity?!" Mercy nearly yelled.

Callum chuckled and wiggled his shoulders back and forth as he smugly said, "Careful, sweetie, that's my sexy genius man you're talking about."

Mercy laughed then had a sudden somber change in her mood. "August still won't move an inch."

Callum's mouth parted, and he said, "Mercy, I'm afraid to say you are just going to have to flip up that sorry excuse of a flimsy shirt and flash him your plump, gorgeous breasts. Maybe that will wake his dumb ass up."

Mercy's mouth dropped open, and she dropped her eyes to her cropped top, putting her hands over her top.

She looked up to Callum and sadly asked, "You don't like my shirt?"

Callum threw his head back and roared with laughter and said, "No way. You look as steaming as a cup of hot tea in that shirt. But it's going to take a little bit more than your toned stomach and a little under-boob action to tip August over the edge. You know what a solid block of stone that guy is."

Mercy sighed, knowing that she was going to have to do precisely what Callum said. She was aching for just about anything serious from August at this point.

This called for drastic measures.

If anyone knew how to do something drastic, it was Mercy.

12

The woman with the blue skin and hair took a deep breath, then sat up with a startle, causing her hair twists and fishtail braids to fall over her shoulders. Blue eyes blazing, she whipped her head around and saw Oz sitting on the floor.

Jael's small frame was asleep next to him on the ground. With his legs stretched out and crossed, Oz leaned back with his hand on Jael's side. He grinned at the blue woman as she whipped her head around, scanning her unfamiliar surroundings.

After taking a good look at the other two people asleep in the pods, she looked down at her traditional clothes, then up at Oz's modern-looking, tactical clothing. When she eventually looked up at Oz's eyes, he was standing and offering her his hand. Jael remained asleep on the floor as Oz connected with the woman with the blue skin.

To avoid frightening her, he started with memories of the camp and what he and Jael had been doing to free her and her companions. He showed her how he and Jael had killed the humans, and how he administered the medicine to all three of them so they would wake up.

Overwhelming gratitude poured from her through the connection, and she moved over so Oz could sit down. He sat next to her on the cot, and it made a creaking sound. He revealed enough of the plan to her that she began nodding in agreement. He could feel her anger growing about her abduction from her home. Oz didn't pass along the information that he had learned from the human woman that he'd drained, but he did pass over the gift of Jael's knowledge and language.

The woman's bright blue eyes widened in awe as the information cascaded into her mind like a waterfall. Oz sensed her overwhelming thanks as the realization of what she now held in her mind began to sink in. The information began seeping in and rapidly spreading, enveloping her brain in a blanket of linguistic hope. He knew she would need a little while to process everything, so he nodded, and she severed the connection. The woman's blue eyes were rimmed with dark blue lashes, and they fluttered as her mind sorted her vast new foundation of knowledge.

When he turned around, Oz found Jael sitting up with a glowing grin. She was a picture of delight and must have been watching when he passed the woman Jael's language.

Remorse crawled up his ribs as he watched Jael's joyful expression. He hadn't told Jael about what he saw and didn't plan on telling her any time soon. He didn't know how to explain what he now knew. To put the things those humans have done to his people into words felt like toxic sludge in his throat. He wanted nothing to do with it.

Knowing he still needed to process the information regardless of his feelings, Oz's stomach was in knots. Swallowing down the sadistic doctor's mind was not going to be pleasant. However disturbing her mind was, she did hold vast medical information for not only his kind, but also Jael's.

They were lucky that they now possessed this second massive wealth of information, he thought to himself. He just hoped he could cope with all the trauma he had absorbed in that moment of weakness. The cost to him would not outweigh the great benefit to his people. As he decided it was worth it, the screams of his people echoed in his mind, threatening to force their pain on him again.

The depravity of these humans was beyond anything he could understand, and he needed more time. Telling Jael, not showing her, was the only option, he decided. The last thing he wanted was to dump his anger onto Jael, especially as he explained everything.

He would not be able to hold back his emotions and keep them from spilling over into the connection. The story was traumatic enough without being force-fed the feelings as well. He wouldn't do that to her or anyone else. She didn't deserve to bear the weight of his pain as well as her own. No one should have to absorb the mind of their people's torturer.

Oz decided he would wait until after they had taken the people they had rescued to the caves near his village. The feelings he'd received from the blue woman indicated she was happy to leave her old life and wanted to seek retribution for her abduction.

If she only knew the depths of her captor's crimes.

Once the beige woman and the brown man woke from their forced sleep, the blue woman calmed the beige woman and, at the same time, Oz calmed and connected with the man.

Oz transferred Jael's knowledge to the dark brown man. His reaction was similar but more subdued. He simply stared at his hands, while his growing smile told Oz everything he needed to know. These people loved this new intoxicating lingual drug as much as he did.

Knowledge is such an addictive, organized presence to behold in a formerly chaotic place of solely abstract thoughts and ideas. It was amazing to allow words to blanket thought and for those thoughts to suddenly have a concrete, buildable structure, with it all falling into place like a solved puzzle. It would allow them to build vast fortresses and castles in worlds unknown, as well as break down the slightest essence of life, seeing inside the building blocks of life itself. All this grandeur had simple beginnings with words and numbers. These beautiful little marks and swirls, when formed in groups, could hold unlimited power.

The power of these symbols equaled that of a God. They now had the ability to create and destroy; to express a thought which has no physical form.

Worlds could be conquered with this power alone.

Once he and the man ended the connection, Oz found the blue haired woman had already taken care of transferring Jael's knowledge to the beige complected woman. He was astonished that the blue woman was able to collect herself so well after waking up in unfamiliar surroundings, especially considering that their species didn't sleep. These people will be perfect to take to the cave to help, he thought.

Oz began pointing to the gear around the room, and the three of them got to work preparing for the journey while investigating what the humans had packed away in the duffel bags.

While Oz was helping his people, Jael was picking through the food and having a feast in the humans' tent. Her appetite had returned after the moment of nausea she experienced from taking her first life. She decided that what she had done didn't deserve her pity or guilt. Jael felt as though she had indeed done the right thing.

She dined in the human's empty tent while Oz began removing the bodies and dumping them in the woods for the scavengers. Everything, including the bones, would be gone by the morning. She tried not to think about that as her second meal was heating on the small electric stovetop.

Jael was nearly bouncing as the little metal tin heated, and her spaghetti dish was finished. Obviously, it was not actual spaghetti, but it looked just like it, and she was always down to pretend that it was real spaghetti from Earth. After eating some kind of fake red meat with a gravy-type sauce, she was still hungry, but not starving like she had been. She didn't recognize the faux meat, but it was good, and she was hungry, so she didn't care. The other humans had been consuming it, so it couldn't possibly be that bad, she hoped.

Mid bite of spaghetti, Oz walked in and widened his eyes at the mess of empty tins and cans around her. She had red sauce dripping down her chin and had no idea. He grinned and tried not to laugh, putting his hand over his mouth.

He dropped his smile and thought for a moment. Still watching her, Oz walked over and sat next to her and put out his hand to connect.

Oz spoke first and said, "I am not going to tell anyone what I saw in that woman's head. Not yet anyway. I need to pick through it first, and it's going to take a while. Through the connection, it was too vivid. I could hear, see, and even smell everything she did to my people. I can't pass that on to you or anyone else. It would be wrong. Just know that I will explain everything once we get to the caves. I'm sure you want to know, but I won't dump that kind of trauma and anger onto you."

"I understand. You're right. I do want to know, but if you don't feel like it's right to share it, I can't fault you for that. I know you, Oz, and I never doubted there was a reason you killed her. I knew what I was signing up for when I came with you. I knew what we might have to do," Jael said with sincerity in her eyes.

Oz grinned but with sadness and a distance in his eyes.

He slid his eyes to his own hands and said, "We saved three of my people and finally saw the faces of our enemy. I informed our new friends that we would need to keep what we saw here a secret until we meet with the others in the caves. We will be heading to our new home soon, and all three of them want to come along with us."

Oz continued, "I don't think it's too presumptive to say this. I don't know how or why I know, I just do. Jael, because of you, my people *will* be free. Everywhere."

13

When Callum and Mercy made it back to the main cave's chamber, they found Jacob and August both soaked with sweat from building the floors and walls with the cement they had made.

Under a few layers of sandy dirt, they had found an area of compressed volcanic ash which they crushed and finely ground. Their people traded with other villages to get lime for soap and mortar for stone fireplaces, so they had obtained several buckets of quality lime when a trader recently passed through.

August's mother swung the deal through someone she knew on the north side of the village. She ensured that the trader would be back with more for her fictitious friend's new stone porch business. Callum had been the actor for her ruse.

Tools clanked and scraped against the cement and wooden molds while Mercy watched August work, entranced. He and Jacob both had their tunics off and were laying concrete on top of one of the leveled areas of the floor.

In order to use less concrete, they laid down flat stones first, then layered the concrete over the top. Afterward, when they cleared the concrete from the stones, it created a mosaic on the floor.

The floor needed to be level and steady for everything they planned to develop in this room, and it also needed to be strong, so adding the flat stones to the flooring seemed necessary. They didn't have enough metal to reinforce the concrete, so they made do with what they had.

Mercy took in all of August's muscles glistening in the LED light that was shining up from the floor on the edges of the room. Then, she noticed the long wires that all headed to the same lava tube. She looked up and saw several long, suspended light fixtures and wiring hanging from the cave's ceiling, but nothing was wired together yet. She wondered how much longer it would be before they would have lights running through the entire cave. She had never seen it herself, but from Jael's memories, it seemed magical. The brightest thing she had ever seen so far was the warm, yellow light of a fire.

Even though their sky never went dark, it wasn't nearly as bright as Earth's. With no sun and only auras to give them light, their world was always cast in a colorful glow of neon green, violet, and fuchsia. She wasn't sure which she preferred. The sun on Earth seemed so warm and inviting, but the constant auras on her planet were entrancing.

August walked by, stealing her attention, and she had a thrilling idea strike her.

Jacob was concentrating on smoothing the concrete, and his back was to Mercy. As Callum walked around Mercy to stand next to Jacob, she met August's orange eyes and winked at him as she raised her right hand to grasp the bottom hem of her shirt. August froze and then darted his head over to Callum and Jacob, then right back to Mercy. With a devilish grin, Mercy lifted the left side of her top and showed August one of her full breasts.

While August was still wide-eyed, stunned, and adjusting himself in his pants, Mercy dropped the hem of her cropped top and blew him a kiss.

She walked over to a chatting Callum as Jacob was nodding yes. Callum was talking about plumbing and how they were going to make the pipes without causing suspicion. Mercy stood next to Callum and listened to his issues about the dangers of fumes without ventilation.

Callum narrowed his eyes at Jacob as he said in a direct tone, "We're not going to be able to do any metalsmithing in the cave or bring more people in to work until we find a way to install a ventilation system. It's unsafe to breathe stagnant air, not to mention the chemicals released during metallurgy."

Callum shook his head, "Don't give me that look, Jacob. I will shut this whole operation down. Don't test me."

Releasing a rough sigh, Jacob rolled his eyes, knowing he would likely end up with the job of creating a ventilation system.

Half listening, August crept quietly around the group and then slipped behind Jacob to stand next to Mercy. The moment she noticed him standing to her right, he slipped his left hand under her plump rear and gave her a soft pinch on her inner thigh. Shrieking and batting at August's arm and chest, Mercy turned back to Callum, who was now staring with a scowl and his arms crossed.

Mercy cringed as Callum said, "Would you two please fuck and get it over with? The sexual tension between you is wearing me out. Well, actually, I'm wearing Jacob out, *but* you get it."

Openmouthed, but with no trace of shock on his face, Jacob rolled his tan eyes once again and got back to work on the floor. Callum just glared at August and then pointed to the door of the cave's chamber. August guessed they were being instructed to take their nonsense elsewhere, so he smirked and tipped his head at Mercy, and she followed.

August needed to visit his mother with Mercy anyway. They needed to recruit more people.

They headed toward the door, and August said, "We will go start the recruitment process. I'm bringing my mother in on this part."

Callum grumbled and shook his head, saying, "Good, we need someone with some damn sense around here. August, sometimes I think you have brain worms."

"Uh, thanks, asshole," August said as he scowled and walked toward the door with Mercy.

Mercy covered her mouth to hold in a laugh and picked up her pace. They made their way through the cave and down the lava tube, ducking under the trip line and jumping up through the hole in the cave's ceiling.

After a reserved walk to August's parents' home, August and Mercy walked to the door and found it wide open, so they went in. August tapped on the wall twice, and his mother came around the corner with a grin. Upon seeing them, she pushed August out of the way to wrap her arms around Mercy in a suffocating hug.

Mercy was the woman his mother had always wanted for August, and she was overly delighted that he was finally giving her a chance. Sarah had wanted August to pursue Mercy since their adolescence.

Mercy was on a throne of gold in Sarah's eyes.

Sarah walked to one of their padded benches and patted the seat next to her for August to sit and connect with her. When August sat down, the bench creaked under his weight, and his mother scowled at him. If he so much as left a scratch on her furniture, he would have to run, so he didn't move around again. August gave her his hand, and Sarah initiated the connection.

Sarah said into August's mind, "Yes, my son, is there something other than bringing my favorite young woman to visit that you needed to speak with me about?"

His mother already knew what he was going to ask, and he quickly realized that this was just one of the many tactics he needed to learn from her.

He replied and said, "I do have something I need help with. I need to recruit intelligent people who want to help work at the base. It's already sealed and soundproof. We need more bright minds and creative hands involved."

"Absolutely. Are there any specifics I need to know?" she asked.

"They need to at least regularly visit a home along the tree line and have an uninterrupted path to the entrance of the base. As long as they live around the village's perimeter or visit somewhere regularly that touches the edge, they can come. We need to ensure that the satellites aren't tipped off to what we're doing. They need to be able to keep a secret from the village elders until the project is far enough underway that no one will be able to do anything about it," August said, with his eyes darting between his mother and Mercy.

"I will pass on the gift to the people I find are a good fit first. Depending on their reaction, I can tell them what's brewing. I'll ask if they want to join your efforts and if so, I'll send them to the lava tube. I can tell them to wait for someone to come out and meet them."

August nodded and said, "That will work, we need at least ten more recruits right now. Don't forget to warn them about the trap set with the single thread of silk. I don't want any of our people to be shot with venom darts."

"As long as I get some new boots for my strolls in the deep woods, we have a deal," Sarah added as she looked down at Mercy's boots.

Chuckling, August darted his orange eyes to Mercy, who held a curious grin. He pointed to his mother and then his boots. Mercy nodded that she understood and would make his mom a pair. August wondered if Mercy knew his mother was only cooperating because he brought Mercy with him. Judging by Mercy's smirk, she had a good idea.

After breaking the connection with his mother, he walked to Mercy and held his hand out to help her up. They headed to Mercy's house to rest, but August hadn't mentioned to her yet that he planned to stay at her house this time.

In all the time they had been friends, August had never rested at her house nor her at his. In their culture, this would be a clear sign that someone wanted more than just friendship.

They didn't go to August's house often. It was rather sparsely furnished, and Mercy hated it. Not liking it much either, August was rarely there. He was at Jacob and Callum's, or he was at Mercy's house. He only bathed and rested at his own home.

Recently, he had spent more time than usual at Mercy's, after Jacob and Callum kicked him out, again. He didn't even remember why they made him leave. It was probably because he had done something stupid, he thought as he walked.

After they left August's parents' home, Mercy began to pull her hand away, but August took her arm and held it while he continued walking. With a small smile, Mercy walked with him all the way to her home. When they were out in the village, he never touched her except for shoulder taps. Thrilled about this change Mercy had trouble containing her excitement.

A group of children rushed by, playing a game of chase, then they passed a busy cart with people all around trying to trade for oranges.

After speaking out loud in the caves, Mercy was dying to be able to talk to August out in the open, but she knew that wasn't going to be possible for a while.

She desperately hoped they could discover who their enemy was, and why they were stealing their people. Nausea boiled in Mercy when she thought about the fate of those who had disappeared. She always wondered what had happened to her parents. The pain of the loss was calloused now, but it was always there, reminding her to stay silent when in the open.

That little slice of heaven in the cave, the place where they could speak? She could thrive there and finally be herself. Endless silence was the worst kind of entrapment she could fathom. Mercy hid her agony well, but it was never far from the surface. It always threatened to spill over if she didn't keep herself occupied.

When they reached her door, she expected August to come inside and then quickly leave as usual. Following close behind her as she went to the kitchen, August headed to her living area. He sat on her bench and removed his boots. Getting comfortable, he set his boots to the side and out of the way.

Stunned and a little confused, Mercy blinked away her surprise, changed her plan and made them both a plate of flatbread and avocado with fruit before sitting next to him on her bench. August was staring into the hearth and slowly eating while Mercy's confusion was growing by the moment.

What she wasn't going to do was ask what he was doing, mostly because August was like a feral tarantula. He was always skittish about her advances, even lately. The only thing that changed after their last argument was that she knew for a fact he cared about her. As she collected their finished plates, she tried to avoid looking at him. She quickly went to the kitchen to clean the plates.

Once she was finished, she turned around, gasped, and leaped when she found August was standing directly behind her. He smirked at her small leap of fright and then took her face in his hands. He looked into her golden eyes and finally put his lips on hers. Mercy was overwhelmed and could barely hold still. The man she had wanted since she was a girl was now kissing her. August turned her around and reached under her rear to set her on the kitchen counter behind them without breaking the kiss.

Mercy set her hands on the counter behind her as August leaned into her. He kissed her along her jaw and down the center of her neck. Hardly able to take a breath, Mercy was throbbing with need as he lifted her cropped top and took a brown peak into his mouth. His hand slid around her breast to hold it as he twirled his tongue. She was already going to come undone and rolled her hips against him. August lifted her up from the counter and carried her, her legs wrapped around him, to her unmade bed.

Leaning over the bed, August pulled her cropped top off in one swipe and then kissed her again as he held a plump breast in each hand. He stroked both of her peaks with his thumbs sending shivers down her spine. Filled with heat, Mercy began wiggling out of her leggings. August chuckled against her lips, then licked her bottom lip before pulling away. After sliding down her body, he pulled her boots off slowly. August reached up for the hem of her leggings around her thighs and peeled them away, tossing them on the floor.

Trembling with the growing heat at her core, Mercy's eyes met August's at her feet, and he grinned as he crawled up to the top of her thighs. She threw her head back and tried to stay calm when she realized what he was going to do. August took a finger and trailed from her knee to her folds before dipping a finger inside and lightly rubbing his thumb in a circle around her bud. Gasping at the contact, Mercy's hips rolled, and August pinned her hips as he continued to circle her bud. She threw her hands to the sides of the bed and squeezed her sheets in her hands as he gave her just enough to reach the clouds but not enough to stroll into heaven. Mercy's breathing was sharp. He pulled his hand away and put his palm over her round lower belly.

Stunned, Mercy threw her head up and stared at August with confusion. He chuckled and smirked before he quickly took her bud into his mouth and flicked her mercilessly with the tip of his tongue. Mercy was shaking and sweat began trickling from her brow as he took her right to the edge and then slowed down. If this was her repayment for her little show earlier, then she would have to give him a performance more often.

This was a punishment she *needed.*

Once Mercy was rolling her ankles and curling her toes, August took her most sensitive place between his front teeth and growled as he rubbed his tongue in one long lick along her bud. Falling over into absolute madness, Mercy slapped a hand over her mouth to muffle her deep throat clicks as waves of pleasure were wrung out under August's tongue.

Still trembling, Mercy lay there attempting to catch her breath as August crawled up next to her and brushed the stray hairs that had escaped from her braids out of her face. Mercy was overcome with joy as August smiled down at her. He hadn't even taken his shirt off, so Mercy began pulling the hem, and he helped her remove it. He quickly slipped out of his pants, and Mercy pulled him onto the bed. She leaned in and kissed him, tasting herself on him, then licked down his throat.

Mercy had been dreaming of this for as long as she could remember, and she knew exactly what she was going to do, especially after she read all of those dirty books from Jael's memory back on Earth.

Mercy was going to make sure she gave August her best.

She licked him between his pecs and then along the center of his abs. Mercy kissed him down his hips and then wrapped her long tongue around his length and slid all the way to the tip. Not expecting her tongue, August clenched his body at such a thrilling, hot sensation. Mercy took her right hand and lightly stroked the softness underneath his length while her left hand assisted her tongue. August was rolling his hips and leaned his head back for the clicks deep in his throat.

He was close, so Mercy pressed in gently under his length and increased her pace. With a gasp, August rocked back and forth a few times as his release poured from him. With the last of his release, Mercy licked the tip of his length, sending a jolt through August that resulted in a high pitch squeak with two wild orange eyes.

Mercy giggled as she headed for the hearth to warm some bath water and left August stunned and satisfied in her bed. After she set the bucket next to the fire, she went back to the bedroom and found August sitting up on the end of her bed, thinking.

She knew that he had been preoccupied with her and not thinking about everything that needed to be done at the base. Now, he was likely doing just that as he looked down at Mercy's old wood floor.

Callum and Jacob couldn't do it all. Jacob was still having trouble with speech and wasn't confident enough yet, and Callum was not interested in leading anything. Mercy knew August was the perfect person for that job. He just needed to clear his head.

August was exactly like his mother, and he just needed to remove all the distractions, like his turmoil with Mercy. Sitting on the end of the bed, the fog in mind finally began to clear. Mercy was his. He didn't know if he deserved her or not.

Probably not.

Definitely not.

But he wasn't going to give her up for anything.

Thoughts about the base rolled through August as he looked up to Mercy, staring at him from the door, still nude and with a grin on her face. She was by far the most beautiful woman in the village. He would never have admitted that when he was with Mazarin, but it was the truth. He always thought she would end up with Oz or Jacob when they were growing up. That was before Jacob met Callum when they were in their mid-twenties, according to Earth years. Jacob and Callum took far too long to end up together, everyone knew it was only a matter of time.

Guilt filled him for stringing Mercy along for so long. Mazarin would have wanted him to move on long before he did. He couldn't believe how idiotic he had acted, holding onto a ghost. There was no way Mazarin was alive, and even if she were, he doubted he would ever see her again. It just wasn't realistic to think she would come back.

He had seen Jael's world. If their enemy was a greater force than Jael's people? How did they have a chance? They had to try to stop their people from being stolen. But getting anyone back? He doubted that was possible.

No one who had been taken ever returned.

Meeting Mercy's eyes, August gave her a half grin as he heard the hiss of the water overflowing from the buckets at the fireplace. Mercy jumped from the wall and leaped over her bench to take the buckets away from the fire. That was not the first time Mercy had left the water buckets too close, leaving August to scrape the ash cement from her hearth.

The memory of the water heating system he'd promised her to hit him like a tree branch while running through the woods. He had forgotten all about it. After they rested, he would build her a water heating tank above her hearth and connect it to her bath. Oz had provided the information on how to do it, but he knew he wasn't Oz, so this would be a task. August could do the work, he just needed specific plans. He sighed as he wished his friend were there to help him, just like he always had during their childhood. He had the memories; he just didn't have the context. Oz hadn't passed on his carpentry skills along with the plans.

After their baths, they would both get back to work helping Jacob and Callum set up the base.

They would both *finally* be able to focus.

14

The blue female, Amelia as she had decided to be called, proved to be more than proficient in medicine. She had been an apprentice to the healer in her village on the other side of the mountain.

Oz hadn't disclosed much, but the human woman he had drained was a physician, and he now held her memories *and* skills. He would pass on the information to Amelia after he explained that she would also have to receive some memories of the horrors that their people endured at human's hands.

He would do his best to filter out most of it, but some of the essential memories were attached to the brutal crimes she had committed.

The human woman also had a knack for chemistry, and that would make things easier for everyone once they had a lab set up in the cave. If he could find a way to separate the knowledge from her actions, he would, but they were intertwined, and he wasn't sure it was possible to peel the two apart in his mind. He wondered if great blessings and good luck always came with such heinous curses and costs.

He wondered what clues they would find at the campsite. Oz knew they only had a short time before they would need to leave. They had already far overstayed their welcome.

He opened the third bag in the north tent, where they had found his people. There, he found weapons that looked like the ones from Jael's memories, but much more high-tech. A wave of nausea rolled through him when he thought about the daunting task ahead for all of them, not just what he and Jael had to do on this mission. His people would be at risk if they pursued freedom, but it was worth it, and he knew that. Even before speaking so much as a single word aloud, he knew he would give his life for the privilege.

For the right.

In the fourth and final bag, he found the doctor's tools he had been looking for. He pulled two devices in particular from the bag and tossed them next to him on the ground. The rest of the tools and equipment would be helpful at the cave, but the devices on the canvas floor would burn with the tents. Contempt for the small machines burned inside of him like a raging flame, heating him from the inside out.

Feeling a tap on his shoulder, he found Jael behind him with her wrist out. She wanted to know about the devices at his feet, but he wasn't sure if he wanted to explain.

Oz took her wrist and connected with her saying, "Those things were used to commit torturous acts against my people. They will burn along with the tents."

Jael said, "Please tell me, if not everything, just about this."

Releasing a ragged breath, he said, "The metal box with the digital display opens for fingers or toes to fit inside. They close the box, and it uses a cauterizing tool to burn the nail root and bed, so the nail stops growing. They can't use us until we are properly de-clawed. The other tool that looks like hooked sheers are for removing the end of our tails."

Nausea filled Jael's gut as what he told her sunk in.

She said, "Do you mean they aren't killing your people like you always thought?"

He replied, "That's exactly what I'm saying. The physician I drained enjoyed using those tools while my people were awake. Her memories were filled with their screams."

At that, Oz severed the connection and put his arms around Jael. She pulled him to her and kissed him. After a few moments to process, Jael finished putting together what she had gathered to fill her pack. Their new travel companions were also prepared with the supplies they'd collected from the camp.

The electronics most likely had hidden tracking devices in them, so they had to leave them all behind. The brown man, Carter, took some of the devices apart and studied them. He expressed through a connection with Oz that they would be able to duplicate the technology if he had suitable materials and some help. Knowing Carter could duplicate the tech was a relief, and Oz wasn't too heartbroken about destroying it all.

Carter suggested they run an electric current through the human's jackets just in case there were hidden tracking devices. Oz agreed, and when the first jacket held together, they repeated it with all of them. Carter had rigged the battery on the ATV, and the process had been quick and easy. They hoped it was enough and they wouldn't be tracked.

To be sure, Oz searched the physician's memories, but

only found knowledge of trackers on weapons and the high-tech devices and nothing about trackers in the clothing. It was too cold to be concerned with it. They would ditch the coats when they reached a more temperate climate to the south.

According to the human physician's memories, her group wasn't due back for another few days. There was a parking lot with multi-wheeled vehicles and trailers where they were supposed to meet to transport the people they had stolen.

Just because they had a few days before anyone would expect the humans to return didn't mean they could stick around. They needed to head out right away and set this campsite ablaze. The satellites might be watching.

None of them could wait to watch the camp burn, but they knew they wouldn't be able to stay once Oz gave the signal to leave.

After Jael signaled to Oz that they had finished piling the entire campsite into the tents, he started and moved the small ATV to the north side of the camp, and into the entrance of one of the tents.

Jael was shocked to see Oz hot-wire the ATV in less than a minute. She couldn't believe it when he drove it like he had been driving modern vehicles all his life. He was sliding it into gear and driving right by her like he knew exactly what he was doing. He parked it smoother than she had ever parked a car in her life. It must be a fancy vehicle or some-thing, she told herself with confidence.

She was glad that he didn't see her surprised expression. Jael had been sure that she would be the one moving the ATV, especially considering she was the only one of them with an actual driver's license. Laughing to herself as she remembered her old tuna can of a car, she hoped, eventually, she could drive something a little cooler than her old whip of a car.

As Jael daydreamed about futuristic cars, Oz and Carter set pieces of highly flammable jade wood, found near the humans' campfire, in strategic places in the tents and ATV. Oz wondered if the humans were bringing the wood back for a purpose, as it was piled to one side of the camp. Maybe they just wanted it for the excellent light and heat it put off. They were all sad to see the ATV go, but they knew taking it meant the risk of being tracked.

Oz took a stick from the still glowing campfire and tossed it into the ATV, right on top of the large vials of transparent liquid that Jael had found in the human physician's tent. The large vials smelled strongly of alcohol, and Oz thought they would likely make a perfect accelerant for the fire.

The group headed toward Oz's village, and a short while after they began walking, they started to hear the crackles and smell the smoke from the fire as it bellowed behind them. Oz darted his eyes to Jael, who softly smiled at him, but he could tell she was troubled by all of this.

Knowing that their enemy was human gave Jael a knot in the pit of her stomach. She dreaded discovering the truth. The possibilities crashed over her like waves as she did her best to keep pace with Oz's long legs. Those menacing devices of torture were part of a bigger picture that Jael was becoming increasingly concerned about.

Had they jumped into a battle they couldn't possibly win? Surely not, she thought, as she looked at Oz and held his eyes as he gave her a small smile.

A smile like the one he used to when she was scared of his fangs.

A familiar tickle of butterflies fluttered around inside her as she thought about how scared she had been of being eaten, just to find out later he was vegan. That seemed like a lifetime ago. She hoped she was as wrong about what they were facing now as she was then.

Why did the enemy have to be human? Oz said they even smelled like her. How did they get all the way out here? Were they from Earth, or elsewhere? Could humans have evolved in more than one place? Somewhere deep in Jael's mind she wasn't surprised it was humans.

Memories from her life on Earth and how she was treated went off like bombs of warning. She knew humans. She knew their tactics and their ways to use -- to hurt and then take --to kill. Oz and his people did not deserve this, no matter the reason for this evil. She cringed as she thought about the medical devices that Oz had dropped at his feet back at the camp, and the anguish held inside of them -- humans and their thousands of years of wars, slavery, and genocide. All these things weighed heavier in Jael's heart than ever. If these humans were like those at home on Earth? She shook her head and swallowed down her dread-laced bile.

When she was still on Earth, the east was slowly declaring war on the west. The old world was in a constant battle with the new world. What no one seemed to grasp was that the maps that they'd poured and strategized over were just simple flat representations of a round globe. If you keep going east or west in any direction, you will always end up back where you began. It was an endless cycle with humans, and they always seemed to find a way back to their wicked ways. History was doomed to repeat, just like the Earth would keep turning and the sun would keep rising.

Guilt began eating at her as she desperately tried to separate herself from those humans, but it was becoming increasingly difficult. Judgment and cruelty were such a human thing, she thought, a human like her. Guilt by association wasn't a healthy way to think, but the thoughts were ruling her reeling mind, and she was unable to shake it. Humans try to portray themselves as altruistic heroes when they're often nothing but a wolf in sheep's clothing.

Her poisonous thoughts about her own species seeped into her heart like an oily black sludge. Jael tried to force away the feelings of panic that accompanied her disdain for her former world, her own people. What if there were more planets with humans? Were humans innately depraved creatures? Was it always going to be a part of their genetics?

She thought about her own behavior in the beginning, when she had first met Oz. She had been horrible to him. She had been judgmental, just like her people were with each other. Bile was growing and churning inside her, threatening to rise in her throat with the reality of the situation.

Noticing her change in demeanor, Oz put his hand out to the group, and everyone stopped. Jael stood and blankly stared at the ground as he studied her for a moment. After slowly approaching Jael, Oz took her face in his hand and brought her brown eyes to his.

His expression seemed to say, "Do we need to stop?" Jael shook her head no and softly smiled at him. He quietly looked at the rest of the group and nodded that they would continue in a moment. Oz kissed Jael on the head and halted the cascade of thoughts pouring through her head about her people.

Dread filled Jael. When they returned from this mission, things would be different. She and Oz would need to have a serious discussion about their relationship. They were going against humans like her. If he was going to play a role in his government and be a leader? He couldn't have a human on his arm, could he? Or would he need her *because* she is human? Jael knew she would have to either back away or play a very uncomfortable role, the thought of either terrified her.

Jael forced nausea down as best she could, but Oz noticed and stopped the group again. This time they all sat down, and Oz led Jael off behind a large oak tree. He pulled her to sit on the ground with him.

He quickly took her left wrist and connected with her softly saying, "I know something is wrong."

Unable to hold back her emotion and thoughts, they all cascaded into Oz, and his eyes widened in shock. A tear slid from her bloodshot eyes, and Oz kissed her forehead, then pulled her into his lap.

After Jael's breathing slowed, Oz said softly, "When we get to the cave, nothing will change. You're not going to back away, and don't worry about the future. What's the point of fighting for freedom if I can't love who I want? As long as you are a consenting adult, it shouldn't matter beyond that. Either our relationship won't matter to my people, or I won't fight. It's that simple."

Appalled, Jael gasped as she said, "Our relationship is not as important as your people's freedom."

Oz replied, "You're right. It's far more critical. Without you, our freedom would have been impossible. You are the *only* reason this is happening. If my people don't see that, then we will leave and go back to the treehouse. They can't get to us there. We were far safer there than we ever thought."

Jael responded, "I know how you feel about it, but I also know how important you are to this. I refuse to let my own wants hold you back from saving your kind. Oz, you're brilliant. I know they need you."

"They may need my skills, but I need you. I won't have it any other way," Oz said as he broke the connection and took Jael's face in his hands. He strung a line of kisses along her jaw, then held her to him.

Within moments, he knew she was close to sleep. Right before her snoring began, he pulled half of the stuff in her pack out with his one free arm while trying to find her mouthguard. She always gave a warning twitch right as she fell asleep, which seemed to buy him enough time.

He chuckled softly, thinking about the late-night television advertisement from her memories that gave him the idea for the mouthguard. The song on the commercial was constantly stuck in his head. He laughed under his breath about how he used to think everyone on her world rattled with the same noise she did. Getting comfortable, Oz patted her head and blew out a deep breath as he leaned back and lay against his pack.

He didn't miss her snoring at all.

He also didn't miss the emptiness he used to feel. He would not give up this little alien woman that he'd found, not for anything.

15

While Callum begrudgingly held up the round air duct, Jacob and Luna attached it to the anchors with hooks along the cave's ceiling.

Cooling and heating wasn't the issue for the caverns. They just needed strong airflow from the sealed area to the outside. The problem with airflow, however, was the accompanying sound flow.

Luna had been an enormous help with coordination since she'd arrived. She was one of the five new recruits from the village. Her white hair made her easy to spot across the vast space in the cavern, so Jacob never had difficulty finding her to ask for something.

With the lights now working and the rudimentary, gear-based thermal power generator creating electric power, Jacob decided to design an electrical mechanism to solve the problem of sound escaping through the air ducts. He developed a system that drew fresh air into the front room with a fan, then alternated between open and closed. It moved in opposition to the vent that went outside of the sealed and soundproofed area.

The oxygen flow would be tested once they had the technology in place. If the seal broke, he had installed a red warning light that would blink if the vent was open.

As the door to the sealed cavern shut, Callum whipped his head around and saw that August and Mercy had arrived and were walking toward them with more buckets of jade tree sap.

August made his way over to Callum, who said, "Now that you're actually helping, can you please get your ass up here so I can have a break. I am sick of this construction work."

Jacob narrowed his tan eyes, and Luna sighed, "You just finished taking a break. How are you already tired?"

Interrupting before Callum could spout out a retort, August said, "It's not about being tired as much as it's about the fact that he doesn't like the work."

With a nod, Jacob shot his eyebrows up in agreement. August chuckled as he climbed the tall wooden ladder next to Callum so that Jacob could go with Mercy and decorate with rolls of silk. They had traded a pair of Mercy's boots for the material, and she had picked multiple dark brown and cream colors for the bedding and furniture.

After Callum climbed down, he and Mercy briskly walked to the command area, where some of the recruits were busy setting up the living areas. Some were constructing the apartments, while others were installing plumbing and lights.

Looking up at the construction, thoughts of Jael ran through Mercy's mind. She couldn't wait to meet her and hoped she would like the apartment. August was convinced that Oz would be voted into whatever leadership position they decided to create once he returned. Oz as leader wasn't her concern. But after him? What next?

Mercy cringed, hoping that whatever government system they picked wouldn't end up corrupt like the governments from Jael's world. She wondered if it was even possible to prevent corruption or if transparency and ethics were always an illusion to those who choose to remain asleep.

Mercy briefly went through Jael's memories about politics, and what she saw was nothing but lies and hypocrisy. It was the same with religion and every other leading institution on Jael's Earth. Everything was always about *control*. Her people needed a system where each person could vote, and have those votes genuinely mean something.

When Oz lived in the village, he was pegged to be the next village leader. August was relieved because he didn't want his mother's responsibility, but Oz didn't seem to enjoy the idea either. She wondered how Oz would feel about still being the best pick, even after being gone for so long.

Mercy knew the thought of leadership had always bothered August. When Oz was banished, August began to act out to avoid having to take up the torch. Mercy would never forget when August ate the purple-stemmed mushrooms and ran through the village stark naked, hiding in various yards, just to leap out and scare the villagers.

Sarah found him and knew immediately he was twisted. She took him by his round ear all the way back to their home. Mercy had been sitting in the window of her room when she spotted Sarah dragging him back. August was easily double his mother's size at the time, and the sight was hilarious. He could have simply stood up, and he would have been out of her grasp.

Breaking her thoughts, Callum blurted out, "You want to include me in that interesting conversation in your head?"

Mercy blinked away her thoughts and realized she was standing in the command living quarters, completely zoned out and lost in her own mind.

Slapping a hand to her open mouth, she giggled and said, "I was just reminiscing about when August went wild after Oz was banished. Do you remember when he ran around naked and terrorized everyone after he ate those purple-stemmed mushrooms? His whole group of friends took up the torch after his mom dragged him home."

Callum threw his head back and laughed, "Now, that was an exciting time. I can't say I was all that upset about a bunch of sexy people running around without clothes."

Laughing, she said, "Of course, you weren't upset. I'm honestly surprised you didn't join in."

Grinning, Callum chuckled as he fanned himself and said, "Yes, it was a hot day, wasn't it? I had a bad experience with mushrooms as a teen. I didn't want a repeat, so I didn't take any until I was much older."

Callum was bold, and she wondered why it had taken so long for him and Jacob to get together. Then she remembered that Callum was terrified to make a move. He wouldn't admit it, but she knew better-- all those looks he gave Jacob when he thought no one was looking. Mercy was Callum's best friend and always had been, so she noticed every time.

Guiding her thoughts back to the project at hand, Mercy decided to go with a darker color scheme for the fabrics since the oak wood of the apartment would be stained lighter. After setting the fabrics to the side, she sat down on the wood floor of the apartment and looked down onto the new modern floor of the command center.

Admiring the work, Mercy couldn't believe what they had accomplished in such a short time. She wondered how fast they would be able to advance once they won their freedom. It was still such a faraway dream. They hadn't even finished the base or put a face to their enemy yet.

She could feel it, though. A storm of a different kind was brewing, and she felt it grow stronger as time passed. Sarah told her that some of the people to whom she had passed the gift mentioned they had been waiting and knew something was coming.

One person, a white-haired woman, had said, "So that is what the feeling I've been having was all about."

Mercy understood. She had been waiting too --for so long.

She could feel it before the village elders sent August on his mission to kill Oz. That deep stirring in her soul, the one that says, get up and be ready. Ready for what exactly? She didn't have any idea then, but she understood now.

When she looked around the smaller cavern, she could feel the power of their movement raining down over her. Glimpses of what the future held flashed through Mercy's mind as she walked to the hole in the wall where the windows of the apartment would be. She peered down at the wooden tables and stools being assembled with large hammers on the floor below. The LED lights shining above made the cavern glow, with the bright white light bouncing off the grey floor and walls.

She felt it now, what Jacob felt. That need to plug into

the power of development and progress. It was a decadent dessert, and Mercy was now thoroughly and hopelessly addicted. To be able to speak and communicate with symbols was to harness the power of their creator.

The creator had whispered into their hearts that they would all be free one day. That voice in their minds said, *I'm here, and you are not alone.* This creator was inside and a part of all of them. They were everywhere. They lit their paths and filled each person with the hope that their faith and undying determination would one day lead to freedom. A grin graced Mercy's face just then, one of empowerment and dreams being realized.

Callum walked up to her and softly said, "It's surreal to look at what we've been able to build so far. Jacob is so driven by this wild goal of total freedom. I've never seen him so happy. This is *right,* Mercy. This feels so right."

"This does feel right. It's like our momentum increases the more we grow with this project. It's growing exponentially, and the thrill of it is like a drug. The lights are just as magical as I wanted them to be, and the indoor heated water? Have you had a hot shower yet? August built a hot water tank above my hearth and ran a line over my bathtub! It's heaven."

August and Jacob came through the door, so Mercy waved them over. Once they were up the stairs and into the top apartments, they headed to the larger one on the right to meet Callum and Mercy and go over the next phase. They all sat on stools around a wood table in the living area. The stools allowed their tails to rest comfortably curled up behind them.

After they were all seated, August adjusted his tail one last time, and began by saying, "Since we have almost completed the construction phase, we need to start running evaluations and tests on everyone to find any particular skills or higher intelligence. After we have that information, we can form work groups. Each group will be tasked with goals that helps with forming the military structures and government systems, building weapons, or developing technology. Eventually, I think we should use the information to form a school. There will be more, but this is what we need to start with, and we can build from there."

Callum responded first and admitted, "What if I don't want to do any of that? I want to design buildings."

The group turned, and all looked at Callum incredulously.

Mercy laughed and said, "Callum, you and I can help in other ways, maybe the school? It won't be that bad."

Deadpanning, Callum said, "Why do we need a school when we have the connection? We can just transfer knowledge."

August spoke up and said, "Because we want to grow organic thought that is formed from learning. When the information is passed directly into to the mind, the natural development of the individual's thought processes are replaced by the processes of the person who passed that information. We want our people to be able to form their own unique thoughts and not be a copy of the next person. We will not grow intellectually if we follow that path."

Staring straight at August, then darting his eyes to Mercy, Callum chuckled and leaned in to say, "Good girl. You screwed his brain back on."

Gasping, Jacob rolled his eyes and leaned his head back. August couldn't help the ridiculous grin on his face. Clearly, Jacob had told August his ideas about organic thought before that little speech, but August wasn't planning to give Jacob any credit. He still hadn't said a thing, and August loved getting under Jacob's skin whenever he could. It was hard to do, but when August found his chance, he always took it.

Trying to change the subject, Mercy asked, "When do we think Oz and Jael might show up?"

Everyone at the table went quiet, then August finally spoke, "They should arrive any time now. No one knows for sure when, or if, they will make it."

"They will make it. I know they will," Mercy said sharply with her brow furrowed in August's direction.

"Either way, we move forward. If they don't end up returning, we will train, prepare, and send someone else to gather information," August said to a scowling Mercy.

Mercy huffed at August's response, and then Jacob turned toward her and spoke quietly and slowly, saying, "If anyone can accomplish this task, it will be Oz."

With everyone in shock at Jacob's first words, Mercy said, "Jacob's right, and we need to have a little more faith that Oz and Jael will be here soon."

After a pause, Mercy continued, "So, who is going to tell Oz's mother?"

Again, the table went silent.

August cleared his throat, then slid his orange eyes to Mercy and said, "When Oz returns, we will bring her to the base, but we will not share any information before then. We are not going to get her hopes up. She's lost two children, and I won't see her grieve Oz all over again, not if I can't help it."

They all nodded in agreement, and Mercy took August's hand under the table. He was finally getting back to himself, or maybe he had never really been himself before. He seemed surer of himself, and Mercy was falling hard. With every look from his bright tangerine eyes, she melted, and she was eager to get him back to her house.

In her mind, they had thousands of moons of time to make up for.

16

Carter halted the group, seemingly out of nowhere, and Jael was thankful. They had been walking until she collapsed, and after she slept, they would wait for her to wake up to walk and repeat the process. She thought she had counted a hundred sleeps so far but knew that was not an accurate way to determine the number of days they had been traveling, even if it was correct.

Oz approached Carter, and they connected their hands. Making a grim expression, Oz nodded slowly and broke their connection.

Stepping over an oak tree's root, Oz signaled to Jael, so she walked over to meet him and gave him her wrist. She had been connecting with Oz in front of the group regularly, and the physician, Amelia, was *always* awestruck by it. Jael made sure to angle herself so Amelia could see, and the blue-haired woman widened her eyes while she watched them. She hoped, eventually, she could be friends with some of the people that they had rescued. She couldn't wait to meet his friends at the cave as well.

Oz was her lover and her friend, but Jael had been yearning for a best friend since she'd lost contact with Sis. Amelia had already shared a handful of kind smiles with Jael, and she was hopeful about her becoming a friend.

Looking up at Oz, Jael wondered what it was that made him develop such a scowl on his face.

After spending much of his downtime riffling through and organizing the physician's memories, Oz had condensed and transferred the physician's medical information over to Amelia. Although he had warned her beforehand, she had been deeply disturbed by the memories Oz sent her. He did his best to remove the traumatic screams and visual memories of the physician's victims, but sharing some was unavoidable.

The medical knowledge that those specific memories provided could be vital to their people in an emergency, so Oz deemed it worth the cost. Shortly after he passed on the information, Amelia ended up vomiting in distress from what she had learned. Jael was beginning to think she didn't want to know the information Oz was holding.

She was thankful he didn't show her that first night after he had drained the human physician. Jael was having enough trouble dealing with killing a man, but these memories Oz held seemed far worse. That man deserved the knife she embedded in his neck, Jael believed, but taking a life and watching the light dim in someone's eyes was a hit to her soul that she didn't ever expect.

How could you hold onto your own spirit while you watch another spirit be severed from its host body? It was a gut-wrenching experience. To know someone will never take another breath because of you. It's enough to make anyone spill their lunch, and her stomach cramped as if in response.

Once she finished her train of thought, Jael gave Oz her wrist, and they connected.

In a concerned tone, Oz said into her mind, "We either need to spend a few days walking around this area or we need to wrap our faces in several layers of silk. We cannot breathe any of the air for about another six miles. Do you remember the program you watched about the fungus that makes ants go insane? The one where the fungus stalk grows out of their heads? They called it the Zombie Fungus."

Already nauseated and shaking her head, Jael grasped her stomach with her right hand and flatly said, "Please tell me you are kidding?"

"Unfortunately, no. Carter lived in the northern village on the other side of the mountain, and a traveling merchant said the mountain people were having an outbreak from a parasitic fungus. This fungus is uncommon in the mountains, but we must be safe. Carter was told this was where the bodies are taken when their people finally die, so the airborne spores don't spread to the other villagers."

"So, we are really going to risk this?" Jael said pointedly as nausea filled her gut.

Nodding his head, he broke the connection solemnly, pulled a shirt out of the bag, then ripped it in half. He wrapped the strips of the shirt around his own face, leaving only his eyes showing, then wrapped Jael's.

Evidently, they were going to run, because the next thing Jael knew, Oz gave his pack to Carter and knelt for Jael to slide on his back. She climbed on, carefully avoiding his curled tail with her pack, and they took off at unbelievable speeds. No matter how tight she gripped Oz around his strong waist and shoulders, the force of his run jarred her with every pounding step. The group had to be running at least thirty-five miles per hour and maintaining that speed. Oz was hardly breaking a sweat, even breathing through layers of silk.

As Jael looked around the group, she noticed they all seemed like they were exerting a negligible amount of energy to achieve their impressive sprinting speed. Amelia had an expression of bored leisure, and Jael could not understand how they all acted like their breakneck pace was *easy*. Most of the group wasn't wearing any kind of shoes, and she was shocked they were able to avoid all the obstacles on the ground with such ease. They may have descended from scorpions, but these people clearly had more secrets in their DNA that Jael couldn't help but be curious about. She just closed her eyes and pressed her head into Oz's back, hoping she could keep holding on.

With the wind whipping the ends of the silk around her face, Jael couldn't stop thinking about how silly she felt about not having a clue Oz could run this fast. This was on another level. Also, she was on his back, with her pack, which meant the entire group was being sorely delayed because of her. With the added weight, Oz wasn't reaching his maximum speed, which Jael was now incredibly curious about.

Guilt hit her about holding them back as they ran, but it was quickly forgotten when she opened her eyes and spotted a rotting corpse. To Jael's horror, there was a three-foot-tall, solid, white-toned mushroom sticking out of the back of the skull, reaching up to the sky. Whipping her head around, Jael pressed her face into Oz's back and swallowed down the bile in her throat.

When she was finally calm again, she made the mistake of looking around, and they were *everywhere*. Gasping inside her silk wraps, she was disgusted to find bodies in different levels of decay, all with various stages of fungal growth from their skulls. The shiny black bones of the skeletons,' which looked human, littered the ground. Jael quickly buried her face in Oz's back to hide from the nightmare all around them.

She hoped this would be over soon, and thankfully it was.

After a short while, they slowed, but Oz didn't let Jael off his back or take the silk from his face. She looked around, and they were all walking at a brisk pace through the massive oak trees. She wondered if they were walking an extra mile or two just to be safe.

Jael's body was aching, and her arms were throbbing from hanging onto Oz when they finally stopped to rest several miles away. She slid off Oz's back and crumpled on the ground in a heap. Everyone in the group sat, one by one. After unwrapping his face, Oz grabbed his pack, then he sat down next to Jael.

He lifted her limp left arm off the ground and connected with her saying, "We should be fine walking from here once you're rested."

Jael was happy not to have to move her mouth to speak, "How can all of you possibly stand my slow pace when you can run like the wind?"

Ignoring her, he said, "We should arrive at my village soon. You will likely only sleep two more times before we make it."

Groaning through the connection Jael said, "Thank

God, I need a real bath. Are you going to answer my question?"

Without missing a beat, Oz sensually said, "I just need to get between those thighs soon, and I'll be fine."

Jael whipped her head around and met sparkling eyes and a wide grin. She just shook her head and plopped it back onto the ground. She reached up and pushed her loose fishtail braids out of her face before looking back up at Oz.

When Jael's eyes met Oz's, she said, "So, no? My question is being completely ignored. Cool, cool. Do you really want everyone to know we're talking about sexy time over here? I know if you can smell arousal, so can they. I really don't feel like being a naughty air freshener at the moment."

"I don't give a damn about them. I would take you right here," Oz said, straight-faced and stern.

Glaring over at him, Jael shook her head again and said, "And you think *I* am the sexual deviant?"

Oz grinned and held back a chuckle, then responded, "My people aren't in the closet about sex as much as your people. We are usually open about it in many ways. August is oddly quiet about his sexuality, but everyone else that I know in my village doesn't hold back. If I started kissing you and made it clear that I had no intention of stopping, they would all just find somewhere to go for a little while."

Jael had never really asked Oz much about his sexual history and wondered about it for a moment.

He said, "You wondered that awfully loud."

Heat flooded Jael's cheeks, and Oz chuckled as he said, "It's not a secret. I don't mind. I only had one serious relationship, but I did have quite a few encounters before her. I could go for any gender, but I tend to prefer women."

Remembering something Oz had said back at the treehouse, Jael asked without thinking, "Have you ever had sex with a man?"

"Would it matter if I had?" Oz replied, sincerely asking.

Jael quickly replied, "I don't believe that matters at all. I'm just curious."

"Not much happened physically, but I have had a few encounters with males. I had my first sexual experience with a male, but I do lean more toward feminine people. Specifically, alien women with little brown spots."

Face heating again, Jael was speechless, and Oz said, "We should rest a while and then get going as soon as you wake up."

Too tired to keep chatting, even if it was only in her mind, Jael nodded as best she could, and Oz broke the connection.

Carter was already resting on his pack with his eyes closed, and Amelia was picking through medical tools and vials. The light tan woman, Zoe, was propped against a tree and chewing some of the remaining dried fruit that they had brought from the treehouse.

17

August followed Mercy into her house after their work at the base. He was relieved to take his boots off and get some rest, but he had some business to attend to first. He adjusted himself in his seat and tried to come up with something special to do with her.

A storm was slowly rolling in, and thunder cracked the same moment Mercy sat next to August holding two fruit plates. She passed August a plate, and he wished they were down in the cave so he could say thank you. He fell back on their old ways and tapped his chest.

Since he had gained the ability to speak, being completely silent was a pensive challenge. He knew their enemies were listening somehow and would do anything he could to prevent breaking his silence. But the idea that there was somewhere he could speak? Where he could say thank you out loud? He was in awe that he now had a word for that warm feeling of thanks.

They quickly ate, and Mercy took their plates into the kitchen. August met her halfway and then tilted his head to ask her to go back outside. His crimson silk-tied hair knots and fishtail braids fell over his shoulders. Mercy looked down at her dirty cropped top and workout shorts, shrugged and decided she didn't mind getting filthier than she already was.

The water falling from the sky would probably make her cleaner, she thought.

August was leading her outside, but she started to turn back for boots. August shook his head no. She sighed, and they headed for the woods behind her house. Barefoot, August took off running, and Mercy followed.

The rain began pouring, so August stopped and pulled the silk ties out of his knots and fishtail braids, rinsing his loose hair in the rain. Mercy had just washed and braided her hair after her last hot shower, so she decided to forego pulling her hair down. She closed her eyes to listen to the rain in the woods.

She tilted her head back and let the cool water from the giant oak leaves above drip onto her face. She hadn't run through the rain in several thousand moons, and Mercy had forgotten how the sounds of the rain in the woods calmed her racing mind. The drips of rain on her face and the sweet scent of the grass that grew all around were enough to erase the worry and stress of their recent work in the cave.

Mercy took in the rain as it fell all around, creating a symphony from the drips and babbling currents from the little streams which emerged with the rains. She heard August padding softly toward her. His deep, masculine pine scent reached her before he did. He nervously wrapped his arms around her from behind and leaned her head to the side, kissing down the side of her neck. The caress of his kiss was warm on her cool, damp skin.

Taking a shaking breath, Mercy felt August's length press into the seam of her behind. She had wondered why he wanted to go back out into the woods. His little plan unfurled in her mind, and her heart leaped. Heat spread through her as he pushed aside her brown hair and kissed the back of her neck and down the other side. With his hands rising to her stomach and crossing, Mercy gasped as he continued and slid them under her cropped top. He cupped her ample breasts in his warm hands and grasped them softly. He continued to kiss her neck while he started slowly stroking her taunt peeks under her shirt with his thumbs.

Rolling her hips and generous rear into August's length, Mercy was nearly whimpering with need. Smiling into her neck, August took one hand and slowly rolled down her skin-tight shorts. She quickly shimmied them down her thick thighs. Once she was free of her shorts, August took his middle finger and pressed on her bud, sending a bolt of pleasure shooting through her body. Mercy arched back against him as he rubbed tight, soft, sinful circles with his finger, and she moaned softly in his ear as he increased his pace.

With his face still buried, kissing her neck, August now had to hold her up. He held Mercy firmly in his broad russet arms and continued wringing out pleasure as the rain fell over them.

Hips rocking and legs shaking, Mercy whimpered as the edge neared and she let out the deep clicks in her throat. August, sensing the coming waves from her throat clicks, flicked her bud quickly, and she fell off the cliff of desire. Mercy panted as he held her and continued to wring out her overflowing pleasure. Mercy trembled and squeaked. He finally relented, cupping her between her soft thighs and feeling the rhythm inside.

Mercy took deep breaths as she found her footing, and August continued to hold her in his strong arms. She twisted her head and pulled him to her, meeting his full lips with a kiss. He pressed his hips into her, and she felt the result of his pleasure on her lower back.

Leaning to the ground, August reached over and pulled her shorts up for her, then they headed back to her house to bathe and finally get some rest.

As they walked, Mercy thought back to Oz's mother. She couldn't get his mother off of her mind. Agony shot through her at the thought of Oz not returning. They would all have to hold in the secret that he survived the jade woods for all those years.

How would they explain the language and Jael? Someone would eventually tell her. Oz had been gone for so long, but no one had forgotten him. What ifs spun around in her mind, but as she looked around the damp forest, she calmed down.

Something deep inside whispered, "He will make it. He has to." Mercy smiled to herself. She wanted to be there when they brought Oz's mother to the base after he returned. That idea felt a lot better than the alternative.

The elders of the village were always so negative, and she hated it. She wondered how they stayed sane with all their worries. Sometimes it angered her, considering that after a certain age, the chance of being taken became non-existent. She wondered when the next person would be taken but stopped herself and that thought altogether.

She had to stay positive, or she would make herself mad thinking about everything that could go wrong. Mercy hoped that through their efforts, at the very least they could stop their people from being taken. She wondered how long it would be before they would all be free.

What would that be like? To walk around their village or stroll through the woods and talk to whomever she wanted, with no fear? To grow as a people? She had so much she wanted to say to August, but when they were at the base, there were too many people around.

Mercy never dreamed she would be seriously thinking about speaking, out loud, all the time. Jael's memories showed television shows with nightclubs full of dancing people, enormous skyscrapers reaching to the clouds, vast water fountains spraying high into the air, and winding roller coasters where people screamed in delight. They spoke and yelled out with whatever they felt, and it made her mind spin with the possibilities.

They could call one another on handheld devices. Humans could simply call a number and obtain loans for school. Anyone could call, they said in the commercial. Her heart raced when she thought about children going to school, her people's children. Learning is freedom, she thought as she recalled the many classes Jael had taken in college. Receiving knowledge and the ability to speak after silence is like gaining wings and flying after all you've ever known to do was to crawl.

If she could have gone to school, Mercy would have been a fashion designer, she quickly decided. She hadn't told anyone, but she had been designing dresses and all kinds of clothes to wear after they won their freedom. She had even sewn a dress. It was a beautiful sleeveless floor length dress with a deep low neck. She would wear it to a fancy ball one day. Mercy knew she had to be careful, so she kept the dress under her bed and only put it on when she was alone with all the windows shut and only her fire to light her lonely barefoot dancing.

Maybe one day she could wear it for August; she hoped.

Maybe one day.

18

As Luna mounted the heavy copper piping on to the cave's wall, her sweaty, tired hands slipped on the metal pipe, and it fell. Jacob was holding the other end and lost his balance, hitting the ground with a growl. The loud clang of metal against concrete sent echoes careening through the cavern as the pipe bounced up and struck Jacob on the back of his leg.

"Luna, I need a med kit. Please find Callum. *Quickly*," Jacob said softly, along with a grunt of pain. Jacob moved his arm out of the way, revealing a massive gash down his calf from the sharp end of the pipe. The copper edge had cut clean through his loose pants, and the cut went deep into his muscle. Thick blue blood was already spilling out onto the paved floor as Luna sprinted for Callum.

Once she reached the command room, she yelled from the entry, "Callum! Come quick. Jacob's hurt!"

Without a second thought, Callum leaped from the second story and onto the paved stone floor of the cave, landing on his feet. He landed with a grunt and ran toward her. Luna turned and sprinted to find the med kits they had prepared in the north wing, then returned to Jacob.

Callum reached Jacob, furrowed his brow in worry, and said, "That looks bad. I think we are going to need to catch a big critter for you."

Jacob shook his head no as he held pressure on the wound and said, "I will not participate in that vile act -- unless I am dying."

Callum knelt, saying gently, "Luna will be here soon with a med kit. Do you need me to stitch it together?"

Jacob darted his tan eyes at Callum and glared at him. He nodded his head in agreement, knowing that Callum had offered so that he didn't have to ask. Jacob hated to ask for help and would do anything to avoid it, something Callum knew all too well. Luna arrived with the med kit, and Callum pulled out the vial of honey as well as a needle and silk thread.

Jacob growled as Callum stitched his leg. Callum looked at him pointedly and said, "If you growl at me one more time, I will hold you down and give you a titty twister right here in front of everyone. Do you really want that?"

With wide tan eyes, Jacob Looked at Callum like he had lost his mind, then scowled and sat back, crossing his arms.

"That's what I thought. Now hush, you big baby," Callum said under his breath as he kept stitching.

Once he was finished stitching the wound, Callum said, "We can stay in one of the lower command room apartments to rest, then I will go back to our house to stage things. I need to run some errands in town. I'll be back after that. Hopefully, Mercy and August will get here soon, and Mercy can come to sit with you."

Callum looked to Luna and said, "Can you help me get him up and to the apartment? He's heavier than he looks."

Luna gave him a half smile, still filled with worry, then nodded and helped Callum lift Jacob off the ground. Once he was up, they helped him slowly walk to the smaller apartment downstairs and get settled in the large bed with brown and tan silk sheets.

Everything had been completed in the north wing except running the last water lines to the living quarters. Thankfully, the medical center was ready with hot water and lights, and was fully stocked with herbs, natural remedies, and medicines from the local healer.

Jacob looked to his left at Luna and said, "We need to obtain some sand, then we can build a kiln to make glass. We will need to find a traveling merchant who sells it, and two people will have to go and get at least four buckets. We will need more, but I think four buckets will work to start."

Callum narrowed his eyes at Jacob and said, "You get hurt and you still can't take your mind off work? Rest here and I'll find some sand. I just have to go visit Sarah."

They helped Jacob onto the soft bed, and Callum propped him up with a few pillows. Callum leaned over and pressed his lips to Jacob's in a kiss before leaving the apartment with Luna.

Loving Jacob had always been easy for Callum. It was putting up with him and his analytical antics that was difficult.

They walked into the general operations chamber, and Callum turned to Luna in all seriousness and said, "Jacob is going to drive you crazy while I'm not here. Please, for me, just walk away and don't smother him with a pillow."

She laughed, "I got it Callum. He's really not that bad."

Giving her a pointed look, Callum said, "You have never experienced a hurt Jacob. We are all in for a *treat*."

Laughing again, she said, "Ok, be careful. I will get some rest until the others show up."

With that, Callum turned and headed to his home, then to Sarah's house. He wouldn't admit it to Luna or Jacob, but he was scared out of his mind. Jacob's wound was deep, and he knew what it meant if an infection set in.

There was no critter big enough to save him from an infection. That remedy only worked for fresh wounds. As his feet crunched the leaves on the ground, fear and irritation brewed inside.

He arrived at Sarah's house, and she swung the door open after seeing him walk up the path. That woman always knew everything, and it boggled his mind as to how she was so observant. He just didn't care that much, he guessed. But he sure did love to hear the latest gossip about the private lives of the villagers. It was basically the only interesting thing to do, in his opinion anyway.

Callum swore she was a psychic or had some divine gift because she always knew who was in what bed, who had been cheating on whom, and who would end up together. It was uncanny how accurate she was about his own pursuit of Jacob. She knew he liked Jacob long before he even admitted it to his own mother.

That reminded him, he needed to visit his parents' old house. He missed his mother and father terribly. They had passed of old age after having Callum late in life. Their run-down old home was now occupied by a young woman who understood his need to visit and would let him come inside. She usually treated him to her neighbor's pies, so sometimes, he had ulterior motives for his visits.

Those pies were so good that sometimes he daydreamed about them.

Sarah held out her hand as they entered her hallway. August's father was in the backyard, shirtless and doing some kind of stretching. Callum dropped his jaw as he looked at the older man's crimson, half-nude, massive body contorting outside of the window.

He was sure that Sarah had been watching him like a show, just like she always did. He was a good-looking person, so Callum understood. He looked at Sarah, her expression questioning.

He connected with her and asked, "We need sand. Four buckets at least. Can you do that for us?"

"Eventually, I am going to want something in addition to seeing your pretty face for all these favors," Sarah said into his mind.

Smiling wide, Callum said, "Of course. You know I'll do anything for you."

"So, you need sand? Is there a reason for the sand?" Sarah said with her eyes slightly narrowed at him.

"Yes. It's to make glass. That's our next goal, according to Jacob."

He continued, "Thank you for all the new recruits. They're exactly who we needed. Luna has been great with Jacob. He's such a grump sometimes." Callum picked at the hem of his tunic as he met Sarah's eyes.

He was not telling Sarah about Jacob's injury because he knew she would worry too much. Deciding not to tell Sarah reminded him of Oz's mother, so he dared to ask her about it.

"Oz's mother doesn't know anything yet, right? No one has accidentally told her or tried to give her the gift, have they?" Callum asked.

"No. I gave specific instructions not to tell her about Oz surviving. He hasn't returned, and she will not be made aware if he doesn't make it home. If I know that young man, though, he will make it. Oz was always my first pick for our leader, which ultimately saved his life when he was banished. If he had been nearly anyone else, they might have just slit his throat. The elders were sure he knew about his love's actions. Now, I hate to think of what would have happened if we hadn't sent Oz to those woods -- if he hadn't been there to save the human woman."

Fear laced through Callum at the idea of never having this beautiful gift, of Jael dying in the jade woods, alone. She was their beloved gift-giver, the woman who gave them the tools to set themselves free. Shaking his head at his fright about what could have been, Callum thought about Oz again, and his next question formed.

"Jacob wants to have a vote for a leader when Oz returns. Jacob and August want Oz to lead even though he's been gone as long as he has. I want Jacob to lead, but I think I might be the only one. Since you refuse to do it, what do you think about all of it? The election and the candidate choices?" Callum asked.

Sarah tilted her head in thought and then said into the connection, "If I have the opportunity, I will vote for Oz. That young man was a dreamer, one like our kind has never seen. All the older children that followed him around the village did it for a reason. They were lost without him when the village demanded his banishment. I love him like I love my own son and like I love you. Watching him walk from the village that day was one of the most challenging days of my life. The second hardest was when Mazarin was taken. If Oz makes it back, I will make sure he leads us. He *will* lead us to freedom."

Feeling Sarah's overwhelming emotions, Callum nodded and broke their connection. Sarah would get them pure sand from the beach from the avocado merchant, and they could move on with this daunting project.

While walking through the village, it struck Callum that it probably had been Mercy who informed Sarah that he had his eyes on Jacob. He shook his head at the thought of his golden-eyed friend and took his time walking back.

19

———

J ael was awakened by her bouncing legs and growing
hunger, but she didn't move right away. The sounds of
the woods, rustling leaves and cracking branches, and
the group's swift footsteps told her they were walking.
Once fully awake, she opened her eyes and found Oz
looking down at her with a grin. She looked around and saw
that he was walking with her in his arms. She rubbed the wet
spot on Oz's shirt where she had drooled on his shoulder
and peered over to see that Carter had her pack. Once her
eyes were fully adjusted, and she was satisfied she couldn't do
anything about Oz's saliva-soaked shirt, she spit her mouth
guard into her hand, and Oz let her down.
   The ground was soft and still covered in the large oak
leaves. After a good stretch, she looked around at the enormous trees that surrounded them. They all looked exactly
the same. She had no idea how Oz and the group knew their
way. She shook off that thought -- it was too early in her day
to form any kind of scientific hypothesis.
   She took a few deep breaths of the clean, fresh air and

smelled a hint of something sweet that she couldn't place. Noticing her sniffing the air, Oz reached out for her to connect, and she lifted her arm to him.

He said, "That scent is from the flowers in the village. We are downwind and circling around the outskirts of the houses, moving toward the caves now. We made it, my love."

A thrill went through Jael at the idea of a meal, a bath, and a bed. She hoped there would be a bed. She would never complain about Oz's hard body, but he was not a comfortable person to sleep on.

Oz, on hearing her loud thoughts, replied, "There will most likely be a bed for us, if nothing else. If I had to guess, I would say that August has most likely completed a lot of work. When he wants to, he can be profoundly focused and efficient. I wouldn't be surprised if he and Jacob already have running water in the cave."

Thinking and looking around, Jael asked incredulously, "Wait. Did you walk the entire time I slept?"

With his eyes searching the canopy to look anywhere but at Jael, he said, "I knew we were close to my village, and the others agreed it was worth it to forego rest and keep going. We should reach the mouth of the cave soon. From what I remember, its location is straight ahead."

Ignoring Oz's sudden interest in the treetops, Jael shook her head, "Well, what are we waiting for? Let's run!" she exclaimed in his mind.

Oz grinned and signaled to the others that they were going to run. Carter handed Jael's pack back to her, and she slid it on. Oz helped her adjust her straps and get it just right so she could run without it slapping her on the back.

Setting a steady pace for Jael, Oz ran in front with her right behind him. The group followed suit and took off one by one in a fast jog. Jael thought it was probably more like walking for the others but tried not to let it bother her.

After a few miles, Jael became heavily winded. They slowed down, and Oz signaled that the cave entrance was close. He had mentioned earlier that the entrance was just a hole in the ground, and could easily be missed. He didn't want anyone to fall into the caved-in lava tube. The group slowed, and Oz whipped his head around at Jael with a wide, delighted grin, and pointed down in front of him.

Approaching carefully, Jael peered down into a dark cave from the lip of a small opening in the ground that could easily have been overlooked, just as Oz had said. Smiling, she turned and saw that Carter was already handing his pack to Oz.

Carter leaped in first, and then Oz tossed his pack to him. Oz took off his own pack and tossed it down next. Once all the packs were in the cave along with everyone else, Oz knelt to let Jael get on his back. Carefully avoiding his coiled tail, she climbed on and buried her face between his shoulders as he leaped into the cave. Although she knew he could easily jump long distances with her on his back, she was still rattled to the core in the moments before he landed on his feed on the cave's floor.

After kneeling and helping Jael off his back, Oz grabbed their packs, and started down into the dark cave. He stopped suddenly, sniffed the air, then dropped the two packs. Oz pointed to something that was strung across the cave. His pointed finger slid along an invisible line from one cave wall to the other. He signaled to everyone to step over it, but Jael was too short, so she went under. Once they passed what Jael assumed was a trip line, the group reached a cave wall, and Oz stared at it for a long while.

He tilted his head to the left and sniffed the air once more, then he looked down at the cave's floor and all around the base of the wall. Tilting his head again, he shuffled and shifted a few feet to his right. He reached out to the cave's wall, feeling along the stone, then began closely sniffing an area of about three feet from the floor.

He knelt, took his right index finger and pressed on the wall. He was able to push his hand slightly inwards with light pressure. The mechanism he had pressed made a faint click. A door popped open and nearly smacked Oz in the face, causing him to snap his head back.

Watching in absolute astonishment, Oz opened the slab of concrete and stone. A whoosh of air smelling of freshly cut wood flowed out from the open door. Turning to Jael, Oz grinned and headed inside the room. Jael followed behind, looking up at the long LED light fixtures and air ducts in amazement.

Once they were all inside the room, Oz closed the door behind him, and it sealed shut. Jael heard a suction sound as the door sealed and was shocked at the perfect fit, made with just concrete and stones. The incredibly heavy door had easily slid open like it was a freshly greased, modern door.

Oz looked around at the group and headed for the next door, but it was locked. Sighing, he slid down onto the ground next to the door, and Jael took a seat next to him. Carter removed his pack and stretched while Amelia lay down on the stone-paved floor. Sprawling out, the vertically blessed Amelia took up a large amount of space in the modest-sized room. She flexed her blue limbs and stretched like she was planning to rest for a few hours in the middle of the floor.

Jael didn't let on, but she thought it was comical. She made a mental note to become Amelia's friend right away.

She couldn't wait to hear what Amelia had to say.

She couldn't wait to hear what Oz had to say.

She couldn't wait to speak.

Jael ran her hand over the newly laid cement and paved stone floor, then smiled to herself, thinking about the lights and the airflow above them. Electric lights were a feat, and Jael was beaming as she thought about what they would find inside the locked door.

They would have a lot more than just a bed ready.

She looked at Oz. His head was resting on the wall, messy hair falling over his shoulders. His eyes were already sealed shut. He had a look of relief about him, which calmed Jael's nerves. She hadn't seen that look since the treehouse.

It was a look she dearly missed.

Soon, someone would come through the door, and together they would begin building a defense against the humans on the dark side of the planet. Their long mission had succeeded. According to Oz, they had achieved something that had never been done before.

They had brought his people home.

The magnitude of the task they had just completed wasn't lost on Jael. She figured that they had to have traveled for several months. She had bled four times while they were on the move, and her last bleed had only ended recently. She hoped the timing of her periods hadn't been affected by the strenuous exercise.

She would have to ask Oz how long they had been traveling in order to know for sure. She didn't like relying on him to be the living computer all the time, but sometimes, it was just easier to ask. Jael knew he didn't care, but she did.

Jael dug through her pack for a bag of something that looked like potato chips, which she had been saving.

They all heard the door click, and the seal released. With a whoosh, the door swung open, and Oz had a smirk prepared on his face as he peered into the dark doorway.

August slowly stepped into the room. His eyes widened with surprise when he saw some of their people with Oz and Jael. Looking back to Oz, August's mouth dropped open, and he pulled a key from his pocket. He quickly turned around, signaling for the person he was with to follow him inside.

One of the most stunning women Jael had ever seen walked into the room with a bright beaming smile on her beautiful face. She was curvy and fit, with long, golden, tan legs and brown hair framing her gorgeous face. She had on a cute dark brown cropped top and tan shorts.

That tan-colored silk was all too familiar, and Jael thought about the sweet spider Rew. Her heart leaped as she thought of the enormous, purring tarantula.

Oz held his hand out to her, and They all rose from their places on the floor, filing into a large, bright cavern. Delight shot through Jael as she and Oz darted their eyes all around the vast, brightly lit cavern. They were amazed at the perfectly level, paved floor; the long, hanging LED light fixtures; the air vents; and even copper water lines.

There were people sawing and hammering away at hardwood. They looked to be making beautiful stools and long, wooden tables. Three people were at a table with large sheets of cream-colored paper, and all were hard at work with what looked like sharpened graphite sticks, wrapped in silk to protect their hands.

This was beyond anything Jael could have ever expected. They had already figured out how to use electricity.

She approached the people who were writing. As she looked down at the paper, she was in awe of their meticulous handwriting and construction plans. Oz came behind her and put his arms around her. Then, he turned her around and grabbed her hand.

Leading her off, Jael was confused but was sure Oz had a good reason to leave. They neared a door at the other end of the cavern, and Oz quickly opened it for her, letting her go through first. He continued on through a narrow area, then went through another door that led into another large cavern.

They nearly ran to a door under a set of stairs. After Oz shut the door, he pushed Jael into the wall and leaned in. Smelling her own grotesque body odor, she knew Oz could tell she needed a bath and didn't understand what the hell he was doing.

With his lips at her ear, he smiled as he softly whispered, "Spots. My little Spots. I've wanted to whisper that in your ear since you taught me the word. I have loved your spots since the day I found you asleep in the hollow of the jade tree. Before I knew how to make words, you were always my little Spots."

He traced his finger down the brown freckles on her nose with, such love in the soft touch. Delight shot through Jael, and she threw her arms around Oz upon hearing his first words.

"Spots? You've had a nickname for me this entire time? Why haven't you ever called me spots before?" she asked, practically speaking into his shirt because of his height.

"What's the fun of that nickname if I can't say it aloud?" Oz asked, sincerity in his eyes.

Nodding in agreement and with a smile growing on her face, Jael said, "Good point. Technically, I already have the nickname Jael, and now I suddenly regret bringing that up."

She quickly changed the subject, asking, "Er, how did they do all of this so quickly?"

Waving her hands around nervously, Jael wasn't used to speaking to Oz like this, and she felt painfully awkward.

Oz laughed and said in his perfect voice, the sound of rich, deep honey, "August and Jacob, I'm sure. I have been waiting for this for too long."

He nuzzled his face into the crook of her neck, and the heat of his breath made her insides melt.

His voice was smooth and masculine, and she felt a sense of peace when he spoke. It sounded the same as it did in her mind when they connected.

Pulling back, Oz showed Jael his handsome face, and she said, "You sound the same in my mind as your speaking voice. You guessed your own voice?"

Giving Jael a half smile, Oz said, "I've secretly hummed a few times while pouring water. I had a good idea of what my voice sounded like. August's, on the other hand, sounded high-pitched, like a female child from your world, and I never said anything. I just let him sound like a baby the entire time."

Slapping a hand to her mouth, Jael let out a boisterous laugh, and Oz joined in. She grinned up at him, and he leaned over and kissed her before pulling away and opening the door.

Jael asked, "So, what do we do now?"

Looking back at Jael as they walked into the main chamber, Oz said, "We will have to speak with everyone else. But I think for now, we will just stay here and quietly build our defense."

Jael nodded and said, "That's all great, but I get to have a bath soon, right?"

"Yes, we both will get a bath soon. A few more days, and we would have had a trail of scavengers thinking they were following a dead body," Oz said softly back to Jael while leading the way.

Jael swiftly stuck her finger between his perfectly round butt cheeks, eliciting a jumping yelp and then a glare from Oz. He protected his rear from her with his tail for the rest of the short journey.

Once they made it back to the main chamber, there was a group of twelve sitting around one of the long wooden tables. Everyone had a blank paper placed in front of them.

They all looked at Oz and Jael as they entered the room, and as they neared, August said, "Oz, we are ready when you are to vote for our temporary President, Vice President, and General."

Oz and Jael sat on the remaining stools at the table, and Mercy smiled at Jael as she handed her and Oz each a blank sheet of paper. Oz slid his hand onto Jael's knee in reassurance.

Speaking boldly as though he had always had the ability, Oz asked, "There are twelve people here. How is this a fair vote? We should wait until we can gather more of the villagers for their votes as well. There have to be a hundred and fifty people in the village. This is less than ten percent of the population. And let me guess, all of them were picked by August's mother?"

Callum set a small stack of papers on the table next to

Oz and narrowed his eyes at him as he said, "That wasn't too hard to figure out. *Sarah*, August's mom, secretly walked around the village and asked those who were aware of the gift who their choices were. She reported them back to me, and I carefully documented each selection."

"Who are the choices?" Oz asked sharply after noticing who was standing next to him.

Cutting in, August said, "You, myself, my mother, Jacob, and Luna."

Laughing, Oz said, "August, we all know if Sarah doesn't win, she *will* carry out a coup."

Everyone at the table laughed, and Jael smiled, not having a clue who most of the people were, other than August and those she'd traveled with. She finally recognized Jacob after thinking back to some of the memories Oz had shared of his youth.

Watching Oz fall back into place so effortlessly with his people filled Jael with joy but left her wondering about her own place in this circle. The man she had met in the woods when she was first transported to this planet was not the confident man sitting next to her. This man was made new by his own efforts, and she'd had the privilege of watching it happen.

Clearing his throat, August said, "So, we just need to pass the graphite around, and everyone will vote by writing down the names and positions."

August leaned forward and took the bundle of graphite sticks, then passed them around.

Oz handed a single stick of the graphite to Jael, and she said softly, "Do I get to vote too?"

Narrowing his eyes, Oz scoffed and said, "It wouldn't be much of a fair vote if everyone didn't participate."

Jael cocked her head at Oz's response. No one even looked up when Oz answered her. She peered at the stack of already cast votes and wondered who would end up in what position.

She took the graphite and her paper, then wrote her votes. She only knew three of the people listed so she wrote down Oz for President, Jacob for Vice President, and August for General.

From what she knew, Jacob was a wise person, and August seemed like he would make an excellent military leader. Jael then folded her paper in half, the same as everyone else. Once all the folded pieces of paper were on the table, Callum collected the votes and diligently tallied them.

Luna rose from her stool and helped Jacob to the apartments in the smaller cave's chamber. Jael noticed Jacob's leg and wondered why they didn't get him a pill bug.

The moment the door shut behind Luna and Jacob, Callum finished his counting and barked a laugh, causing everyone to turn sharply to look at him.

"Well, big fucking surprise. August, you're our new General," Callum said in his calming deep voice, with a smirk.

Luna gave August a light fist bump to the shoulder. August smirked at his new title, and Mercy grinned from ear to ear. Jael already liked Mercy and wondered if they would have a chance to get to know each other.

Callum continued while making eyes at Jacob, "Vice President is my Jacob."

Oz chuckled at Callum, who looked over sharply at Oz and said, "And you, Ozias, are our new President. Congratulations, *asshole*."

Oz's face fell as his shoulders squared, and with a sharp tone, he asked, "What?"

Did Callum just call Oz an asshole? Fear spread down Jael's spine, and the threat of unprovoked conflict tasted bitter on her tongue.

Narrowing his eyes at Jael and then rapidly shifting them to Callum, Oz said, "You had to have counted wrong. There is no way you're correct. I just got here. How could the people in the village vote for me when they didn't even know if I would return or not?"

August cleared his throat, and Oz shot his wide eyes over to his best friend.

With a kind smile, August replied, "Not one person doubted you would come home. No one forgot you."

Nodding his head, Callum said, "Only one person out of thirty-three didn't vote for you to be President, and that was me because I voted for my love. I also didn't pick you for Vice President or General if that makes you feel any better. I don't like you."

Jael looked over at Oz, whose mouth was now hanging open. Ignoring Callum's last comment, she had to grip the round top of her stool as she lost it, laughing until tears poured from her eyes. A few people at the table began laughing along with her, the first being Mercy.

Jael squeaked out, "I knew it!"

Jael howled with laughter. She knew Oz would end up in a leadership position. They'd had argued about it for months, and she was going to relish her victory.

Oz just crossed his arms and shook his head at her. Mercy threw her head back and laughed with Jael. The rest of the table erupted in booming laughter, and August grasped Oz's shoulder, jostling him as he wiped away the tears from his own deep laugh.

"I think, you have all lost your minds. I have been banished to the jade woods for thirty thousand moons, and you think I will accept being the President of our people like this? I haven't even been here long enough to take a bath!" Oz exclaimed while throwing his hands up in protest.

With a deep chuckle, Callum said, "Well, I hate I'm admitting this, but if we've all lost our minds, then it sounds like you're the only one sane enough to lead us, *Mr. President*. Oh, and you have a bath and shower in your new apartment, so you can bathe however you want. But *please* do so quickly because you are all ripe." Callum pursed his lips in disgust, plugged his nose with his right hand, then waved his left hand in front of his face.

Bringing his hands up to tuck the loose hairs behind his ears, Oz sighed then turned to Jael and said, "Well, are you ready to see our new home?"

Filled with energy that Jael only wished she had, Mercy clapped and squealed, then said, "Follow me! We are so excited that you are both finally here!"

Bouncing out of her seat, Mercy half walked, half skipped, all the way to a door that led to a long narrow hallway.

While they followed Mercy, Jael leaned over and said, "I knew you were going to be elected, and I am not sorry about laughing. You were clearly well-liked before you were sent away. We've been over all of this, and I win."

Scoffing, Oz smirked as he said, "We will see how sorry you are for winning."

Oz then winked as he took off, jogging after Mercy.

Heat filled Jael at Oz's words. When she opened the

large door to the cavernous chamber, she saw Oz and Mercy entering the apartment on the top, right. Following behind on the stairs, she found them waiting for her next to the door.

"Callum and I picked everything out, so it didn't end up looking like August's house," Mercy said in all seriousness.

Oz threw his head back and laughed, then asked, "Is August's house still empty?!"

Mercy giggled and nodded, then said, "He's never there. He is exactly the same as he was when you left."

Turning to Mercy, Jael asked, "Are there some clothes we can borrow until we can clean ours?"

Eyes widening, Mercy said, "Oh! I made you some new clothes. They are all over here."

Mercy led Jael to a tall, wood built-in cabinet in the bedroom and opened it, showing her all the clothes she had made. Since she was smaller than Mercy, Jael picked up a pair of leggings and held them up. They looked like they would fit perfectly -- too perfectly.

Jael looked to Mercy with a curious expression and said, "How did you know my size?"

"August shared some memories about you from the tree-house. I hope you don't mind. I couldn't wait for you to get here," Mercy said while she was rocking on her heels.

How did she manage to get her size from just August's memories? Jael was impressed and had no idea how she had guessed her size so accurately.

Jael could tell that Mercy wanted to be her friend, and she couldn't help feeling giddy about it. She hadn't had a best friend since Sis, except for Oz. Her curly-tailed man was much more than a best friend, though, so he didn't really count.

She didn't know what to say, so she just nodded and smiled.

While looking through the clothes, Jael realized that Mercy must have investigated current fashion trends back on Earth and added her own spin to the styles. These clothes were incredible, Jael thought, as she held up a cropped top and blushed, doubting she would ever have the confidence to wear it. She carefully folded everything back the way it was and closed the cabinet.

"Mercy, this is all too much. How could you have done all this so quickly? And how did so many people know we would make it back?" Jael asked, her eyes roaming over the lovely furniture in the room.

Smiling softly, Mercy said, "We don't sleep, and there's nothing else to do."

Grinning, she continued, "You didn't know Oz before he was sent away. He was always the guy who would help anyone in need, and he was so creative and intelligent. We all thought he would be the next leader of our village, even though he always hated that idea."

"So, how exactly did you decide on a leader without ever speaking to one another?" Jael asked.

Pulling her lip in a half snarl, Mercy said, "It's so primitive to think that we communicated that way. I can hardly believe any of us understood one another at all. We just always followed one person, and I think we all decided on our own that the next person was Oz. There was a lot of passing around memories and feelings."

Jael said, "You did develop a type of communication, but it was made up of simple hand gestures and expressions. We have a game called charades on Earth, and that's what I always felt like we were playing when Oz would tell me stories."

Tilting her head with a confused look, Mercy asked, "Oz was able to tell you stories *before* your ability to connect? See what I mean? No one else in our village is quite like him. How did you two figure out the connection anyway?"

Jael had known that question would come up eventually. How would she explain how she and Oz figured it out? The memory of swimming through the water, believing Oz would kill her, was all too real. She could smell the salt in the air, and her heart rate was soaring.

Jael, frozen in place, quietly said, "That will have to be a story for another day."

She would need to talk to Oz about it before she said another word. They had an understanding, but this was much more his secret than hers. She wouldn't change what happened, but she would be lying if she said that it didn't cause her emotional pain. Occasional nightmares about Oz trying to kill her would sent her into an all-encompassing panic. When she would wake, Oz was always there, holding her sweat-soaked body close. She had never once woken up from her nightmares to find his face dry and free of tears.

He knew precisely what she dreamed of, and why.

Nodding, Mercy looked over to see Oz standing in the doorway and then quickly said, "I am going to go and check on Jacob and let you two get comfortable."

She bolted out of the apartment and shut the door with a click.

Keeping his eyes on Jael, Oz walked straight to her and said, "Take off your clothes."

Her breath hitched, and she looked at him incredulously as she said, "We need a bath first."

Laughing, Oz said, "Yes, that's mostly why you're undressing. You are going first so I can watch."

Cheeks burning with heat, Jael suddenly felt self-conscious, the treehouse was usually dark, and the lights in this modern-looking bathroom were painfully bright.

And Oz could *speak*.

With a devilish grin, Oz said more firmly, "Jael, take off your clothes. *Now*."

A thrill went through her. This would be the first time they had been intimate in a long while. The only difference was that this time, they could both communicate in the open.

Sitting on a stool, Jael took off her boots and set them aside while Oz slowly walked over to the shower and turned it on. He never took his burning yellow eyes off of Jael.

Oz had that hungry look about him, and her heart was pounding before she even peeled off her shirt. She took the hem and pulled it off, then unbuckled her belt and pulled it out of her belt loops. She dropped her belt on the floor, and she met Oz's eyes again. Solid black eyes met hers, and she trembled as she unbuttoned her pants, and they fell to the floor.

Her breath hitched as Oz closed his eyes and rolled his head back before dropping to the floor and removing his boots. She tested the water and got into the abstract, grey quartz-tiled shower just as he tossed away his second boot.

Jael watched Oz stalk closer and step into the stream of water under the broad showerhead, pinning her to the wall. Barely breathing, she looked into his eyes and watched the yellow edges fight for control as he slid his hands up and down her body.

Shaking his head and taking a deep breath, Oz stepped

back and took off his sopping wet shirt then took the bar of soap and lathered his hands. His unbraided hair was now resting on his shoulders, and he had the top of it pulled back with a silk tie. Jael loved his hair this length and was tempted to ask him to keep it this way.

Starting with her neck, he rubbed her down her arms with soap and then back up to her chest, pausing over her small peaks. As he circled each a few times, and Jael shivered at the sensation combined with the cold quartz of the wall at her back.

Pulling away for more soap, he said, "Turn around and put your hands up on the wall."

Hardly able to breathe at his commands, Jael turned around and put her hands on the wall.

He leaned into her ear and said, "That's good, Spots."

Lightning shot down her spine at the heat of his words in her ear.

Starting on her back, he ran a single soapy finger down her spine, and she wiggled and gasped. He slipped his hand down the center of her rear, and Jael squealed as he brushed her back entrance with a soapy finger, nearly jumping with the contact.

Chuckling, Oz continued down her legs. He quickly soaped himself up before turning Jael around and pulling her under the stream with him. He pulled the silk bindings from the fishtail braids in her hair, and shook them out, massaging her scalp as he went. She unbuckled his belt and began pulling it out. While she started removing his now-soaked pants, he took the soap and washed her stomach.

Circling his finger around her navel, he heard her gasp sharply gasp, and he gave her one of his typical naughty smiles. She slipped his pants off his hips, letting them drop, and he kicked the soaking pants into the corner. Jael took the soap from him, and he turned around, letting her lather his back. She took her finger and softly ran it under his tail, making him shiver. Before he could respond, she slapped his perfectly round behind.

Oz whipped his head around and narrowed his eyes at her.

"Oh, you're a bad girl Spots."

Quickly taking the soap from her, Oz lathered his hands thoroughly before tossing it behind him. He took one hand and washed his length and then slipped his hand between Jael's legs, finding his way between her hot folds. Unprepared for Oz's hand, Jael gasped and tried to jump back. Knowing what she would do, Oz grabbed her by her hips and flipped her upside down before she could make a sound. He held her under stream, rinsing the soap from the apex of her thighs.

"Oz what are you doing?!" Jael squawked as she desperately tried to hold on to his muscular waist.

Squealing, Jael's body tried to seize as Oz pressed her into the freezing cold shower wall and pulled one of her legs behind his head. His tail uncoiled, and Jael nearly stopped breathing when she felt it wrap around her knee to help hold her in place.

She could feel Oz's hot breath over her entrance, melting her insides into lava as shivers rocked her from the cold of the wet, quartz shower wall on her back.

Looking at her from above, Oz smirked and said, "Let me know if you get dizzy." He descended and his tongue sank deep inside of her.

Upside down, holding on to his sturdy waist, Jael's hips shook and rocked as Oz tasted her inside and out. He took the tip of his tongue and flicked her bud, then began circling with a soft rhythm. He was relentless, and Jael was already close to the edge. Legs now firmly wrapped around Oz's face, he took her bud into his mouth and ran the length of his tongue along it, back and forth.

Unable to hold back, Jael moaned as she shattered, and her release slammed into her. Oz held her firmly and flicked her mercilessly, drawing out her waves until she cried out and began shaking uncontrollably.

He flipped her over. While catching her breath, she said, "I think I'm dizzy now."

Laughing, Oz kissed her neck while he carefully laid her down on the shower floor.

Leaning over to her ear, Oz whispered, "My little spotted alien," before he swiftly slid his length into her.

Arching off the cold floor, Jael moaned as Oz fully seated himself. He took her legs, draping one over each of his forearms, and leaned back as he swiftly entered her again and again. Her lips parted in a breathy gasp as she was close to shattering again. She could feel her body beginning to clench, but she knew Oz wasn't finished yet. Jael came apart with a gasp, as his continued strokes kept her waves moving.

As he quickened his pace, Jael cried out at the pleasure exploding with every delicious thrust. With deep clicks in his throat, Oz released into a writhing Jael with a groan.

20

When Mercy walked into the bottom apartment where Jacob was staying, the rotten scent of his wound hit her, and she pinched her nose tight.

Trying not to gag, she quickly headed toward the back and found a feverish Jacob. How had they not smelled his infected wound while they were all sitting at the table? Nausea flooded her gut.

Looking down at his wound, she saw it was oozing greenish-yellow puss. She said sharply, "Jacob, your wound is infected! You should have drained a bug when you had the chance! Why didn't you say something?"

Mercy didn't wait for his answer. She ran to the medical area and found Amelia, the blue-haired woman who had returned with Oz. Amelia held the extensive medical knowledge he had gained from the human he killed. Mercy found her emptying a large black bag of medical supplies and tools.

Mercy ran up to her with heaving breaths. "Hello! I am Mercy. You are the healer, or I mean, the doctor, right?" she said frantically as she tripped over her words.

Amelia's dark blue hair was knotted and pulled back, showing the angles of her shoulders. She was wearing a tight-fitting shirt and some of the village's traditional, loose pants.

All her attention now focused on Mercy, Amelia answered, "Yes, are you OK?"

Mercy's words caught in her throat.

"Yes. No. Oh! I think Jacob's wound is infected. He has a fever, and the skin is swollen, plus something green is oozing between the stitches. It looks gross and smells even worse." Mercy was nearly in tears, her emotions threatening to spill over.

She had watched people in her village die from this. They didn't last long after the fever started. She tried unsuccessfully to convince herself to calm down, but her fear continued to force her heart to beat faster.

"I found one single vile of the human physician's antibiotics for our kind out in the supplies. Let me save a small sample and gather my things. Take a few slow deep breaths. I'll see what I can do. We may have to sedate him and drain the wound on his leg."

Moisture gathered in Mercy's eyes as she said, "Thank you! He is in the bottom left apartment in the command area. I need to go find Callum."

After running out of the medical area, Mercy headed down to the north wing, where she found August finishing up work on a bathroom shower fixture.

In a rush, Mercy said, "August, where is Callum? Jacob's leg is infected."

"His leg is infected? He was just at the table with us. Why didn't he say anything? Callum just went to the village to make an appearance, then he will be right back."

"Ok, if you're sure Callum is coming right back, I am

going back to check on Jacob. Do you remember the man down the path who died from the infection on the back of his head?"

"He is not going to die, Mercy. Oz said that bitch of a doctor had extensive medical knowledge, and he gave it all to Amelia. I'm sure she can fix his leg. I'll be by when I'm finished, then we can go home."

August paused with his eyes wide and awkwardly said, "I mean, go to your house."

Mercy smiled and said, "It's your home too and it has been for a long time." She turned and walked back toward the command area and Jacob.

When she arrived at the apartment, Amelia was already preparing a syringe with the solution that the humans had used to tranquilize their people. Draining the wound on his leg would be excruciating without it, and Mercy was so thankful sedation was even an option.

Jacob was sitting up and scowling when Mercy met his eyes. His straight, black hair was loose and draped over his broad shoulders.

"Callum went to the village. He should be back soon," she said.

Amelia looked over at Jacob, who seemed upset, and said, "Do you want to wait for him?"

With a slow and effort-filled nod, Jacob said quietly, "I will *not* go under without Callum here."

Nodding, she walked over to grab her medical bag and said, "I'll be in the medical area waiting. When Callum arrives, I will inform him of Jacob's condition, and then we can begin."

Amelia headed out of the apartment's door, and Mercy followed behind her to sit on the stairs. Mercy watched three of the new recruits as they sanded the last table for the open command area and then cleaned up all the dust. A tall, dark brown man, a light cream woman, and a person that was reddish bronze-toned, like August, worked to complete the job.

The light cream woman dragged a bucket of diluted blue ink over to the unfinished table and began staining the surface with silk rags. The blue color was giving the table a grey tone that Mercy liked. As she watched their meticulous work she thought, either Sarah knew how to pick recruits, or their people were generally gifted.

So far, each one of them had such profound skills and talents.

Mercy knew she was going to design clothes one day. The idea made her light up inside, and she couldn't help but smile thinking about the future. Their people would have a real future where they could grow and develop as a society.

She loved Jael's memories of the arts and music. She knew Callum also loved the idea of music. They had already discussed his future dance club for hours, and she saw that same spark of light shining in him when he spoke about it. He had told her all about his plans for the upscale club and restaurant, and Mercy loved every detail. Her favorite idea was a home he wanted to design for himself, Jacob, and their future children.

Mercy wondered if Oz would wait for Jacob to recover before talking about what he had learned about their enemy. She was curious to know exactly who they were up against.

Just then, Mercy heard a door above open and saw Jael and Oz emerge from their apartment.

Quickly standing, Mercy said, "Oz, Jacob has an infection in his leg. Amelia is just waiting on Callum to return from the village before they put him under to drain it."

A solemn Oz furrowed his brow, nodded his head, and said, "I'll assist Amelia, go get Callum and tell him what's happening. Tell the doctor we are starting now."

Mercy cocked an eyebrow and said, "Are you sure you want to piss off Callum *and* Jacob?"

Oz said flatly as he walked by Mercy, "Sure. If I have to be the President, then we are doing things my way."

Mouth gaping, Jael darted her eyes over to a stunned Mercy. She then followed Oz into the apartment where Jacob was sitting up on the bed with his arms crossed.

When the scent of his wound wafted around them, Oz held his nose and turned to Jael who was trying to hold back a gag.

In a nasally voice and with his brow still furrowed, Oz said, "Can you run to the kitchen and grab a silk rag, please?"

"Yes. Are you still irritated they voted for you as the first leader? Why are you so surprised? I knew it would happen before I met everyone," Jael scoffed a bit under her breath as she walked to the kitchen.

Jacob opened his eyes and quietly said, "Really, Oz? Are you still on that? She's right. We warned everyone in the village before the vote that we may have to vote again if you didn't return. They decided to wait until the base was finished to give you more time. The elders still don't know, but I'm not planning on telling any of them anything. The less they know, the better."

Oz sat on the stool next to the bed and let out a frustrated sigh before saying, "Listen, if I must be president, and you are my Vice President, we are not waiting on Callum.

We are doing this procedure now. You're vital to us pulling this off. I sent Mercy to the village to send him back. He will be here when you wake up."

"I am not going under without Callum here," Jacob responded in an irritated tone.

"You will have to deal with it. We need you too much, and this infection is risky. We are starting as soon as Amelia arrives," Oz said flatly.

Huffing with a scowl, Jacob said, "Callum will be furious. I'm taking back my vote for you. You came back a prick."

"Thanks. I'll deal with him," Oz said right as Jael walked in with a silk kitchen towel.

Oz ripped off two strips of fabric and twisted them into his nose. The look on his face was serious, but with the two strips of silk rolled into his nose, Jael burst out laughing. Even Jacob chuckled softly, despite his irritation.

Narrowing his eyes at Jael, Oz said, "What is so funny? His wound smells terrible! This is worse than the fresh guts of that giant scorpion. That giant octopus was a close third after its second day on the deck."

Shivering at the thought, Oz shook his head at the gross memory.

Still giggling, Jael said, "I can't smell his wound like you can, but I could smell the scorpion guts. That was disgusting. I am so glad I never have to touch a scorpion's dried organ again."

Laughing and sending the rolled silk in his nose flailing, Oz said, "That reminds me, I still can't believe you caught that pill bug. It weighed almost as much as you do!"

"Well, to be fair, I jumped out of a tree and landed on its back. That armored bug slammed me into four different trees before I could get enough rope around it to flip it over. Those damn little legs move so fast!"

Oz and Jacob both laughed, and Oz said, "It is too bad that I wasn't able show you the easy way to do it."

Jael glared at both Jacob and Oz, then with a deliberate tone, asked, "The *easy* way?"

Jacob covered his mouth with his hands to hide his smile, and Oz said, "Yes, if you soak a dried scorpion heart or stomach in water first, the scent will travel farther. Then, the creature is so busy with eating its meal, you can walk right up and wrap the rope around it. Once the rope is tied, you can then easily pull the rope to topple it over and force it into a ball."

Eyes wide in shock, Jael just gaped at them while Oz and Jacob had a good laugh.

The apartment door creaked open, and Amelia quickly walked into the bedroom, looking at Oz with concern.

"Oz, I think we need to wait for Callum," Amelia said.

"No. We are starting now. Let's get washed up," Oz said firmly, and Amelia looked at Jacob sympathetically before following Oz to the kitchen.

Once they washed up, Amelia looked at Jacob with remorse before giving him the first injection in his shoulder. He was out cold in less than two seconds. None of them could believe how fast it worked. That must be how they were taking their people so effortlessly.

Amelia checked Jacob's breathing and, under her breath, said, "That was fast. No wonder we don't remember anything."

Oz stood next to Amelia and handed her tools, while she cut Jacob's stitches, laying his wound open. Jael held her nose and did her best not to gag when greenish-yellow and white puss gushed from the wound and onto the silk rags under his leg. Oz quickly gathered the soiled towels, replacing them with new ones as Amelia irrigated the wound thoroughly.

She was no expert in anatomy, but Jael was shocked at how similar the muscles inside their legs were to human muscles. She closely examined Jacob's exposed calf muscle. She wasn't squeamish, at a distance of course.

Blue blood ran down the sides of the wound as Oz firmly squeezed the area to remove any additional pockets of infection. Finding none, Amelia finished irrigating the outside of the wound. She took a different solution that was a deep violet and irrigated the wound once more before Oz handed her the tray with the prepped sutures.

After sewing up the wound, Oz handed Amelia a small wooden jar of honey, which she applied before bandaging Jacob's leg. Oz began cleaning the area, removing the silk sheets from under Jacob and piling them into a large silk bag for washing.

Just as they finished, Callum came flying into the apartment and said, "Is Jacob OK? Why in the hell is he unconscious!"

"He is fine. We had to sedate him for the procedure. We are going to wake him now, so you have perfect timing," Oz said calmly, hoping Callum's anger would be defused once he saw Jacob awake.

"Perfect timing would have been waiting for someone to come get me. Mercy almost knocked me over, then tried to pull my arm out of the socket to get me to come back to the base. All she could manage to communicate when we connected was that Jacob was being put under. I had no idea what that meant," Callum growled with a cold scowl on his face.

"It needed to be done, and we couldn't wait. We can discuss this later. Right now, we need to wake him up," Oz said while maintaining his focus on Amelia and Jacob.

Amelia tapped Jacob's upper arm and began injecting the solution from the second prepped syringe. Callum finally gave up and lay down on the soft bed next to Jacob.

Looking up at Callum's worried blue eyes, Amelia said, "It will be a little while before he fully wakes up. Once he does, please come and get me."

After the second syringe, she took the third and said, "This contains an antibiotic. I only have one vial, and it will take weeks to make more. If his leg doesn't look like it's healing and free of infection immediately, he will need to drain a creature. If the infection comes back, he won't be able to win this fight. We might have to amputate his leg if he starts to decline and the infection spreads."

Callum nodded and curled up next to Jacob, glaring at Oz like he was mentally berating him.

He was *definitely* mentally berating him.

After pulling his floppy makeshift nose plugs from his nostrils and tossing them in the trash, Oz turned to Jael and tilted his head for her to follow.

They quietly walked up to their apartment, and once inside, Jael asked, "Why did you not want to wait for Callum?"

"Jacob, August, and I are all in leadership roles. We are now responsible for freeing all our people. I'm not waiting for anything if Jacob's life is in danger. The bacteria from the wound were already seeping into his bloodstream," Oz said flatly.

"I understand. I need to ask you a question. I hope it's not overstepping. When will you tell everyone what you learned?" Jael asked, a hint of worry in her eyes.

Oz lowered his gaze to the floor and said, "I will as soon as Jacob recovers. That's not a conversation I am looking forward to."

Jael paused, "Is it because I am human?"

Oz whipped his head around to look into Jael's eyes as he said, "No. It's because of many reasons, but none of them are you."

Jael bit the side of her lip and then said, "I have another question that I've been avoiding asking you. How do I explain how we discovered that the connection works with me? Mercy asked, and I didn't know what to say."

Darting his eyes to Jael, Oz thought for a moment then said quietly, "I can't lie to you. I have been avoiding those memories. What I did to you weighs on me far more than having to tell my people that humans are taking us. I honestly don't know what to say because I still feel like my actions were inexcusable. Forgiven or not, I'm afraid most of my people won't understand, primarily because of our rules about it. What I did to you was a violation because it was done without consent."

She walked over to gently grasp his forearm and said, "I won't say a word, if you don't want me to say anything. I will lie and say you had my consent. I am not a liar, but I will lie about this, if that's what you need me to do. This is a tense situation, and you need your people to believe in you."

With a shaking breath, Oz nodded and said softly, "I don't deserve you."

She scowled and shook her head as she said, "I'm

nothing special. You don't have any idea what a loser I was before I was transported here."

Smiling sadly at Jael, he asked, "You mean you transported yourself? And I was a banished criminal who stalked you through the jungle while naked, remember? I still can't believe I didn't at least put pants on before I tracked you. I am pretty sure I was winning at the loser race."

She threw her head back, laughed, then said, "OK, maybe you win!"

Grinning, Oz kissed Jael on the head, and they sat on the bench as he quietly sighed while closing his eyes.

She rested her head on his shoulder and said, "It's pretty incredible you could speak so quickly. How did you do it?"

"The ability to speak is intertwined with language enough that muscle memory is transferred as well. I am only guessing. I'm not sure we will ever know," he said with his eyes still closed.

Oz then cleared his throat and started again, saying, "*Latine loqui quoque.*" I can speak Latin now too.

Jael sat up and stared at Oz with wide, shocked eyes, "Did you just say something in Latin?!"

Chuckling, he opened his eyes and said, "Yes. I stole it from the human physician. It should come in handy. Isn't it odd for the humans that take us to speak a language that's been dead on your world for centuries?"

Her curiosity was overruled when her mind went back to the fact that it was humans that were taking them. Jael asked, "Yeah, about that, how am I going to be able to face your people when they find out that my kind have been taking them?"

"Easy. You will be with me when I tell them. I told you, if they reject you, they reject me. We will return to the treehouse and grow old together, and that will be it. Fuck everyone else. You are the only reason we have this chance for freedom. You are by far our people's most valuable asset, but you are mine first. I don't care how selfish it is. I will walk away from it all for you."

Stunned, Jael quietly said, "I think that's the nicest thing anyone's ever said to me."

Sliding his arm around her and pulling her into him, Oz said, "Jael, you were pushed aside by others your entire life before you met me. That's never happening again. You are my first priority, so get used to it, Spots."

Lying her head on Oz's rock-hard shoulder, she said, "So, what do we do now?"

"First, you sleep, and I rest. Then, we find the quickest way to get sand. We need a lab and clinic for Amelia. On one of the times we connected during the journey, she said she could make antibiotics if we could build her a lab. I'm not sure how we will figure out a microscope for her, but hopefully, Jacob will recover soon, and he and Carter can work on that."

"What do I do?" Jael asked.

"You will be working with Carter, learning about how the electromagnetic (EM) drive works. You transported here with it, and we need to know everything about it. We are not sure what kind of space propulsion the humans here are using, but we are going to explore our own either way. When we eventually head to the dark side of the planet, we will need to understand space travel, so it made sense to get you on that team. I will explain more once I discuss everything with Jacob and August."

Turning her face up to look at Oz, Jael said, "Are you

serious? You want me to work with your geniuses? I think Carter might be even more intelligent than you are."

"He is, no question. So are Amelia, Jacob, and Mercy. And yes, why not?" Oz said flatly like that made perfect sense.

Confused, Jael nodded and quietly said with a small smile, "Alright, I'll take the job. It is my dream job, after all."

21

While sitting with August, Mercy quietly said, "I can't believe Oz made Amelia put Jacob under without Callum there."

"Why? Oz had a reason. I'm sure he's in a bad mood. He is still irritated that we made sure he was elected. You know that was my mother's idea, right?" August said with a smirk.

Feigning surprise, Mercy asked, "What?"

August laughed at her faux shock and said, "You knew that. Don't act surprised. You know my mother is tired of being the one who always has to coordinate everything. The last time the elders were arguing, I thought she was going to set fire to that old, forest-green man's flowers. She's ready to just tend her own garden with my father, and that's it. I was shocked to hear it at first, but after she explained, I understood the reason she insisted that we made sure Oz won."

Jumping up and grabbing August's broad arm, Mercy said, "August! We need to go get Oz's mother!"

"What do you think Callum was doing in the village earlier? He had just finished giving Oz's mother the gift. When he passed it to her, he told her that her son was alive and in the caves. Callum was headed to tell my mother all about it when you found him. You do know he tells her everything, right? Sometimes I think that's how she gets most of her information. I can't get anything past her." August said flatly.

With a look of genuine surprise, Mercy asked, "Do you mean Oz's mother could arrive anytime? Why didn't you tell me?"

Looking around at anything but Mercy, August nervously said, "I haven't had a chance. The people who traveled with Oz needed a shower right away, so I had to finish up their plumbing. The only time I saw you was when you were in a panic over Jacob."

Mercy tilted her head in agreement saying, "Oh, I guess you have a point. When is she supposed to be here? Have you talked to Callum yet?"

"No. I got back to work after the vote. No reason to piss off Oz any more than he already is. He said to frame this apartment next, so that's what I'm doing," he grumbled.

With that, August returned to hammering a support beam onto the framing of the apartment that he had been working on before Mercy arrived.

She said, "Do *we* get one of the apartments in the command area now? Since you're the General?"

August stopped suddenly and turned to her slowly, knowing that the next words he said were important.

He noticed that' she emphasized "we" then said, "Yeah. Yeah, *we* do." He gave her a wide grin before turning back and slamming the hammer into an iron nail.

The nail drove into the wood with a single strike from August's hammer, just like all the others.

Smiling, she said, "I'll meet you in the top left apartment when you need to rest. We should probably go to my house and spend some time there soon, though; you know, smile for the cameras."

Nodding, August turned and got back to work. He had hammered in seven nails by the time she reached the new med room. With Sarah sending new recruits all the time, the construction was moving more quickly than before. The sounds and smells of a new building were constant and would be until they had all the labs and offices they needed to move along with their plans.

Now that most of the decorating was finished, Mercy wondered what she would end up doing next. After she passed the finished med room, she looked in the other direction through the construction framing, and toward the entry door for the base. She could think of it as an actual base now that they had elected officials.

She wondered when Oz's mother would show up. Mercy was desperate to see that reunion. She had been thinking about it for years. On more than one occasion after his sister had been taken, she had begged the creator to bring Oz home. It always broke her heart to see Oz's mother around the village. She looked just like Oz. It was a reminder akin to a slap in the face.

Mercy couldn't fathom losing not one, but two children.

Oz's mother was never quite the same after Oz was banished. Then she lost her daughter? Mercy felt old grief gnaw its way back to the surface.

She hadn't known Mazarin well. She only knew her because Oz and August were so close. Mercy couldn't stop the twist of pain in her gut as she thought about how tough Mazarin's loss was for August. Even though Mazarin was August's former partner, anything that hurt him mattered to Mercy. More than anything, he was her friend, and that love ruled.

Mercy sighed and headed toward the apartments in the command room. When she opened the door to the command area, she found Callum sitting on the stairs blankly staring at the floor.

Slowly, Mercy walked over and then softly asked, "Are you OK?"

"Jacob's fine, but I'm still furious with Oz. He could have easily waited," Callum said with a seething viper's tongue. In contrast to his usual calm and collected demeanor, it was chilling.

"I know you're angry, and I'm sorry. Do you want to go for a run with me?" Mercy offered.

Callum met her eyes and said, "No, I'm saving my animosity for Oz."

Mercy's eyes widened. She walked over to pick up a stool and sat next to Callum.

"Oz was elected President because we all know he is the right person for the job. Jacob has a vital position now as well. I would be angry if I were in your shoes, but I also think I understand," Mercy said softly.

"Well, good for you. I don't care. I am owed an explanation, and I will get it," Callum snapped.

Sitting for a few more moments, Mercy finally gave up and walked up the stairs to the apartment that was across from Oz and Jael's. She just hoped that when Oz came out, Callum wouldn't do something he would regret.

Inside the apartment, the smell of the sea creatures' inks

that were used as stain was faint against the orange oil cleaner they used for the floors. The smell of the stain would be gone in a day or so. The scent reminded her of the ocean, salty and sharp.

The silk bed sheets were so perfect. She didn't want to disturb the order of them. Unable to go without rest, Mercy pulled the covers back and slid inside, getting her tail and limbs situated just right. She turned the lights down with the switch next to the bed, and closed her eyes, emptying her mind of the day.

Shortly after Mercy got comfortable inside the bed's slick sheets, she heard August come in, making her heart leap.

Leaning against the bedroom doorframe and smiling down at Mercy, August said, "I was hungry for some fruit, but I'll gladly have you for dinner instead."

With that, August leaped from the doorway and landed, straddling Mercy. Mercy let out a squeak as August flipped up her cropped top and tasted her peaks while sliding her leggings down her hips.

August grumbled, "I like these flimsy shirts," as he moved from one peak to the other.

Just as he started moving down and mumbling something about easy access, a knock sounded at the door.

With a deep, angry growl, August shot his head up and furrowed his brow. Mercy laid her head back and groaned while she pulled her shirt down and August slid off the bed with a grunt.

Grumbling, "If Callum is at the door, I'm going to...," August trailed off as he opened the door to find Oz casually leaning against the doorframe.

With arms crossed and impatience marring his face, Oz

said sternly, "Time to talk. Get Jacob and tell Callum he and I will talk later. You, Jacob, and I have things we need to discuss."

August turned toward Mercy, but she cut him off and flatly said, "I heard."

Before August got the chance to say another word, Oz was already halfway down the steps, heading toward a table in the command area August walked out to get Jacob from his apartment.

He knocked on Jacob's door, and Callum swung it open with a scowl before the second knock.

August stepped inside and said, "Oz said he would talk to you later. This is important. Is Jacob awake?"

"Yes, I'm awake," Jacob responded from the bedroom with a grumble.

Walking out slowly, Jacob turned to Callum and kissed him sweetly before leaving to meet Oz. The moment Jacob wasn't watching him, Callum returned to his expression of irritation.

August thought Callum was acting like Oz had trampled his flower garden. He did understand why he was upset. August just didn't want to get into the middle of it. He preferred to watch drama unfold rather than be a part of it.

Once August and Jacob were seated, Oz sighed and said, "Before we start, I want to make something clear. If we are doing this, we are doing it right. You somehow convinced the village to elect me, so that means we are doing this my way. None of us will delay medical care for any reason. We are servants of our people now, and I want a vow here and now that both of you understand this. We will free our people, even if it is at the cost of our bodies, minds, and personal lives. We will lose people we love. If you're not ready to sacrifice everything for your people, there's the door."

August nodded in agreement without hesitation, and Jacob followed after a moment of thought.

Oz closed his eyes and took a deep, slow breath before saying, "Our planet is called Sclavus Three by our enemy. It's one of six original slave planets. Of the six, only two are still being used, this planet and Sclavus Six. Our people were transplanted onto Sclavus Six."

He continued, "The primitive beings on the other slave planets died off long ago. Our planet has been functioning the longest of the six. Our people have been farmed for servants and laborers, likely long before we developed the connection. We are by far the most resilient of any slave species on record."

August and Jacob were still as death as Oz went on, "Our people are referred to as Blattae Aurea, which means golden cockroaches. We are the most desired of all those labeled as primitive enslaved people. We are silent, hearty, and relatively intelligent, and when sold, we are worth a small fortune. Our people are obedient to a fault, and we remain silent without a fight, unlike the others."

"Primitive slaves? What are our people used for?" August quietly asked, not sure he wanted to know the answer.

Oz cleared his throat, closed his eyes, and softly said, "Everything."

Both August and Jacob quietly gasped. They sat up straight and waited for Oz to continue.

"The three people we brought back are under strict

orders not to discuss what they saw at the campsite up north. I don't want it getting out yet. Our enemy is an ancient race of humans that began so long ago, they don't even know where their home planet is. Their language, Latin, is something Jael recognized, and it's in her world's history. Latin and the connection to Earth are still a mystery. The physician I drained and gathered this information from had no knowledge of Jael's world. It is like it never existed, but clearly, this ancient race of humans have been to Earth at some point."

With wide eyes, August quietly asked, "Oz, did you say you drained a human?"

Snapping at August, Oz said, "Don't look at me like that. I did what needed to be done."

August shivered as he looked over to Jacob. Oz continued, "When they take our people, the humans wear high-tech cloaks which make them virtually invisible. They give a sedative to those that they capture. It was made for our species and is the same thing we used to put you under, Jacob. We were also able to obtain syringes containing a substance that counteracts the sedative. Amelia will start research on the solution that wakes our people. Maybe she can even find something to prevent the effects of the sedative. She needs glass instruments for her lab to do all of this."

Jacob spoke up, "Sarah said it wouldn't be much longer until she can get the sand that we need. The man with the avocado cart should be here anytime. It will take some experimentation to figure out how to make the glass strong enough for the lab, but that shouldn't take long."

"After we finish the base and have at least a hundred

people recruited and ready, we will take a small, trained team and head north to take back our planet," Oz said.

"What are we up against exactly?" August questioned.

"There are at least a thousand soldiers posted in various camps and approximately two hundred people who run the base and processing port. Our people's holding cells are underneath. The port is only used by our enemy, and the soldiers are mostly unaware of what planet they're on. They were forced to sign agreements never to reveal what they learn, under penalty of death."

"A thousand?! And just how do you expect a hundred of us to take down a thousand of them?" August asked with a furrowed brow and lips pulled back in aggression, showing his teeth.

"We will face them with fifteen or fewer. We have exponentially superior mental processing power, we don't need sleep, and we are predators by nature. Our bodies are bigger and stronger. We are faster. With a solid strategy formed from the tactical intel I have collected, we will find a way. We will only take a handful of people north to take the UTC's north base. The rest will remain here and defend our base.

"We have to win. There are millions of our people on worlds all over the center of our galaxy." Oz stopped and took a long slow breath before continuing, "That's as far as I am willing to open up about the information on our enemy for now. It will take some time to sort out more of her memories. Jael's mind was much more structured than the physician's, so we will have another meeting once I have organized more information."

Oz laid out his plan, "We need to spend as much time and energy as possible preparing. August, find someone in our village who is willing to ride along with the traveling avocado salesman when he arrives. We must spread the gift of language to the villages across the mountain and tell others that we are building a resistance."

"I can do that, no problem. I'll get my mother to help find the right person," August said.

Oz continued, "Once the walls are up, we will need Jacob to gather the recruits and assign jobs. We need to immediately develop weapons, medicines, and technology. Carter will help with the tech. He studied the humans' technology before we burned it. He said he could build better tech based on what he learned. According to him, we won't need a sealed, clean room to build our computer chips."

Jacob nodded, and said, "We need to discuss how best to pass information through the connection. Would it be beneficial under these circumstances to transfer Carter's observations to me to save time? We all understand that organic learning is pivotal, but I think an exception should be made here. I would also suggest transferring Latin to those who are in charge at the base."

Nodding, Oz said, "I agree. If that's all, I am going back to my apartment."

Both August and Jacob nodded. Oz headed up to his apartment and shut the door behind him.

The moment it was closed, August quietly said, "All those missing people are out there somewhere."

Jacob looked back toward Oz's apartment, and while holding his gaze there, he said, "At best our people are being used as servants and laborers. Who knows what horrors they have experienced. Oz is obviously disturbed by what he saw in that physician's mind. They are likely torturing us before we are sold."

Anger laced through August at the thought of Mazarin

out there, somewhere, having gone through whatever Oz couldn't share, doing who knows what as an enslaved person in silence. Sensing August's brewing anger, Jacob hobbled inside his apartment and quickly shut the door.

When August became angry, he was a force of nature and could clear a room with a single growl.

22

Oz watched through the doorway as Carter wrote out the lines and lines of code that he had memorized from hacking the devices they'd found at the campsite. Everyone agreed that Carter was the most intelligent out of everyone they'd given the gift to so far. If Oz's brain could process like a computer, as Jael had put it, Carter would be on a different plane of existence.

Oz watched as Carter carefully pealed the long paper from the wall, rolled it up, and set it in the corner, then unrolled another to put in its place. Carter started again, and this time he drew electronic schematics for a computer he was designing.

Briefly looking over his shoulder at a focused Oz, he returned to his drafting and said, "I will be finished drawing up the plans for the computers soon, then I will need to start training a team right away. Please ensure Luna is on my team. Her computations are exquisite.

"Developing technology will be simple with the right

minds, materials, and tools. Luna and I have an idea for a holoscreen, and I think it will work well with the available materials."

Oz nodded, not at all surprised by Carter's update.

As Oz strolled down the hall toward the command room, he spotted Mercy walking toward him.

Stopping as she neared, he said, "Mercy, I would like for you to take some of the tactical gear we made before our mission and duplicate it. Make it better in any way you can. I plan to give you a team of people to work on uniforms for recruits, but I want you to begin designing now. Would Callum like to join you, or is he still enjoying his errand duties?"

Whipping her head around to check and see if Callum was in the hall, she quietly said, "You just earned a spot on Callum's shit list. Why are you trying to jump your place on it? I'm pretty sure you're top three already!"

Chuckling, Oz said, "I've been on Callum's list for a long time. It doesn't worry me. I think I know why he's pissed at me, and its old news. Do you think he would like to design uniforms and tactical gear with you? I want him involved in at least one project since he's with Jacob. It looks bad to new recruits if he's not participating."

Glaring at Oz with her hands on her hips, Mercy's golden eyes narrowed. She was trying to hide her excitement about her new job. She bit the inside of her cheek and pretended to still be thinking about Callum, "I honestly think he's interested in architecture. When he talks about the future, all he does is describe the structures he wants to build. I know there's not a need for that yet, but I'm sure he *would* like an actual job on one of our projects at the base."

Mercy considered this while tapping her foot, "I'll ask him. How is Jael? No one has seen her in a while."

Darting his eyes around, Oz said, "She's still exhausted from our journey and has been sleeping a lot. Thank you for being so kind to her."

"How could I do anything else? She is why we have this chance."

"I wish she saw it that way," Oz said softly, giving Mercy a half smile then heading toward the command room and is apartment.

Once Oz reached his door, he sighed before opening it. Jael was still in bed. He didn't know if she was asleep or not, but he didn't dare bother her yet.

He didn't understand why she didn't see her value. She was the most beautiful being he had ever encountered, and she had given him everything he could ever want. Her insecurities were eating at her like cancer, robbing her of the joy of her extensive accomplishments in life. It was as if the rubber band holding her together had finally snapped, causing her formerly organized parts to spread out in a jumbled mess.

He wasn't sure if it was because she found out that humans were the enemy, or she had killed a human male. It could be her fear that she's just not good enough, something stemming directly from being passed around as a child. Before the anger began burning, Oz shut down those thoughts and focused solely on the woman he loved.

Standing in the kitchen and staring at the bedroom door, Oz wondered what it would take to pull her from the dark place she now found comfort in. Sighing, he turned around and made her a plate of fruit, salted buttery-ripe avocado slices, and flatbread before he headed into the bedroom.

He sat on the bed next to her and gently stroked her back to wake her. After a few moments, she stirred. Jael stretched out, reaching out with her limbs as far as they would go.

She looked over at the small bedside table and saw the plate of food Oz had brought her. Her stomach was in knots, and she knew she should eat, but she just wasn't hungry.

As a human, she didn't deserve any of this kindness.

Never had she dreamed that she would feel this way after meeting Oz's beautiful people. They were too perfect. She was nowhere near their level of intelligence and beauty.

Jael had gone from being on a planet where she had above average mental capacity, to a place where she was likely the least intelligent being on the entire planet. Her brain and knowledge had always been her prized possession, so what now? Her entire identity was painstakingly built on her intellect, and in an instant that had been blasted into a cloud of fine dust. She'd had nothing else to lean on back on Earth; no support system, no family, and no people around worth befriending.

Funny thing, perspective... *everything is fucking relative* she thought sarcastically. She almost smiled as she added *Einstein was a prick*.

She groaned and sat up, looking into the yellow eyes of a solemn Oz. The lights were dim, and the light-grey-toned wood of the room had become a dark charcoal shade with deep shadows. The bright lights she usually loved were nothing but an eyesore.

Handing her the plate, Oz gently said, "Please. Just try."

Jael hadn't seen pain in his eyes like that in a long time. They mirrored the pain that was once found in her own eyes. If there was anything that could wake her from a haze of despair, it was the look of pain on her love's face.

Sitting up, she took the plate and quickly shoved the folded flatbread with avocado into her mouth. Her stomach ached and twisted at the unwanted intrusion, but she forced it down. With relief in his gaze, Oz watched her eat every bite and then got up to run her a bath.

When Oz padded back into the bedroom, he sat next to her, meeting her eyes, and said, "Do you know why my people chose to call the transfer of your language 'the gift'?"

"Because language is a gift?" Jael said quietly.

"Yes, but that's not why. We call it the gift because when August transferred it to Mercy, they both considered it to be your gift, Jael. Soon, all my people will know who gave them a fighting chance. *You* were the key, and *you* are our gift. Why you ended up here and if we deserve it, I am still unsure. But there is undoubtedly one thing I know more than anything else. I would still be running around naked in a treehouse if it wasn't for you."

Unable to help the explosion of laughter, emotion finally spilled over, and tears flowed with it. She threw her arms around Oz, and he held her until her breathing calmed. He helped her to her feet so that she could go and take a bath.

Her joints and muscles were still recovering from the grueling journey, and she knew she couldn't miss any more meals if she was going to heal properly. She would struggle but vowed to start small.

Memories of her time at the treehouse slid into her

mind. When Oz was suffering from the tree's chemical burns, he had tried to lie down and gave up, so she knew that he understood. He just wanted her back, the real Jael, not the shell she had become in that bed.

After walking to the bath, Jael quickly got in, and Oz sat next to her on the bathroom floor.

Slipping into the hot water, she said, "Thank you for everything."

Sighing, Oz said, "All I did was run you a bath."

"No, you made me find my way back from that dark place I'd found myself stuck in, in my head," she said as she soaped up her hands.

Narrowing his eyes at her, he said, "What does that mean?"

"It means I'm going to stop grieving the loss of my old self and life, because I have someone much better to become. I am in a better place than I was. I just need to get used to being in a different role than I was before. I know that now," she said as she passed him the shampoo bottle he was reaching for.

Smiling, Oz took her head in his hands and brushed his lips against hers. As she bathed in the deep tub filled with hot water and bubbles, Oz sat on the side of the tub and shampooed her curls.

After she was clean and dressed, they sat on the bench in the living room, and Oz said, "If you need more time before you start working, you can take as long as you need. You will be expected to do something, though. You are the President's wife, and we are the first, first couple, so we are setting the bar."

There was a knock at the door, and Oz jumped up to get it.

As he walked away, Jael whispered to herself as she looked down at her open palms, "The first of many."

She focused on her left palm and made a fist.

When Oz opened the door, he found Callum on the other side, and he internally groaned, hoping he didn't come to confront him.

"You and Jael have a visitor waiting for you at the base entrance," Callum said, then he smiled at Jael.

Oz said, "Thank you," as Callum quickly walked off.

Narrowing his eyes at Callum as he shut the door, Oz said, "It looks like we are taking a short walk. Are you up for it? He said the guest was for *us*."

Jael rose from the bath with a forced smile and dressed herself quickly. She met Oz at the door, and he walked ahead of her, leading the way.

Once they crossed the command room, they passed through the narrow hall leading to the main operations room. Looking around at the four buildings dividing the large cavern's four distinctly carved walls, she couldn't believe how much progress they had made. They had stripped the cavern of metals as they carved the shape of the walls, then poured level concrete floors as they excavated. Periodically, the building teams added support beams wherever Jacob claimed they were needed. The beams were primarily in the excavated areas and had become a part of the frames of the buildings that Jael was admiring on their walk.

The floors of the labs and offices were finished, and there were doors and windows that opened to the large hallway. Without glass, they were built with the same solid window coverings that Oz had used at his treehouse, just not quite as thick. Air ducts and branching copper water pipes ran along the ceiling. Stairs in the hallways led to a second story which mostly held supplies and was used for storage.

Jael was so busy looking around she hadn't noticed Oz slowing down. He came to a halt and Jael peered over at his stunned face, then trailed her eyes to where he was focused.

An olive-toned, black-haired, pretty woman stood in the hallway. Oz darted his eyes at Jael and then smiled from ear to ear before he sprinted toward the woman. Jael walked behind Oz and watched as he threw his arms around her.

Slowly approaching, Jael wondered who the woman was. Then it struck her. This was someone that Jael had longed to meet. She hadn't thought this moment would ever be possible.

Oz turned around with tears threatening to spill from his eyes and said, "Jael, this is my mother."

His mother grinned, and Jael looked at two strikingly similar smiles. She leaned forward and wrapped her arms around Jael and held her close. His mother's hair smelled like citrus with a hint of cucumber.

Heat spread in Jael's chest, and tears sprung in her eyes when Oz's mother didn't let go.

His mother whispered to Jael, "Thank you. Thank you for bringing my son home."

Tears welled in Jael's eyes, not because of what his mother said but because of the love emanating from this kind woman. She was everything Jael could have imagined Oz's mother to be. Oz's mother's warmth was engulfing, and Jael felt a calm wash over her from the contact.

For a moment during that hug, Jael got to experience what it felt like to have the unconditional love of a mother. It would be a moment in time that she would cherish for the rest of her life. Unable to find the right words, Jael remained silent.

When she pulled away. August was there to greet Oz's mother with Mercy.

"Did you have any trouble getting inside?" August asked.

"No, it was easy with all the memories Callum shared," she said with a broad smile and glittering eyes.

"Have you chosen a name yet?" Oz asked.

"I was hoping you would help me with that," she said with a sweet smile.

"I like Faye," Jael said quietly.

The kindest of all her foster mothers was named Faye, and it fit Oz's mother flawlessly. Knowing exactly where the name came from, Oz slid his eyes to Jael, and a corner of his lip tipped up in a smile.

Oz's mother twisted around with a grin and said, "That's perfect. Faye, it is."

"It is fitting. Let's all go to our apartment so we can speak in private," Oz suggested as he looked around the wide hallway and all the open windows.

They followed Oz through the main hallway toward the apartments in the command area. Oz headed straight for his apartment door and opened it for everyone to come inside.

Faye sat next to Jael on the backless, padded bench and took her hand. Jael was overwhelmed by her sincere affection. She had never experienced having her hand held by a loving mother, except for a few times when she was a child, and that was by her one extraordinary foster mother, Faye. This time though, the love Jael felt was not something that she knew she would have to give up.

Faye kept holding her hand and looking between Jael and Oz.

In a sincere and sweet tone, Faye said, "I have to admit, I'm not all that surprised my son fell in love with an alien he found in the woods."

Everyone except Oz laughed. He just smiled and rolled his eyes before he crossed his arms as he leaned on the wall across from Jael and his mother.

"Did Callum tell you we elected Oz as our President?" August said as he slid his eyes to Faye.

Faye's mouth dropped open, and she threw her head back laughing. Jael knew that laugh. It was as sweet as a melody. Jael truly loved this time with Oz's mother. She was a lot like Oz but much wiser and more refined.

Once she calmed down, Faye quietly looked at Oz and asked, "How did you manage to survive all that time in those awful woods?"

Shrugging his shoulders, Oz said, "After clinging to a tree through the first tidal wave, I built a treehouse from the jade wood. I planted some fruit trees, and I found a wild young tarantula. August, where is Rew? Please tell me she's not at your house."

"She's at Mercy's, and good luck getting her back," August teased as he narrowed his eyes at Mercy.

"I love her! I'll give her back if I must, but it would mean a lot if I could keep her at my house. I am hopelessly obsessed with her silk's color. I have never found a silk that matches my skin tone so perfectly," Mercy said to Oz.

After thinking for a moment, Oz said, "Keep her for now, but we might have to work something out after this is all over. Maybe we can talk about breeding her eventually. They live for 200 years or more, so we have plenty of time."

Mercy smiled, nodded at Oz, and said, "We better get back to work. It was good to see you, Faye."

Mercy and August each hugged Faye and then quickly left the apartment.

While still looking toward the door, Oz sighed and then slowly said, "They named her Mazarin. Well, August named her."

"You mean your sister?" Faye asked, pain lacing every word.

"Yes. My sister," Oz said when he finally looked over at his mother.

"It's a beautiful name," Faye said softly while still holding Jael's hand.

There was a knock at the door, and Oz walked over and opened it a crack.

Luna, on the other side, quietly said, "The sand has arrived."

Nodding his head, Oz said, "Thank you, Luna," before quickly shutting the door.

Oz turned to Jael and said, "After Jacob figures out how to make glass, he can make Amelia a microscope. We should have antibiotics soon after that."

"Do you see why you both are so important?" Faye said, in a bolder tone than she had spoken yet.

Looking down at his mother, Oz sighed and said, "You've always thought that."

"I also thought one day you would lead our village. Looks like I'm two for two." Faye looked over at Jael and winked at her.

Rolling his yellow eyes, Oz slid down the wall and sat on the floor with his legs spread and tail straightened underneath him. Jael knew he couldn't sit like that for long, and he was only stretching his tail. With his action, Jael was reminded of their time at the treehouse, and she smiled slightly to herself.

While keeping his eyes on Jael, Oz said, "When we lived in the treehouse, we went out a long way to find honey, and one of the young jade trees *ate* me. Jael sprinted all the way back to the treehouse, got my ax, then ran back to the jade tree and hacked the damn thing in half to get me out. I am not even sure how she lifted my heavy ax once, much less over and over."

He continued, "I think there was another trip back to the treehouse during all the chaos. She somehow dragged me back in a wooden basket, then hoisted me up on the pulley system I had made for the treehouse. I wanted you to know that Jael saved me from being eaten alive twice in the course of just a few hours, first by the tree, then by the hundreds of scavengers that followed us as she pulled me home. I owe her much more than my life."

"After all of that, she prepared everything all by herself for us both to make it through the next flood. Only days before the flood arrived, she caught a pill bug that was almost as big as she is She brought it to me, saving my life a third time." He smiled proudly at Jael.

With her mouth in a faint smile, Faye squeezed Jael's hand and slowly turned her head to meet Jael's blurring, tear-filled eyes. Oz had hardly said anything about that time, and Jael was unprepared for it. Emotions threatened to force her tears to spill over. Jael sniffled and tried to calm herself after the memories of that time flooded her mind.

Faye squeezed her hand gently and said, "I meant it earlier when I said that I'm not surprised Oz found an alien in the woods and fell in love. He was always a dreamer, and as a child, he would try to rescue every hurt creature he found. Once he..."

Oz cut her off while he rolled his eyes, setting his head back on the wall as he said, "Please, not this one."

Faye chuckled and met Jael's brown eyes as she continued, "Once, he found a pill bug with some of its back legs injured. He rolled it home and hollowed out some sticks to attach to the bug's broken legs. Well, he didn't realize the bug was not going to be keen on letting him fix its legs. I wasn't aware of what was happening until I heard a crash and looked out to find Oz with his head stuck inside the closed-up pill bug. He was pushing on the bug, but it wasn't going to budge. I had to pry the bug apart with the neighbor's help to get his head out!"

Jael and Faye laughed, then Faye said, "I have missed you, my son. I still cannot believe you're really sitting right there. This is a miracle."

"It may all be a miracle. I've felt that since I found Jael asleep and snoring, hidden between some tree roots," Oz said as he looked at Jael with admiration in his eyes.

A puzzled look crept up on Faye's face before she asked, "How did you figure out how to connect? I've wanted to ask since Callum passed me your gift."

Nervous about the truth, Jael blurted out, "I asked Oz over and over to talk to me somehow. After a long while, I finally wore him down and made him find a way."

Standing across from them, Oz stood silently, with no expression. Faye slid her eyes from her son to Jael's broad smile, and Jael could see a twinge of curiosity at Oz's silence. Faye knew they were hiding something. Not one thing escapes the questioning eyes of this sweet woman.

"Interesting. Once our people are free, I wonder if we

will eventually lose the ability to connect?" Faye asked, changing the subject.

Oz broke his silence and said, "I don't think we will ever know exactly when or how it developed, but we know precisely why. We should attempt to keep it as a reminder of our history. It might have resulted from our manipulated evolution, but it has become the path to our future."

23

"How is your leg healing?" Mercy asked Jacob, who was hard at work leaning over the elaborate geothermal water pump system.

"I've been healed for over a week. If you don't mind, I need to get back to work," Jacob said pointedly as he looked over his broad shoulder at Mercy.

Sneering Mercy headed back to her office. So much for an interesting lunch break visiting with friends. She had been sure that this whole speaking thing would lead to a lot more, well, talking.

Her mind wandered all the way into the cosmos as she walked right by her door and nearly made it all the way to the command hallway before she realized what she had done. Huffing in annoyance at her own mistake, she turned around and headed back to her office.

Mercy hated this entire concept of time. Since Jacob had discovered how to make glass, everything was happening in a rushed, domino effect, one discovery after another. Scouts were now scouring the lands with lists of necessities from Jacob, Carter, and Amelia.

Mercy was stuck in an office with Callum, watching the hands on the clock twist around in a circle. She thought the concept of time was pure madness. She hated being tied to something that kept moving no matter how much she wanted to pause it. Time was one concept she could have done without, she decided with a huff.

On her planet, they had never had this all-encompassing concept of time, other than tracking the movements of the moons. Now everything was converted into some modified ancient calendar from Earth. She understood why it was essential for them to keep time, but she hated it. Days, hours, minutes, they could all go to hell. She wanted her freedom back.

She realized that this one freedom was the cost of a greater freedom, in the end the ultimate freedom. She held onto that thought as she entered her large office containing wooden mannequins. Callum was working and deep in thought, looking at a mannequin wearing a pair of tactical pants that were nearly ready to be sent for testing.

"Well, Jacob's leg is better," Mercy said as she sighed.

Callum slid his eyes to hers, narrowed them, and said, "I could have told you that."

Rolling her eyes, Mercy said, "What are we supposed to do on lunch breaks anyway? What's the damn point of talking when no one ever wants to talk? And I hate this time nonsense. I liked it a lot better when we could just be. Now we are either late or early. I haven't been on time *once*. It's unnerving and uncomfortable. I hope it's not a forever thing."

Callum replied, "Jacob doesn't even want to talk to *me*. I

think you just picked the wrong person. I don't like time either. After all of this is over, we are ignoring time entirely, forever thing or not. Have you thought any more about what you want to do after we win our freedom? Still on the clothing idea?"

Mercy nodded, "Yes. Since I want to eventually design clothes, I've started making some dresses and other clothes during my time off."

Mercy scowled at the tactical pants and continued by grumbling, "Cute clothes. Not these invincible clothes that Oz wants."

"Have you seen the makeup her kind wears? It's like colored mud they cake on their faces. They all have different styles. It kind of creeps me out. Why would they paint their faces?" Callum asked, genuinely trying to piece it together.

The idea of having something smeared on his face was odd and caused him to absent-mindedly rub the skin on his cheek.

"I like it. I would wear those big lashes and add shimmer to my cheeks. I would love to see my hair curled like they do," Mercy said with stars in her eyes.

Callum just shook his head, "It's like they all want to hide who they are behind a mask. Some of the humans' feminine practices are really strange."Looking at the pants, he tried to focus back on work. "I wonder if we could figure out how to make snaps so that these pants won't need so many buttons."

"That's a great idea. You should ask Jacob about it. I'm sure he can design little metal snaps, or maybe we can use magnetic strips. How are we going to make the winter clothes that Oz wants?" Mercy asked Callum, who was still studying the tactical pants.

"One disaster at a time, Mercy," he crooned, not looking away from the mannequin's legs.

Sighing, she said, "We have to be here for four more hours, until the shift is over. Are you going to stare at those pants the entire time? I promise they won't magically turn into a honey-drizzled flatbread."

"Don't act like you would be upset if that happened," Callum snapped back with a furrowed brow, glaring at Mercy.

"Hm. Good point," she said reluctantly before continuing, "I wonder, if we took multiple layers of sap-stiffened silk, could we somehow make a bulletproof vest? I assume our enemy probably has guns, right?" She asked.

"That's a damn good question. If we're making tactical gear, we need to know what we're up against. I think it's time Oz told everyone the details he found out about our enemy and quit being so damn secretive," Callum said flatly.

Mercy turned to leave. "I'll be right back," she said as she left the office.

She decided to find August and get some answers. Mercy turned left and headed to their apartment. She had seen him walk that way earlier and hoped that's where she would find him.

She walked in a found August exactly where she thought he would be -- eating all of flatbread that she had just picked up from her neighbor the day before.

Standing with his arms crossed and still chewing, August stared at Mercy with his brows pinched together as she spoke, "We need more information about our enemy to make the gear we need. We can make generic tactical gear, but we could make more specific items if we had more information."

"I can't reveal anything. Oz doesn't want the information to get out yet. We can't risk our people giving up before it begins," he said in a whisper.

"I'm not asking you to go against Oz. I'm asking you to talk to him. Everyone knows we are facing a powerful enemy, but how are we supposed to give our all if we don't know the facts?" she argued.

Sighing deeply as he leaned his head back, August relented. "Fine, I'll ask him. I thought that after he saw his mother, he would be in a better mood, but nothing has helped. He came back from the jade woods different. I knew he would, but there's a piece of him that's darker than it used to be. *That* I wasn't expecting. I think he went through something out there that he hasn't told anyone about. Sometimes I think it was the time he spent alone, but the longer he's home, the more I think something else happened to him."

"I agree. He was always so warm and happy. Now he seems so quiet and cold. Do you think it might be Mazarin?" Mercy asked.

"No. I noticed he was different before I told him about Mazarin and all the missing villagers," August said quietly, the thoughts of his former love brought pain to his orange eyes.

Mercy reached out her hand and laid it on his crossed arms as she softly said, "I'm sorry."

August wrapped his arms around Mercy and whispered in her ear, "There's nothing for you to be sorry for."

Nuzzling his head into her neck, August soaked up her warmth and affection. He still felt guilty for how long he had strung her along. Refusing to face the truth nearly cost him the attraction he could now feel growing between them.

August had known that Mercy wanted him for a long time. Still, she was always distant and respectful of his decision to pursue a relationship with Mazarin, even if that relationship had been short. Mercy had gone so far as to act happy for him and Mazarin. Pain at that thought laced through him, and he held Mercy tighter, knowing that watching him and Mazarin must have been excruciating.

Because of Mercy's feelings for him, during his youth he had avoided any casual hookups with her or her friends. August secretly had several sexual encounters, but none were serious until Mazarin. They had sealed their new relationship just days before she was taken.

Stopping his thoughts, August felt it was wrong to think about Mazarin at that moment.

He dared not think about his love for Mazarin when he felt so much admiration and care for the woman now in his arms. He wasn't rushing anything with Mercy. She deserved all of him, not the half-healed, sad sack that he was when no one was around. August always had a pretty smile for Mercy, but it quickly faded with her exit. He would not tell her how bad he really felt, not now.

The thought of Mazarin crept back into his mind. Thoughts of her alive and being used for hard labor made his breath catch. He didn't know how he was going to endure keeping the secret of their people's fate.

Mercy was right. He had to talk to Oz. This was a burden no one should carry alone. The truth of the crimes against their people was too heavy and vast for just a handful of people to be tasked with keeping as a secret.

Their little village contained about three hundred people up until shortly after the time Jael arrived at the treehouse. With so many loved ones freshly missing, maybe telling their people the truth would inspire instead of discourage them. Maybe they should tell everyone that the people Oz brought with him were rescued by him and Jael -- that there was a chance they might see their loved ones again one day.

Mercy smiled softly and walked out the door. Taking a deep breath, August prepared himself to go next door to Oz's apartment. This was not going to be an easy conversation, and his throat felt like it was growing tighter by the moment.

Audibly swallowing and trying to relax the panicking muscle in his throat, August knocked on Oz's door. August was physically larger than Oz, but since Oz's return, August feared him. Oz had been broken then somehow healed.

August thought as he heard Oz's firm footsteps approaching the door.

Oz opened the door wide, and August could see Jael in the kitchen preparing a meal. Oz was partially dressed, wearing only his pants. Both were preparing for their work shifts by the look of it.

August said, "I need to speak with you about something."

Oz looked over to Jael with a blank expression, and she smiled and nodded before Oz walked outside with August and shut the door.

"I think it's time to talk about our enemy with the people working in the base, so they know what we're up against. We've hit a few walls, and I'm concerned about our inability to move forward with our preparations. Just now, Mercy asked if they have guns so she can develop gear that will protect our people. I think it's time we told everyone the truth. It might inspire instead of instilling fear and despair like we initially decided."

Sighing, Oz said, "You're right. We can't keep everyone in the dark forever. They need to know the truth, and the time is now. We need a transparent government, and this is how it's done. Tell Jacob and have everyone gather in the command center in fifteen minutes."

August nodded and headed straight for Jacob's apartment.

Jacob didn't answer his door, so August headed for the research lab. Passing through the brightly lit hallways, August wondered how long they would be in hiding. How long would it take them to be fully prepared? Would it be enough? Is it possible to defeat the human colonizers from the dark side of the planet? How could they possibly defeat such a massive force? The humans had advanced beyond their people by hundreds of thousands of years. He blew out a shaking breath and tried to calm his nerves.

Understanding why Oz had held back the truth was not in question. How he would deliver the truth without killing their people's spirits and will to fight was beyond August. He was just glad he didn't have to come up with that speech. Over the years, August had certainly been envious of Oz at different times, but at this point in their lives, August wouldn't want to be in Oz's shoes for any reason.

Approaching the research lab, August hesitated a beat before knocking. This was the calm before the storm, the moment before everything changed. The recruits would know the truth, and the extent of the fight inside their people would be evident.

Releasing a heavy breath, he knocked. Jacob quickly opened the thick wooden door, and he was covered in soot and ash. August peered behind him, wondering what they were doing in there.

August cleared his throat and said, "It's time to gather everyone in the command center. Oz is ready to talk. We have about ten minutes before he will be ready."

Jacob stared into August's eyes, slowly nodded in understanding, and said, "I'll ring the bell."

24

The dinging bell caught Mercy off guard as she was stitching the hem of a newly designed set of tactical pants. Three dings meant the President needed everyone gathered for an announcement.

Had August convinced Oz to tell everyone the details in less than thirty minutes? There is no way August talked him into it that fast, she thought while she wound up her spool of thread and slipped her sewing needle into a scrap of silk. This had to be about something else. Maybe they were getting new recruits or starting a new project. She rose from her spot and filed out into the open hallway of the cavern, staying behind Callum as they walked.

Jacob was at the end of the hallway next to the open door of the command center. He was stoic, as usual, and covered head to toe in grey ash and black soot. When his eyes found Callum, his shoulders lightened and the slight scowl on his face melted away like honey in hot tea. Mercy hoped that one day August would love her as much as Jacob loved Callum. She will never forget the look on Jacob's face after he met Callum for the first time. She had been standing behind Callum in the market that day.

From what she knew about Jacob, he hadn't had many relationships, with only a few flings before Callum. Mercy remembered he had only been with a couple of people when he was young, but he lost interest in dating all together for many years.

With his conservative demeanor, Mercy could see why. She decided a long time ago that Callum was by far the most interesting person she had ever met. She wasn't all that surprised when the two ended up together. Callum needed Jacob's focused presence just like Jacob needed Callum's love for life and his creativity. Mercy was just sad they had not become a couple sooner.

Your circle of friends is painfully small when you don't have the option to speak, she thought as the thick sludge of longing and anger broke free from her heart. The seed of helpless despair can so quickly grow from the knowledge of what *could* have been.

Mercy wondered, was it all for a reason though?

There had to be at least forty people in the command room after everyone filed in. Mercy sat down at a table, and then Callum plopped down next to her a few moments later. Sliding her golden eyes to Callum, Mercy slapped a hand to her mouth to hold back the raucous laughter threatening to spill over her sealed lips.

The entire area surrounding Callum's mouth was covered in thick black soot and grey ashes. Mixed with what she knew was his freshly reapplied facial oils, it had made an opaque paste. They must have snuck away for a kiss.

"What?!" Callum hissed.

Holding her right hand to her mouth, she reached up

with her left hand, took a finger, and ran it down the side of Callum's mouth. She turned her finger around, and he gasped, then grabbed her finger to look at it closely. Callum shot his eyes at Jacob, who was walking up front, leaving a dusty trail of ashes as he went. Callum furiously rubbed his face with his dark grey sleeve but only managed to smear the grey ash and soot all around his face. The contrast of Callum's blue skin against the grey ash was painfully obvious, and Mercy was desperately trying not to laugh. Callum finally gave up with a quiet huff and crossed his arms when he realized he was making it much, much worse.

Mercy could hardly keep from snorting as she slowly exhaled her held breath, all in a failing attempt to calm down. Finally able to stop her laughter, she looked up to find Oz silently glaring at her and Callum.

"Oh shit," Mercy said under her breath as she nudged Callum in his ribs.

Once Callum noticed Oz was staring at both of them in the quiet cavern, he took a sharp breath and sat up.

When did Oz become so terrifying? Mercy thought, as a freezing chill from his glare slithered down her spine. Her skin felt like bugs were crawling under the surface as she looked into Oz's blazing eyes.

Roaming his piercing yellow eyes around the room, Oz cleared his throat and said, "Now that I have your attention, it's time that we discussed our enemy."

Mercy sucked in a sharp breath as she realized August had gotten through to Oz, and her request was being honored. No wonder Oz had looked for her in the small, crowded group.

After taking a visibly pained breath, Oz continued, "Our desperation for communication dove deep into our DNA and eventually gave us a way to share our thoughts through our neural connection. Through this intimate connection, Jael was able to give me the gift of her language and knowledge. I passed this gift on, and as you know, that's why we all have found ourselves here today. Jael is a human, and she is from a planet called Earth. As many of you are aware, she was accidentally transported to our planet by her EmDrive when a lightning bolt struck just outside of her lab.

When Jael and I recovered three of our people from our enemy, we learned something which we initially found confusing and excruciating for both Jael and me. Even before I knew all the facts, I didn't question Jael and her humanity. I hope I can trust all of you to have the same consideration and that you will allow me to fully explain before making any decisions or judgements."

"Our enemy is *human,*" he said flatly.

"They come from a different planet than Jael's. The humans on the dark side of our world have been stealing and enslaving our people for more than ten thousand years. These humans have existed here for so long that at some point during their million or so years of rule, they lost their own home planet. It has been missing for more than seven hundred thousand years.

Since they discovered our planet, we have been considered the most prized of all enslaved creatures. We remain silent, and as so-called lowly insects, our so-called simple minds could only learn the languages of our enslavers well enough to respond to commands. In our entire history as enslaved people, there have only been a handful of instances when our people fought their rulers on the planets they were taken to. These rebellions have all ended with our people's brutal deaths.

"The humans claim the right to own us as a species, and they have kept our planet a secret from all other worlds and intelligent beings. We are not the only slave planet. The other, Sclavus Six, has the majority of our people, numbering in the millions.

"We are drastically outnumbered here on our planet, and we don't have close to the same resources as our enemy, but we do have intelligence and skill. They cannot outrun us, they cannot outsmart us, and they can no longer keep us quiet. We will match their guns and tracking technology with our minds and bare hands. We *will* take back our planet, and then we will prosper as a free world and people."

Who was this man that returned from years of solitude in the jade woods? This was not the bright and kind man Mercy once knew long ago. This man was a leader, and she knew at that moment, with a chill running down her spine, that her people chose their President well.

Mercy's eyes slid over to Callum, who looked speechless for once, with his mouth hanging open, and she whispered, "Oz is a *lot* different than I remember."

"Yeah, me too. I knew him pretty well when we were younger," Callum replied quietly.

Mercy wondered what exactly that meant but didn't have time to think about it because August walked up and said, "I guess we can answer some questions with what we now know. Bulletproof clothing would be beneficial. They use ammunition shot through weapons similar to the guns on Jael's world, but they are actually miniature versions of a railgun."

Mercy's mouth gaped open in shock, then she said to Callum, "Well shit, so much for the bulletproof idea."

Twisting his lips around, Callum looked at her and said,

"Maybe not. Let's talk to Jacob. Knowing him, he has already built one of their weapons. I'm sure we can use one of his prototypes to test our designs."

"We would still have to come up with a concept first," Mercy said as she rolled her eyes.

"You don't give us nearly enough credit. If anyone can figure this out, it's us," Callum replied before turning and heading back toward their office, ash still smeared around his mouth.

Fair enough, she thought. The ideas cascaded into her mind like a waterfall as she thought about the properties of the mature jade tree's sap. Maybe they could somehow use the fact that it is a non-conductive material?

If the suit had a non-conductive base layer to protect their skin, they could run wires through the exterior of the suit and electrify the outside. This wouldn't stop the blunt force of a molten round, but maybe it would catch and redirect it?

Or, turning the entire suit into a railgun that could collect, aim, and shoot the rounds itself would even be better. Mercy had the idea buzzing in her head but wasn't sure if any of it was practical, or even possible.

"Callum, I have an idea. We need Jacob and maybe Carter. It's worth it. You go clean off your face and find Jacob. I'll go get Carter next door," Mercy said.

"That fast, huh?" Callum said in a snarky tone with a smirk.

She stared at Callum blankly before he winked at her and walked out. Yes, that fast, asshole, Mercy thought as she walked to the office next door and knocked.

"Yes, Mercy, how may I help you?" Carter asked in his crisp deep voice.

"I have an idea. What if we could catch the molten rail-gun's rounds anywhere on the suit and redirect them? Then, the suit could be programmed to send the round anywhere you want." Mercy beamed as she told Carter her idea.

Carter stared at Mercy as the thought rolled around in his head before he said, "That's a brilliant idea. It's possible, as well, using the new computer chips we just developed. I'll meet you over in your office after I finish up here. It will only take a few minutes."

Nodding, Mercy smiled, walked back to her office, and began drawing the outline of a suit. Moving along, she imagined the wires as a thin mesh, but she wasn't sure. That was Jacob and Carter's part. Hopefully, they could help make this a reality, because the idea of having armor that worked as offense as well as defense was a game changer.

Once everyone was gathered in the office, Carter began, "Mercy has an idea for a suit that, at the very least, could repel the enemy rounds shot from any angle other than straight forward."

Mercy looked over at Carter, wondering if he had already built the entire thing in his head and tested it. He had an almost otherworldly talent.

Without changing his expression, Jacob said, "That's precisely the kind of thing that we need. Maybe we can build a shield into the armor with the same technology Carter, what do we need to develop in order to pull this off? Besides the obvious portable energy storage that we are already working on."

Looking at Jacob, Carter said, "We have what we need regarding the tech. We just need to apply it to her idea. Please inform Oz that I'm only a few hours away from our testing. He requested that he be present when we flip the switch."

Nodding, Jacob said, "I'll let him know."

Turning to Mercy, Carter said, "As soon as we work out our end with the tech, we will meet with you and incorporate it into your design for the suit -- should only take a day at the most."

Mercy just sat and grinned ear to ear as everyone filed out. Once she was alone, she danced around the massive office and let herself go, dreaming about her future fashion career.

25

While heading toward Carter's office, Oz heard strange banging noises coming from Mercy and Callum's office. He shrugged it off because, between those two, they would be lucky if any work got done. They were both eccentric, almost to a fault. It was good for ideas but not productivity.

He entered Carter's dimly lit office, and at the back of the room he noticed a large flat blackboard with wires connected to an extensive network of circuit boards on the table.

"Is this what I think it is?" Oz asked with a smile growing on his face.

Carter simply said, "Yes," and then flipped the switch.

Bright blue light flooded the room, and the mechanical parts and fans on the circuit board began to whirl and spin. The small circuit board was connected to a small, thin, off-white mat, around six inches long and hardly an inch wide. The small mat burst to life with color, and then the air above it seemed to shimmer.

In absolute awe, Oz watched as a full-color, holographic screen appeared. Carter reached up and tapped an icon, and a file with written code opened.

Carter looked to Oz and asked, "Did the human physician's memory show you that they had this technology yet?"

Chuckling in disbelief, Oz said, "They just recently developed it, but they haven't even integrated it into their fleet ships. How close is Jacob to stabilizing the H-cell battery?"

"He will be finished with the H-cell battery testing tomorrow. I'm surprised he hasn't updated you. Don't you live across from his apartment?" Carter asked, confusion written on his face.

"Yes, he lives across from me, but they have been spending a lot of time at their home to keep up our ruse," Oz replied with grin he couldn't wipe from his face, even if he wanted to.

"Check with Mercy before she finishes her shift. She has some news for you," Carter said as he switched off the computer and holographic screen.

He headed for the door and tipped his head to Luna, who was quietly sitting in the corner working. She nodded, began gathering her belongings, then got up from her seat and followed them out, her long white braided hair swishing behind her.

Oz followed Carter, then stopped at Mercy's door and said, "Have your team develop a communication system for us, preferably one that's run by touch, like the tablets from Jael's planet. We need to be able to communicate with anyone in the village when they're off shift so that we can call them in if needed."

Nodding, Carter walked down the hall, and Oz slowly

opened the door to Mercy and Callum's office. Peering inside, he found Mercy prancing around and humming to herself. The fishtail braids and knots in her brown hair bounced behind her as she danced.

Oz cleared his throat to get her attention, and Mercy whipped around, looking stunned to see him in her doorway.

"I hear you need to speak to me?" Oz asked, still smiling from Carter's progress.

With a broad smile and heavy breaths from dancing, Mercy said, "I came up with an idea to give us some protection against the railguns. Instead of thinking about heavy metal armor, we could electrify a suit that would deflect the molten rounds with the same tech used by the railguns."

Mercy watched as his smile faded. Oz spun the idea around in his head and considered the implications of the design.

Tilting his head to the side, a grin spread to one side of his mouth. "Brilliant idea, Mercy. Does August know?"

She answered quickly saying, "No, he doesn't know yet. I have another hour until my shift is over."

"Go home now and take tomorrow off. You've more than earned it," Oz said as he smiled and headed toward his next stop, Jacob.

His footsteps tapped against the cold paved floor. Oz stopped for a moment to take in the grand accomplishments already made by his people. They didn't even have a proper name for their people yet. The Latin word Glisco, meaning freedom, blaze up, and kindling came to his mind. That one didn't feel right, though. Maybe Iungo, he thought, *to connect*. What a fitting name for his people, Iungo, Oz thought as he continued to stroll down the wide hallways.

He would add this to his list for one of their upcoming meetings.

Presidential duties such as adding government positions and forming the physical training program, would be next on the agenda for his meeting with Jacob and August.

He hated this.

All of this.

Times like this made him want to retreat to the treehouse, to a time even before he and Jael had learned they could connect. Spending all that time with Jael alone was the happiest he had ever been.

The time away from his people was a punishment for which he had committed no crime.

He hated that he had to make Jael work; that she couldn't run on the jade treetops with him in the nude at any time they wanted; that he had to be away from her -- her feel, her scent.

Jael hadn't begun working yet. He wasn't entirely sure she was ready. It had been just over a year since she transported here, and life had been nothing but chaos for her the entire time.

Most of the time, he walked around wanting to take her and run back to the treehouse. He knew the humans were afraid of the immature jade trees. They would leave him and Jael alone, but he knew it wouldn't be the same for his people. He could not abandon them. He was not a coward and would not run from this responsibility, no matter how sweet the memories of Jael and their time at the treehouse were -- how sweet their freedom was.

Her freedom.

His freedom.

But it was all just an illusion.

To achieve the absolute freedom he desired, he would have to fight and could end up dying for it.

His people believed they had elected a kind and fair leader, but he wasn't that young man anymore. He wouldn't admit it to anyone but Jael, but the time he spent trapped in the jade tree was a hell no one should ever endure. To have life sucked from you while you were being eaten alive, a layer of skin at a time, was a horror that he couldn't forget.

While trapped inside, his spirit broke. He had accepted his fate and was mere seconds from allowing the tree to pull the rest of the neural energy from his body, letting himself die. Tears had poured from his eyes as he said his last goodbyes to his little spotted alien. Until he heard Jael's screams of anger and felt the force of the ax against the wood, he had truly believed he was about to meet death.

That's all it takes, though, just one moment in time when your spirit breaks, even if it's just a crack in the shell. The heart is like a stone, and life is like the water of a babbling stream. It washes over the rock, refining the rough spots and moving it along.

Forcing it to continue.

But once the heart is broken, life enters the cracks, filling them with silt and water. Then comes the freeze, the trauma and pain, the real test of the heart. The once gentle liquid expands in the cracks, it easily fractures the stone, and it breaks into pieces. One can press their heart's pieces together, but to truly mend the cracks and breaks? That would take superheated molten rock from deep inside the planet.

An impossibility.

The heart will *never* be the same again.

Even if one could mend the heart with that molten rock, scars would always be there.

Thicker.

Evident.

Sometimes he could still feel the acidic sap eating away at his skin and searing his lungs with every shallow breath. The only thing that pulls him out of it are the memories of Jael's cries of fury as she slammed the ax into the tree that final time, causing it to spit him out onto the ground.

When he looked up and saw Jael standing over him, slick with sweat, heaving with pained breaths, and still holding his ax, he felt something more. Just for a fraction of a moment, something told him there was more, and he had to live. Jael wasn't aware of it, but she saved his life in more ways than one that day.

She saved him from being eaten alive on the inside as well as the outside.

Jael made him feel worthy.

Finally reaching the door to Jacob's lab, Oz prepared himself for what he might find on the other side. No one ever knew what you would find when popping in on the organized chaos. He chuckled recalling Jacob when they were young. Nothing had really changed.

The door opened silently, and Oz peered inside, finding Jacob sweeping up a pile of ashes. Kicking a table leg into the pile, he stirred up some of the ash he had just swept. The cloud of ash finally settled, and Oz stood with his arms crossed.

"Was that a table?" Oz asked curiously as he tucked a bit of hair behind his ear.

In reply, Jacob said, "Yes. It was a necessary sacrifice. I needed to test the new ventilation scrubbers and emergency sprinklers. Both work exceptionally well, as expected."

Chuckling, Oz asked, "And there were no scrap wood piles you could have, er, never mind. How is the H-cell development going?"

"Once the final testing is complete, we will be ready for production. We need about a ton more sand. And that's a literal ton, not one of those Earth human figures of speech. We should send a secret team out with a cart to bring back the enormous load. I did the math myself, and we can easily fit one ton of sand into a standard cart. We are at a standstill once this last bucket is used up. These ancient volcanic lava tubes have proved to be filled with every precious metal needed for our technology, but without the silica from sand, we can't move forward."

"I'll put together a team and go myself. I know the best way to avoid the jade woods and the immature trees on the border," Oz offered with a half-smile.

Clearly not entirely OK with the idea, Jacob smoothed loose black hair out of his eyes and said, "You are *not* going by yourself with Jael. You two would never come back."

Oz threw his head back and laughed, then said, "OK, you're right. August can accompany me. We will need Mercy here, though. She has extensive work on a project ahead of her."

"Callum can go as well. Mercy and I both need to focus," Jacob said flatly.

Oz reared back a bit, lifting his right eyebrow, and said, "Are you sure that's a good idea?"

Jacob narrowed his eyes at Oz and said, "Whatever is going on between you and Callum, please figure it out. Callum's incessant loathing of you will soon cause me to eat a handful of purple mushrooms and get lost in the woods for a week. I believe at this point he might complain if he saw you eat flatbread the wrong way. I see how you glare at him. I know the feeling is mutual. Sort it out."

Oz considered what Jacob said, "Is there a wrong way to eat a flatbread? I mean, I guess there could be. I already explained why it was important to start the medical procedure right away. Is he still angry about that?"

"No. It's not the procedure. Although *I* am still irritated with you about it, Callum is not. It's something else, and he won't say a word about it. Maybe being stuck with you for a while will make him figure it out or get over it," Jacob said as he turned back to his papers that were plastered all over a wooden tabletop.

Oz had an inkling as to why Callum would still be so upset. He disregarded his thoughts and said, "Fine. He can come too. It might take a few weeks to get there and back. Find someone to build a cart, then bring it to the edge of the woods using one of the main routes into the village. Even better, have them take it to your house, and we can leave from there. I'll meet them in the woods on the way."

Without turning around, Jacob said, "I'll make sure you have everything you need."

With that, Oz headed off to tell Jael about their new task. He was itching to leave the base anyway. He bet that some fresh air would help tremendously. Being forced to hide in this cave was against Oz's very nature.

Once he arrived at their apartment, Oz walked in and got right to the point, "We need sand, so Jacob decided we are sending August, Callum, and the both of us."

With a scowl and a snarl on her full lips, she said flatly, "I thought Presidents didn't go on secret sand missions."

While trying not to laugh, Oz said, "Jael, there are just enough people in the base to get the necessary jobs done. We can't waste time sending people who are already working on projects. Carter recently made a holographic, interactive screen, so there's no way I'm sending anyone from his team anywhere. You get the point."

Oz shrugged and leaned against the wooden wall of their apartment.

With her eyebrow cocked and her mouth hanging open, Jael shook her head and said, "And you wanted me to work with Carter? Are you insane? It would have been a room full of genius scientists working with a dodo bird who had just figured out how to put-on pants! And I promise, I would not have been one of the scientists in that scenario."

Throwing his head back and laughing, Oz wrapped his arms around her as he kept saying, "I'm sorry! I'm so sorry!" while continuing to laugh.

At that point, Jael was laughing too. There was no reason to deny that she was easily the least intelligent being on the planet. She may have been the spark that lit the fuse, but she was a mere sparkler among dynamite when it came to brain power.

With her face partially muffled in Oz's shirt, Jael said, "Do you think your people developed such high intelligence because you were forced to be silent for so long?"

Becoming very still, Oz thought for a moment and then said, "I absolutely think the hindrance of one sense can heighten others. After living in silence for so many generations, I could see that hypothesis being more than plausible."

Jael asked, "How can all of you go from speaking freely to utter silence so quickly? I am still not OK after months of not talking. Oh, and if I haven't mentioned it today, thank *fuck* your people developed clocks and adapted the Earth's human calendar. Your moon system was making my eyes cross."

Chuckling and running his hands up and down Jael's back, Oz asked, "Are you going to be OK going with us? Or do you want to stay here? You are more than welcome to stay here with Mercy if that's what you want. I spent most of my life silent. For me, it's not as bad as it would seem. When you've never had the option of something, even after just a taste, it's not quite the same as losing something you've always had. We've always had silence, and as much as we longed for more communication, the worn-in silence can still be comforting."

"I guess that's true. Wait, why would Mercy want to stay with me?" Jael asked sincerely.

Leaning back to see her face, Oz tilted his head at her and said, "Mercy has asked about you multiple times and has been begging me to invite them over for a meal. She wants to come over so she can get to know you."

Jael's heart raced at the prospect of making a new friend, and she blurted out without thinking, "OK, I'll stay!"

With a growing grin, Oz asked, "Really? You want to stay and get to know Mercy? I could swing letting her off for a few days while we're gone. She has done exceptionally well at her job and deserves it. I have to be honest, though. I wish she would have worked with Carter and his team because of her genius design skills and creative mind. August said she has no interest in tech, so instead, I relented and put her on uniforms. She ended up designing us some profoundly advanced armor, and I can't say I'm surprised. Time will tell, but she may have tipped the scales in our favor. We were never friends or anything, but she was August's neighbor growing up, and she always seemed nice. I think she is a perfect person to introduce you to more of my people as well. I hope you two will have fun. We will need to leave right away."

Nodding, Jael reached up and took Oz's lips against hers, giving him a passionate kiss goodbye.

With her eyes on Oz's, Jael said, "I love you, and thank you for making me feel important, even though I am this planet's top dummy."

Once again, Oz tossed his head back and laughed. After wiping his laughter induced, weeping eyes, Oz kissed Jael on the head and quickly gathered his clothes in a bag.

Before walking out of the door, he embraced Jael and said, "I love you for me, but I also love you for all my people. Don't forget, you've given us the keys to freedom. You are the reason for our hope."

26

Feeling a light tap on her shoulder, Mercy whipped around and found Oz and August standing behind her as she was in line to get a meal. They had finished building the mess hall, and anyone at the base could come in and eat or take a sack of rations back to their workspace or apartment in the base. Mercy had been deep in thought about how convenient it was that they had set up a place to get food inside the base. It felt so modern, even more so than the building itself.

Clearing his throat, August met Mercy's eyes and said, "We need to go to the coast with Callum and get Jacob more sand. We're taking a cart, so it will probably take around four weeks."

"Jael said she's staying here and would love some company. You've earned a day off a week until we return, so you two should have some extra time to spend together," Oz said, smiling kindly at Mercy.

Grinning, Mercy hugged Oz quickly and then threw her

arms around August. He leaned down and softly kissed her goodbye before they walked off to find Callum and head out. Mercy turned toward the tables after Oz and August walked away and found everyone who was sitting and eating now silently staring at her. As she looked around the room, she wondered what everyone was looking at. There wasn't one scowl or odd look, just all eyes on her.

Feeling a bit awkward, Mercy reached down, grabbed a silk sack with fruit, avocados, nuts, and flatbread, then slipped out and headed to the command area and Jael's apartment.

After she climbed the stairs, Mercy knocked on the door, and Jael answered almost immediately, swinging the door open. With a smile plastered on her face that showed every tooth, Jael couldn't contain an ounce of her excitement.

"Hi! I'm guessing Oz spoke to you already?" Jael asked.

"Yes. I brought us a ration's bag. Want to have dinner together since everyone else is gone?"

Still smiling so wide her cheeks hurt, Jael said, "Come in!"

Mercy walked in and went straight to the kitchen, placed the large rations' bag on the counter, and began unloading the food. With the food spread out on the counter, Mercy pulled a small bag from her pocket and set it down next to her.

Turning around and slyly eyeing Jael, Mercy said, "I'm just going to throw an idea out, and you promise you won't judge?"

Creasing her brow in question, Jael crossed her arms and slowly asked, "Go on?"

First clearing her throat, Mercy peered at a skeptical Jael

and said, "I think we should have a nice quiet dinner, and then we should drink some purple mushroom tea."

Throwing her hand up before Jael could speak, Mercy continued and nodded as she flared her eyes wide, "And yes, I mean *those* kinds of mushrooms."

With her mouth open and eyes wide, she let what Mercy just said process a moment.

Jael chuckled and threw her hands over her mouth. Finally dropping her hands, she said, "Really? I mean, yeah! I would love to! That was the *last* thing I thought you were going to say!"

Mercy beamed, clapped her hands and flipped around to get to work on their dinner. She pulled a small bottle from the bag and set it down, then she tossed the bag onto the stool at the table behind her.

"What's that?" Jael asked inquisitively.

"Some kind of grain alcohol. We need to mix it with the juice carefully. Amelia gave me instructions," Mercy threw over her shoulder with a smirk.

Again, Jael's mouth was agape, "You have alcohol?! And we're going to drink mushroom tea?! *Is this real life?!*"

Jael would never admit it aloud, but she was nearly in tears. Mercy was everything she had ever wanted in a friend. The perfect best friend for her now stood in her kitchen, and Jael couldn't compute the odds of what had just happened. Sis would have loved this beautiful curly-tailed woman.

A thrill shot through her at the idea of a *real* friend that was interesting and fun. How did she get so lucky? Jael closed her eyes for a moment and said a tiny prayer of thanks. She knew anything could happen during a friendship, but this was a *chance*.

Just having the chance to make a real friend was reason enough for her to be ecstatic.

Back on Earth, she had so-called friends, but not *real* friends -- no one she ever truly wanted to spend time with. Other than Sis, she had always been in superficial relationships, and she never had much in common with anyone back on Earth.

Mercy was gorgeous and full of energy. No one like her even *existed* in the desolate, West Texas town she was from, Sumner, Texas. She shivered and shoved that thought away. That town had almost entirely ignored her. She had been an invisible woman who simply blended into the background noise.

Good riddance to being *unseen*.

Smiling over at Mercy, who was preparing their meal, Jael approached the counter and said, "Is there anything I can help with?"

Looking over at Jael, Mercy perused her lips then nodded, "Why don't you make our drinks?"

"Sure. How much alcohol do I add to each cup?" Jael asked as she looked down at the little bottle.

"Amelia said just a couple of spoonful's. She was glaring at me, acting like if I fucked it up, we might die, so be careful."

Taking the small bottle of alcohol and holding it up to look at it more closely, Jael said, "I knew Oz used mushrooms as a teenager, but I didn't know..." drifting off, Jael wasn't sure she knew how to ask what she meant.

"My people, for the most part, still party as adults, if that's what you're wondering. Just wait and see once we are all free! Our people will have these woods full of nightclubs, dance studios, music halls, art galleries, theaters, and restaurants. I'm sure there will be tattoo parlors on every other corner, as well. I already have one I want. Callum and I talked about his dream to be an architect. I think he just wants to build anything that has a water fountain and one of those walls with plants in a pattern all over it. He talks about what he wants to build like it's going to happen; it's never an if."

A nightclub? Tattoo parlors? She was going to love it here, Jael thought to herself as she measured the alcohol from the glass bottle with a spoon and poured it into the wooden cups. No wonder Callum had asked her so many questions about the places she had been. Too bad she hadn't ever been anywhere nice.

With her hand still resting around the glass bottle, she thought about how Oz's people had come so far. She felt a sense of calm fall over her that she had only experienced before with Oz. Smiling to herself, the excitement about her evening's events was just settling in.

Mercy began humming, and Jael asked, "What are you humming? I don't know that song?"

"Oh! Carter has developed a few computers already, and he has been working on condensing them for practical use. I think he has one of the smaller computers already built. Anyway, one of his team members wrote a synthesizer program and some music-producing software. They've been playing with it after their shifts are over, and the music is outstanding!" Mercy explained.

Psychedelic's? Alcohol? Music?

"Your people really do like to party," Jael said with a chuckle, unable to hold back her grin.

"Hey! That's a great idea! We should throw a party! I love dancing." Mercy nearly leaped as she whipped around toward Jael with a plate of cut mango, raspberries, roasted nuts, sliced avocado, and some fluffy flatbread.

"Shouldn't we wait for Oz and August to have a party?" Jael asked.

"You mean Callum? Oz and August won't care either way. We just have to convince Jacob and that's easy. Jacob's like that old stern dad who you can convince to do almost *anything* with enough pestering," Mercy explained, waving her hand as she spoke.

Taking her plate, Jael took a seat on the padded bench, and Mercy sat next to her.

Adjusting her tail behind her and then sweeping her fishtail braids off her shoulders, Mercy said, "After we eat, let's drink our mushroom tea, and then we can go to Carter's office to find out about some music."

"OK. Um, are you sure the guys won't get mad about us throwing a party?" Jael asked, with her brows lowered, peering at Mercy through her lashes.

Mercy responded, "We are not just having one party. And Callum will only be upset because he got left out. He will get over it."

"No, I mean Oz," Jael said a little quieter.

"Oh, you mean, as his woman, are you going to be in trouble for partying without him?" Mercy asked.

"Well, yeah, I guess that's just about right. I feel pretty called out," Jael said and then blew out a breath with her eyes wide on her plate of food.

Mercy threw her head back and laughed, then said, "Honey, you have a lot to learn about our culture. Most of us are not jealous at all. We've never had enough of anything to get jealous anyway. I think something more evolved. Something more than our fast-processing brains and the neural connection since we were forced into silence."

Nodding her head in agreement, Jael replied, "That's what I think about all the time. Not the jealousy part. I didn't know that, but it makes sense. The fact that I can't do the calculations your people *all* seem to be able to do -- not even close for me. I think your people evolved more complex brain structures after being forced into silence during your entire evolution. Not having language meant that your society's creativity was never able to develop. I'm sure personality was deeply affected as well."

Jael shivered with the after thoughts of her own statement but peered over to find a smiling Mercy.

"You are the *perfect* person to do mushrooms with!" Mercy blurted out with a broad shining smile on her face.

Jael and Mercy both laughed. Mercy looked down at her plate, then at Jael, and said, "I'm going to finish my plate in the kitchen while I make the tea. It *is* going to taste vile. But it's worth it, I promise."

Jael rose from her place on the bench and followed Mercy into the kitchen, hopping onto the counter to sit while she watched Mercy make the tea.

"So, I'm assuming these are going to be strong?" Jael asked, looking down at the dried purple mushrooms sitting on the counter.

Mercy slid her eyes to Jael and smiled as she said, "They're probably like everything else on this planet, *wicked*."

Mercy handed Jael her finished tea, then Mercy began smashing the mushrooms into the bottom of her own mug and poured hot water over it. Jael was already gagging in her mind and had no idea how she was going to choke this down. A hint of the smell of her tea hit her nose, and she gulped, wondering if she should drink it over the sink or trash can, just in case.

"Shouldn't we, like, I don't know, plan the party and get everything together before we drink this?" Jael asked and then took a closer sniff of the bright violet, rotten-dirt-scented liquid.

Jael made a disgusted face at her steaming mug of gag-a-licious tea.

"No, that's the whole idea," Mercy said, like that made any sense at all.

"What?" Jael asked quickly, right as Mercy downed her steaming tea.

"Oh, fuck it," Jael said right before downing the hot, grainy, violet concoction.

Jael looked down into the empty glass and immediately regretted drinking it hot. Her stomach promptly rumbled in protest.

"Why did that have to be hot?" Jael asked, right before a small gag squirmed its way up her throat. She grimaced with the sensation. It tasted *very* illegal and somehow -- violet. Closing her eyes, Jael said a silent prayer.

Mercy just threw her head back and laughed, drawing a giggle, then a boisterous laugh out of Jael. Grabbing her stomach, Jael threw a hand over her mouth to avoid losing her dinner.

"Hurry, finish your food, and let's get to Carter's office before we can't find it," Mercy said flatly, again, like that made any fucking sense to Jael.

Jael grabbed her plate and shoveled food into her mouth as fast as possible, and Mercy did the same. Once the two finished gorging themselves to take the edge off the stomachache, Jael hopped off the counter and went to slip on her boots. Mercy put her hand on Jael's shoulder and shook her head no.

Confused, Jael asked, "I can't wear my boots?"

"No way! You have some cute shoes that I just made you to wear with some high-waisted leggings and a cropped top. You will look great, I promise. I know you don't like dressing out of your comfort zone, but I think you will like it. Plus, that's what I'm wearing, and I want to match in case I lose you tonight -- which is a strong possibility, even if we're in the same room," Mercy said as Jael stared at her like she was glowing.

Mercy just barked out a sharp laugh and then said, "Follow me!"

Jael followed Mercy to the closet. She had a feeling that tonight might be one for the books. She hoped someone had built a camera, because they definitely needed to document this.

Mercy pulled out a navy-blue cropped top and a pair of grey leggings, handed them to Jael, then stood there waiting for her to change. Jael realized Mercy wasn't going to leave and so again, Jael just said fuck it, this time in her head. She started stripping off her navy leggings and grey tunic. Mercy took them from her and dropped them on the floor like they were soiled, and she was disgusted. They aren't that bad, Jael thought.

She quickly dressed and, with Mercy satisfied with her attire, they headed toward Carter's office. After they passed through the second large door of the hallway, Jael began feeling different.

Mercy seemed so far away, but Jael knew she was close. Before Jael understood what was happening, she was sitting in a chair in Carter's office giggling and Mercy was badly explaining the plan to an eager group of people.

Jael vaguely heard "music" and "let's party" before she was ushered out of the door in a heap of excitement. She wasn't sure how her legs were working but they seemed to be moving on their own just fine and clearly knew what they were doing, so she didn't worry about it.

"Why do I have to go? Jacob said Mercy and Jael are staying here. Do I not even have time to properly say goodbye to the man I love?" Callum ground out at August and Oz.

"No, you don't have time to 'properly' say goodbye. That would take a whole day with you. We do not have the luxury of time, as I have already made clear. When we win our freedom and independence, we will have plenty of time for that," Oz stated flatly with his arms crossed.

Callum briefly closed his light blue eyes and said dryly, "Fantastic. We have to fight an impossible war where we're all going to *die, and* I must gladly give up properly fucking my man for an entire Earth month. Thanks a lot, you two. Please kindly suck on a scorpion tit and get fucked by her stinger. I hope she forgets to spit on it."

Shaking his head as Callum walked toward the door, August leaned his head toward Oz and, with his eyebrows raised, said in all seriousness, "Well, this is gonna be a fun trip." Then he walked toward the door and collected his pack off the floor.

August closed his eyes for a moment; he knew bringing Callum was a bad idea, but Callum was the most available candidate from all the projects going on in the base. He knew that he would probably end up being forced to confront Callum about why he was still so upset with Oz. Maybe it would be for the best. Jacob and Callum came as a pair and apparently had for a long while. Oz needed to make peace with Callum and that might as well happen sooner rather than later.

Callum and August headed to the village to get some supplies and ready the cart. They didn't want to stay out of sight during the journey, so staging was the best option. Oz traveled alone toward the rendezvous point in the woods where the other two would pick him up.

After an uneventful slow walk through the woods, Oz leaned back on a tree against his pack. He adjusted his tactical pants to give his tail more room and sat down with his tail stretched out under him. He was the only one who could wear any of the new gear because he was not supposed to be seen. Callum and August had to wear their people's traditional attire.

He wondered how Jael and Mercy were getting along. He hoped they could be friends, and Jael could have the one thing she'd always wanted. The nice thing about knowing everything in her mind was how simple it made finding ways to make her happy by just picking around her memories. He noticed that she would fixate on certain things. For example, she always paid more attention during television shows that featured friends laughing together. Books about beach trips were her favorite. The irony of her love for alien romance books was not lost on Oz.

Oz put his arm behind his head and leaned his head back. He wondered how he had gotten so far in such a short time. Just over an Earth year ago, he was a naked jungle man in a treehouse. He often wondered how he had managed to convince Jael to be with him, especially after everything he had done. Her bubbly, happy spirit was what Oz fell in love with and he in no way felt deserving.

Now that he knew what a mountain goat was, he decided the name, Jael, did fit the best. At heart, she was definitely a wild mountain goat. He had never known anyone like her, and she owned his heart. She was his home.

He wondered if she knew she was mispronouncing her name.

Oz began pondering the rocket idea he had shared with Jacob right before they left. If they could eliminate the enemy satellites, they would remain unseen when they headed north to take over the UTC base. They still needed a real plan, and he hoped that was it. The real question was, would there be enough time. After some deep thoughts about rockets and crossing the mountains, Oz finally heard the distinct sound of a cart rolling through the woods. The leaves under the wheels crunched, and the wooden wheels creaked as they slowly rolled down the path.

When they finally arrived at the tree where Oz was sitting, August was scowling, and Callum looked like he was having a fine time. He began ignoring Oz the moment they made eye contact. The sheer magnitude of feelings that could be perfectly conveyed in utter silence was amazing to Oz, and he wondered if Callum would scowl at him the entire trip.

Callum jumped into the back of the cart to take the first ride and rest. Oz peered back at him and narrowed his yellow eyes. Callum was in the long wooden cart with his arms crossed, leaning against the side that faced away from the front of the cart. He made it clear he was going to be resting for a while, so Oz and August didn't argue.

They each grabbed one of the handles jutting out from the arms of the long cart, and the four, large, eight-spoked wooden wheels started rolling. The cart was new and hadn't been broken in yet, so the pull was a little rough, but they made do. The wheels groaned and whined as they began turning. Close enough to connect, Oz reached out for August's hand and connected with him just like they had thousands of times before when growing up.

"So, what did you do to make him so mad at you? I know you did something," August asked without daring to look back at their irritated friend.

"He has always been this way," Oz said into the connection while giving August a side-eye.

"Right. He's only this way with you. I don't know what you did, but it was definitely something. I'm not sure I *want* to know the details."

Then August asked, "How are we going to make it to the north and raid the base when we are being watched constantly by satellites?"

"The satellites, thankfully, only track visual, and somehow, auditory information. So, we are going to have to do something about that. We will need to find a way to get to the continent on the planet's dark side, and we will need to travel over the mountain range after crossing the sea," Oz replied coolly.

"Are you out of your fucking mind? They will see us," August said into the connection, interrupting Oz, all while staring at him with disbelief.

"No, they won't see us. Because we are going to shoot down their satellites with guided missiles," Oz said.

August snapped his head to the side to look Oz in the eye and, after a beat, said, "You're not kidding, are you?"

"No. Honestly, part of why grumpy pants is coming with us is so that Jacob won't be distracted. He has a lot to do in a short time. Jacob thought you were distracting Mercy, so that's why you were picked.

"To answer your question, after Carter began teaching Jacob about the tech from the UTC campsite, I did some thinking about our upcoming journey. Right before we left, I decided they should find a way to get some rockets into the air to take out those satellites. If not, we will have to find a way to hack into them, which will take much longer because there is a different security code for each satellite. It could take years to crack their systems."

With an air of smugness, August said, "Now *I know* you did something to Callum. That all makes sense, especially the part about me distracting Mercy, because I'm hard to resist, of course. Wait, what the hell is the UTC?"

"The United Trusts and Colonies. They are part of the enemy, I finally began sorting through the doctor's other memories, and I've been learning a lot. It's hard to get through her memories because of what she does to our people, but thankfully most of her personal memories aren't so brutal."

Remembering the disturbed looks he received from Jacob and August in their first meeting about their enemy,

Oz continued, "She personally maimed every one of the villagers who were taken from our village and hundreds more over the years before that. It may be in the thousands. She worked on Sclavus Six before she gained enough clearance to come to our planet."

Shaking off the gut-wrenching thoughts of Mazarin being subjected to whatever maiming might mean, August asked, "The rest of the plan is to build a boat to get across the sea, the sea with all the giant sea creatures? Are you OK? Did you take some mushroom tea when you decided that? Or maybe bonk your fucking head?" August asked while pointedly looking at Oz with his orange eyes blazing.

Chuckling, Oz said, "No, I didn't drink any mushroom tea, and no, I did not hit my head, *August*. Carter's team is planning to develop a sonar system so we can see underwater. And we will have a motor. They won't be able to catch us."

With his gut in a knot, August said, "I honestly think you lost your mind in the jade woods."

"I may have, but your mother and everyone else made sure I was President of our little *cockroach rebellion*, so now you have to deal with it. We haven't even drafted our laws, so all of you did this backward and accidentally gave me absolute power. You're damn lucky I'm not a tyrant."

"I'm sure we could just get Amelia to poison you," August replied while smiling at Oz.

Rolling his eyes, Oz sighed and flatly said, "Jael would kill all of you."

August furrowed his brow, then raised them and said, "Hm, good point."

"Once we get through the mountains, I think we will

make our way northwest and stake out the base to learn the guards' rounds. Hopefully, we can get inside and shut off the main power before we are spotted. The holding cells and common areas for our captured people are under the UTC base. We will need to make our way to the bottom through the vent system in order to release our people because the base will lock down and go on backup power when we cut the main power. We won't have the captives helping us take the base. We will face fierce resistance when we reach the generators at the bottom level. Both the primary and backup power sources are heavily guarded."

His face set with confusion, August replied, "You are aware that the mountains are snow-covered and freezing, right?"

"That's all you have to ask about the preliminary plan? And don't remind me. We will make sure that we have plenty of winter gear for the journey. The dark side is frozen, but it's not entirely dark. There is a glowing, brown dwarf star that suspends our planet in place between itself and the black hole. It casts a dim red glow on the ground, but it's not close enough to provide any heat."

"A brown dwarf? I've been wondering about our solar neighbors since you shared Jael's knowledge with me. Does she know yet?"

"No. While I was sitting by the oak tree waiting on you and Callum, I came across the doctor's memories of how she got off the planet. The pull of the black hole gives their engines a hard time, so instead of wasting fuel, they slingshot off the brown dwarf into a wormhole they created."

"I was with Jacob and Jael yesterday after my shift, and we discussed the doctor's knowledge of the rest of the galaxy, so I'll need to brief you on what I've learned. It might as well be now. The doctor was only a doctor for humans and our species, but apparently, there are many different types of intelligent beings that have evolved on many different worlds. The humans seem to have one of the oldest civilizations and have always been in charge of the UTC."

The humans claim they are superior because they evolved independently on more than one hundred worlds. Twenty worlds have beings who are anywhere close to modern-type humans, but only a few are civilized. Of those twenty, only four are spacefaring, or close to spacefaring. One is Jael's world, and another is in a system fifty light years away from here. The UTC has been observing it for over two hundred thousand years.

"Their original home world and the first human-origin planet were abandoned and lost over a million Earth years ago when they colonized a second young world with no creatures of higher intelligence, Novum Donum. They lived there for around three hundred years before discovering a planet in a system just under fifteen light years away which had also independently developed humans called Genil."

The Genil were advanced enough to build a rocket to send to the ancient humans' newly colonized world on Novum Donum, and they formally introduced themselves. That's when the UTC was formed, and the humans began searching the galaxy for other worlds with intelligent life, especially humanoid life. That was several hundred thousand years ago, at least.

"So far, they have found more than a thousand planets with non-human, intelligent life at various stages of evolution. These beings did not evolve from primates. Most intelligent life comes from marsupials, dinosaurs, or avians. No two intelligent beings have evolved from the same rudimentary creature as humans did. *Supposedly.*"

"Once we gain our independence, I want to visit every world I can," August replied quietly.

Oz nodded his head and said, "Me too, August. Me too."

28

When the lights in the command area slowly dimmed, Jael fell from her zoned-out, slumped spot on a chair near Mercy and the group setting up the food and drinks.

"Oh, shit! Jael!" Mercy yelled.

Jael laughed while sprawled out on the floor. She pulled Mercy down with her, and they both laughed while Mercy unsuccessfully tried to get back up.

"Mercy, how much mushroom tea did you give Jael?" Amelia asked as she leaned over the giggling pair, giving Mercy a scrutinizing look.

Leaning up with her nose scrunched, Mercy replied, "Just a regular cup. I only put a few in the bottom."

With her dark blue fishtail braids falling around her face, Amelia sighed then said, "I don't know how strong psilocybin mushrooms are on Earth. Ours contain so much of the psychoactive ingredient that the interior of the dried mushroom is entirely filled with the compound's signature clear crystal."

"And that means?" Mercy asked, leaning her head up and squinting her eyes in an attempt to focus.

"They're strong as fuck!" Amelia proclaimed, throwing her hands up, pulling a bubbling laugh out of Mercy.

"Doc, why don't you get a cup of mushroom tea and join us? They will be starting up the music soon! Some of the people on Carter's team have been working on it during their off time! It's so, so good. Promise." A smile so wide that she couldn't see graced Mercy's face.

With her hands on her hips, Amelia sighed at Mercy's grinning face and said, "Oh, to hell with it. Where are the rest of the damn mushrooms?"

"On the counter in Jael's kitchen!" Mercy was so excited she jumped up from the floor and threw her arms around Amelia.

"They are in a little silk pouch. The little spout on her sink to the right has boiling water."

Amelia couldn't believe that she was heading off to drink mushroom tea. She stalked off toward the apartment. Mercy kept her golden eyes on Amelia's mess of dark-blue fishtail braids as she walked away and thought that Amelia was quite possibly the most beautiful woman she had ever seen.

Amelia was tall, taller than Mercy, and she was a deep cerulean blue with a lean muscular build. The angles of her face were sharp, and her piercing blue eyes were tipped up like large, glittering almonds. Mercy was not nervous around anyone, but something about Amelia's presence made her breath catch and her heart race.

Sliding her eyes down to the giggling form below her, Mercy sighed as she leaned over and pealed a limp Jael off the floor. Once she was standing, albeit slumped over, Mercy handed her a cup of water. Jael downed it, drinking only from the side of her mouth, then handed back the cup.

Mercy took the cup from her and said, holding back a grin, "Try to keep it together long enough for the music to start. Then we can dance, and you won't have to lay on the floor and laugh by yourself."

"I was by myself? No, I wasn't! There were little sparkly fairies down there with me! They told me you are my new best friend, but I already knew that. They also said August would see a bright star soon. I don't know what that means, but they were super serious. I wonder if they know I'm not on Earth anymore. I should tell them. Oh, and they said I need to eat more apricots, so I don't get anemic."

"Apricots, huh? They said apricots specifically?" Amelia asked while chuckling from behind Mercy, startling her and sending her heart racing again.

Putting her hand on Mercy's shoulder, Amelia leaned in and said, "Apricots on our world are exceptionally high in iron. I'll have the foragers gather some extra Apricots for Jael next time they go out."

Confusion struck Mercy as she tried to process the words and information being exchanged, the mushroom tea was settling in for the ride, and her comprehension was twisting.

Grinning, Jael kept her eyes focused somewhere in the distance and seemed to be entranced. Jael's short life went flying through her mind, filled with mundaneness and longing. Then like a bomb went off, there was Oz, pulling her into the safety of their beautiful treehouse. With the soft hints of a drumbeat gathering in the distance, Jael began to sway. As soft and deep melodies encircled her very soul, she began dancing, raising her arms and swaying to the colors dancing around her. Jael felt like she was back on the river of light that had transported her to this planet.

The strong beat of the music filled the Command room, and Mercy reached over and took Jael's hands. The walls seemed to sway and jump as they moved, dancing along with them. Guiding her to the middle of the room, Mercy grabbed Jael's hips, and they swayed together as the rest of the people gathered for the party.

Swaying and dipping, swinging and rolling, electronic music swallowed up the darkened room as Amelia and Luna joined Mercy and Jael on the dance floor. Luna leaned over and took Carter's hand, and the two swung around and away from the group to dance alone. Shifting away, Jael followed the beat of her own music as Mercy and Amelia fell into a rhythm of twists and steps. As more people joined in, the temperature rose, and sweat began glistening in the dimmed lights.

Seeming to move as one with Mercy, Amelia allowed herself to submerge her senses in the delightful tones and beats that were enticing her mind and body. Rocking her hips, Amelia hadn't ever known such sparkling joy. The effervescence in her heart combined with the decadence of this colorful noise swimming in her ears was sending her mind into a state of pure ecstasy.

Why had she waited so long for this?

Mercy slid her eyes around the room at all the laughing, smiling people. Her people, these were *her* people. Golden-tinged tears gathered in Mercy's eyes as she took in the beauty of what she witnessed.

The precious gift from Jael was a vessel of hope provided by chance. A revolution, the spread of language, the birth of art, music -- all were products of Mercy's beloved people.

There was an emergence of creativity born from eternal reticence. Unbounded and free, their expansive minds had broken free from iron chains.

Like the first bite of a forbidden apple, this knowledge unlocked their potential for experience.

These were all things that they had longed for so deeply. Just months ago, they could not have fathomed such wonders even existed. This was the beginning, and Mercy was part of it. She felt connected to her world and her people, and she knew they were all meant for more than just winning their independence and freedom.

More than just taking back their planet.

The fight gathering their wills was building like a perfect storm. It was congregating and churning above peaceful seas before slamming down and raging with monstrous force. Their power was a chamber of searing hot water, exploding into thunderheads and striking down with a cement fist.

More was coming for them, for all of them.

More than just this place, this world.

She felt it deep inside, the calling.

It dragged its surly claws across her speeding heart, the need crying to escape.

Amelia slid her hands over Mercy's shoulders and whispered into her ear, "Mer, look at Jael."

Pulling herself from the reeling recesses of her own mind, Mercy reluctantly slid her blurred eyes to where Amelia was pointing. When her eyes focused, she could see Jael's small form facing the wall. With her hands up and feeling all over the natural cave's wall, Jael looked as though she was thoroughly entertained. A giggling, Mercy and Amelia slowly and quietly walked over to Jael and tried to listen to what she was saying without disturbing her.

With her hands pressed to the cold stones, Jael said clearly and concisely, "The blind can see inside. The silent can speak inside. The answer is so clear. Energy cannot be created or destroyed. It can only be changed, transformed! The scales were out of balance. They deserved more. They received it in the end. Chaos becomes order. Order becomes chaos. The end is truly the beginning. The start of it *all*."

As if she were coming out of her trance-like state, Jael sighed and then, in a whispered tone, said, "They really are the great wizard, and this is not Texas anymore, Rew. I should have named myself Dorothy. Damn it. That really *would* have been perfect."

Turning around, Jael found Mercy and Amelia staring at her, a set of gold and a set of light blue eyes wide and intent on figuring out her meaning. They approached her, and Mercy smiled in the sweet way she always did.

"What did the spirits tell you?" Amelia softly asked.

Mercy whipped her head around to look at Amelia, who simply looked at Mercy then back to Jael, ignoring Mercy's utter shock at her question.

Furrowing her brow, Jael answered, "They said a lot, actually. I saw more than I heard, though. The stone was so bright and loud. They must have been inside these stone walls somehow. They showed me you deserved the gift I brought. They showed me that you deserved the extra smarts, too, I think."

Halting, Jael tilted her head and took a deep breath, and closed her eyes before softly saying, "Your people deserve so much. The spirit said it believes that we will all be given a gift."

Amelia kept her eyes on Jael, and when she stopped speaking, Amelia finally turned to Mercy and whispered,

"She probably won't remember any of this, but we will. Don't forget what she said. Sometimes people receive visions while in a fevered state. I think Jael might have genuinely connected with our creator.

"There was a dying child. His infection was moments from claiming him, and I connected with him to comfort him in any way I could. He transferred the most beautiful visions of light and joy. Then he transferred what I now know as a night sky, but the stars in the sky from his visions don't match any patterns from Jael's knowledge. They were moving so fast that they seemed to streak by. The boy was surrounded by a hot light."

Mercy gaped at Amelia as Jael blurted out, "Stars move, but so do we all," then walked off toward the table with food and drinks.

Following Jael, Mercy asked Amelia, "How long ago was that?"

Amelia answered, saying, "In Earth years? It was over five years ago. The young boy died shortly after, but I showed his mother the visions he passed on to me, and she smiled for the first time since the child had become sick. I thought the visions were for her from her son, but what if they weren't? What if they were a message for now, and I just didn't understand at the time?"

29

August hated resting in the hard, wooden cart. After just a few moments, he decided he was done with it and made Callum and Oz stop for a rest.

He had no idea how those two rested in the shaking wagon, and he was not having it. He felt like his brain was going scramble into mush and slide out of his ears. After a good head shake and a lingering stretch, he grabbed his pack and slung it over his shoulder as he walked to the small clearing in front of the cart.

While August prepared his spot on the ground, Oz and Callum sat propped up against an oak tree, next to one another but far enough apart to allow Oz to raise his elbows without them coming near Callum.

Seemingly out of nowhere, Callum rose to his feet and walked off into the woods, leaning his head back to stretch when he was far enough away that he thought they couldn't see him.

Rolling his eyes at Callum, Oz took the opportunity to rest, and he began thinking about the UTC base and how they could find a way in. The doctor was a dense person who had no interests other than hurting his kind while she processed them in her office at the base. He knew the doctor *chose* to hurt his kind instead of knocking them out. She deserved the end she got.

She had tortured hundreds over the years, maybe up to a thousand, and believed his kind had a severely inferior intellect. All humans believed his kind had the mental capabilities of dogs and only showed signs of intelligence after training. All the worlds belonging to the UTC believed that they were helping lesser creatures and saving them from back-breaking, fruitless lives on their home planet, Sclavus Six. Little did the people of the UTC-controlled planets know, but Oz's people originated here on Sclavus Three, not Sclavus Six.

Or so it seemed. He hadn't dug any further into those memories yet. He wasn't ready for what he might find.

The doctor had little knowledge of the layout of the building except for the top level. The top level had precisely nothing of importance, and Oz sighed in irritation at another dead end. He needed to find out where they generated their main power and where they kept the data. The only thing the doctor knew was that the generators were on the bottom level, and that was only from one memory in which she overheard someone in the mess hall talking about it.

Oz hated having to comb through all her thoughts to pick out pieces of information they needed. Some of the extracurricular activities she participated in were vile and disturbing.

Great columned arenas were filled with cheering humans while the spectacle ensued. The shows all resulted in a mass slaughter of enslaved people and animals. Oz was disgusted with their torturous games and hoped that those they selected were, at the least, criminals. He shuddered at the thought of his people dying by such cruel butchering, unable to have a chance at survival.

All for the cheers of the rich who gathered to watch.

Suddenly, Callum comes running toward Oz with his eyes wide. The moment their eyes met, he pointed behind him then dove toward them and behind the cart. Callum was not the type to be violent and never had been, so Oz knew there was a threat. Following suit, August and Oz crouched behind the tipped-up, large wood cart. Callum grabbed Oz's hand, connected, then said into his mind, "The humans. They didn't see me. They're invisible."

Callum sent Oz the fresh memory.

Fear laced through Callum. The thought of being taken away from Jacob brought bile up his throat.

Before he dropped Callum's hand Oz said, "Stay here and wait. If they catch us, run back to the base."

Oz grabbed August's hand and connected, saying, "Humans with guns, follow me."

Like a flash of lightning, Oz flew up a tree, and August wasn't far behind. The two gracefully leaped from tree to tree without rustling a single leaf. They smelled the humid air of the woods for the direction of the humans, and both simultaneously slid their eyes north. Oz shot his yellow eyes over at August and tipped his head in a nod. August followed close behind as Oz leaped from branch to branch. Finally, Oz paused and whipped around to signal the humans were below.

They couldn't see the humans, but they could smell them.

August watched the ground and saw six separate steps

slightly indented in the soft ground. He waved a hand at Oz and then pointed to the spot where the humans were walking, cloaked with some kind of tech. Their forms were entirely invisible. August held up three fingers, and Oz nodded.

At the same time, Oz and August silently slipped off the branch and leaped from the tree, slamming into the three unsuspecting humans. All five of them crashed to the ground in a heap. Dirt flung around and onto their cloaks, making the humans partially visible. Oz and August leaped to their feet and carefully watched the ground, making out the humans' forms as they moved.

August jumped in first, grabbing one by the arm and slamming him to the ground while a dart whizzed by his head. A pained yelp came from him. August ripped at the cloth hiding the human, revealing a horrified man trying to raise his arms, a dart gun in hand. The gun was a fraction of a second from being pointed in August's direction. August tilted his head to the side, looking at the man's fearful expression, and then slammed his fist into the human's pale face. Red blood spurted from the man's flattened nose, and he cried out in agony, dropping the gun while grasping his face.

While August was ripping the cover from the man he fought, Oz slammed his fist into the gut of the human on the ground resulting in a loud feminine grunt and then the sound of a vomiting heave. The partially visible form under the cloak slumped and groaned as the ground gathered where she pulled her legs into her. Oz wasn't taking any chances, so he grasped what he believed to be her neck and squeezed until he felt her head drop.

August already had the third human in his clutches and

was ripping off the cloth, which still had the ground projected onto it. He found a shaking man underneath, and August swiftly slammed his fist into the man's temple, knocking him out cold.

The fearful whimpers from the man with his nose bashed in were the only sounds remaining in the woods. With all three of the humans unconscious or incapacitated, Oz and August stripped them of all their gear and tied all of them to a tree with their own rope. They all slumped against the ropes in their undergarments.

They were headed toward the village. Oz began searching through their gear, and he quickly found exactly what he was looking for. More guns with darts that all contained small vials of the solution that knocked Oz's kind unconscious.

He scoffed at the liquid sloshing in the chambers behind the sharp darts and dumped them on the ground. Oz then crushed them under the sole of his boot with a crunch. He found some GPS devices and turned them off before he took all the food from their bags and put it in a pile. August joined him in sorting the gear, but they mainly found clothes and camping supplies.

After they piled up everything they didn't want, Oz handed August his flint to ignite it. August spilled the humans' rubbing alcohol over the gear, then showered it with sparks. The resulting flames roared to life.

Joining the group after a whistle from Oz, Callum collected all the food and sorted it into a spare bag they had brought with them. He then returned to watch the fire as the humans began to groan and rouse. The first human awoke, his crushed nose still oozing as his eyes grew wide with realization. The man looked down and then shifted his gaze over to Callum. Already glaring with a look promising death, Callum sneered and showed his fangs when the man made eye contact. Fear drained all color from the human's already pale face, and he quickly began trying to wiggle free from his rope bindings to no avail.

The man let out a fearful squeak as Oz walked silently around the tree, wearing modern tactical clothing and gear. The human man began visibly shaking when Oz approached, and an observant Callum was smirking and reveling in the human's fear. August followed Oz around the tree, making himself known as well.

Urine spilled down the man's shaking legs as he took in the knife strapped to Oz. Sparing no time, Oz reached around the man's head with his right hand and held his head to the tree with his left.

Callum and August watched as Oz connected with the man, eliciting a blood-curdling scream from him as Oz's specialized nerve dove into the man's spinal column to form the bridge between their minds. Tears poured from the man's eyes as Oz forced his way in, quickly blocking out the human's ability to move or make a sound. The other two humans began to wake when they heard the scream, and they both looked around wildly at the scene.

Silence fell, and Oz began his search.

Oz peered around in the man's mind, finding out that the team of humans had the task of stealing one of the people from the village. They had been sent to make up for the three that got away. This was their last one. The UTC thought the three who escaped had also killed the four humans.

Reviewing the man's memories, Oz figured out how they managed to transport people such a far distance unnoticed. They were using a small device that worked with the same camouflaging fabric the humans were wearing. The device hovers, and the six points of a fabric sack are fed into the bottom. The device lifts the occupant, creating a floating teardrop, then it travels along with the humans as they head back to their slave processing center in the north.

The human man had begun to sweat profusely as he stared, his gaze frozen onto Oz's eyes with absolute terror. He could feel the intrusion as Oz began searching. The woman next to Oz's captive, began to weep, and a sob left her lips.

Staring blankly, Oz continued to riffle through the man's mind.

Finally, he happened upon information he was looking for.

The little hidden rebellion was still a secret.

The human man knew nothing of the cave system or the progress. He had no idea why Oz was dressed like a modern human, a fact that caused the man deep distress. Oz could sense the man's blood pressure rising through his palm that was around the man's neck. The human's thoughts came cascading through, and Oz was having trouble ignoring them to get the information he needed.

Having had enough of the man's racing thoughts through the connection, Oz commanded, "*Tacēte!*" Silence!

With that, the man froze in terror, confused as to how Oz could possibly know the language. The man's breath was becoming short as Oz plunged back into his mind. Something told Oz this man was on the verge of a heart attack, and he needed to move more quickly, or he would lose his opportunity. The veins on the human's face were bulging, threatening to bust, and his nose began to flow with crimson blood once more. Oz let up on his neural hold over the man's body. He didn't want the human to die while he was trying to get information.

The human man, late middle-aged, was a squad leader and knew information about some of the more interesting parts of the UTC base, including the slave processing areas. Oz only took in what he wanted and blocked the rest. He didn't want everything, as he had taken from the doctor. That choice had been a mistake made in the heat of anger that had given him a mind full of the screams and torture of his own people.

Can the satellites hear them speak all the way from space, or did the humans plant hidden microphones that pick up the sound?

Do they track his people by heat or just sight?

Right when Oz thought this man didn't know anything, he found what he was looking for. This man, Zeno, had snuck into the command center of the UTC base and watched the villages on the monitoring screens. There were lists of sounds that were picked up from the village, and they were displayed behind the screens on a chart with red numerals listed next to them. There were corresponding red numerals with dots showing points on the screen where the sounds originated from.

They were listening with microphones on the ground.

From what Oz could see, there were no heat maps or anything other than raw visuals with sounds feeding in. He noted that they only had microphones around the homes. It looked as though the range was limited to the village perimeter. He didn't know from what distance the microphones could pick up sound, so he decided they should avoid speaking unless they were at least a mile from the village.

This meant they could speak during their current journey for sand. Good to know, Oz thought, considering how tempting it was.

With a shaking breath, Zeno, whispered, "*Blatta, agama liquid si amovēbis clabum habēs in cerve mē. Narrābō tē aliquid optatum, place exire. Non ferre diutius. Cor meum est infirmus et non capit tensionem.*" Roach, I will do anything if you will remove the spike you have in my neck. I will tell you anything you wish, just please, get it out. I cannot bear it any longer. My heart is weak and cannot take this stress.

Tears began rolling down the man's face and Oz nodded in agreement.

Jael had explained that when he picked through her brain, she was mostly unaware of what he was doing, so this man didn't know what was happening. When Oz pulled his hand from Zeno's neck, the brown-haired human let out a pained whimper of relief.

The other human male softly whimpered as his mind cleared and he became fully aware of what was happening.

With his eyes narrowed, Oz asked aloud, "*Sane, Zero habeo quaestionēs.*" Alright, Zeno I have some questions.

"*Satellens supra tollent nobis vocēs aut habes microphone sererit ubique paga? Memor Zeno, scīrer responsum.*" Do the satellites above pick up our voices, or do you have microphones planted all over our villages? Be mindful, Zeno, I might already know the answer.

Oz glared at him. "*Verum merēbit finem celerem tibi. Mendacium merēbit dolorem. Electus tuum omnino.*" The truth will earn you a swift end. A lie will earn you agony. Your choice entirely.

With an audible gulp and a shaking voice, Zeno answered, "*Non rogāns quomodo scīs nomen mihi, sed non mentīrī tibi. Iuro omnis benedictiōnēs ab Iupiter, satellēs modo vidit. Microphona fundantur in arboribus circum pagum. Tollent sonum usque ad decies, nequaquam."* I am not going to ask how you know my name, but I will not lie to you. I swear on all my blessings from Jupiter, the satellites only see. The microphones are found in the trees around the village. They pick up sound up to ten paces, no more.

In his head, Oz easily converted the paces into meters and nearly scoffed at the short range of the microphones. They barely reached a few yards into the woods. A whimper sounded from the other man as the woman continued to weep. Oz shot them a sharp look, and they both went silent and shook with fear.

"Bene. Nunc, narra mē plus satellibus." Good. Now tell me more about these satellites, Oz demanded as he looked back at Zeno.

Zeno gulped in a breath of air and then swallowed audibly before clearing his throat. Blood from his shattered nose still flowed and slid down his neck to his bare chest. He spat to Oz's left, trying to rid his mouth of blood before continuing.

"Non scīo mutum. Ego princeps manipulus est comphreonis locī, unitas quinque. Scīsne linguam nobis et cur vestīris similiter? Tu opinari esse insecta stupida. Quid perfututum?" I don't know much. I am just the squad leader for ground capture, unit five. How do you know our language and why are you dressed like that? You're supposed to be stupid insects. What the fuck is going on? Zeno demanded, his pale skin further draining in color.

Snapping his head back and laughing, Oz leaned in close to the man and showed Zeno his sharp fangs as he whispered, *"Zeno, capesne me pro stultum perfutum?"* Zeno, do you take me for a fucking fool?

Trembling violently and trying to pull his face away from Oz's, Zeno responded with a shaking voice, *"No, non omnino. Quo fit ut rogābam. Videri tam intellegentem quam aliquis hominem. Id est exadverso omniorum docuisse. Amplius decem milia anni, UTC academiae docuit tironēs ud vobis sunt cimices stupidās quis genus mutabant esse callīdus satis perficere pensa prima. Docēbant creātus es de parte cimiorum et planetārum."* No, no, not at all. That's why I asked. You seem as intelligent as any human. This is the opposite of everything we have ever been taught. For more than ten thousand years, the UTC Academies have taught the recruits that you are stupid bugs who were genetically altered to be smart enough to perform basic tasks. They taught us you were created from parts of bugs and plants.

From the doctor's memory, Oz had learned that she inadvertently discovered a secret DNA file in the data archives containing information about his people's unique genetics. Hence, he refrained from asking Zeno more about it. He knew the man wouldn't know anything; the physician who had found it didn't even know what it meant.

He knew there was a dirty secret about his people's genetics hidden at the UTC's base, one he would need to find when they raided the headquarters to the north. That minute bit of information would be helpful later, and the level of secrecy surrounding the file was all he needed to deduce this fact.

The UTC had no idea how intelligent Oz's people were. Despite being highly skilled, all his people chose to be wholly mute and maintain their silence. The fact that they remained silent even though they were enslaved on speaking worlds, changed his heart about their mission. He knew he could not turn away from helping his people after finding this out.

No matter how badly he wanted to run and hide with Jael.

"*Immo Zeno, quid cogitās vere hic factum est?*" Well, Zeno, what do *you* think is truly happening here? Oz asked.

"*Cogito confundī essēmus.*" I think we might have fucked up, Zeno admitted.

"*Quis et quid habes perfutum?*" Who, and what, have you fucked up? Oz asked.

"*Cogito nōs hominēs exercēris UTC confundī essent nobis et casū creabāmus monstra, unī habēmus minoris aestimābāmus aperte.*" I think we, the people running the UTC, have fucked ourselves and accidentally created monsters, ones we have clearly underestimated, Zeno stated, like the point he made wasn't an absolutely scathing insult.

With that, Oz wrapped his hand around Zeno's throat and broke his neck before he had the chance to utter another word. Oz might have gone back on his word for a swift death if Zeno had continued. The other two humans whimpered and cried when they saw their comrade being killed so easily by Oz.

After this was all over, Oz's people would face thousands of years of bigotry. Internally cringing at the thought, Oz shoved it away for another day and looked over at August, who was watching intently with his large bulging arms crossed.

"We don't have to stay silent. They only planted microphones around the villages. They hardly reach into the woods," Oz stated, still facing the tree and the slumped-over, dead human man.

Callum let out a, "Whoop! Thank fuck," and began walking around the humans' burning gear toward August.

Out of the group, Callum hated the silence the most. It ate at him far worse now that they knew how to speak.

Now that he knew what he was missing.

August rolled his eyes and said, "So, what do we do with the other two?"

"You already know the answer to that. They've helped steal hundreds of our people over their long careers. If that's not enough for you to be OK with me ending them, then remember they will tell their friends we can speak now," Oz explained, head angled back at August, eyes trained on his friend.

"Well, get it over with so we can go," August said with a solemn face and walked toward their cart, not wanting to witness his friend killing people.

Callum gave Zeno's dead body a kick with his foot and hissed before following behind August. Shrugging, Oz reached over to the frightened woman and snapped her neck. The remaining man lost consciousness at the sight of the woman's death. Oz reached over and pushed his head to the side, breaking his neck as well. He pulled his knife from his belt and made a single slice at the ropes before continuing after Callum. The three dead humans slumped into a heap on the ground.

The scavenger bugs would pick the humans clean in a matter of hours. Nothing would be left; not even their bones would remain.

30

"We have a giant bed. We should all stay at my apartment," Jael announced to the group.

Mercy answered first, "Sure. Amelia, Luna, are you coming?"

Amelia shrugged and said, "I don't see why not."

Luna nodded and said, "I am exhausted. I could use some rest. I've been working for days."

"Yes, sleepover!" Jael yelled as she took off toward her apartment.

Beaming, Mercy followed behind her matching her pace. Amelia and Luna trailed after them more slowly.

Once they were all seated on the floor in various places around the kitchen, Mercy pulled the alcohol and juice that Jael had mixed up from the cooler drawer. She drank some of the sweet drink, then passed the cup to Amelia, who took a few gulps before handing it to Luna.

Jael shook her head "no," then fought to open her eyes as she said, "Uh, well, I think my eyeballs have had enough action for one day. I thought I could hang out, but I think I need to go to sleep before I fall over and start snoring."

After a dramatic yawn, she peeled her eyelids up and found Mercy with a wide grin. The rest of the group had not seen a yawn yet and were mesmerized by it.

Laughing, Mercy said, "Jael, it's OK. Go to sleep. We know you need it. We will all be here when you wake up."

Smiling, Jael headed for her bedroom and mumbled, "My fairy godparents from the floor were right."

They all waited until Jael shut the bedroom door to hold their faces in quiet laughter. Jael's first mushroom experience had been the group's focus for the night, and it had been thoroughly entertaining.

Mercy would make sure to remember not to give Jael quite as much next time.

Stretching and then looking over at Amelia, Mercy said, "After we finish the alcohol, I am going to lie down too. Are you two coming?"

Amelia answered first, saying, "Of course. It's much better than the floor."

Laughing, Luna said, "Yeah me too. I don't mind squeezing in."

"Her bed is gigantic and can easily fit all of us. It's settled, then. Let's go get some rest," Mercy said.

At that, Luna downed the remainder of the juice cocktail, set it in the sink, and followed Mercy and Amelia to the bed. They all crawled into the enormous bed with a passed-out Jael.

As Mercy lay there, she thought about the things Jael had said throughout the course of the party and everything she had said to Amelia.

What did she mean by it all?

The things Jael said resonated within Mercy, and she wondered if there was some profound truth to her words.

Something moving below the surface.

Several long hours later, Jael began squirming, and one by one, they all got up from their pile of limbs to find a meal. They headed down to the mess hall and found a table while Luna grabbed a few bowls of cut oranges, roasted nuts, and a plate of salted, sliced avocados with fresh flatbread. Amelia sat next to Mercy. Jael sat on the other side of Mercy, leaving one chair open for Luna.

When Luna returned to the group with a feast, they silently devoured the food as if they had been starved.

After guzzling water, Amelia said, "Make sure you eat plenty of avocados, Jael. You went too long with an exceptionally narrow diet. It would be a good idea if you allowed me to run some tests to make sure you're not deficient in anything. It also might be a good idea to see if the planet has had any other effects on you. It's doubtful Earth has the exact same oxygen content as we have."

Confused, Jael asked, "Run some tests? You already have testing equipment? How in the sunless hells did you develop a lab that sophisticated so quickly?"

"I had plenty of help from Carter and Luna. After Jacob developed the right way to create tempered glass, it was just a matter of time. Luna was the one who helped develop the software, and she has been trading her time between Carter's team and mine. I've been able to develop several antibiotics for our kind. We have some other modern medications as well, including an anti-inflammatory which works for both of our kinds. We just identified penicillin, which I know is a human antibiotic. Once we can culture more, we will have plenty. It's just nice to know we have it available for you if we need it," Amelia explained, a hint of a smile on her blue lips.

"That's incredible. I'll be happy to come in and have some tests done," Jael softly said in awe.

"Great, we can go after we are finished eating. Drink at least four cups of water, so your blood draw goes smoothly."

Nodding her head, Jael agreed and downed her water. Modern medicine -- Jael hadn't had such a wonderful thing available to her since she was on Earth. An anti-inflammatory would be a blessing for her next period. She sighed with relief at the thought. It had been well over a year of painful periods, and Oz still acted like she was on her deathbed each time. She had felt like she was dying inside, so she guessed his reaction wasn't too far from being warranted.

They finished their meals without another word, then everyone followed Amelia to her clinic which was in front of the north wing. The north wing was comprised of nearly empty general housing, except for the apartments of Carter, Zoe, and Amelia. Sometimes Luna stayed in the general housing, but Jael assumed she was just crashing when she didn't want to go all the way home after work.

They all filed into a sterile, well-lit lab with two exam tables in an otherwise empty room. Jael took a seat on the table to the right as Amelia prepared her instruments.

"I have never had a physical in my life. I hope you don't find anything bad," Jael said flatly, looking down at her arm where Amelia would be taking her blood.

"Oh, I doubt I will find anything too bad. I want to test your lung function because I'm almost positive our air has more oxygen than Earth. Other than that, I am just looking for deficiencies. I think I will test your blood sugar as well. I *should* do more than just basic testing, but I'll save the rest for another time. I guess you could say this is a basic physical," Amelia said without turning around.

Amelia set up her implements on a tray on the exam table. Jael held still while she drew a few vials of blood. Amelia then asked her to pee in a small cup, so Jael used the lab's bathroom.

Once she was finished with her blood draw and urine sample, Jael wearily looked around and said, "I am still exhausted from last night. I think I am going to go back to my apartment and go back to sleep."

Mercy smiled and said, "OK. Oz said I could have Mondays off for a few weeks while they're gone. Let's plan to meet at Jael's apartment Sunday after shift."

Amelia nodded and Luna said, "I'll be there! Carter said I've earned some days off too."

"I'm not taking off work, but I'm coming anyway. I can rest later." Amelia said.

Jael smiled and then headed out of the lab in a daze, slowly walking straight to her apartment.

"Amelia, I don't regret that I talked you into the tea. I hate that I need to go get ready for my shift. I had so much fun dancing last night. Luna, I'm glad you hung out with us. I always liked you when we were kids," Mercy said as she moved to leave the clinic, but she paused when Amelia looked over at her.

Luna smiled at Mercy and said, "Me too!" before walking out the door with a wave.

After propping up the tubes in her frosty, geothermal water-cooled refrigerator, Amelia walked to Mercy and hugged her, then said, "Dancing was just what I needed, we need to plan another party soon. I had a great time."

"I'll see you later," Mercy said as she headed to her apartment to shower and change clothes.

She had another hour before she had to be on shift, so she walked through the command center and cleaned up the chairs before heading into her apartment. The room had been cleared of trash and party remnants, but the chairs were still strewn about, and a table was on its side.

Mercy entered her dark apartment and looked up at the ceiling where the lights hung as she flipped the switch.

It never seemed to get old.

She turned on the water to her shower and reveled in the heat. Taking down her braids, she shook out her hair and washed it thoroughly.

While rinsing her hair, Mercy realized that she hadn't thought about August once since he'd left.

31

Poking through the bags of food, Callum found some interesting options. He decided he would save most of them for Jael since this was human food with the possibility of meat, but he found a couple of desserts that were unbelievable. One had a small, spongy round white cake with strawberries and a red sauce, and Callum had no problem licking the remains out of the bag with his long tongue. He was in heaven with all the sugar and suddenly not so upset that he had been dragged on this wretched trip.

His stomach gurgled and groaned, likely protesting the pure sugar. Deciding he was finished eating for now, Callum peered around the side of the cart to where August and Oz were sitting against a tree and talking about the satellites and how they would take them out.

August had a scrutinizing look about him as he said, "How in hell are we going to come up with a fuel that will propel a rocket from under the ground all the way to where the satellites circle the planet?"

Oz nonchalantly replied, "What do you mean we? Jacob found a perfect biofuel from algae that one of his scouts came across in a puddle near our old swimming pond. Why did you think Jacob was covered in ash at the last meeting? It has tested within the explosive ranges we need. The satellites are stationary and were only set up to watch over this side of the planet. They only have propulsion systems with solar radiation converters that provide minimal power to keep them in place."

August's mouth dropped open then closed again before he said, "And you think Carter's team will be able to write the code for a ground-guided rocket with multiple missiles to take out all the satellites?"

"That's what he said. The plan is to launch our own satellites and the missiles within the same rockets. They will lose their surveillance on us and their global positioning, all at the same time."

With a furrowed brow, August asked, "Oz, do you *honestly* think we can pull this off? How are we going to do a test run for the rocket? What if it blows up before we get a chance to knock out the satellite surveillance?"

"We are forming backup plans, but we didn't have anything solid before we left. We only had one conversation about it. Are you saying that you would like to suggest something?" Oz asked.

"Yes, you fucking prick, I would very much like to suggest something.

You are all insane!"

"The rocket should not be plan A! It should be plan C or D, at best. We should rely on our stealth and current numbers to cross the bridge up north. We have almost seventy-five people working at the base now, and we can increase the physical training. Oz, you said it yourself, the UTC base is not far from the bridge," August seethed, eyes wide with irritation.

"The *entrance* of the UTC base is not far from the bridge, but there is nothing but barren land for miles on the mainland after the end of the peninsula. The fog is no guarantee for cover, and we still don't know if the area has satellite surveillance or not. Jael and I may have just been lucky," Oz said, his head tipped to the side, wondering if August was going to continue to have a problem with their new plan.

After making his way over, Callum stood in front of them and asked pointedly, "We gain the ability to speak *outside,* and you two are blabbering on about plans? Do you have no desire to sing or dance? Tell jokes? Dream about the future? Be happy? What the fuck is wrong with both of you?"

August froze, and his dark red eyebrows shot up with the simmering strife snaking its way through the humid air.

Narrowing his yellow eyes at Callum, Oz said flatly, "You do remember we are called the *Golden Cockroaches* by all other known intelligent life in this galaxy, right? Until that changes, I die, or you elect a new President, I will continue to discuss our plans and do my fucking job."

Sliding his wide orange eyes to gauge Callum's reaction to Oz's comment, August pursed his lips, waiting patiently for the reply.

August wasn't going anywhere.

Closing his eyes and leaning his head back, Callum released a frustrated sigh and then brought his head back to face Oz., "You haven't changed in twenty years. Still all about *business* and no fun. You are lame as fuck, and you always have been." Slightly shaking his head, Callum crossed his arms and leaned against a tree, his blue eyes continuing to glare at Oz.

Rising to his feet, Oz pointed to Callum's face and seethed, "You are just upset that I didn't want to *fuck* you behind August's house when we were sixteen. We shared a moment in time, Callum, a *moment*. It meant nothing. We were both tripping our nuts off on mushroom tea, and you were hot as hell! *So fucking what?!*"

With his bright eyes sliding between Oz and Callum, August slid a hand over his gaping mouth, desperately hiding a grin.

He was really glad he had stayed seated.

"You acted like I didn't exist after that. We did more than just twist tongues you inept fuck. You were my first serious crush, and I had wanted you for a long time before we had our *moment*. You didn't care at all. You tossed me away like I meant nothing," Callum exclaimed, becoming quieter with every word.

Sighing, Oz said with a calmer demeanor, "You're right. I didn't care, Callum. That's why I didn't continue to pursue you. I never felt the way you did, so I cut it off before it went any further. We were hormonally engorged teenagers. I don't understand why you won't just get over it. It was *twenty years* ago."

Still watching from his seat leaning against the tree, August wished he could reach the bag of the human's dried fruit snacks sitting on top of Oz's pack.

Watching them bicker back and forth called for snacks.

"Why Oz? Why were you just a hormonal teenager, but all the other people I hooked up with were interested in *at least* a short relationship? What you did was just fucked up. You *had* to know I liked you," Callum said flatly and continued to glare at Oz, his light blue eyes sparkling in the reflected light of the bright auras.

"Listen, you were hot, and the person I was attracted to at the time was not an option. I wasn't ready for *a girl* at the time," Oz said.

"So, you're saying you hooked up with me *because* I am a male? That makes no sense. I know you've been with our tan-haired friend who kept his hair in three braids, at least a few times."

Oz's cheeks heated as he conceded saying, "Oh, yeah. He was really hot too. I missed him when he and his family moved. I genuinely liked him. I was a little older then, and even so, we didn't take our physical relationship much further than you and I did."

Now fully invested, August had his leg stretched out behind Oz and onto Oz's pack. Moving the bag around with his foot, he managed to turn the edge of the bag to face him. August began pulling the bag of dried fruit toward him with his toes, a grin blooming on his face. Callum began getting upset again, so August shot his head up to watch the action, his bag of snacks finally in hand.

"How is that supposed to make me feel any better, Oz? *How?* You never gave me a damn chance. You used me," Callum said, his blue eyes blazing.

"Fine! I hooked up with you, a random hot guy because I was horny. I couldn't be with a girl because I was fucking scared of being *eaten* by the girl!" Oz yelled out, instantly regretting his revelation.

Silence filled their small rest area between the tall oak trees, leaves rustling slightly in the wind above. The absence of sound grew to envelop them.

None of the three were breathing when Callum finally

broke the silence and said, "You thought," he coughed, cleared his throat, then continued, "That if you hooked up with a female, she would *eat* you afterward?"

Oz responded by staring blankly back at Callum.

A long high, pitched wheeze left August as he leaned toward the ground. With his eyes closed and a grin already plastered on his face, August hit the soft ground with a grunt and began laughing, so hard tears sprouted in his eyes.

After overcoming his initial shock, Callum snapped his jaw shut and squeezed his eyes shut with a cringe of a smile on his face. Slumping to the ground in a heap next to August, Callum joined him in rolling in the dirt, laughing.

Callum always knew Oz was hiding something. He just didn't know it would be *hilarious.*

Rolling his eyes, Oz went looking for a snack after peering down at his pack and noticing August had stolen his. Once he found what he wanted, a bag of the human's freeze-dried blueberries, he returned to Callum and August, who were finally catching their breath from their laugh. They wiped tears from their eyes and tried not to look at each other lest they both fall over laughing again.

Oz sighed and sat down by August next to the tree.

"Why the hell did you think a girl would eat you after you hooked up with her?" August asked with a sly grin, desperately trying to hold in a chuckle.

Rolling his eyes, Oz leaned his head back to rest it on the tree and replied, "I knew this wasn't over. When I was a little kid, I saw two scorpions mating from my bedroom window. The female *ate* the male afterward. I didn't have a father, so for most of my childhood, I thought my mother had eaten him. I also thought she ate my sister's father.

"It turned out, she just wanted to be by herself and also

wanted to have children. You should have heard the laugh when *my mother* found out what I thought." Oz shook his head at the memory of his mother's booming laughter.

"You really led me on and *murdered* my boyhood dream of being with the one and only *Mr. Popularity*, all because you thought you would be *eaten* if you hooked up with a girl? Are you saying that, when we kissed, if I would have tried to take a bite of you, you may have turned out celibate like your mother?" Callum asked, a broad grin on his face.

"First of all, *fuck you*, and second, probably," Oz admitted with a sigh, shoulders shrugging with the confession.

All three began uncontrollably laughing as they tried to get up from the ground and pack up their gear to continue.

Callum put his hand on Oz's shoulder gently and chuckled as he said, "I'm just delighted we could have this talk, Oz."

"Oh, fuck a scorpion tail, Callum," Oz replied, shaking his head as he brushed Callum's hand off his shoulder and headed to the cart.

With a satisfied grin, Callum grabbed his pack from the ground.

It was August and Callum's turn to pull the cart, so they tossed their packs into the back, then found their places up front. Not wanting to bounce around in the cart, Oz decided to walk in front instead.

Once they were ready to take off, Callum asked, "Doesn't Jael's world have horses? What the venom happened to our horses? Why don't we have that, Mr. President know-it-all? You do know, right? Or do I need to run back and ask Jacob? I'm sure he knows."

"I thought we just got over our shit?" Oz asked as he furrowed his brow over his shoulder at Callum.

"We did. I just don't like you," Callum responded, as though it made perfect sense.

Oz glared back at Callum and said, "To answer your question, I don't know for sure, but I have a guess. I think there was some type of mass extinction event in our world's ancient history that wiped out the first mammals. Our planet is also missing amphibians and reptiles. I assume it had to be something massive, and that it moved too quickly to allow anything to take cover or hide. There might have been some kind of radiation burst from the black hole when it ate our original star. I won't know anything for certain until I can dig through the archives in the lower levels of the UTC base."

"Maybe that's why they call us cockroaches. Those can live through a nuclear blast, right?" August asked.

"I do think we're called cockroaches because we're hardy and challenging to kill. I don't think they thought that much about it. They do think we are as dumb as actual beetles, though. Our people refuse to speak after they're taken and learn the truth. I'm not sure why," Oz said flatly.

Rolling his eyes, Callum said, "Cockroaches cannot survive a nuclear blast. That seems far-fetched, August."

"Really Callum? Did you not investigate anything in Jael's knowledge except trash television shows and smut books?" August asked.

"She didn't read any books about architecture, so what do you expect? At least I'm not fucking an alien I found in the woods! Literally, Oz, you found a dirty alien in the woods, brought her home, and had sex with her. What the fuck, bro."

Callum held up a hand before Oz could respond and said, "It gets better though, because, before Jael was an alien here, she read naughty books about humans fucking blue aliens. I don't understand how your relationship even works with that history. You know, she really liked those books. She read *seven* of them."

"And August, you are too much of a slippery slug to properly rail *your* woman. So, your digs don't bother me," Callum said pointedly.

Grinning with pride, Oz turned his head around to Callum and said, "She was just preparing for the real deal, and I always saw August as more of a red-horned beetle."

Scoffing, August turned to Oz and said, "A red-horned beetle? I am offended. They roll and eat balls of shit!"

After they all shared a laugh, they quietly walked for hours until they smelled the sea on the breeze and stopped for another rest. According to Oz's solar-powered watch, they were four days ahead of schedule and could afford to rest. No one got any decent rest in the cart, so they were relieved to work an extra stop into the schedule.

Once they were ready to get going again, August and Callum filled the back of the cart with sand while Oz collected avocados and oranges under the cover of the trees. He had put the filled bags into the cart and gone to forage for more, when he found a hill with a single olive tree, so he filled a bag with olives. He had never seen olives grow so large and wanted to plant some of the seeds around the woods near the mouth of the cave. He thought back to the olive tree he had found in the jade woods. He had been thankful to find the versatile fruit.

After August finished filling the cart with sand, he took the small vials that Jacob had sent with him to collect algae samples from the shoreline. While collecting the samples, he peered out onto the water, and in the distance he could see massive sea beasts breaking the surface of the water in a frenzy. Something enormous must have died, and the giant scavengers were fighting and feasting. In the warm, humid air, August shivered, thinking about the predators in the water and how they would soon be crossing this very expanse of sea.

Dread brewed inside, and August scrambled to finish the samples so he could get back to the cart. He wanted to get away from the water as fast as possible.

Once they had everything they needed, Oz asked, "Do we want to get back in a week, or should we keep taking extra rest stops?"

"I don't know why you asked me that. You already know my answer," Callum said without looking at Oz.

August just nodded and found his place in front while Oz and Callum prepared to pull the cart. The added weight to the cart wasn't a big difference due to the balanced design, so they quickly got it moving and headed off into the woods and back to the base.

32

It had been three weeks. Oz, August, and Callum should be home soon, Jael thought as she stared at the holoscreen while Luna sat in the chair next to her, explaining how the guidance system worked.

"This area here in the top left corner is the wide-angle view where each small red dot will represent a rocket. The larger area, here, is where you will see the smaller missiles break off. The small green dots will need to be guided to the satellites, which will be marked in orange. Once you get close, the guidance system will automatically switch to a camera mounted on the top of the missile. You will then maneuver the missile with your controls here." Luna pointed down to the keypad, where Jael noticed the four arrows and a small, rounded ball in the middle.

While watching Jael scan the screen a few times, Luna played with the ends of her single long, white fishtail braid.

Dropping her thick braid to point at the screen, she said, "The bright blue button that says ARM, right here, in the middle at the top? This is to start the five-second timer to trigger the electric current which detonates the highly explosive chemicals inside the missile."

"Will there be anything we need to watch out for? Will they be shooting back at us?" Jael asked, not taking her eyes from the simulation.

Picking her white braid back up and rubbing the ends between her fingers, Luna answered, "We are assuming that is the case, so we are launching over triple the number of missiles we need. Their job will be to stand as decoys if the enemy needs something to aim at. If they shoot one of the missiles we are guiding, the program will automatically send your camera views and controls to the next closest missile."

"Was this really Oz's idea right before he left?" Jael asked, in a breathy whisper, her eyes trained on the screen.

"That's what Carter said. I wasn't there," Luna answered with a shrug.

"This is intense. I can't believe how advanced your people have become in such a short time. Why are we guiding the missiles ourselves and not a program?"

Luna turned to look at Jael and said, "You mean *our* people? It was something about the fact that computers aren't as clever in a pinch. I got a little distracted when Carter was explaining it."

Smiling, Jael said, "Yeah. I mean our people. That makes sense if anything went wrong with the program or if the enemy was more prepared than we realized. Manual control for the most critical part of the plan is logical."

After spending time with Luna, Amelia, and Mercy, Jael had finally been coming to work for her shifts on Carter's team. If that was Oz's intent, it worked like a charm. Jael still felt inferior and was simply floating along and trying to keep up, but she loved it. She loved it more than she ever dreamed

-- to be part of a larger unit, to be able to work in a room full of brilliant minds for the goal of freedom. She didn't want to miss one moment of work.

Carter's team was incredible. She was catching on to the team's project's inner workings and even understood how some of the newly developed tech worked, but she knew deep down that she was not on their level. She could learn all she wanted about their technology and software, but when it came to helping develop it?

There was no way.

Jael didn't necessarily feel *inadequate* about that part, but she didn't know why they wanted her input. She didn't understand why it was so important that she participate in tech development, but she did it anyway because she knew it was the right thing to do. During development, when shift first began, she felt more like a little kid sitting in on a college lecture than a participant, but she smiled and acted like she knew what was going on anyway. Maybe her participation was meaningful because she was with Oz, and she had some kind of obligation to help the cause in an open and active way.

Ah, politics, Jael thought to herself as she practiced with the missile guidance software. Her fingers moved quickly over the keys, and she was easily able to maneuver the dots on the simulation.

She hoped the real deal was that simple.

After looking at the clock, she went ahead and turned off the holoscreen and grabbed her lunch bag before heading to the door. She planned to stop by Amelia's office and thank her for the bloodwork again.

The results showed that she had low iron, but other than that, she was in perfect health. After adding some extra apricots to her diet, she had not felt any different but was hopeful she would notice a difference eventually. She had multiple deficiencies as a child, and one of the worst was anemia.

Thinking back, that may have been part of why Jael was so clumsy and always felt so sick. Jael stopped walking to look down at an old, faded scar on her arm, one from a particularly rough fall on some outdoor iron stairs at one of the last foster homes. The back of her forearm caught on a twisted piece of rusty iron that protruded from one of the rails as she fell. The memory of the pain from that slice and the antiseptic afterward was enough to snap her out of the memory, and she got back on her way to the clinic.

During a meal with Mercy the day before, Jael noticed that her usually light-brown skin had paled. She abruptly realized her body needed vitamin D. She wasn't sure how worried she should be and wanted to ask Amelia about it.

When she walked into the clinic, she found Amelia working in her lab with Luna. Looking back out the door behind her, Jael wondered how, aside from teleporting, Luna had reached the clinic before her. She distinctly remembered seeing Luna still working when she left the tech lab and headed straight for the clinic.

"Luna, you really do split *all* your time between here and the tech team office. When do you rest? And how did you get here so fast?" A confused Jael asked, whipping her head back around to the open doorway one more time.

Sighing, Luna chuckled and said, "I walked right by you while you were zoned out in the hallway. Honestly? I don't get much rest. I know I'm needed, so I just make it happen. I can rest when I'm dead."

"I don't know if we deserve you, Luna. I don't know how you do it all," Jael said.

"Thank you, but we all deserve my undivided dedication, my friend," Luna replied with a smile.

"What can I help you with, Jael?" asked Amelia, finally turning from the holoscreen she was working on.

Looking down at her arm and then at Amelia, Jael paused then asked, "I was wondering, do I need extra vitamin D since there is no star shining on this world? And we also don't know how long we will need to stay underground."

"Your vitamin D levels were normal when we did your testing. You should be fine without a supplement. I have found that most of our fruit and vegetables are higher in nutrients than the ones on your world. I've been running tests on the foods, and they're exceptionally nutritious. They are filled with vitamins and minerals," Amelia explained.

Shifting in her seat, Amelia turned a timer off and selected some options on a device that Jael thought looked like a centrifuge, causing a hum to slow and stop.

Amelia turned back around to face Jael and continued, "You may have noticed the flavors of our produce are bold in comparison."

"I bet they are several times more nutritious. Everything tastes so much better here. The avocados taste like clouds of cream, and the almonds are so sweet and have a slight metallic after taste. It sounds weird saying it out loud, but it's delicious. Now the vegetables, on the other hand, are so pungent I don't know how anyone eats them," Jael explained, frowning at the thought of the carrot Oz convinced her to try the day before he left.

It had been almost as bad as the mushroom tea...almost.

Laughing, Luna said, "They're disgusting. Usually, only the old people in the village grow and eat them. They lose vision in one eye and suddenly think, 'I should eat the most rancid vegetable stew I can tolerate.'"

Looking around at Amelia and Jael staring at her in confusion, Luna continued, "I was raised by my grandmother."

Amelia and Jael both uttered a simultaneous, "Ah."

Jael made a face of pure revulsion and said, "I'm really glad I'm not the only one who thinks the veggies are gross. Oz talked me into grabbing a carrot the other day in the mess hall, and it was horrendous. I've never eaten something that smelled and tasted so strongly of foot and root. It was like someone concentrated the carrot color and flavor way too much, or just compacted the carrot somehow. I don't spit things out. I am a trooper, and I swallow even if it's nasty. The chewed carrot *fell* from my mouth. My tongue just said, *no*."

Laughing, Amelia said, "I could try and make a soup at home, or we could cook a soup for you in the mess hall? I would highly recommend eating them three times a week at least for additional vitamins. They will make you feel a lot better too. I know the flavor is strong, but I promise after one bowl of vegetable soup you will not regret it."

Jael shivered in disgust and said, "If you say so."

Amelia chuckled and said, "Let's see if Mercy is hungry, then we can all meet in the mess hall for afternoon soup."

Rolling her eyes and groaning, Luna curled her lip at Amelia and said, "Fine, I'll go get Mercy."

"Good. We will see you there," Amelia said, smirking as Luna filed out of the clinic.

Amelia hung up her lab coat and followed Jael out the door, toward the mess hall.

The long, brightly lit hallway was slowly filling with people, and their boots tapping on the stone floor began filling the space. The second shift of the day had just ended minutes prior. No one seemed to pay Amelia and Jael any mind as they walked through the bustling hall.

The people working in the base left in small groups to avoid a large number of people suddenly appearing in the village at once. Many of them used the time to socialize before returning to their reticent lives.

Watching their kind go from bright and filled with hope to stone-faced and silent as they approached the base's door was heartbreaking. At that moment, it made sense to Jael why they maintained such determination working on the daunting task of freedom. They had a daily reminder of why it was essential to keep pushing themselves, to keep developing and completing their plans.

Once they reached the mess hall, Amelia grabbed herself and Jael a bowl of soup and sat down at a table in the middle of the room. After retrieving her bowl from Amelia, Jael sat down next to her on a stool.

One whiff of the soup nearly made tears gather in her eyes.

This was going to be a test of her will.

Staring at the steaming soup, Jael kept repeating in her head, "It's not as bad as a centipede," over and over, but that was accomplishing absolutely nothing. Mercy and Luna both pulled their stools out from under the table and sat down with their bowls of soup. Luna reached back and adjusted her tail before giving Jael an exasperated look. Mercy looked downright sad, and Jael thought Luna seemed like she was getting angry at the soup the longer she looked at it.

Amelia thought, "It is just soup!"

Why were they all so damn upset about it? Amelia looked around, confused.

"It's not that bad! Plus, I know none of you have eaten a single vegetable in over a month. You owe your body something that's good for it," Amelia explained.

Grimacing, Jael brought the soup to her lips, plugged her nose with her left hand, and dumped the concentrated green-grass-tasting mush into her mouth. Swallowing in one gulp, Jael released her nose then thought she was going to wretch when the powerful scent of the carrots and celery hit the back of her throat.

She had never wished to be back at the treehouse with Oz more than at this moment.

"Are you sure I can't just smell the vitamins right out of the vegetables? I feel like I can get plenty, just from the smell," Jael explained as her hand snaked up to hold her nose again.

Laughing after swallowing her fifth gulp of soup, Amelia said, "No, it unquestionably does not work that way. Just pick up the bowl and drink it if it's really that bad. I think you're all making a much bigger deal about this than it is."

"We are not," Mercy defended, in a gravelly tone while grimacing at her steaming soup.

Luna was busy choking down swallows, her feet tapping the floor with every gulp and her long tail unraveling behind her for balance.

Amelia rolled her eyes and said, "All of you will thank me for this."

"Sure. Right. Worse than my grandmother's vegetable

stew, without question. This better give me superpowers because this is *super* nasty," Luna croaked, one hand up in the air speaking along with her.

Everyone laughed, then Amelia collected the mostly empty bowls in a stack and took them to the mess hall's kitchen.

"When are the guys supposed to return with the sand?" Luna asked, before downing her tall cup of water.

"They said it could take four weeks, and it's been about three. We have been so busy, I've hardly noticed the time passing," Jael admitted.

"You haven't missed me?" Oz called out with a hand on his chest from the door of the mess hall.

Jael forgot everything as she knocked her stool to the ground to run and leap into Oz's open arms.

Slowly setting her down, Oz took her face in his hands and kissed her, slipping his tongue along her bottom lip before whispering, "I can't wait to get you in the apartment. We are taking a few days off, so go home, and I'll meet you there in a few minutes."

The sweet, breathy whispers near her ear sent lightning down her spine and heat between her legs.

Before heading off toward the apartment, Jael smiled up at Oz and said, "I did miss you. Too much."

While strolling out of the mess hall, she passed by August with Mercy pressed to the wall.

August slid his hands up and down Mercy as he pinned her to the cold wood wall and ravaged her mouth with his tongue. Mercy was overwhelmed with heat and panting by the time he pulled away. August dragged her off to their apartment like he had been without her for years. Mercy looked back at Amelia and waved before she disappeared around the corner.

With a flat expression, Amelia waved back, and then her arm flopped back at her side. She slid her attention to Oz and Luna as she headed back toward the clinic.

Oz signaled to Luna that he needed to speak with her. As she approached Oz, he said, "Please have a few people go and unload the produce. Then, have all the sand transported directly to Jacob's lab."

"No problem. I just had lunch, so I'm back on shift now," Luna replied.

Oz said, "Thank you, Luna," before heading off toward Carter's office.

Once he arrived, Oz knocked, and Carter opened the door before he could knock a second time.

With a large smile, Carter said, "Oh, fantastic! You're back! I wanted to tell you. Jael has been an excellent addition to the group."

"Thank you. I appreciate you including her on your team. She was so nervous about going to work before I left. Do you know what changed?" Oz asked.

"Yes. Jael, Mercy, Luna, and Amelia struck up quite an inseparable friendship in your absence," Carter explained as he slid his hands into his pockets.

Warmth filled Oz as Carter's words sunk in. *Jael had made new friends.*

"What job has she been training for?" Oz asked, a smile on his face from Carter's explanation.

Carter beamed with pride as he said, "She has joined the team that will guide and fire the missiles after we launch the rockets."

"You've already designed the software and formed a team?" Oz asked, astonishment evident on his face.

Nodding, Carter explained, "Yes, we already have the simulation training in progress. We finished writing the software and code for the rockets a week after you left."

"I have to say I am impressed your team is working so quickly and efficiently." Oz said as he tucked a loose hair behind his ear.

"Our people are proving to be reasonably consistent with our high intelligence levels, and all of us have the same driving motivation. If you haven't spoken to Jacob yet, he has begun assembling the first rocket and plans to have the project finished within the next four months. That includes excavating the tubes to lay the rails for the launch," Carter said with a smile.

"So, Jacob is going with the electric-rail launch idea? Did he find a way to prevent the mounting projectile from melting?"

"Yes and no, he discovered an alloy that can withstand the heat, but the rail works more efficiently if the projectile is allowed to melt. It will simply fall away after the rockets' engines move them into an upward angle. All simulations and tests have pointed to the rails being the most effective launch method."

"Great. So, we *will* be able to launch more than one?" Oz asked.

"Yes, we have three planned. Two will contain our satellites and missiles, and one rocket will house only missiles. We will keep the rocket filled with missiles in orbit for protection," Carter said, closing the door behind him as he walked out of the lab.

"I am going to be taking a few days off. Please don't

expect Jael to come in until later this week," Oz said over his shoulder, as he headed toward his apartment.

During the short walk, the anticipation of spending several days with Jael nearly sent him into a run.

After pushing open the door of his apartment, Oz found Jael in their kitchen preparing him a meal.

"I heard you made some new friends and that you've done well at work. Carter seemed impressed," Oz said while setting his pack down by the door.

Jael turned around with his plate and said, "I had way too much fun with Mercy. Amelia, Luna, Mercy, and I have been meeting daily in the mess hall, and we had a few parties while you were gone. I drank mushroom tea!"

Laughing nervously, Oz asked, "OK? Well, how did that go?"

"Uh, about as bad as you are probably imagining. I fell off a chair and talked to a wall for a while. There were little dancing lights that I thought were talking fairies. Amelia seems to think I have some kind of spiritual connection. Then there were these spirit things moving in the wall. Everything was talking to me. I had so much fun! We all danced for hours, and then they all stayed here while I slept. Don't worry. I wore my mouth guard and didn't scare them with my snoring," Jael explained with a beaming smile.

Grinning, Oz said, "I'm so glad you had fun and made some new friends. I knew you and Mercy would get along great. I remember Luna from the village when we were kids. She was always working on something."

Sitting down on the padded bench, Jael asked, "Did you have a decent time, even though you had to be quiet the entire trip?"

Surprise was written on Oz's face as he said, "Oh, Jael! I

haven't rested and nearly forgot. We came upon three humans in the woods and got some great intel. The microphones are only used to listen around the village, not out in the woods. We can talk openly if we're not within a certain radius of a village. We are going to try to put up some kind of markers in the woods, so we know when to fall silent."

With her mouth gaping with surprise, Jael asked, "We could go camping! I'll see if Mercy can make us a tent!"

Considering her words, Oz furrowed his brow in thought and said, "I think that's a great idea. I'll try and plan a few days off in about a month, and we can go on a short camping trip. We plan to head north in four months, so we should definitely plan a few weekends for us before then. I'll make sure everyone going north with us takes some time off to spend with loved ones before the journey."

Oz paused momentarily, then said, "We've already come so far. I think we should have a celebration and dinner for everyone. Why don't you, Mercy, and Callum plan the party."

Beaming, Jael said, "Yes! I'll see Mercy tomorrow and tell her."

33

"Instead of our normal food, let's make special dishes, like fire-roasted fruit tarts and maybe some avocado-stuffed, pan-fried flatbread," Callum suggested while he leaned his hip against the heavy wooden table that they were all sitting around in the mess hall.

"What if we make some of the Earth humans' deserts too?" Jael chimed in, excitement thrumming in her chest at the thought of a cookie.

Mercy swung her head to Jael and said, "Great idea. I'll ask Sarah if she, or any of the other villagers who enjoy cooking, have found ways to make any of your planet's deserts."

"You know, Sarah has already been baking cakes and cookies. Everyone who passes by her house can smell them, but she swears she isn't doing anything new or different. I'll go visit her when I go home. I will have to break it to her that I can *literally* smell her lies. She has been trading for a lot of bananas, and I think she's been using them in place of the eggs your world uses in cakes," Callum explained, finally pulling out a stool to sit on and adjusting his tail after taking a seat.

Unable to control her giggling, Jael said, "I never thought I would eat a cookie or cake again. If either, or something even remotely close, ends up at the party, I will be squealing while I eat it."

"It's that good?" Mercy asked, interest written on her face.

"How did you pick up language's muscle memories but not receive my taste memories? Did you get my scent memories?"

"We just got your accumulated knowledge, the muscle memory for speaking, and some auditory memories. Touch, taste, and scent weren't shared. Oz easily could have shared all your memories but didn't, probably to ensure your privacy," Mercy explained while Callum nodded in agreement.

Looking from Callum to Mercy, Jael scoffed, "Privacy? Oz didn't have to share all the spicy novels I've read!"

Reaching to lay a hand over Jael's, Callum laughed and said, "Oh Jael, we, as a people, don't care about that. As much as I don't like Oz, and it pains me to say this, he probably didn't think the books' sexual naughtiness was a bad thing. Those were very entertaining books, by the way. Not all of us are strictly science nerds like Carter and Jacob. I love Jacob's analytical side, but the guy needs some excitement in his life. He could talk about the biofuel he's developing for days."

"Yeah, some of us like to have *actual* fun," Mercy included with a wink.

Jael laughed and said, "When we lived at the treehouse, Oz was hilarious - never serious like he is now. I think I developed a set of abs just from laughing. Since we've been back, he's been so stern, but I think after we win our freedom, he will loosen up again, I hope."

"I'm sure you're right. He was wild when we were kids. I remember he and some other kids always played a chasing game in the woods. It's like hide-and-seek, except the one searching is blindfolded, and everyone tries to force the other players to make noise so they will get tagged. Oz always won because he would either make you scream in fright, or he would make you laugh and give yourself away, then he'd run off to the next person and do the same. Even blindfolded, he would find all the kids in the trees. At first, no one else could climb like him. Our people used to spend a lot of time in the trees, but we haven't done that in more than ten thousand years. August eventually learned how to climb as well as Oz, but then the tag games ended because they were always on a team together," Mercy explained while she rolled her eyes.

"That sounds just like him," Jael admitted, shaking her head.

"Has someone asked Luna if she knows someone on one of the tech teams who can make us a colorful light system? And who is going to mix all the alcohol? Did Amelia harvest enough mushrooms for the tea?" Callum asked, making it known that he was finished talking about Oz.

"I haven't asked Luna yet, and I will gladly mix the alcohol myself if we can't find someone else. I'll ask Amelia about the mushroom harvest after we finish our meeting. She was wanting to do some studies on them anyway, so I'm sure she has plenty," Mercy explained as she shifted on her seat.

Jael spoke up and said, "I can ask Luna. I have a shift with her soon."

"OK then. It's all settled. I'll gather a few people to set

up in the command room before I go home, then I'll visit Sarah. I'll see you two later!" Callum said as he walked toward the door of the mess hall.

Mercy and Jael followed behind, each heading to their shifts. Jael walked on, and Mercy stopped at the clinic. Amelia had a patient, so Mercy waited outside the doorway until they could speak

Amelia finished up and her patient left. Mercy walked in and found her with a new, side-cropped haircut, buzzed on the sides and longer on top. It was a big change from the long, dark-blue hair she had previously worn. The cut was very different from their people's usual long, fishtail-braided and knotted hair.

"You cut your hair!" Mercy couldn't help blurting out the obvious, excitement shooting through her.

"I feel like it suits me better. It's a lot easier to take care of," Amelia explained with a smile, her baby blue eyes bright.

"I love it!" Mercy said with a grin. "Oh! I almost forgot why I came by. Did you harvest and dry enough mushrooms for tea at the party tonight?"

"Yes, of course, they're right here," Amelia said as she handed Mercy the large navy-blue bag of dried mushrooms.

"Thank you, I'll see you tonight!" Mercy said over her shoulder as she walked toward her office.

As Mercy walked, she spent the time wondering who came up with the barbering tools that were used to cut Amelia's hair that way. Her people were adapting to modern ways so quickly, that she wondered if something would be lost along the way... some of the deeper parts of progress.

Is it supposed to move this quickly, or are their people a speeding bullet heading for a target, nearing their end?

There are so many things they were up against. They had

never fought back against the humans. Rebelled maybe, but never fought back. After thousands of years of being farmed for servitude, they had lost their most daring people and those willing to risk being taken for standing against the eternal silence. The genetic impact on their people was overwhelming to think about.

What if their souls yearned to fully express themselves so desperately that their bodies eventually had to respond, giving them a way? What if it was their own desire for more that drove them to find a way to make that the first connection?

Is one little rebellion all it takes to spark a revolution?

That's how it happened in Earth's history books.

If they did it, we can do it too.

The way hope can sneak its way in, just like doubt... hope is like a light cloud of thin vapor, that barely seems to do or hold anything. Yet these whispers of support, of possibility, hold the power to change worlds.

Sometimes when those light vapor clouds of hope combine, they form a booming thunderhead.

A thunderhead that could wreak havoc on their enemies, their captors.

Mercy entered her office and slid her eyes up and down the prototype for her armor design. Jacob had finished the H-cell batteries and Luna had helped Carter design the power grid mesh, Now, she was finally able to get on with her design work.

She took her hand and followed the seams from the shoulder all the way down to the waist of the mannequin. They had developed a high-tech mesh that concentrated enough power in a single area to catch and re-route a railgun's blast just as she'd imagined. The entire process would be so fast they wouldn't see it. It had been through preliminary testing, and it worked.

The image of the test was still fresh in her mind. The mannequin that was wearing the armor didn't so much as shake as the suit easily caught the round and shot it right back at the railgun. Jacob had to duck to miss the returning round, and his whoop of delight filled his lab.

The integrated sensor system simultaneously located the incoming rounds and pre-locked the target for the return. It worked perfectly.

The armor Mercy designed was a simple, sleek bodysuit with flat points on the front and back of the torso made from a series of plates. Jacob had come up with the perfectly positioned plates, which each emitted a massive electromagnetic shield pulse that slowed the molten metallic rounds down enough to be caught. The plates also served as solar panels, and contained rechargeable, H-cell batteries. The suit had exactly enough power for one week of maximum output.

There were still issues with the batteries. They had to work out how to recharge them on the dark side of the planet and in the caves.

They would need a long-lasting battery when they were on the dark side of the planet and they hoped the one they had developed would be enough. Only infrared and red wavelengths would be available, and they would need to get the most battery life they could for the size.

The suit could stay charged for months if stored on the surface under the auras and would fully recharge in a short amount of time on the light side of the planet. This was *only* true if they stayed above ground.

In the cavern, the batteries drained far too quickly.

Something in the rocks sapped battery power. They hypothesized that it was some kind of low-level radiation. but they didn't have time to look into it. This meant that the armor had to be charged right before it was used for anything inside the base.

Batteries in general had been an issue in the cave due to the constant drain on power that they had yet to explain. Endlessly charging the suits drained the main power supply, so they needed to remain un-charged until they were used for practice. They were only pre-charged for a mission.

The suits would never be used inside the base for anything but practice anyway.

The tech teams helped make Mercy's ideas come to life, and her final design fit her vision seamlessly. They added a thick, heated liner inside the suit to keep them warm in the cold and included extra warmers in the bottoms of the boots that extended up over their toes to prevent frostbite. The gloves had extra warming liners for the same reason. The base material was a synthetic Jacob had designed, and he claimed it could be sealed by issuing a command in the helmet. In less than a second, the suit would be airtight for the vacuum of space.

Carter designed the entire suit, including the helmets, to be run by voice commands to a screen in the face shields. Mercy loved that the information screen didn't seem like it was in her face and shrunk to fit the user's needs. The information seemed at a perfect reading distance but was invisible to anyone on the outside. The face shield could be shaded, then made completely clear in an instant. The glass-based material could be retracted or dimmed if needed. The information screen remained fully visible during any of the helmet's settings.

When Callum missed work, she liked to waste her entire break times dancing around her office in the helmet. The colors and sharpness of her vision were enhanced, plus Carter had added a music selection to the helmet's internal hard drive.

Mercy was beaming about her design and backed up to look at it.

As she added the final change to the suit's magnetically activated bottom hem, she realized her shift, which usually dragged, had been over for twenty minutes. It hadn't felt like it had been long enough, but she wasn't complaining.

Rushing out the door, Mercy couldn't wait to get to the dinner and party they had planned.

34

"Now that everyone is seated, I want to start by recognizing the hard work Amelia, Jacob, and Carter have been dedicating to this project. We will succeed at our daunting task because of the hard work you and your teams have put into making advancements for our people in medicine and technology."

"Jacob, I am especially commending you tonight for your efforts at designing and engineering the rockets, which will ultimately set our people free. Everyone has made incredible contributions, and tonight, we are going to celebrate with this private dinner and later with a party.

"We each had seemingly impossible tasks, but all of us have fulfilled the need and more. With every ounce of effort we show toward the fight for our freedom, our collective hope grows.

"We will soon set up a team to decide our military structure, and I plan to have Luna lead the team since she has completed her medical training with Amelia. Now that all the business has been wrapped up, let's eat," Oz said, then he grinned and took a seat at the head of the long table.

Jael was seated next to Oz, and he laid his hand on her leg after he sat down on his stool. The feel of his touch was warm and comforting. She settled the turmoil of the day and was able to finally relax. The hardness on her face faded, and she slid her gaze to Oz.

Jael leaned into Oz to kiss him gently on the cheek and said, "You speak so eloquently. Sometimes I can't believe you spoke your first words just a few months ago."

"I had a hell of a teacher," Oz whispered, his hand gripping her thigh under the table.

Grinning, Oz kissed Jael on the forehead then began eating his plate of fruit pastries and fried flatbread stuffed with salted and spiced avocado. The meal Callum came up with turned out delicious, and everyone began devouring their food.

Turning to face August, Mercy said, "I'm almost finished with the final prototype of the armor. You should come by and see it."

"Alright, sure. I'll come by this week sometime. It was a great idea. I'm glad they put you and Callum in charge of the team creating the gear. It was a great idea to not just deflect the railgun's ammunition but shoot it back at the enemy. That's my favorite kind of genius idea," August said with desire burning in his eyes.

Grinning, Mercy took a bite of her fruit tart and did her best to ignore the heat of August's gaze.

"The armor idea was brilliant, Mercy. Much of what we have developed has been based on technology that I duplicated. Your idea was purely organic. This is the reason we decided organic learning is far superior to using the connection to pass on mass amounts of information. Your genius idea is the proof. The suits will help even the odds with our enemy, and you may have given us the extra boost we needed to win back our planet," Carter explained while keeping his eyes on Mercy. His dark brown eyes were full of pride and care.

Carter had been begging Mercy to join his team and help develop new technology, but that just wasn't her thing. She knew she was better suited for armor design. Her spatial abilities were her strength, and she knew that she had found the right place for her within their grand plan.

With glittering tears gathering, Mercy said, "Thank you," quietly before stuffing her mouth full of fruit pastry in an attempt to soothe her overwhelming emotions.

Mercy had always been misunderstood, but today, she was not only understood, but her mind and ideas were being commended. Holding her breath steady, Mercy wasn't sure another soul in the room could guess how deeply she felt at that moment.

Absolute joy and fulfillment engulfed her.

Keeping her eyes on Mercy, Amelia leaned toward Carter, and grasped his forearm. She quietly said, "That was very kind, Carter. We have so much to be proud of tonight."

Smiling, Luna downed her tall drink then loudly blurted out, "I don't know about any of you, but I am ready for some mushroom tea and loud music!"

"Fuck yes!" Callum said before he downed his cocktail in only a few gulps.

Jacob shook his head and said, "Am I going to end up having to track you down and carry you back home after the party? Please don't get wasted and disappear. I hate when you do that."

"Not gonna lie. Probably," Callum said dryly as he set his emptied cup on the table and grinned over at Jacob.

In addition to the broad grin, Callum's eyebrows raised in a way that said he was not sorry in the slightest.

With his face deadpanned, Jacob said, "Great. Carter, you said one of your team members finished making the lenses on the recording camera, right? Are the lenses installed yet?"

"Yes, they are assembled and ready to use, my friend," Carter said with a chuckle beginning.

"I'm going to need to borrow one tonight," Jacob said, still stone-faced, to Carter while keeping eye contact with Callum.

Callum rolled his eyes and harrumphed before saying, " You can record me all night. I don't care."

Releasing a long dramatic sigh, Jacob crossed his arms, seeming to give up on the subject, for the moment anyway.

"Oz, are you going to drink any mushroom tea tonight?" Luna asked from the other end of the table.

Sliding his eyes to Jael, he grinned and said, "Of course, it's not a party without mushroom tea."

"Really? You're going to drink some of the tea tonight?" Jael asked Oz quietly, her hand slipping over his on her thigh.

Oz looked back at Jael with a narrowed brow of disbelief and said, "I know that at some point you've heard stories about me from someone at this table. Are you really all that surprised?"

"Well, I guess I'm not. I did hear some stories," Jael admitted, shrugging her shoulders and chuckling.

Laughing sardonically, Callum said, "Yeah, let's talk about what happens on mushrooms. That's a great topic."

Groaning, Jacob leaned his head back and let out a dramatic exhale.

Oz mumbled under his breath toward Jael, "Here we go."

"Oh, your feelings are hurt because he didn't want to hit that behind my house," August shot back, his lips in a mocking smile and eyes focused on Callum.

Sitting at the end of the table, Luna's bright yellow eyes were wide. Jacob couldn't hold it in and threw his head back, laughing and smacking Callum's leg. He knew something had been going on; he should have known it had to do with Oz being an asshole and Callum not getting over it.

August just chuckled and crossed his arms over his broad chest while continuing to stare at Callum.

"You just had to bring that up again," August said, shaking his head at Callum and smiling.

Callum blurted out, "Oz thought a woman would eat him after they fucked."

Everyone turned to Oz and laughed as he rolled his eyes and tried to hide his embarrassment.

Jacob sighed and quickly said, "Callum is scared of spiders."

Callum's mouth gaped open as he surveyed the room filled with his laughing friends.

Unable to hold back his laughter, Oz cleared his throat and then chuckled as he said, "That's some mighty fine information to know, Jacob. Thank you for that one."

Glaring at Jacob, who was still chuckling uncontrollably, Callum furrowed his blue eyebrows and said, "You are going to pay dearly for that."

Jacob winked at him, patted his leg, and said, "Oh, I hope so. I'm looking forward to it."

After fanning herself, Amelia said, "Sorry to change the steamy subject at the other end of the table, but the party is in an hour and some of us need to prepare. I smell like a lab rat."

Looking down at her own outfit, Mercy chimed in, "Yeah, me too. I need to freshen up."

35

Stroking a single finger down Jacob's chest, Callum followed the ridges of his chiseled muscles down to his abs and hooked a finger in the waist of his pants. Jacob exhaled roughly as Callum popped the button on his pants. Callum's lips met the angle of Jacob's neck, just under his jaw.

With a breathy, "Just five minutes, I promise," from Callum in his ear, Jacob melted, hoping Callum's promise of paybacks from earlier wasn't going to end up leaving him on edge for the rest of the night.

Leaning into Jacob against their kitchen counter, Callum kissed down his shoulder, slid his hands around Jacob's thick muscled waist, and tugged down his pants by their belt loops. Sliding down his body, Callum kissed a trail down Jacob's hard stomach and ran his tongue from the top of his hip to just above his leg. The sensation of Callum's lick sent shivers of electricity across Jacob's skin. He had no idea what Callum was doing, but he had a good idea it had come from those naughty books.

Taking Jacob's length, Callum ran his tongue along the thick seam underneath, resulting in a tremble and breathy moan from Jacob. Wrapping his tongue around Jacob's tip, he slowly slid his head down and caused a shaking Jacob to grip the counter's edge with white knuckles. If Callum stopped, Jacob thought he might die.

Increasing his pace, Callum took Jacobs's softness into his hand and pressed in underneath.

Jacob threw his head back and let out a high-pitched, breathy whisper before rasping, "Fuck Cal, that fucking mouth!"

Callum took his finger and circled the tight spot in the rear. A moment later, Jacob seized with pleasure and leaned his head back, releasing deep clicks in his throat. Callum brought his hand up to join his tongue in stroking then wrapped his lips around the tip of Jacob's length as his pleasure spilled over, lapping up every bit.

Releasing a low, shaking moan, Jacob swung his head back and slammed it into the cabinet door. "Cal, babe, how am I supposed to go to a damn party after you sucked the life out of me?"

Still on his knees, Callum chuckled and said, "I couldn't help it. You know I can't keep my hands off you."

Callum squeezed Jacob's thighs in a loving gesture and looked up at his dark-haired man. Grinning, he handed Jacob his pants which were still bunched at his ankles.

"I can't wait to return the favor later. I'm going to be thinking about this for days," Jacob said as he reached for his shirt on the counter.

After Jacob buckled his pants and put his shirt back on, they headed down to the party.

As they walked down the stairs, Oz and Jael were right

behind them, closing their apartment door.

One of Carter's teams was setting up the room, moving tables and chairs to the edges. Zoe's tech team was working on the lights, and Luna was setting up the speakers.

Oz noticed everything seemed to be wireless, so he asked with genuine curiosity, "Jacob, did you put the new H-cell batteries in everything?"

Stopping and turning around, Jacob looked at Oz and said, "Yes, we've already made enough rechargeable batteries to last us many Earth years. The entire base is now run with H-cell technology. We have to take them outside to charge though. This cave blocks all wireless signals, so we don't charge them until they're ready to be used. Outside, they're wirelessly charged with the clear solar panels we hid high in the trees above the base. We've also discovered a slight static charge from our planet, which we've harnessed into the batteries' technology to keep them charged much longer. I think it has to do with our exceptionally powerful magnetic field and the radiation from the black hole. The cave blocks all of it, thankfully, or we wouldn't have been able to build electronics down here. The only downside in the cave is the power drain."

With too much excitement to contain, Jael blurted out, "That's why my tablet was fully charged! I knew it was odd!"

Everyone turned and looked to her for an explanation, and with her excited expression fading, Jael realized none of them knew what she was talking about.

"When I was transported here, my electronic tablet was fully charged. It freaked me out at the time, but I understand now. It had technology built into it that made it possible to absorb the electric charge from a wireless charging pad. When I laid the tablet on the pad, it would charge quickly. The planet's charge must have been what filled the battery on my tablet," Jael explained, hoping that what she was saying to a room of geniuses made sense.

"That's exactly right, Jael. I know you've joined the guidance team, but would you mind coming down to my lab to chat about some engineering projects I'm working on?" Jacob asked with his eyes narrowed on her inquisitively.

Oz slid his arm around her waist as she took in a sharp breath before slowly smiling and quietly saying, "I would love to."

Releasing her, Oz walked over to grab a filled cup from a table. His black hair was finally past his shoulders and braided into five fishtails, all knotted at his nape.

Smiling back at her, Jacob asked, "Why do you seem so surprised? Am I missing something?"

Callum leaned in, took Jael's arm, and looped it into his, "I told you so."

"Thank you," Oz said with sincerity in his eyes, something Callum had yet to see from Oz.

"When is Carter coming back to the party?" Mercy asked as she walked up, her hair freshly braided in a plethora of small, brown fishtail braids that she had pulled together and let fall over her shoulders.

The first sounds from the speakers that were being tested filled the room.

Jacob answered and said, "He and a small team are setting up the bases for the external surveillance system. When he's finished, he'll join us."

"I feel bad that he doesn't get to start the party with us," Mercy explained with a frown, irritation about Carter being left out written on her face.

Luna spoke quietly behind Mercy and said, "Trust me he doesn't mind. Carter is probably totally in love with his work. I think he would form a romantic relationship with his computer if he could. The man is glued."

Laughing and leaning his head toward Mercy, Jacob said, "Luna's convinced Carter hasn't rested in a month."

"He hasn't!" Luna said, trailing off and sealing her mouth shut, seeming to avoid saying more.

"Did we all come to this party to gossip about Carter's computer love life and rest schedule, or are we going to start the music? The mushroom tea I just forced down is bound to take effect any minute, and no offense, but I don't plan on talking much tonight," Oz said while tugging Jael to his side and holding her there tightly.

Callum tipped his head and raised his brows in agreement, saying, "Now that's a statement I can get behind."

Mercy quickly made her way over to the table with the sizable holographic computer screen, and the music blasted to life in the large cavern. The vibrations from the beat rang through them from the floor, and bodies began moving.

After the melody of the music began, Mercy fed it through the newly installed, base-wide speaker system long enough to send a clear message. People from all over their secret base began filing into the room. Jacob dimmed the lights just as Luna started up the colorful light show for the party.

Looking up, Luna watched Oz move behind Jael and engulf her in his embrace. It warmed her to see such sweet affection, then her mind shifted to Carter, wishing he would put down his work and join the party.

Taking Jael by the hips, Oz held her close and said into her ear, "Dancing with you will always remind me of when you sang to me on the deck back at our treehouse. I had never even imagined music. Now, here we are, dancing together, speaking, and listening to music. It's like a dream coming true, before the dream ever found its way into my mind in the first place. We, my people, were merely existing before, and now we are living."

Throwing her arms around Oz, Jael felt the tea begin to take effect. She slid her hands up to his broad shoulders, and he leaned down to kiss her, his lips possessive. Oz took her hips in his grip and forced their bodies together before he began moving to the beat of the music.

An eerie feeling fell over her as she remembered the dream she'd had almost eight months before, the one about dancing with Oz in a nightclub. The only thing missing was the sparkly minidress she had been wearing. She refocused on Oz and quickly forgot all about it as the tea took her mind to new places.

They moved to the music, Jael entranced by Oz's movements. Heat burned inside for this man of hers as he swayed and moved them around the dance floor. Oz's hands moved along her form, finding every place she loved to be touched, and his lips caressed her neck.

In that moment, Jael truly allowed herself to *live*.

As more people joined them on the dance floor, the tea dipped its fingers into the depths of Jael's most wild essence. She knew that there were people around, but all she could understand was Oz and his body moving with hers. The walls of the cavern began to shift and wave like they had when she'd ingested the tea before.

Looking past Oz, Jael saw Mercy at one end of the room, moving toward August. Then, her vision blurred, and all she could understand was sound and the soft touch of her love pressed against her.

Once she was finished setting up, Mercy peered around the room, found August and began pulling him toward the middle of the room for a dance. He seemed stiff, and Mercy was more than determined to make him loosen up. His body was a stone compared to hers. She twisted her body around in front of him to get his attention, and it certainly did. Moving closer to her, August smiled at her as he began dancing, and Mercy was relieved. Releasing a deep breath, she tried to force herself to calm down.

Something inside was gnawing at Mercy. Did August want to be here?

She had foregone drinking mushroom tea and hadn't drunk any alcohol yet. She planned to have a few drinks later if all went well. Hopefully, she thought, August was just tired, and it was all her imagination. Something about his eyes tonight...he seemed distant. He must have had a long, hard day. She wondered if there was a way that she could make it right.

Looking around the room as she danced, Mercy spotted Amelia standing with Jacob. She almost wished August would be honest about not wanting to dance so she could dance with her friends. Slapping on a faux smile, Mercy looked back to August and did her best to enjoy herself.

After a few moments, August leaned in and asked, "Are you thirsty? You've been working all day. I'll go get you a drink. Mango juice cocktail?"

Smiling, Mercy nodded and said, "Sure, I'll go talk to Amelia and Jacob."

Nodding, August walked toward the crowd around the bar. The loss of the heat from his body sent a shiver down

Mercy's spine. She looked down at her own hands and wondered if there was something wrong with her.

As Mercy walked over to her friends, she could hear Amelia speaking to the group.

"So far, we have developed several powerful antibiotics by culturing the rich soil around the cave; one mild, topical anti-fungal to treat the ringed flesh-eating fungal infections; a pain reliever; and a second type of anesthesia. I even found a compound in cashew fruit that I think may help our people's late-onset memory loss. I was already close to a treatment when I was taken from my village on the other side of the dead volcanoes, and with the tech I have now, I can create a real medication. I have had excellent results testing the cashew fruit in its basic form. As a concentrated medication, I think I will see a much stronger effect. But as far as the nanotech, it is still at a standstill until we can find a way to make them move," Amelia explained to Jacob.

"Can we get started on some kind of a treatment or vaccine to keep us from going under when we're shot with the darts?" Jacob asked, black brows raised, eagerly waiting for confirmation.

"Yes and I also have a numbing injection in the works. Some of my scouts discovered a miniature vine version of the coca plant from Jael's world, but it's a mild variation. I was able to easily duplicate the chemical structure to manipulate it and create multiple anesthetics. My new medical team is fantastic, and they've caught on so quickly. We will start working on a method to keep us from going under soon. Did you say it was Sarah who sent the word out through the village about our need for healers?" Amelia asked, all while sliding her eyes from Jacob to Mercy and then back to Jacob.

"Yes, it was August's mother, Sarah. She has been instrumental in the recruiting process. The spread of language in the village has been slow, but only a third of our own people are currently without the gift. Only those who have the gift know about the base. I wish we could recruit from other places. I estimate there are no more than five thousand of our people living in villages and towns on the planet. We are the only village on this side of the dead volcanoes, but the town on the mountain is large. There must be over a thousand people living up there since they are so rarely taken. I would like to send a team up to see if they have anyone they can spare," Jacob said as he trailed his finger along the condensation of his drink.

Approaching the group, August caught the last part of what Jacob had said.

"I wonder how they're doing after that brain fungus attack. I hope it's over, but something tells me they're being flushed out," August said as he handed the drink to Mercy, who was standing next to him.

"Thank you," Mercy said to August before turning to Amelia and asking, "Do you think we should try to find a cure and send it up to them?"

Amelia turned to look at Mercy with her blue eyes wide, "Yes, absolutely. I have already been working on one. I have found one mild anti-fungal, but it's only topical. Unfortunately, I've found that most substances which are toxic to fungi are also highly toxic to us. It is quite complicated to find a treatment that could work for something as aggressive as cerebral fungal infections. I am also not entirely convinced the fungus was not bio-engineered by the humans. That fact would complicate matters significantly. I am testing as many soil samples as the team can get to me."

"I can assign more people to the effort," Jacob said as he looked at Amelia.

Nodding, Amelia looked at Mercy and said, "Should we go dance and let them talk?"

Beaming, Mercy looked at August. He just smiled at her as Amelia took her hand and dragged her off to dance. Luna and Zoe were already on the dance floor, and Mercy couldn't wait to join them with Amelia.

August watched as Amelia escorted Mercy to their friends, and he warmed at the look of utter joy on Mercy's face as she began spinning with excitement.

"Was the fight between Oz and Callum as bad as Callum made it seem?" Jacob asked August, breaking the short pause.

"No! It was hilarious. I stole Oz's dried fruit snacks from on top of his pack and watched the whole thing. It was way too interesting to walk away from," August admitted with a smirk as he shrugged his shoulders and took a sip of his cocktail.

Unable to control his laughter, Jacob said, "You have to be kidding! You didn't just sit there and eat snacks while they yelled at each other, did you?"

"They didn't look at me once," August said, also unable to control his laughter.

Rolling his eyes while he chuckled, Jacob pushed his long, blue fishtail braids off his shoulder and said, "I'm just glad they didn't throw punches. I thought someone was getting hit on that trip."

"Who got hit?" Callum asked intently as he walked up to Jacob with two cups filled with a new watermelon cocktail that their mess hall cook, Risk, had come up with.

"Oh, nothing, Cal. It's not important," Jacob said

nonchalantly as he took the cup from Callum and pressed a kiss to his cheek.

Peering at Jacob with narrowing eyes, Callum said, "Whatever, just down your drink so we can dance, and I can finally grind on that ass."

Reaching over, Callum slapped Jacob on the rear, causing him to choke on a sip of his drink. Jacob coughed a few times and glared into his partner's bright blue eyes.

Callum laughed before throwing his cup back to down his drink, then he pulled an unprepared and stiff Jacob onto the dance floor. Jacob looked back at August and shrugged a shoulder just as Callum spun him around.

"I showed up just in time, I see," Carter said in his deep voice from behind August.

Looking around at the now-emptied area, August said, "So, I guess you did."

"Have I missed anything eventful?" Carter asked, a drink in his hand, which surprised August.

He hadn't taken the usually focused Carter as someone who enjoyed a drink, but he guessed he had a lot to learn about his friends. During their life of silence in the village, their people had such meager opportunities to get to know one another. August now made a point to start paying more attention to his friends.

"Nothing too exciting. Jacob was almost busted talking about Oz and Callum's argument in the woods," August admitted, a smirk spreading on his lips.

Chuckling, Carter said, "That is something I'm sad I missed."

"How are you doing with the tech for the cold plasma swords? I've been itching to practice with them," August asked, his orange eyes alight with excitement at the prospect of such a powerful weapon in his hands.

He loved the movies Jael had watched with epic space battles and swords made of light. Not knowing that he was pitching an idea at the time, he had told Jacob all about the light swords, which August found so fascinating. All he wanted to know was how such a device could be possible, and Jacob took that to mean August wanted a similar weapon. August had no intention of telling Jacob or anyone else the truth, as his dream sword was now becoming a reality.

"It's almost finished. Jacob did an excellent job bringing your idea to life. It needs an extended handle for the extra battery space, just in case you need it to last for two weeks."

"I know the battle suits' batteries will last quite a while, but I wanted the cold plasma swords to last longer since Jacob said there's a drain when they're used for cutting," August explained, sure they would run into situations where the sword would be used for cutting through whatever may block their paths.

"I understand. I'll have the team extend the handle then. You should be able to start training with the weapon within the week, and twenty more will be completed before next week. I'll have a schedule made to ensure the batteries are regularly charged for your practice sessions since they keep dying in the cavern."

"Great. I have a good idea of who I am pulling for the tactical team that's heading for the human base up north. I want the tac team trained with them first, and then we can begin training those staying behind."

Nodding, Carter looked out onto the dance floor and smiled to himself. Following suit, August did the same and spotted Mercy. She was dancing, smiling, and laughing with Amelia and Luna. Her beautiful brown fishtail braids were half up and pinned to her head in a halo.

Mercy was glowing, and August couldn't tear his eyes away from her. She had become such a pillar of strength in his life; he felt like he owed her. If it weren't for her, he wouldn't have made it through his loss of Mazarin. Mercy pulled him from the depths of his despair. He had lost so many friends over the years but losing Oz and then the woman he loved, Oz's sister? It nearly broke him. Mercy had been the one who didn't give up and forced him to emerge from his cocoon of pain. She deserved so much more than the miserable existence in the caves and the silent world above.

They *all* did.

Mercy slid her golden eyes over to August and waved for him to come dance. Shrugging his shoulders at Carter, he jogged to her and joined the group that was dancing with Mercy.

Taking her in his arms, August fell into the rhythms of the music and rolled his hips along with Mercy's. Turning her around and pressing her backside into him, August's excitement was becoming evident, and Mercy could feel it against her rear as she pressed against him.

August leaned over and whispered into her ear, saying, "Keep doing that, Mercy, and..." he trailed off as he snaked his hand under the hem of her skirt from behind, making her shudder. She ground her hips against him, and he softly slid his finger down the seam of her heat before gently pinching her inner thigh.

Without thought, Mercy grabbed his hand and began pulling him to their apartment, nestled in the cave wall.

36

Sitting at the front of the large room, August watched as the team began filing in and finding seats. Luna stood next to the whiteboard at the front of the room.

August noticed that Zoe was in the group, as well as a few other people he knew from the village. The team was mainly selected by Carter, and they all seemed eager to get started.

"As you all know, we have been selected to set up the military's structure. This will be essential for our people's offensive against our enemy. Our skills and technology have advanced to the point that, it's now time to establish a command structure and begin training," Luna explained, brushing her unruly white fishtail braids behind her shoulder.

A dark-green man with knotted black hair, who August didn't recognize, spoke up and asked, "Will we also establish the military's laws, or will Jacob's government formation team be taking over that task?"

"What's your name?" Luna asked, her bright yellow eyes shining in the bright white lights of the room.

"Pike."

"Pike, our only objective here is to set up the structure. You've all been selected by Carter because of your superior organizational skills. Jacob's team was selected based on their incomparable analytical and engineering skills," Luna explained, while walking to the whiteboard to write the ideas and suggestions from the group.

With an open marker in hand, she turned and faced the room. Pike nodded his head in understanding, and Luna saw nods from a few others, so she continued.

"August was voted General in the initial voting process, and he will be the commander of the ground forces since that's the branch we're beginning with. *When* we succeed in taking back our planet, we will establish a space branch for our military, but for now, we will focus on the existing need."

"We should have specialty branches within the ground forces for technology, education, physical training, medicine, as well as the main branches of physical and digital infantry," Zoe suggested while tapping a pencil on the table.

Luna lifted a single brow, slid her eyes to August, and said, "Carter clearly picked the right people for this team."

Luna began writing the suggestions down on the whiteboard as more hands shot up. After she finished writing everything, Luna turned and noticed August looking contently at the whiteboard.

"Do you have any suggestions to add?" Luna asked August.

"We need a special team made up of those who are physically and mentally able to handle the journey to the human's base," August said with his hand still rubbing his chin in thought.

"We should probably select the team and start training immediately. It will take at least a month to get everyone familiar with the new weapons and battle armor. How is production going?" Zoe asked, still tapping her pencil.

Luna answered, "We are fully stocked, and more uniforms will be issued once we are finished here. You're right, Zoe. August, I'm sure you have an idea of who you would like to be on your team, but I would also suggest allowing others to tryout after we conduct testing for placement."

"My thoughts exactly. I think you all have this down. I am going to head out to see Carter and Jacob and let them know we are ready to start testing," August said before rising from his seat. The stool scooted back with a screech against the floor.

Luna nodded and said, "It looks like the week I blocked off on the schedule for this work won't be needed. We should be finished today by the end of the shift."

August began walking toward the door and looked back with a smirk as he said, "I'll leave you to it then."

Heading to Carter's office, August began thinking about the people he wanted on his team. This would be a harrowing journey, and he needed nothing but the best.

August walked into Carter's office and found him preparing for a class. Carter was looking forward to teaching it after the military branches were established.

When Carter looked up, August said, "Luna's team was well selected. They should be finished by the end of shift today. She said to let you know we're ready for base-wide testing to begin."

Lifting his black eyebrows, his fishtail braid fell over his shoulder as Carter turned and asked, "It's just now 11:00 a.m. That only took a few hours. The project was taken seriously?"

August shrugged and said, "Zoe seems to understand most of the needs and immediately listed everything. Not much to decide after that. I'm going to Jacob's lab after I let Mercy know that she and Callum will be heading up uniform distribution. I want Zoe as my second. Something tells me she has grit."

Nodding, August started to walk away, and Carter said, "A wise choice. We should have more parties if this kind of productivity is the result."

"Carter, only you would say something so square about a party," August scoffed quietly with a smile as he rounded the corner.

He could hear Carter chuckling at his comment as he walked down the hall to Mercy's office. Sometimes August wondered if Carter's stoic façade would eventually crack, or if it really was his true self.

Tapping his knuckles on Mercy's office door, he heard her moving things around and mumbling.

The door swung open, and Mercy said, "Oh, it's you. I thought for sure it would be Callum coming back just to be an ass and pester me about which of the blue alien books is my favorite."

Mercy stuck her head out of her office door and looked both ways, expecting Callum to pop out. They'd had a silly disagreement over which of Jael's romance books was the best, and neither of them could give it up. Mercy loved the first in the series the best, but Callum liked the fourth. Callum had walked out when Mercy told him he only liked that one because the woman in it had red hair. He growled something under his breath about the "uncivilized wild brute" and "parallels" before he briskly walked off.

Callum had dated a beautiful red-haired woman in his early twenties who disappeared a year after they ended things.

Mercy quit thinking about it and continued doodling her fashion designs.

"You and Callum will oversee uniform distribution. It is up to you what that looks like; just make sure it happens. You can deliver, or they can come by and pick them up, whatever seems more efficient. Everyone should receive two sets. If you run out, we will reassign a few people to uniforms' construction for a couple of days," August said, his eyes narrowing.

August was still confused as to why Mercy and Callum would be arguing over a book but quickly decided to leave that alone.

He had already learned a valuable lesson -- never get between two people who are upset with one another. He wanted to be there for the show, but he didn't want to be a part of the drama. He knew precisely how petty that was and didn't care in the slightest.

"Alright. I will probably just deliver them myself. Since we finished up the battle suits, my job has become a bit slow. Plus, I'm not sure when Callum is coming back or if he will go home early, so I'll just do it all," Mercy said, a smile hinting at the corner of her lips.

Nodding, August said, "I'll see you later at the apartment. I'm headed to Jacob's office. Get ready. We're ready to start testing people for military branch selection, then comes the physical trials to see who's going on the mission to the human base."

Mercy's face dropped as fear blossomed in her chest. She nodded then said, "What if, um...what if I don't make the team?"

His face twisted and a snarl formed on his lips. "What? Mercy, you've got to be kidding me. You're one of our most agile people. I'm honestly surprised you said that."

"Why? Most people are not built like me. I just thought that since most are built more like you, they would be automatically selected over a person like me. I know I'm capable of plenty, don't get me wrong. But, don't we *want* to send our physically strongest people? I'm not trying to demean my own body type. If you were going to arm wrestle, wouldn't you want the biggest arm?"

August furrowed his brow and said, "Physical ability is only part of the equation, and you are just as valuable a soldier as me. Some of our people are physically smaller, but that does *not* mean the members of the team will be tall and have big muscles. Jael, Amelia, Thorne, Zoe, and Luna are all agile people with several different body types and will all be going and fighting alongside the rest of the team. They are just as capable as you and I. Physical size or capability has nothing to do with the power inside of a body.

"Not to mention, you designed the armor. They might need your expertise," August explained with a wink.

Smirking with pride, Mercy said, "That does make sense. I hadn't thought about it that way. I guess I've just been too nervous about it to think correctly."

Pausing to breathe, Mercy looked up into August's bright orange eyes and softly said with a shaking voice, "The thought of being separated from you...it terrifies me."

Unable to hold back the rush of fear, panic settled in her chest, and it tightened to the point of pain. Struggling for breath, Mercy slid her eyes shut. August grasped Mercy's chin and tilted it up toward him, and she opened her eyes.

Looking into Mercy's golden eyes, August whispered against her forehead, "Mercy, that's not going to happen. It would take an army to keep me away. I would conquer *worlds*."

Tears sprung into her eyes, and August tilted her head back to press a kiss against her lips.

"Now, you better get to work distributing those uniforms before Callum shows up, and I have to pretend to look for something while I listen in on your ridiculous disagreement."

"You are *exactly* like your mother," Mercy said. August threw his head back and burst into laughter.

Shaking her head and narrowing her eyes, Mercy slowly closed the door as August chuckled to himself and walked toward Jacob's office. He had never felt so called out in his life. He may have his father's reddish bronze skin, but he had certainly inherited his mother's personality.

As he neared the door of Jacob's office and reached to open it, with no warning, his body was in the air then slammed against the wall across from the door. August sat stunned as loose pieces of the cave's ceiling began falling to the ground, along with a thick layer of dust. Coughing from the force of the impact, dust billowed up and temporarily blocked his view of the door.

Vigorously shaking his head to loosen the dust from his braids, August looked up at Jacob's office and leaped to his feet. He sprinted into the lab and found Jacob on the charred stone ground, slowly rising to his feet. He left a perfect imprint of himself on the soot-coated floor. He was wearing a fully sealed, formerly white, suit connected to an airline. From the round shape of the lump running over the top of his head, he was also wearing a helmet under the suit. He was alone in his lab and walked over to the transparent blast wall to open the door. He entered the containment zone, where he began taking off the suit, then he put it inside the sterilizing bay.

Once he removed his helmet, he opened the containment zone's outer door and casually said, "Bad news. I may have blown open access to a new cavern, and we're going to need to do some construction."

Furrowing his dark blue brow, he stopped and then seemed to speak to himself as he said, "We can use it for the launch tubes and ramps. Yes, that's exactly what we will do."

Looking up at a gaping August, Jacob excitedly explained, "The good news is, the new biofuel is more than explosive enough to power the rockets! This will easily create enough thrust to get the rocket out of the atmosphere and into orbit. I only used a spoonful."

"How big was the spoon?! Is testing for the biofuel over?!" August asked wildly, his orange eyes blazing from the shot of octopamine that was pumping through his blood after the blast.

Laughing nervously at August's demeanor, Jacob said, "Yes, thankfully I was able to get a reading and *not* blow up the sensor before the data could be collected."

Moving like a bolt of lightning, Oz came flying through the lab door and yelled, "What the fuck just happened?!"

Straightening himself with his eyes wide enough to show the white all the way around his irises, Jacob said, "The biofuel test went a little *too* right."

Deadpanning Jacob, Oz said with deadly calm, "Next time you do explosive testing, you will let me know *beforehand*."

After a deep breath, Oz seethed, "I thought we were being bombed!"

Turning to storm out, Oz scrubbed his hands over his face and shot his arms down at his sides before he took a step.

"Why do engineering geniuses have to be so God-damned stupid!" Oz whispered to himself as he stalked out of the lab.

Without skipping a beat Jacob whipped back around to August and said, "I think we need to make a sap collecting trip so I can fireproof the lab. I've burned half of the lab down, four times now. I think Oz might be getting irritated."

"You think?" August said sarcastically, with his eyebrows furrowed at his socially-oblivious friend.

37

Back at her house, Mercy visited Rew and refilled the spider's fruit bowls. Rew had somehow figured out that Mercy loved it when she made silk. It couldn't have been all the dancing around that Mercy did when Rew wove a new sheet of silk, could it? The sweet spider had been going wild with her weaving, and Mercy kept returning to a silk-filled home.

Rew's silk was one of Mercy's favorites. It was getting to the point that she could trade it since she had so much. Her back room had folded stacks of it, taking up every open space on her craft table.

There was an unfamiliar knock at her door, and Mercy had a sick feeling in the pit of her gut. She turned and stared at the door a moment, wondering who might be on the other side.

She slowly opened her door and peered outside to find Luna masked with layered silk, another one in her outstretched hand. Looking from the mask to Luna's fearful eyes, Mercy slowly reached up, took the mask, and promptly put it on. Once it was tied behind her head, she looked at Luna with fear in her eyes.

A mask could only mean one thing.

The fungal infection that had struck the mountain town was now somewhere in their village.

Panic filled Mercy as she quickly checked the ties on her mask, tested the tightness on her face, then invited Luna inside. Luna stepped inside her door but didn't shut it.

Sticking her hand out to Luna, Mercy initiated the connection and said, "Please tell me it's not the fungus."

Luna peered into Mercy's eyes and lowered her brows before saying, "It is. We confirmed five cases in the village, with one more suspected. We've already quarantined them, but we don't know whom they've come into contact with. Everyone above the base must stay above, and everyone below is staying below. We can't risk the airborne spores getting into the base."

"Who is left topside? Anyone, that I know?" Mercy pleaded, hoping the rest of her friends were safe inside the base.

Shaking her head and then leaning just inside Mercy's door frame, Luna said, "Just me. It was a shift change, and I managed to stop everyone at the mouth of the cave."

"Thank the creator for you, Luna. Will you stay at your house, or do you want to stay with me?" Mercy asked, hoping she didn't have to watch Luna walk away.

"We should stay separate since we don't know who could have been exposed. I'm sorry. I should probably go," Luna said as she finally looked back up at Mercy. The fear in her eyes was overwhelming.

"Shit, I have to stay here by myself?" Mercy asked, disappointment evident in her eyes.

"I'm so sorry, Mercy," Luna said as she broke the connection and stepped out of the open door.

Luna looked back at Mercy before she left and rotated her wrist to signal that she would be back to check on her. Luna slowly shut the door. Mercy had to know it wasn't personal. She wouldn't risk her friend; she couldn't.

Luna set off in a jog. When she reached Sarah's house, she found her and August's father closing the wooden window covers. Sarah saw Luna, and they walked around the house to be under the cover of the back porch to connect.

"We heard. Is Mercy OK?" Sarah asked, worry marring her gaze.

Luna looked at her with sadness in her eyes and said, "I couldn't bear the look on her face. I had to shut the door and leave. I'll check on her. She knows I'll be back."

Sighing behind her mask, Sarah shook her head and said, "Are you saying you're offering to be the courier for the base?"

"Yes, of course," Luna said, nodding and not understanding why Sarah wouldn't be happy to have a courier.

With a pointed look, Sarah said, "You should quarantine and let someone old do it. There's no reason for you to risk yourself. I knew your mother. She would never forgive me if I didn't at least try to stop you from doing this. Please, Luna."

"You know I can't do that. My grandmother was a healer, and she taught me never to walk away when I'm needed, even if I'm risking my own life. *Always* risk it." Luna said with her eyes steady on Sarah's.

Sarah's eyes softened, and she grasped Luna's arm, then softly said, "Luna, you are everything our people need to win this war. People think impossible wars are won by bravery, and that's not necessarily true. They're won by the *selfless.*"

Luna broke the connection and nodded her head to Sarah, her former village leader. Luna didn't want Sarah to see the emotion welling in her eyes. She still didn't understand why Sarah didn't want to be President. She would have been elected unanimously if she had run. Sarah wasn't old by any means, so it must be because of one of her famous "feelings."

No one ever questioned Sarah's intuition. Her wisdom lay in something deeper, Luna thought to herself as she headed toward the base. The leaves crunched under her boots, and the wind whistled between the trees as she walked. Luna did her best to keep her faith and hold it together, but inside she was screaming in fear.

Cerebral fungal infections spared no one, and the person's end was torturous. There was much to be feared from this infection, not just death. In the final stages of the disease, people hunted down other people and attempted to eat them alive. They would need to keep track of the infected, or they could have far more deaths than just those from the infection.

Once she arrived, she used the small hidden view screen inside the lava tube to call Jacob and give him an update.

"Luna, how is Mercy? And what did Sarah say?" Jacob asked as his head formed out of thin air in front of her on the holoscreen.

"Sarah already knew and was sealing her home when I arrived. I told her I was the courier for the base, and she wasn't exactly happy about that. Mercy is OK. She's upset. I'll keep checking on her. Next time I go see her, I'll bring her the communication tablet you mentioned before I left.

When do you think Carter will have the new wireless network up and running?" Luna asked, hoping for some good news.

"It will be finished later this afternoon. Stay in the area, and I will signal to you when the bag with the devices is ready to distribute. They will be set up to be entirely silent and have text communication, so the microphones around the village won't pick anything up. Carter mentioned that there would be video options once you're a safe distance from the village. Have you finished your original mission to locate and loop the village's microphones' sound feeds?" Jacob asked as he pushed his hair away from his forehead.

"No, I learned about the fungus right as I was scanning the first zone. I saw a child with a mask on running through the village in the distance while banging sticks," Luna said as she shifted from one foot to the other.

Jacob nodded and said, "Continue your mission as best you can. I'm sorry it's you stuck out there, Luna. We're all sorry."

"If it wasn't me, it would be someone else," Luna said as she adjusted her mask.

"Amelia will be working around the clock with her team. We made an exception, and she shared her physician's knowledge with a few of her most promising team members. We should have some kind of treatment soon, we hope," Jacob explained, exhaustion written all over his face.

Luna nodded, and Jacob signed off. She walked away and jumped out of the lava tube onto the ground. The rustle of the leaves in the woods was her only company. Luna slid down an enormous tree trunk as she took a seat to rest a bit before heading out to finish scanning the trees for the microphones.

Taking deep breaths, Luna tried to calm her racing heart.

Once they got their new, hidden antenna up and running, Carter had said that he was confident they could identify the rest of the microphones' signals.

The new antenna was assembled inside the hollow of a carved-out tree. It was wired to thin, clear solar panels that were attached to the canopy's tree branches. It had a wireless signal that connected with another antenna camouflaged inside the lava tube. The antenna in the lava tube was hard-wired into the base. It would also serve as a hub for the cameras' extensions that were soon to be installed for the surveillance system.

After a short rest, Luna rose from the ground and grabbed the bag with her instruments in it. She pulled the signal tracker from her bag, switched on the small transparent device, and it lit up in her hands. She looked around the map on the screen and headed back toward the village to get her work done.

No sense in just sitting around while everyone else was scrambling, she thought to herself. Her pounding heart wouldn't allow her much rest anyway. After a few minutes of walking, her tablet showed a red dot blinking about a half mile away, much closer to the village.

She had found one. After she recorded the location, Luna could hardly contain herself as she headed back to the base with her discovery.

38

August, Jacob, and Jael were setting out supplies for Luna when she returned from the edge of town with the first microphone's location. Mercy had made a tent weeks ago, and August and Jacob were setting it up in the woods a little way from the entrance of the base. Jael was sorting food for Luna.

Luna's heart dropped when she noticed that August and Jacob had masks to protect them from the deadly fungal spores, but Jael didn't.

"Jael! Where is your mask?" Luna asked, the stress in her tone building with every word.

Throwing her palms up, Jael just smiled and said, "It's alright. According to Amelia, I am immune. You don't need to worry about me at all."

With the relief sinking in and tears gathering in her eyes, Luna's voice cracked as she said, "Thank you, all of you, for doing this."

Without hesitation, Jael threw her arms around Luna and said, "We love you. You should know you are so much more than simply our friend. You're our family. How could we just leave you out here with nothing?"

Chills ran down Jael's spine at her own comment about being left out in the elements with nothing. Images flashed in her mind of finding the scavenger bugs feasting on Oz's oozing, burned body. The fear threatened to overtake her, and she shook as she forced herself to swallow down a deep breath. Blinking away the dryness in her eyes, she focused on Luna and tried to regain her bearings.

"I presumed I would come back to a pile of camping gear. Not a tent being erected with everything I could possibly need. Thank you, and I love you too," Luna said with a grin behind her mask.

"We will get through this. Amelia knows you were exposed, and she's not going to stop until she finds a cure. She said you could come inside after seven days, but we all know that you're going to go help the village instead, aren't you?" Jacob asked pointedly, one black eyebrow raised.

Staring back at him, Luna sighed as worry etched itself across her brilliant yellow eyes. Quietly she said, "Yes. How can I not go help them? Who else is going to nail the ropes to the trees when we run out of empty houses?"

Closing his eyes tight, Jacob forced a breath from his pinched lips. The memories given to him by his long-passed aunt about the last outbreak were equally heart-breaking and terrifying. His chest tightened as the images of gnashing teeth and the chittering of those near death rolled through his mind. Those who lasted the longest would have mouths full of broken teeth after having eaten their own tongues in desperate hunger. A few would become ravaged enough to consume their own arms, leaving gaping wounds that revealed their shining black bones underneath. Gulping air through the thick mask, Jacob shook his head, trying to rid himself of the intrusive images.

"I know my parents are already arguing. My father is probably preparing to go help them too. His grandfather did the same thing during the last outbreak, and he eventually caught that damn fungus," August said, his intent more than evident.

Unable to hide the fear in his tan eyes, Jacob looked at August and said, "I am sorry for his loss. I remember receiving memories of him from Sarah more than once as a young man. He was a great man and leader. Once when I was a child, I was caught exploring too far from the village, and my aunt shared her memories from that same outbreak with me. Those images have disturbed me ever since."

"Amelia will find a cure. She just needs a little time," Jael said just above a whisper.

Turning his head around to Luna, Jacob said, "Jael's right. Amelia is going to find a cure. And maybe even a vaccine if it pans out. She's working on several different options. I heard her say she needed a sample of blood from an infected person to test a new antifungal. One of her team members found a promising soil sample in a boggy area a few days ago. If I get you a med bag, can you get those items for her? She doesn't know that I am sending you. She will be angry, but I know you would be mad if we sent someone else."

"Yes, get me the med kit right away. I'm sure the infected man has already been restrained. He has a few days, maybe, before he passes, and then they will have to haul his body away. I think we should utilize the area where the mountain people are depositing their dead. The place is in a valley, and there isn't as much wind. It's the best place I know for this," Luna said as she kept her eyes on Jacob.

A wind blew through the trees and rustled the leaves, knocking a few from their perches high above and sending them floating to the ground around them.

"Why can't you just bury or burn the dead person?" Jael asked, not understanding anything and filled with fear over their comments regarding the course of the parasitic fungal infection.

"The fungus stem will just grow through the soil. Burning the body doesn't work on the spores, just like burning doesn't kill the parasites on this world. We don't have the time or resources to build an incinerator right now anyway. Much of the microbial life here can't easily be killed," Luna explained, hoping this time she was wrong.

After August finished with the tent, he walked over to stand by Jacob and said, "Plus, we would have to find patient zero, and that could take weeks. We need to head back inside. Luna, we will send out the med kit as soon as we can get our hands on one."

Nodding, Luna entered her tent with her bags and began setting up her cot and bedding. They had given her plenty of tech to work on. She looked over at the tablets -- she needed to distribute those right away. Mercy was alone and had to remain silent.

Guilt wrapped around Luna, and she headed off to take the tablets to Mercy and Sarah and give Sarah the others to distribute. About a third of the people working in the base were trapped in their homes. Though she knew that she should stay put, Luna quickly talked herself out of it and headed back to town.

Once she reached Sarah's house, she set the wrapped

bundle of tablets on her back porch, then headed to Mercy's to do the same.

The village was silent, the kind of silence that makes one's skin crawl.

Not one window was open, and not one person was outside.

She knew her senses were not to be trusted, and any sound caused her heart to pound within her body. When she reached Mercy's house, she could only hear the rustling of the trees and the rumble of a storm in the distance. She placed the bundle of food and the tablet on Mercy's doorstep and knocked before backing away.

Footsteps sounded, then Mercy swung open the door, delighted to see Luna. She waved at her and grabbed the pack before swiftly shutting the door.

Alone once again, Luna blew out a breath and headed back down the path toward her house, then to her campsite in the woods. Her home had been empty for months. It was being used as a spot where her friends could access the woods behind the village without causing suspicion from above. As she walked through, she placed her hand on the wall. Luna wondered if she would ever see the wooden walls of her home again.

Returning to the campsite after the deliveries, she plopped on her cot and turned on her tablet. Peering over at the high-tech helmet that sat near the end of the cot, Luna gave it an appreciative pat before the light in her lap grabbed her attention. Quickly flipping through the holoscreens, the blue light shined on her face and engulfed her in the darkened tent.

Her feelings over what her brilliant team had accomplished were surreal.

Then, she heard a woman's voice call out from the woods, "Luna?"

Popping her head out, Luna spotted Jael and waved her inside the tent. The thunder cracked in the sky above, and she knew a downpour would begin at any moment.

"I brought you a fruit pastry. We had some left over from the party, and I figured you could use them. I also brought the med kit. Please be careful. I don't know what we would do without you, Luna. I, I don't know what *I* would do," Jael said, shaking her head and unable to finish.

The words, without *you*, fell silent on her tongue as tears gathered in her eyes.

"I will survive this. I promise. I have unwavering faith in Carter's team. They developed and tested the airtight helmet thoroughly. I am sure the helmet can keep the airborne spores out," Luna said while reaching out and holding onto Jael's clenched fist.

She may have sounded confident, but inside, her heart was breaking at her own faux faith. The fabricated words of strength went sour on her tongue.

Sitting down on the cot, Luna cleared her throat and brought her eyes back up to her standing friend. Jael said, "I made sure to pass around the first stack of finished tablets to all our friends. You can text or video call any of us anytime. We all have permission from Oz to take your call, even on shift. He is worried about you. And Mercy."

"I'm worried about Mercy," Luna said as she squeezed Jael's hand.

Sitting down next to Luna on the cot, Jael said, "Me too. I wish I could go visit her. It makes me sick to think about her all alone in her house, not able to speak."

"Do you think we are being attacked by the fungus because of the humans Oz and August killed?" Luna asked, her white eyebrows furrowed in thought about her own words.

Looking like she had seen a ghost, Jael said with a shaking voice, "That's exactly why, Luna. Oh my, I, uh, I need to get back inside and tell Oz what you just said. Right now."

"Let's call him. It'll be quicker," Luna offered.

Nodding, Jael took the tablet from Luna, quickly scrolled to Oz's information, and dialed his tablet.

Light burst from the tablet, forming a holoscreen floating in the air above it.

"Luna?" Oz said, his hologram face suddenly displayed in the space above the transparent tablet.

Jael slid her brown eyes to Luna's and said, "Tell Oz what you just said to me."

Wearily, Luna turned her head and looked over at Oz's hologram.

Through her mask, Luna said, "Do you think we are being infected because you and August killed those humans in the woods?"

Tilting his head to the side, his irises dilated as he said, "Interesting. We are receiving *retaliation*. Fuck, I was so busy helping Amelia in her lab I hadn't stopped to think of why it was happening."

"We need those samples for Amelia. Do your best to get them, but please be careful. We haven't broken the news to Amelia that we're sending you to do this. I would like for you to be back at your campsite and unmarred before we break the news," Oz said, one corner of his mouth lifting in a sad smile before hanging up.

The holoscreen faded into thin air while Luna and Jael stared into the space where Oz's face had just been.

Wrapping her arm around and hugging Luna, Jael said, "I love you. Make sure to go and check on Mercy for me. I already miss you both."

As water droplets tapped her forehead, dripping from the leaves of the soaring trees, Luna heard groaning and knocking sounds coming from inside the home she was slowly creeping toward. She knew the man inside was infected. The fungus caused a terrifying change inside a person's mind.

The fungal spores settled into the brain once they pierced the blood-brain barrier. As the disease ran its course, people would chitter and gnash their teeth at anything that was alive.

As the infection sank its claws deep between the neurons, people became mentally unstable, and their gazes were filled with violence and thirst. Like sprawling vines, the fungus' tendrils wove themselves through the living brain matter. Her people were already blessed with powerful physiques, and this cerebral fungal infection only amplified their strength.

Her brow was damp with sweat mixed with rain droplets from the oak leaves high above. Luna's mind went to the knowledge from Jael's world about a similar infection among insects. After reviewing Jael's memories of zoology class, she found that it was called the Zombie Fungus on Earth, and she didn't want to admit how right that was. A shiver snaked down her spine in the humid warmth of the air.

She looked between the leaves at the auras and prayed to the creator that the infected man wouldn't bite her while she tried to collect the blood sample.

A bite was the easiest way to transmit the infection, aside from inhaling the spores that poured into the air from the man's nasal cavity and mouth. Eventually, as the body died and cooled, some of the spores growing inside of him would take root on the decaying flesh and grow into three-foot fungal stems that protruded from any holes it could find in the skull.

Sometimes it burrowed its own holes.

If the air was cool enough, the stems would begin their growth before the victim was dead. Disgust rolled through Luna, and she brought her forearm to her face, breathing deep and attempting to rid herself of the intruding thoughts.

Desperately blinking away the images her mind was cruelly fabricating from her growing fear, Luna slipped around the house and under the tree cover. She stopped and closed her eyes before she put on the airtight helmet that Jacob had lent her. The helmet slipped over her head and seemed comfortable. She noticed the view inside was astonishingly wide as she gathered her thick hair and pushed it inside the back.

Luna smirked at the ingenious addition. Jacob must have known his people would refuse to cut their hair and had left an area in the back of the helmet for a bundle of braids or a bun. Reaching under the soft fabric lip in the front, she pulled the cloth mask off her face and sealed the malleable bottom edge with a quick horizontal touch to the material. The helmet was supposed to be space ready, and she was about to find out for sure in the ultimate test of her own will.

After the high-tech helmet was sealed around her neck, she felt her ears pop from the change in pressure. A soft but confident feminine voice said through the speaker, "Luna, this is Zoe. Are you prepared to enter the house?"

Whispering, "Yes," into the airtight helmet was nerve-wracking, but she audibly swallowed and clenched her fists, while assuring herself she could do this.

Zoe spoke again and said, "I am back-up, and your open line to the base. I am watching from the camera above your line of sight, and we have Pike on your rear camera. We will send someone in after you if things don't go according to plan. Just get that blood sample and come back to us."

After a bit of rustling, Pike spoke up and said in an entirely too cheery voice, "Hi, Luna."

With a dramatic sigh of relief, Luna took one more deep breath and exhaled slowly before saying, "Thank you. Thank you both."

Approaching the back door, Luna squeezed her eyes shut then opened them slowly.

She could do this.

Her friends were with her and had her back.

Turning to face the living area's window, she pulled her knife free from her belt. After hooking her short knife into the edge of the window cover, Luna slid it inside the crack and opened the window with a faint creak. Then, she reached around inside to unhook the lock on the door. She could have just walked in through the man's front door, but she would not have been able to wear the high-tech helmet. The back of his home was hidden by tree cover, but the front was visible from the sky.

As she dropped the wooden latch, it made a scraping noise against the door. The banging started back up at the wall to her left. With her heart pounding, she eased open the door, and it made a loud scratch against the floor. The sound elicited a high-pitched screeching whine from the next room, sending fear shooting through her nerves like lightning.

Closing her eyes, she whispered, "Fuck," under her breath.

She heard Zoe inhale sharply before quietly saying in encouragement, "We are right here with you."

As she walked into the bedroom, she was something a little more than *thankful* for the helmet. The infected man had dropped his bowels more than a few times in the last few days, and the contents were now smeared around and ground into the silk mattress below him. Unable to keep from sneering her lip in disgust, Luna did her best to ignore the filth.

The man was hissing and writhing on the bed as Luna sighed and scanned the scene. Pulling free the rope looped around her belt, she moved closer so she could tie his shifting torso down onto the bed. She planned to take some blood from one of his legs to avoid getting anywhere near his face and those sharp teeth.

As she sat on the floor on one side of the bed and scooted in, the man stopped thrashing and slowly leaned over as far as the ropes around his arms allowed. His eyes remained on her as he moved, and his pale honey-colored irises shook wildly while trying to focus on Luna. The bone-chilling chittering of his teeth began as she crept along the floor toward the foot of the bed.

With shaking hands, she tossed the rope over the bed, and the man snapped his cracked teeth at her lifted arm. As she swung the rope to slide it underneath the bed, it kept getting snagged on something.

Audibly sighing, Luna twisted around and stuck her legs under the bed to kick whatever it was out of the way. Against her boots, it felt like some kind of sack filled with silk-wrapped rocks. Her grandmother had a collection of sea creature fossils she kept wrapped under her bed and wondered if the man did the same thing. He suddenly became more of a victim instead of just an infected man, and Luna sunk her head at the thought. She tried not to think about the gut-wrenching chittering and the hiss of the air he sucked between his teeth.

The man once had a soft, sandstone skin, and he had honey eyes.

He had been her neighbor.

His skin was greying in places, and the color of his eyes had grown pale when compared to their old luster.

After she retrieved the end of her rope, she stopped and thought for a beat before tossing it again. The dark room was only visible because of her helmet, and she was thankful for the night vision, but she still couldn't tell if the area under the bed was free of whatever was blocking her rope.

Checking to see if the area under the bed was clear, she stuck her leg out and moved it around under the bed.

The space she needed seemed to be open.

Suddenly, the lights on her helmet turned on, causing her to leap out of her own skin in fright. As she settled from the startle with a deep breath, she scanned the room from her spot on the floor.

"I just realized you didn't get briefed on everything the helmet can do, so you probably wouldn't have known there were lights," Zoe said quietly, sounding reluctant.

"Yeah, thanks for the warning, Zoe. The lights help a hell of a lot. Now I can see my old neighbor in bright detail. Gross. Thank the mother scorpion, the helmet filters smell. The bed is covered in his shit," Luna said, resisting the urge to gag at the look of him.

The last thing she needed was to puke in her helmet.

She knew damn well that Jacob didn't have a magical tech solution for a helmet full of her breakfast, so she swallowed down the bile creeping up her throat and gripped the rope in her unsteady hand.

He snapped at her hungrily and watched with his sallow eyes, fighting the restraints. His wrists and ankles barely had a shred of skin left. His blue blood was oozing from around the restraints and dripping down the ropes.

Luna felt horrible for him.

He had been a good neighbor.

Deciding she was done reminiscing, Luna tossed the end of the rope under the bed and then stood up to retrieve the other end and repeat the process.

As she walked around the bed, Luna looked down and then quickly shot her head up, her breath shaking as she tried to find her words.

Stopped at the foot of the man's bed, Luna asked with a meek, trembling voice, "Zoe? Can these helmets record video?"

"Yes, do you need to record something?" Zoe asked as

she and Pike searched their holoscreens to see what Luna was referring to.

"Yeah. Um, yeah, I, I need to record something," Luna said softly, with her breath continuing to shake.

The camera switched on at the push of a button on Zoe's holoscreen. Luna saw the recording indicator pop open right as she heard Zoe gasp in horror.

Luna could hear Pike whisper to Zoe, "Where?"

"Right there," Zoe whispered as she trained her eyes on what Luna was seeing. Luna moved her head so the helmet camera could center on what she was looking at.

Pike scoffed and said, "Oh, fucking hell."

The heavy thing that Luna kicked out of the way?

The thing under the bed?

It was a *girl*.

She was maybe twelve Earth years old, and Luna had never seen her before.

She had a thin build, with brown hair, and her grey-toned skin was in a state of early decay. Her tail's tip was missing, and she lay limp on the floor, no longer in a curled shape.

Growing out of her swollen mouth and eyes were three fully formed fungal stalks. Each stalk had a plump cap on the top, filled with deadly spores.

"What the fuck do I do? I think I am looking at ground zero. Should I wrap her and drag her body to the dumping area right now or finish with the blood draw first?" Luna asked, her hands shaking as she gripped the rope.

Shivers racked her body as she looked over at the man. He continued chittering and snapping his teeth at her.

Luna heard the tenor of a man's voice coming through the speakers in her helmet. "Luna? This is Oz. If you can find a way to get the corpse that is hemorrhaging spores to the valley, you could potentially save the lives of many of our villagers. We already have a report that one of Sarah's neighbors has a spiking fever. If you can't do it, I'll need to send someone. Amelia has offered."

"You tell Amelia to *fuck off* and keep figuring out a cure. I got this," Luna hissed, her brow furrowed and determination sinking in at the idea of her best friend coming to drag the corpse to the valley.

"Luna, this is Amelia. Get the sample from the man like you were instructed, but please get one from the girl too. Where was she found?" Amelia asked Luna through the speaker in the helmet.

Luna listened as Amelia didn't wait for an answer, but turned to Pike, Zoe, and Oz and said, "After this is over, we are all going to have a chat about why the *fuck* no one told me what Luna was off doing until two minutes ago."

Smiling to herself, Luna answered Amelia, "She was under the bed. I kicked her out of the way. Otherwise, I would never have known she was there. I didn't recognize her, and I don't think anyone in the village has a girl her age. No one had been reported missing recently, right?"

Oz spoke, "No, no one has been reported missing in a while. I'll pass the video around the base and see if anyone recognizes her. Be careful, Luna."

"I will. I'll contact Zoe once I'm on my way to the valley with her. I'll need someone to come topside when I get back and sterilize me. I kicked her body with my boots," Luna said, holding back a gag.

The deranged man chittered behind her, and Luna did her best to steady her breathing.

"No problem. Jacob and someone from Amelia's team is already at work on a sterilization method," Oz said.

"Thank you," Luna said with relief.

Luna continued around the bed and finished tying down the man. He hissed and chittered his teeth as she cinched the rope around him. After he was more secure, she took a scalpel from the med kit and made an incision along his calf. He tried to fight the ropes, but Luna had secured him tight enough to ensure that his movement didn't keep her from being able to collect her blood sample from the oozing slice in his leg.

Next, she pulled out a syringe with a long needle and took a blood sample from deep within the girl's chest. Luna then tightly wrapped the girl in some fresh bed sheets she found in the man's closet. She broke off the fungus' stalks and wrapped them inside the sheet with the girl, then she dragged the bundle out of the back of the man's house.

Luna returned for the med kit and shivered as the man continued to fight his bindings and snapped his teeth at her. She was so glad this nightmare with her neighbor was almost over.

Backing away, Luna moved her feet as fast as she could as she exited the house.

She didn't know how she was going to get this memory out of her head enough to ever rest. She needed to drink some alcohol, she thought as she picked up the end of the wrapped silk bundle.

"Zoe?" Luna asked.

Clearing her throat, Zoe said, "Yes, Luna?"

"Can someone bring some alcohol to my campsite when I get back?" Luna asked.

"Why? You didn't hurt yourself, did you? You're not bleeding, are you?" Zoe asked frantically.

"No! No, I just need something to drink. Sorry, I probably should have said that," Luna said with a grimace, her nose crinkling.

Giggling, Zoe said, "I can see your face."

With wide eyes, Luna laughed and said, "Oh! No wonder Oz said he would send someone else if I couldn't do it. I didn't know he was watching my face!"

"Are you sure you're OK, Luna?" Zoe asked.

"Yeah, I am OK. Not great, but I'll make it. Seeing a dead girl with a huge mushroom growing out of her face was not exactly on my bucket list," Luna said sarcastically.

"Aren't you still dragging her through the woods?" Zoe asked.

"Yeah. *Looking* at her is what was terrible. I mean, I know she's back there, but she's dead, *and* she doesn't know she's dead. Only *I* know she's dead, and I also had to look at her. Both are not good things for me or her," Luna explained.

"Yes, I'll make sure you get some alcohol. It sounds like you need it," Zoe agreed as she chuckled.

"That bad, huh?" Luna said.

"No, just relatable," Zoe explained.

"I'm so glad they put communication devices in these helmets. Maybe we should give one to Mercy," Pike said.

Zoe answered, "August already offered it to her, but she said texting was fine. She said that she wanted to get used to using the keyboard."

Nodding in agreement, Luna trekked on and was over a mile away from town before she took a break to rest. Her mouth was dry as a bone, but she didn't dare remove her helmet until she could sterilize her body. Not to mention the fact that she was dragging a girl with fungus growing out of her face behind her. After a short rest, Luna looked over at her unwanted, silk-wrapped hiking partner, and rose to get started on the rest of her journey. She decided that she wasn't taking any more breaks, and continued on until she noticed a change in terrain.

Reaching the valley, Luna let out a relieved sigh and said, "Hey, Zoe? I made it."

After dropping the girl's body and watching it roll down a slight slope, Luna asked, "Can you turn on the camera to record?"

Zoe turned the camera on. Luna saw the icon pop up in the corner of the helmet's screen and made sure she kept as steady as she could while she was filming the disturbing scene.

There were bodies everywhere.

The town in the mountains had lost fifty people or more, just based on the bodies she could count. There were skeletal remains scattered around the bodies in various stages of decay, and she wondered if her first guess was far too low.

"Remind me to thank everyone who worked on these helmets. It stays airtight around my neck no matter how I move. How did you fit enough oxygen in it for hours of use?" Luna asked, confusion evident on her face.

Zoe paused a moment then said, "Carter said they break down the carbon dioxide in the back of the helmet. Something about a laser and a tiny carbon filter. He just walked by me and said you missed that when you were assisting Amelia with Jael?"

Laughing, Luna said, "He means hanging out with Jael.

That's when Oz, August, and Callum left to get the sand Jacob needed. Did you not go to that first party?"

Zoe paused and then said, "Um, yes?"

"Do you, honestly, even like parties?" Luna asked.

Zoe replied, "Between you and me? Not really. I would rather read a book. Our people need to quit partying so damn much and write some good fiction. I love to learn, but I would kill to read something juicy. Reading Carter's coding is just not hitting the right spot, you know?"

"Yeah, you're telling me. I've got Carter *and* Amelia. She is just as bad. I swear, next time there is an election, I think I am voting for Amelia for President. She would be an effective leader. You should see her with her medical training team," Luna said.

"I heard she had a few people already fully trained as *doctors* before you went to collect the blood samples," Zoe said, apparent astonishment in her tone.

Unsure if she should say anything about what she knew, Luna just said, "I think they're just in training but probably smart enough to retain the information required to be doctors. Perhaps."

Clearing her throat, Zoe said quietly, "You should probably work on your poker face."

Luna furrowed her brow and said, "What's poker?"

"Oh, my bad. I forgot that we're all in different places reviewing Jael's memories. Poker is a game on Earth. It's played with cards, and it looks fun," Zoe explained.

Luna smiled and said, "You really went straight for the low-key entertainment, didn't you? Did you read Jael's alien smut yet? It's *fantastic*."

"I am honestly pissed off she didn't read more for fun, especially sci-fi. I think the gray alien book was my favorite.

The alien that was bionic was dreamy. That one vampire series was good, too. She read a couple of fantasy books that were *great*. Did you read those yet?" Zoe asked.

"What? No? There were more books like the blue alien books? Callum just told me about the blue alien books! That holdout!" Luna scoffed.

"I think we have plenty of footage. Should you get some more samples in case the mountain town's fungus is different?" Pike asked.

"I think all of this fungus is the same species. It's all white with smooth vertical ridges and a rounded top with no other markings. The exact same as the three on the girl. But, I think I'll get a sample anyway, just in case. I don't want to come back here," Luna said with her eyes flared wide.

"OK, I'm standing by," Zoe said before the speaker in the helmet went silent.

Luna peered around and decided she would collect her sample from a fresher body. Kneeling, she took out the syringe and plunged it into the side of a body with no sign of the fungus. After she took some of the blue blood from the face-down corpse, she sealed the entire syringe in a hard case then stowed it away in her sack.

Heading away from the grisly scene, Luna shivered and took off jogging. Knowing she wasn't going to run out of oxygen made her feel a little better, but the helmet was becoming very small, very fast.

She wasn't going to waste any time sprinting back to the base.

40

Jacob had already set up the tall, solid white sterilization booth before Luna returned. The random white rectangle looked out of place in the thick of the woods. It consisted of two sets of long, UV-LED strips inside of a thick, solid tent made of reflective fabric. The thick fabric was gently flapping in the breeze.

After the intense lights turned off, there was a spray from above that covered Luna and slightly stung any exposed skin. After she and her gear were sterilized, she headed toward her tent, which was still around half a mile away.

Luna finally arrived at her campsite and was able to remove her helmet. With her first breath outside of the helmet, she was thankful for the fresh air. She took several gulps of the clean air and closed her eyes as her breathing evened out.

Picking up her tablet with unsteady hands, she called Jacob, "I'm back, and everything has been sterilized. You can send someone up to collect all the samples."

"Someone will be on their way in two minutes," Jacob said, before signing off.

Before she could finish changing her clothes, she heard the rustling of leaves and quickly pulled her shirt on over her head.

Jael poked her head inside with a broad smile and said, "Surprise! Immune lady gets to collect the samples."

Chuckling from behind her mask, Luna said, "I'm so glad it's you and not someone I don't know. I feel like I've fallen from a tree and hit every branch on the way down."

"I'm not going to lie. You do look pretty rough. I can't stay, but I wanted to see you for a few minutes. Are you, um, OK after everything you just had to see and do?" Jael asked, slowly finding her words.

"No, but I will be. I'm just glad I don't sleep or dream like your people do. Today would haunt me forever," Luna said as she stared at the ground in her tent.

"If you need to talk, I'm just a call away," Jael said before pulling back the tent's opening to head back inside, the med kit in her hand.

A breeze rustled the leaves above them, and the top of the tent gently swayed and rippled. Nodding her head, Luna waved without cracking so much as a smile.

Jael nodded, headed back toward the base. The sound of the leaves crunching under her boots was a comfort.

Reminiscing about the long walks she used to take on the trails back home on Earth, she looked up at the giant trees and squeezed her eyes shut. She was riddled with anxiety for Oz's people. Their future seemed to be in jeopardy. Her heart pounded with fear that grew with every passing moment.

She watched carefully for the mud on the wall that

marked the trip line in the lava tube, and made sure she ducked far in advance. She still wasn't sure what happened when someone triggered it, and she wasn't too keen to find out.

When Jael arrived at the base's door, she quickly opened it, and Oz was on the other side to help her push open the heavy door.

"Thank you," Jael said as she walked by him.

"Did you find the trip line OK? How was Luna?" Oz asked, concern marring his face.

Jael looked up at Oz and said, "I put a bit of mud on the wall so I could find it. Luna was as well as can be expected, I guess."

They walked in silence the rest of the way to Amelia's lab. Once they arrived, Oz again opened the door for Jael, and they went through the sterilization process. Amelia was waiting on the other side, and she and her team were ready in full biohazard gear. They were all attached to a tube that ran along the ceiling and provided fresh air, just like Jacob had in his lab.

The off-white suits were inflated, and Jael thought they looked like marshmallow people. If the mood had been lighter, she might have even laughed about it.

Jael handed the sealed box to Amelia, then headed back toward the door for sterilization. After a medical tech put a seal on her eyelids, she walked through the door, the lights blazed, then the spray that followed stung her skin. She hissed at the sting and couldn't wait to wash it off. Oz was next, and once he was finished, they both changed clothes and continued to their apartment. Jael waved at Amelia as they passed by the large glass wall.

Now that the samples were in hand, Amelia knew it was time to get to work.

"Hazel, open the boxes, and I'll remove the syringes inside," Amelia asked.

"Do you want to do the spore separation and extraction yourself?" Hazel asked, the puffy suit making it difficult for her to see Amelia.

"Yes," Amelia replied as she looked inside the first case at the syringe filled with blood.

Taking the syringe into her gloved hand, she took one drop of the sample, placed it onto a glass slide, then placed the slide on the stage of her large microscope. Leaning back, she moved the slide around and found what she was looking for, the bright white living spore within the blue blood.

"This sample is filled with spores. Get started with every antifungal. I want testing to start right away. Ensure that the samples are kept at body temperature, so the spore thinks the victim is still alive. The boxes were designed to maintain that temperature. If the temperature drops at all, the spores will split and form roots for the stalks that protrude from the victim's body. We have plenty of blood to test for now, but we will need to culture more of these spores soon."

Hazel nodded solemnly and swallowed before she said, "I will make sure that the spores stay at a constant body temperature."

Amelia watched as the medical team took the samples and added the various antifungals that they had helped discover and develop. She hoped this was enough. They had to find a treatment and maybe even a vaccine, if they got lucky.

To develop a prophylactic treatment, she would need at least one survivor.

The fungus decimates the person's immune system before it ever has a chance to fight. The spores wage an all-out war on the blood vessels in the brain, trying to force themselves through the tissue. The patient develops fungal meningitis, and symptoms of encephalitis begin shortly after. Once the swelling in the brain begins, it's just a matter of time before the individual fungus cells break through the vessels and spread inside the brain. The spores work individually until the body cools, then the strongest and fastest grow and emerge from the victim's body.

If the samples contained antibodies that could be harvested, those could possibly prepare the immune system. Maybe they could keep the fungus' spores from multiplying and stop the infection in its tracks?

Everything hit Amelia at once as she wondered if she could induce an immune response in a scorpion.

She held her arm up and said to the room, "Someone get me some small scorpions, *now*. We need airtight cages. Hazel, please go to Jacob's lab and tell him what I'm doing."

Two people leaped from their stools, and one called Zoe on the coms, requesting small scorpions. Hazel scrambled to the door and started sterilization.

Amelia could tell that Hazel was *not* a fan of the safety suits.

While waiting for the tiny creatures, her people's biological cousins, Amelia had a member of the team process the samples from the mountain people. She directed another team member to process the samples from the girl that Luna had found under the bed. After the samples were ready, she put them under her microscope to see if she could find a difference.

They looked identical, and she wasn't sure what that

meant. Amelia didn't have genome sequencing technology yet, so she would have to test the treatment and vaccine on both strains. She hoped genome sequencing and nanotech would be ready soon but it was doubtful.

Jacob dropped off the airtight cages with a nod to Amelia, and shortly after, someone knocked on the lab door and set a large box of writhing scorpions outside. Amelia got to work immediately, putting them in the airtight cages Jacob had just dropped off. Amelia infected half with one fungus sample and half with the other. She hoped that after a few hours, the scorpions might start to show an immune response to the spores.

Could she find a way to kill the spores but maintain enough of their structure to trick the immune system? Or discover the target antibodies? She just knew she could trick an immune response.

It would at least give the strongest of their people an edge against the infection. The physician that Oz had taken the knowledge from had little experience in mycology, and Amelia was cringing inside as she racked her brain for the answer. Her eyes began pounding from concentration, and she raised her arm to rub them. With her hand up, she just stared at it through the screen of her biohazard suit.

After shaking her head at herself, she got back to work.

She finished infecting all the scorpions and began testing their blood every hour. By hour thirteen, she had isolated a handful of samples, and was already mixing a solution to inject into a test scorpion.

Test after test and failure after failure, Amelia didn't give up. With five people dead and ten more with fevers, she was running out of time. She worked for two weeks straight and went through over a thousand scorpions before she finally had one survivor.

One.

Her hands shook as she reached into the cage and took the creature out to take a blood sample. The scorpion struck her thick gloves with its stinger to no avail.

Amelia faintly smiled as she whispered and said, "Little girl, you might save us all." She set the scorpion back in her cage after obtaining the sample.

Amelia walked over to her microscope, and the slide came into view on the holoscreen. Joy filled Amelia, and she nearly screamed with delight. There were dead spores floating all over in this little scorpion's blood. She knew she could find antibodies for the fungal infection if she had the right equipment.

They had found the anti-fungal medication.

Amelia began shaking as she took slow breaths, and tears sprung into her pain-filled, blue eyes.

The other fifteen scorpions with the same anti-fungal are due to be cleared in six hours.

Not one had died.

Heart pounding in her ears, Amelia shot to her feet and shouted out to the team, "We did it! Get in here! We did it! We have our first survivor!"

The team gathered around, and all cheered from inside their puffy white suits. Someone was already at the panel calling Jacob to tell him the good news.

"Now, we just have to trigger the same immune response in a volunteer. I need the sealed cages removed and replaced with a medical bed immediately. Get to work, team. Our job isn't over yet. I will volunteer first. Oh, if anyone tells on me, you're off the med team. This is my damn choice; do you all understand me?" Amelia said as she walked with wide strides toward the clinic.

Looking back, Amelia saw nothing but solemn nods from her team, her friends.

When she reached the sterilization lights, Amelia let out a sigh and closed her eyes as the lights shined.

They had *finally* done it.

Now, it was time to infect herself.

41

Banging on the glass wall of the lab, Mercy was back in the base and had fury in her eyes. She was furious that Amelia had decided to make herself the Guinea pig. Mercy could not believe Amelia had given herself the cerebral fungal infection.

Amelia was still feeling fine, and the anti-fungal was working. She rolled her eyes and tapped her ear since the room was soundproof.

Growling and grimacing, Mercy had no idea what to do with her anger. Why had Amelia taken it upon herself to expose herself like that? Mercy was at a loss. Amelia had become one of her best friends, and Mercy couldn't lose her. Out of the corner of her eye, Mercy saw Luna walk up, arms crossed and a scowl on her face.

"Did you just get back inside?" Mercy asked as she looked over at her friend.

Luna answered without looking at Mercy, saying, "No, I went and took a shower in an apartment before coming down here."

Releasing a deep breath, Luna went on, "I know why she did it, but I'm pissed too."

Mercy started to calm down and asked, "Do you want to go over to Jael's for dinner? She sent me a message. You probably just got one too."

Luna looked down at the tablet under her arm and saw the notification, "Yes, I got it. I'll come. I just need to go say thank you to Zoe before I head over. She kept me from losing it when I was stuck in that damn helmet for nearly a day."

Nodding in understanding, Mercy said softly, "I'll see you there."

Looking back, Mercy found Amelia's blue eyes were already focused on her. Mercy furrowed her brow in irritation and walked off toward Jael's apartment with her arms crossed. She was glad they might be able to develop a treatment, but Amelia was reckless to infect herself when there had been only one scorpion survivor. She could have waited until she knew the other scorpions weren't going to die. Fury coursed through her body as she walked. Her boots tapped on the stone floors, sounding louder than usual in her ears.

As she approached Jael and Oz's apartment, she looked over at her own door and shrugged. She wondered what August was doing. He had hardly been home since she returned to the base. She guessed that he and Jacob were working on something together because Callum was by himself doing an intense workout of some kind in his apartment.

His apartment door was wide open. She could see him doing handstand pushups with his legs in the splits. Could she even do a handstand? She knew she could as a child, but she hadn't tried in a long time.

Jael swung the door open and said, "Come in! Oz said August is working late with Jacob on the rocket assembly project."

"Thank you for inviting me. What Amelia did gutted me. I kind of needed some company," Mercy said, looking down at her crossed arms and wondering if Jael had seen Callum's hellish pushups.

"I understand, though. I would have done the same thing if I were in her position," Jael said as her lip quirked in a half smile.

They heard a knee bump into the bed frame, followed by Oz yelling from the bedroom, "Like hell! Over my dead fucking body. You would *never* ..." he trailed off as they heard him moving something.

Rolling her eyes at Oz and whatever he was doing in the bedroom, Jael turned to Mercy and said, "It was ultimately her choice, and she decided to be the hero. After testing ten thousand soil samples between fifteen people on the medical team? And after they were all working around the clock for days on end? I'm sure she was more than ready to be finished with it."

Oz came around the corner, picking at something stuck in his eye, and said, "What's done is done, and she can hopefully inoculate the entire village with her antibodies. *If* it works anyway. This is all still a hypothesis. We talked earlier, and once she has finished here, she will be heading up to the town in the mountains to distribute the antifungal. There might be more villages on the other side of the mountains under attack by the fungus. We will need to check with a traveling salesman next time one comes around. I think we're due for the orange cart soon."

Out of nowhere, Oz yelped and looked at something between his fingers before he grumbled, "Stupid hair was still attached."

He rubbed the side of his temple where he had accidentally pulled out his own hair and scowled.

Chuckling, Jael turned to Mercy and said, "How is Amelia doing? Have you talked to her?"

"No, not yet. I did bang on the glass, and I made sure she knew I was pissed off at her, though," Mercy said with her arms crossed and a scowl marring her face.

Mercy found a seat on the padded bench while Jael walked into the kitchen with Oz. Jael brought Mercy her plate while Oz carried both his and Jael's plates to the living room. It was a mix of nuts and grains, with avocado and mango pieces. Oz passed around a bundle of brown silk with warm flatbread inside. There was a honey-based, salty-sweet glaze on the flatbread, and Mercy was nearly drooling before the first bite. She leaned down to smell the food and had to hold back a groan of pleasure at the scent.

"Who made this?!" Mercy asked as she greedily shoveled another bite into her mouth.

"Oz made it for the first time a few weeks ago, and we've been eating a lot of it," Jael said between bites, not giving away Oz's secret recipe.

Mercy wondered if it was just salt and honey mixed together but didn't ask. She planned to experiment and make some at home later.

After they finished their meals, Jael collected the plates and headed to the kitchen to wash them.

"Are you going to try out and go on the mission?" Oz asked Mercy, who looked stuffed from her meal.

"I was planning on it. Part of me does want to stay here with Jacob and Callum, though. I love Callum, and he's my best friend, but he has Jacob. I feel like this mission is a lot more critical than my fashion designer dreams," Mercy said, followed by a breathy sigh.

"This mission is what will make your dreams *possible*. I understand how you feel, though. I, quite honestly, hate my job. I wish I could be working with Jacob or Amelia, but I'm stuck *deciding* and thoroughly pissing everyone off. I'm trying out too, because I couldn't stay here and play President even if Jael wasn't necessary for the mission," Oz said with an irritated undertone.

Rolling her eyes at Oz, Mercy said, "You're doing a hell of a lot more than playing President. Everyone has been more than happy with the job you're doing. You were always set to be the leader of our village after Sarah anyway."

After stretching her tail out behind her, Mercy shifted in her seat on the bench, hoping she didn't just poke a resting scorpion.

Jael sat back down next to him. Deadpanning Mercy, Oz said, "Everyone keeps saying that, and it doesn't change the fact that I hate it, and I decline."

"Oz, you were already voted President. You can't just decline after the fact," Jael said while giggling.

Scoffing, Oz said, "Excuse me, who here is President? Oh yes, that's me. With no laws or regulations set up prior to election, I have total power. Total power means I get to say that I decline. I am *playing* President to appease, but I will be quitting this parasitic job promptly."

Mercy slapped a hand to her mouth and let out a chuckle before saying, "What do you want to do instead?"

Shifting his eyes to Jael, Oz said, "Well, first off, I would make a lot more time to fuck my woman."

With her whole body now simmering, Jael slid her hands up to cover the heated embarrassment that was surely shining on her face.

"Second, I would want to work with Jacob on the rockets and probably with Amelia in her lab too," Oz explained as he slid his eyes back to Mercy, who sat adjacent to them.

Looking over at Jael, Mercy burst into laughter at the shock in Jael's eyes.

"You have nothing to be embarrassed about. I know this won't help, but at least you're getting laid, right?" Mercy said with a sly grin.

"I don't think I will ever stop being embarrassed," Jael said with her eyes still open wide, looking somewhere in the middle of the floor.

Oz leaned over and whispered in her ear, using a deep tone, "I love it that your skin becomes hot when you get all bothered."

Flushing with heat all over again, Jael nearly shivered at Oz's words. Snapping her eyes to Mercy, Jael elbowed Oz, causing him to squeak and rub his side.

"Ow!" Oz said as he kept rubbing where Jael had stuck her elbow.

Laughing as she walked to the door, Mercy said, "Thank you for dinner. I'm going to go and find August. Maybe afterward, I'll go and bang on the med room's glass wall and scowl at Amelia again."

42

With Mercy scowling at her from the other side of the glass, Amelia finished up storing the last of her own blood samples in a geothermal cooler, then headed over to open the door. It had been another week, and Amelia was now beginning transfusions from her own blood to test how effective the antibodies would work if used as a prophylactic for the rest of the base. She knew it would only be temporary, but it might buy them some time to get ahead of the disease.

The antibiotics had worked for those who had fevers, and no one has come forward as ill since, so she hoped they were out of the woods. They had lost thirteen people in the village. The fungal infection had a variable incubation period, and it was hard to tell if others would eventually fall sick.

"So, you can finally come out of your glass test tube?" Mercy said with much more attitude than she intended.

Exhaling through her pursed lips, Amelia looked at

Mercy and said, "I wasn't trying to hurt you, Mercy. My blood type can be used for any of our people. It just made sense for me to be the one."

"I know why! I don't fucking care! You're my best friend! You, Luna, and Jael are all too important for me to lose. I don't know what I would have done if the antifungal hadn't worked," Mercy said as her voice cracked. She was hardly able to get her words out as tears sparkled in her eyes.

Reaching out, Amelia grabbed Mercy and wrapped her arms around her before she pulled away and said, "I'm sorry, Mercy. I shouldn't have made such a rash decision. I hadn't rested in days."

"I forgive you, but don't do that shit again. Are you going on the mission?" Mercy asked quietly as Amelia pulled away but kept her hand wrapped around Mercy's arm.

"Yes. Are you planning to try out?" Amelia asked, her head slightly tilting to the side.

Mercy said, "Yeah," as she looked back behind her. She thought about how she had told August she would stop by and see him at work.

"I need to go find August. I'll see you later," Mercy said quietly as she turned and walked toward Jacob's lab.

Mercy still felt like Amelia's actions were a betrayal. She just couldn't shake the hurt.

Before she arrived at the door, she heard banging that rattled the frame of the building and wondered what the hell they were doing in there.

Cautiously, Mercy opened the door to Jacob's office and went inside.

As she walked over to the glass wall, Mercy said under her breath, "They need some kind of supervision."

Looking out into the enormous lab, Mercy could see

that they had built further into the newly discovered cavern. The spotlights shined on the shiny metal where Jacob and August were working and moved along with them.

Suddenly it occurred to her what she was looking at. As her eyes adjusted, Mercy saw the three massive rockets being assembled in their entirety. She slipped on a pair of ear protectors and a hard hat before stepping out into the open cavern. Jacob's original lab was large, but this third cavern was enormous. They could easily fit the three rockets that Jacob had designed inside and have plenty of room to build the launch tube and electrified rail tracks.

Workers were already paving and framing up the launch tube at the end of the cavern. She knew that by using the new tech they recently developed, Carter's team had plotted the best place from which to launch the rockets. According to the plans on the massive holoscreen, there were people above busy felling a few trees.

The simulation video of the plan was playing on a loop, so Mercy stopped for a beat and watched. They were planning to pull up the root systems so they could build a nature-covered, rollback deck. The deck would split and lift, then slide to either side. The rockets would shoot into the sky along the track. They would move one by one through the launch tube.

She recognized some of the engineering for the tracks. It was railgun tech. They were planning to shoot a rocket into the air, at top speed, from under the ground.

It was genius. All of it was absolutely genius. Mercy was in awe. She peered up onto the side of the rocket where the lights shined and found August suspended and carefully bolting electrical panels to the side of the middle rocket.

"This is incredible, August. I can't believe it's coming

together so quickly," Mercy said, her head pointed in his direction.

"It wasn't my brain that designed it. You can complement our quiet engineer. Jacob made such precise instructions, the team could build the rest of it without his help," August said, pride beaming in his voice at his friend's ingenuity.

Jacob had quickly become August's best friend after Oz was banished.

They had been close friends before that, but Oz's absence in both of their lives drew them together. They had developed a brotherly relationship, and August often needed Jacob's endearing strength and calm. Even long before the gift, Jacob would design something useful, and August would instantly beam about his friend's accomplishment. Their kind of friendship was something Mercy had always wanted. Their type of friendship was something that Mercy finally had.

Maybe that was why what happened with Amelia was so hard.

Slipping down the ladder to the ground, August walked over to Mercy, and they took a seat on a nearby bench. Mercy lifted the ear protector, then slammed it back down onto her ears with her eyes narrowed in irritation at the noise. Crashes and screeching saws on metal in the background made it impossible to talk, so Mercy stuck out her wrist for them to connect.

"I guess this is still useful, huh?" August said, looking down at their joined hands.

Mercy looked at August with narrowed eyes and said, "I can think of a couple of reasons to keep it around."

Lifting his brows at her, August wondered if that was a hint. She didn't look back at him, so he didn't think about it further.

"What's going to be on the physical test? Do you think I'll be able to handle it?" Mercy asked, finally looking over at August.

"It's graded on a curve, based on your size. I'm testing for what you can hold up for your own body type, not some imaginary normal. Then we can practice based on each team member's needs," August said into her mind, with a gentle tone.

"When does it begin? Do we need to have some kind of practice beforehand?" Mercy asked.

August was quick to answer, "No, you don't need to practice or train to prepare. We will start formal training as soon as I've selected everyone on my team. Have you been sticking to the base's current exercise schedule?"

Jacob approached and said, "Taking a break in the middle of shift? What the hell, you prick?"

Plopping down next to Mercy, Jacob put his arm around her as he slid her ear protector to the side and said, "How is Amelia?"

August pulled his hand away from Mercy and broke their connection to take off his ear protection and hard hat. Jacob had noticed Mercy come in and sent his team on break so the noise would die down.

"She's better. The anti-fungal worked, and she thinks she can find a way to make some kind of a preventative treatment from her natural antibodies," Mercy said, with irritation laced in her tone.

Tilting his dirty face toward Mercy, Jacob said, "A way to

prevent the infection would be terrific, but I'm just glad we have a treatment for now. Amelia gave us a hell of an edge."

"So, Jacob, are you going on the mission?" Mercy asked, wanting to change the subject.

"No, I have to stay here as head of the base and work on recruiting. It's better this way. I have a feeling Oz will attempt something unhinged on the mission. He hasn't mentioned anything that would make me think that. I just know him and his bullshit," Jacob said, as Mercy noticed a hint of an eye roll.

Nodding her head, Mercy said, "That does sound like him."

She went on, "I'm assuming Callum will be staying then? Or are you getting tired of Callum's daily workout party of one? How do you deal with all of the noise?"

Smiling, Jacob just tapped the ear protectors now resting at his neck and said, "I bring them home every night. It's quite a nice show he puts on, actually."

Throwing her head back and laughing, Mercy said, "You really are a genius!"

August just shook his head and, with a scowl, grumbled, "I'm so glad I have the top apartment."

A light flashed on Jacob's tablet, and he walked over to his desk and lifted it up to see what the message said.

From Amelia:
"Luna and Carter's nanotechnology is working. Come to the medical lab when you can. This changes EVERYTHING!"

Walking back around the corner toward August and Mercy, Jacob smiled and said, "We have nanotech up and running. We should all clean up and head to the medical lab."

Clearly astonished, with wide golden eyes, Mercy asked, "Nanotech?"

Nodding, Jacob pointed his thumb over his shoulder to the rockets and said, "We needed to develop the large and the small. We didn't have a lot of confidence in the nanotech, so we haven't discussed it much. That is until now I guess."

August and Jacob headed to the wash stations, so Mercy rose from her spot on the bench and said, "I'm not filthy like you two. So, I'm going to head to the lab now. See you both there."

Setting the hard hat and ear protector back on the rack, Mercy looked back at August. He was staring at her from the wash station as he toweled off his face. Mercy smirked and then headed toward the door. The handle clicked behind her as the door closed, and she headed for the medical lab.

Mercy thought she remembered Amelia mentioning the nanotechnology project in passing, but she didn't know they had been able to get the program working yet.

Arriving at the lab, Mercy found Amelia giving one of the villagers the second round of antibiotic injections.

He said, "Thank you."

After she withdrew the needle, Amelia placed a bandage over the single droplet of blue blood that had pearled on his arm.

Amelia finished with her patient and then walked over to Mercy while pulling her tablet from under her arm, saying, "You got here fast. I don't think I even messaged you yet."

Amelia scowled as she looked through her tablet, and Mercy said, "You didn't. I was with Jacob. I hardly even remember you saying anything about nanotech. How did you figure out how to get it to work so fast?"

"It was entirely by accident. I sent Carter a message about the nanobots while the tablet was sitting next to them. I looked back into the microscope and found them all moving to the left and raising their right robotic arm," Amelia explained with a smile.

Carter and Oz entered the lab right before August and Jacob arrived. Zoe filed in right behind Oz with Luna in tow.

Amelia looked around and said, "Now that most everyone is here, plus some, I'll get started."

Clearing her throat, Amelia turned on the viewing screen and showed the left-turning nanobots with their right arms raised.

Dropping his mouth open, Carter said, "I'll get working on it. This will be simple. I'll have your nanobots dancing by the end of the shift."

Smiling, Amelia said, "Thank you, Carter. This means I can treat a variety of diseases that are immune to treatment. These nanobots have an arm that infiltrates a cell and are designed to re-order the base sequences of the genetic code. Since we needed nucleic acid sequencing during the fungal infection, my team got on it, and we just finished putting together the equipment. Now that we can program the nanotech, we can figure out how to tell the arm to mimic the specific signal protein we need."

Tapping his foot in thought, Oz said, "In more simple terms, you mean you can now manipulate genes with microscopic robots?"

Amelia smiled and said, "That's precisely what I am saying. After Carter discovers and programs the specific frequencies for each filament, we can control them from a tablet. In their most basic application, they could be used to assist clotting in a hemorrhaging artery and maybe even repairing mortal wounds on the battlefield, if it comes to that. I will be able to make a vaccine now. I just need to isolate the base sequences that will trigger the correct proteins from an immune response. It won't take long since I still have the surviving scorpions and blood samples from our test group. I just need to compare them to samples of people who have not been infected."

Jacob whistled and said, "This is exactly what we need to get ahead. Put everyone we can on this."

Oz nodded and said, "Absolutely. Carter, pull anyone you can spare that isn't already working on the project and send them to Amelia's lab. I think combining the two fields of thought might speed up the process."

"I agree. I'll get on it right away," Carter said before walking straight to his office to tell the nanotech team.

Exiting the medical lab, Mercy said, "Those tiny robots are so small they can alter genetic code? Is that something the enemy humans have? Or did our people come up with that entirely on our own?"

Oz answered, "The humans have had the tech for many thousands of years, but according to their people, only the richest have access and know how to use them. They use them in strange ways and are very secretive about them. We were just lucky that Amelia set her tablet down when she did. It was an honest accident but no less a great discovery."

Nodding her head, Mercy continued to her office. Her shift was one thing she had hardly been around for lately. Since the armor for their journey to the north was designed, and they had finished production, there wasn't much for Mercy to do.

Looking down at the stones in the floor, she wondered what the mountains would be like. What creatures they might encounter, what secrets they would find at the humans' base to the north.

43

"Are you absolutely sure you found the gene that will prevent the sedative drug from putting us under completely?" Jacob asked.

"It's a resistance gene, and I think it's something relatively new from an evolutionary standpoint. I can simply turn on our resistance to the compound with the nanobots by changing the base sequence. I have enough to dispense in our village now, and I can have enough made for the mountain village in a few days. They're self-assembling, and we can make trillions a day. I think we should send a small team up to the mountain town with them, as well to help. The villagers might be willing to help us in return," Amelia explained as she pulled out her tablet.

"I think you're right. Let's send a small group to the mountain village. I think you, Mercy, and August should go," Jacob suggested.

Amelia nodded and said, "No problem. I'll send Mercy a message if you want to let August know."

"Sure, I'm heading there now," Jacob said as he walked out of the medical clinic and headed toward his lab.

Amelia: Looks like you, August, and I are going on a little trip to the town on the mountain."

Mercy: "What? Since when?"

Amelia: "Since just now. We need to dispense the nanotech."

Mercy: "Why am I going?"

Amelia: "No idea. Maybe Jacob wants you to be there because it's the first time we'll be using the tactical suits in the field?"

Mercy: "Damn! If I knew that I'd have to go on such long field trips, I wouldn't have signed up!"

Laughing, Amelia wondered if Mercy was serious.

In just a few days, they would be heading out for a long hike up the mountain. Amelia estimated the journey would take about two weeks, at the least. If they stopped and rested only once each day, the town was only around a four-day walk.

Packing up her vials and tools, Amelia wondered how the hell she was going to get through this journey with the two love bugs. She had hoped that Jacob would just send Mercy, but she understood that they needed some trained protection. Amelia was proficient with small blades, not large ones, not yet anyway. Not to mention, she recalled hearing that August had some impressive scorpion kills under his belt.

They'd had large scorpions in the village she was from, in addition to sinister flying beasts that took people and let their larvae eat the bodies while the victims were still alive.

She blinked. The memories of her old life were tucked away, back in their dark hiding place.

The main mission's tryouts were today, and Amelia was nervous. She knew she had to go no matter what, but being tested physically was not on her list of favorite things to do. She liked a slow, steady workout, not pushing to maximums. She knew Mercy was nervous too but didn't understand why. Aside from Oz and Callum, she was probably in the best shape out of everyone in the base. Amelia knew because she had conducted all the physicals.

After packing her things, she headed to the command room to meet the tryout group. Amelia opened the door to find she was the last to arrive. There were already around thirty people seated -- rows of curled tails behind cross-legged people sitting on silk-stuffed workout mats.

Clearing his throat, August stood up front and said, "Thank you for trying out. This mission is going to be grueling, but it's critical to gaining our freedom. We have a few tasks that we think will determine if you have what it takes to make it through the journey.

"First, we will test your physical skills with simple strength-to-body-size tests. Second, we need to test your stamina and speed, so we set up a course that reaches the jade woods. You will be asked to bring back a bucket of sap within a certain amount of time.

"The third is my personal hell -- Cold tolerance. I almost failed that test, so good luck with that one."

Someone on the front row asked, "Will we receive weapons and armor training after we make the team?"

"Armor training, yes. Right now, we are only training those going on the mission on how to use the armor. Weapons' training is something everyone will be participating in. We are figuring a lot of this out as we go, so if anyone proves particularly excellent with the plasma sword, we will likely select them to be a trainer," August explained.

Several nods from the group bobbed up and down before August continued and said, "I have group lists available on the table up front here. We do have some people who are required for the journey, and they will not be subject to the testing. They have already been selected as imperative to the mission. They will find their names on a separate list here," August pointed down to a paper on a different table.

Mercy ran to the exempt list and took in a sigh of relief when she found her name.

Amelia walked up behind Mercy and asked her, "You're going on both missions?"

"Yes, it looks like you are too!" Mercy said, beaming with her usual excitement.

Sighing with relief, Amelia realized that Mercy had just been joking about not wanting to go on the mission. She looked up and saw Jael approaching them.

Jael walked over and said quietly, "Please tell me I don't have to try out."

"No, your name is on the exempt list. I wonder if they will want you to sneak into the human's base?" Mercy asked, eyes wide in realization.

"If they want a secret agent, they will be sorely disappointed. I'm not sure I could hide a fart, much less my whole identity!" Jael declared a little too loudly, prompting heat to flood her cheeks as she shifted her widened eyes around the room.

Laughing, Amelia said, "You would do well with some training. Plus, we don't know if that's the plan yet anyway."

Rolling her eyes, Jael said, "Knowing Oz, it will start out

being a mildly hair-brained plan that turns out, at the last minute, to be completely deranged."

Behind Jael, August threw his head back and laughed at her comment, "Damn, now that's the *truth*! We wouldn't have it any other way, right?"

Scoffing and looking around at everyone, Mercy said, "Wait, has Oz actually lost his mind? Because I think we should maybe talk about this."

Laughing and putting his arm around Mercy, August said, "No. He just wants to get back to some kind of a normal life. He was banished for fifteen years. I'm sure all this chaos was the last thing he wanted to come home to."

"Sometimes, I think all he wants to do is take me back to the treehouse and hide," Jael said, honesty in every word.

The look in Jael's eyes told everyone that she wouldn't necessarily mind it if that happened.

Chuckling as he walked over to stand in front of the first test group's table, August threw over his shoulder, "I'm still worried that he's gonna do that!"

After his laugh, he turned around to the large open room, and yelled, "OK, line up if it's your group's turn to test now. Groups two and three will test tomorrow before I leave. Luna will be in charge of your training until I return."

Amelia, Mercy, and Jael walked into the hallway outside the command room and back to their jobs.

Amelia slowly stopped and slid a hand up to her forehead. Her face went grim. She turned around sharply while quietly asking, "Do you want to come to my lab to see something before I announce it? I found something interesting about our DNA. I want another set of eyes on it to ensure I didn't miss anything."

In unison and with wide eyes, Jael and Mercy said, "Hell yes!"

After Jael and Mercy had a good laugh, someone opened the command room's door at the end of the hallway, and sound flooded in from the room. The three took off down the hall, making their way to Amelia's glass-walled lab inside the clinic. As they walked, Jael began to see a shift in Amelia. Something was wrong.

Once they were inside, Amelia closed the door and dimmed the clear glass to a dark grey. She pulled the holo-screen up and selected a file named "Buttons."

An image of DNA popped up on the screen, and Amelia pointed to several spots on the double helix which were lit up in red and blinking. "These represent all of the genes that we share with the animal kingdom on our planet."

Then Amelia twisted her hand to move the 3D image that had popped out of the screen. The DNA showed several small spots which were now blinking blue.

"This is all the DNA we share with Jael," Amelia said with her eyes on the double helix.

Completely deadpanning on the outside, Jael could only breathe. Not so much as a single thought could break through her entrenched shock. She wasn't sure Amelia understood how bad this was.

"I can tell by your expression that I should probably just continue," Amelia said as she slowly turned back to the screen.

"We share around sixty percent of our DNA with various plants and creatures on our world. We also share almost fifty percent of our DNA with humans. I don't know if this is because we were genetically engineered or not. I honestly don't see how this could occur organically,"

Amelia turned with worry on her face, looked at Jael, and found her mouth dropped open.

"We should, um, probably get Oz. This is beyond my comprehension," Jael said as she walked over to the lab's communication panel.

"Hi, you should probably come down to Amelia's lab," Jael said, the shock of what Amelia had explained still roiling through her, spreading its tendrils of angst and fear.

Oz nodded and said, "I'll be right there," and the holo-screen disappeared into thin air.

It took less than three minutes for Oz to come barreling into the darkened lab. The open door sent light from the hallway pouring into the lab and caused Jael to squint.

Amelia quickly caught him up. More to himself than the group, Oz said, "I had a sneaking feeling we were engineered. This is going to make it a lot harder to gain our freedom and *stay* free. The leaders of the First Humans, or Primi Homines, might legally claim us as property if their ancestors did in fact create us. Even by combining DNA with a single animal, the act lays out a legal claim for ownership."

With the heat slowly draining from Jael's skin, she said with a hushed voice, "What do you mean *legally*?"

Looking over at Jael, Oz said, "I've been reviewing more of the physician's memories. Are you sure you want to hear this right now?"

Nodding, Oz gave Jael an agreeing tip of his chin before he grabbed a stool and sat down.

"There is a council made up of the planets' leaders called The United Trusts and Colonies, which decides on the major laws that affect all planetary systems with space-faring beings. Slavery is legal as a way to collect debts of all kinds, including life debts. It applies to genetically engineered species but not to naturally evolving creatures. The idea behind the law is that a genetically engineered being owes its existence to its creator, therefore owing a life debt," Oz explained, concern marring his face as he tucked some loose, straight hair behind his ear.

"Are you saying we will have to fight for our independence from a bunch of royal and political leaders *after* we win our planet from the First Humans?" Mercy asked, her brow furrowed and her mouth in a scowl.

Oz nodded and said, "That's exactly what I'm saying. We will have to find out the truth first -- were truly engineered or not. If we *are* engineered, we will have to fight a hell of a lot and most likely still won't ever gain our freedom. If we are *not*, then we can possibly plead our case to the UTC, if we can gain an audience, that is."

Looking positively sick, with bile churning in her gut and creeping up her throat, Jael roughly swallowed and said, "What happens if we find out you've been engineered? Does that mean the First Humans will come back and take over again?"

"Yes. At that point, the First Humans will have the UTC backing them. They have infantry numbering in the millions. We will not stand a chance," Oz said, a cold quiet in his tone.

44

Standing before the table, Oz started the meeting by saying, "As you all know, our people up in the mountain town are dying from the cerebral fungus. We need to send you three to spread the anti-fungal to anyone who is currently sick; give everyone immunity with the nanobots; and begin passing around Jael's gift. Hopefully, in the week or two that you're there, you can plant the seeds we need sown. If we can talk the town leader into helping us recruit, we can build our resistance further," Oz said as he nodded to Amelia, Mercy, and August.

Amelia cleared her throat and said, "Are we going to use a signal booster so that our tablets will be in range of the base?"

Nodding affirmatively, Oz said, "Yes, that's the plan. The booster is small, and to ensure the signal reaches, tech team one is installing two more signal towers inside trees that are much closer to the base of the mountainside. Your tablet will have the ability to transmit programming signals to the nanobots at close range. You will be able to work with the nanobots just like you do in the clinic."

"Mercy, Carter uploaded a diagnostic data collector to your tablet and put sensors all over the suits to track everything. The three of you will wear the armor up until you reach the town. Once you've set up a base camp outside of town and upwind, you will change into inconspicuous street clothes."

Mercy nodded, and August turned on his stool toward Amelia and asked, "Amelia, did your team ever finish the portable anti-microbial scrubbers for the tent? Immunity be damned, I'm not OK with breathing in those spores. I don't want to be stuck wearing a helmet for two weeks while we are creeping around the woods, even if it does look wicked as *fuck*."

"Yes, they finished developing and building them last week. They've already been packed with our gear," Amelia explained, smiling at Mercy's proud expression at August's words about the helmet she helped design.

Beaming as August's words sunk in, Mercy looked over at August and quietly asked, "You like my armor designs?"

"Are you serious? The armor looks like some kind of sick space-battle gear. I love it," August said as he smiled at Mercy.

A wide smile bloomed on Mercy's face as she said, "Thank you," while she adjusted herself on her stool, her curled tail rolling tighter behind her.

"If you're all prepared, I'll have your packs and armor bags brought up to the cave's door," Oz said.

August nodded as he looked at their small team and answered, "Yeah, I think we're ready."

Rising from his chair, August turned to face Mercy and asked, "You did bring your old clothes from home, right?"

Rolling her golden eyes as they walked to the command room's door, "Yes August, I brought my old ugly village girl clothes. I don't see how they could possibly know what I'm wearing all the way from space!"

"You would be surprised what they can see," Oz muttered under his breath as he walked up to the door and opened it.

Thoughts of he and Jael's shared moments on the deck of the treehouse ran through his mind, and anger rose in him over the intimate violation he knew to be true.

Someone had been watching the entire time.

Quietly, the group passed through the long hall that led from the command room into the wide, bright hallway that led to the cave's door. As they approached the door, Mercy saw Jael and ran up to her with a smile.

Throwing her arms around Jael, she pressed her face against her curly hair, and whispered, "I'll miss you so much."

Jael said, "I'll miss you too."

When Mercy finally released her, Jael looked up at Mercy and said, "Carter told me he sent a map for you to upload to your tablets. The armor and helmets will show you where all the transmitting microphones are hidden in the trees around the village, as well as their ranges. After Luna found the first one, Carter's team was able to identify the signal and quickly found the rest of them. That way, you can easily find the best place to speak openly to each other. You can also use a small holoscreen in the forearm of your armor, just like the one in the helmets," Jael said.

Oz started outlining the mission by saying, "We can't

map out the microphones around the mountain town, so rely strictly on your helmet's communication when you get there. Since all of you are now immune to the fungal infection, your main challenge will be to convince the people to accept help and remain silent. Good luck. We will see you back here in a few weeks.

"Oh, and don't worry, Mercy, I sent my mother to get Rew from your house. She will take care of her while you're gone," Oz said with a smile. Then, he opened the door that led into the lava tube.

"Thank you, Oz. I love that spider," Mercy said as she turned and walked through the door.

They made their way to the opening in the ground to leap out. Mercy and Amelia each had a large round bag with a magnetic seal around the top, cinched shut and waiting for them under the mouth of the lava tube. Mercy snapped her pack to the magnetic mounts on her back and smirked at the genius design. August had an enormous duffel bag filled with their tent, and it had magnetic strips along the middle to attach to his back. They quickly dressed in their battle gear and tested their helmets.

The communication software in the helmets was intuitive. The programming could isolate communication with one or more people by simply looking at them, saying their name, or by using any other group designation, verbal or not. Mercy was loving the clean air that was a constant in the helmet. By design, it could infinitely recycle air as long as it was in range of any kind of electromagnetic or electrical power source. The energy hitting the surface of the planet was even strong enough to charge the helmets if given enough time.

August looked at the group with pride, and for the first

time, he truly felt like they could really accomplish this --
they could win their freedom. This wasn't just a dream
anymore. This was becoming real, real fast, he thought.

Even though Oz had told Jacob about in their last meeting, August *knew* they were not genetically engineered.
Something deep inside told him they would win their planet
back, and then win their people's freedom everywhere.
August couldn't quite put his finger on it, but he thought
he had encountered a creature in Jael's memories that had a
mix of DNA from other plants and animals. If only he
could find it again. It was like looking for a single black
grain of sand in a sea of red. His heart began pounding in
his thick body as he shifted his thoughts back to the
mission.

Swallowing down his feelings, August turned his head to
Mercy and Amelia and said, "Ready?"

Both nodded their black helmets and picked up their
packs before leaping from the lava tube and onto the ground
above. Grabbing his own heavy pack from where he had
tossed it moments before, August slung it over his shoulders
to lock it into place on the back of his armor and headed in
the direction indicated on his helmet.

He wondered, if he turned off the guidance, could he
find the mountain town the old way? After assuring himself
he could, he watched Mercy who had her hands out, playing
with options and settings on the suit and helmet. He
wondered how she would do on their journey, knowing she
could handle the terrain as well as he could. He just wished
she knew that.

Mercy was always one of the village's most athletically
gifted members, but she never cared much about any of it.
Amelia, on the other hand, he wasn't sure about. She seemed

to be athletic, but then again, all his people seemed capable in that way.

Even those born without limbs were agile and just as formidable as those who had all their limbs. He smiled to himself as he thought back to his great aunt, who was born with a malformed leg that had to be amputated when she was six years old. As an adult, she had saved four children from a young ground wasp and made it out alive herself. Pride filled August as he remembered his beautiful great-aunt from childhood.

August quickly set aside his thoughts over whether or not he should have physically tested Amelia before they went on the mission. Not that it would have mattered, since she was needed to run the nanotech.

August asked, "Amelia, do you have any prior experience in the wild? Did you ever go out foraging around your village across the mountains?"

Nodding roughly, Amelia said in a sharp tone, "Yes. I've killed a scorpion that likely weighed over a thousand pounds. I only had my sting to kill the beast. Does that answer your question, *August*?"

With his eyes wide, August nodded and said, "Um, yes. I would say that more than answers my question. I'm glad you have the extra experience."

With a flat tone, Amelia quietly said, "I'm not," and took off walking much faster to put some distance between her and the group.

Whipping her head around, Mercy asked, "Uh, August? Did you just say something fucked up to Amelia?"

Dumbfounded, August said in an inquisitive tone, "Well, I didn't think so. Shit! It's been less than fifteen minutes, and I've already pissed someone off. This is *not* a good start."

Shaking her head, Mercy said, "Damn it, August. Next time just *shut up*."

August slung his head back and sighed as Mercy jogged to catch up to Amelia.

Once she drew near, Mercy asked softly, "Amelia? Are you OK?"

Looking back at August, Amelia then shifted her eyes to Mercy and said, "Yes, I'm sorry. August just brought back some painful memories. That's all."

"Do you want to talk about it?" Mercy asked as she took Amelia's hand to slow her brisk walk.

"August asked if I had any experience in the wild. I explained that I had killed a massive scorpion with my venom. He said he was glad I had experience, and I said I'm not. Because I'm not glad. Not at all. That vicious scorpion killed the woman I loved, and I was too late. I would do *anything* to have not had the experience," Amelia said, tears gathering in her eyes as she thought of the pair of beautiful brown eyes she missed so desperately.

Not saying a word, Mercy threw her arms around Amelia and held her tight until August walked up.

Amelia looked at August and said as kindly as she could, "Don't worry, it doesn't have anything to do with you. I'm sorry I made you think that."

Nodding in understanding, August quickly walked on ahead to give Mercy and Amelia a moment longer. The leaves under his boots crunched as he headed around a felled tree, avoiding the line of sight formed by a gap in the trees.

Looking back at them in an embrace, he hoped Mercy

could help Amelia mend whatever great pain she was harboring.

"Are you OK?" Mercy asked as she pulled away to stand in front of Amelia.

"Yeah, I'm alright. I just haven't had time to think about her much since I woke up in the human camp. I lost her several years ago, but the memory of that day is always still as fresh as it was the day it happened when I'm reminded of it," Amelia said, the weight of her loss prevented her from taking a full breath of air.

"I am so sorry, Amelia. I had no idea you lost someone you love," Mercy's breath was sharp, and her gut was in a knot over her friend's pain.

"Most of us on this world have lost at least one special person. In one way or another, we all have our own motivations to change things here. I want to open a medical practice one day and ensure our people have access to antivenoms. I just *know* that if I had the tech I have now, I could have saved her. I don't just want to change this world for us. I want to change this world for her. We don't have to be forgotten to time anymore. We have names and legacies now," Amelia said quietly, as her voice cracked with the pain of each word.

Tears silently fell as Amelia kept her visor darkened.

45

Jacob was excited to have some time off with Callum after they visited Sarah. They hadn't been home together in so long that Jacob felt their apartment at the base was more his home than the house he had lived in since he was a child...before his parents were taken.

With most of the rocket's components designed and tested, the hard part was finished. All they needed to do now was assemble it and beg the creator it worked. They would take out the enemy satellites and implement their own in a matter of minutes, if everything went according to plan that is.

Sliding his hand into Callum's, he hoped he would enjoy the plans he had made for them. If they had to be silent, they could at least have some fun.

Approaching August's mom's home, Jacob held up his hand to knock, but Sarah opened the door before his knuckles had the chance to hit the wood.

A bright smile graced Sarah's elegant face. Her light-brown fishtail braids fell over her shoulder as she opened the door for them.

Since he was a young boy, Jacob thought Sarah was the most incredible woman he had ever met, but he would never admit it to August. He always thought he wanted to find someone like her, someone with poise and power behind their demeanor.

Someone distinguished.

He looked back at Callum, the man who changed his life.

His love, the man that exuded power and grace -- the man who pushed by him one day in the village, and that was all it took.

Jacob had been with a few people in the village but had stayed to himself and his stone path for the most part. Then one day he dared to venture to the other end of the village. He fell in love the moment Callum shouldered him out of the way while he was trying to trade some wood tools he had crafted for oranges.

Jacob reached back and squeezed Callum's hand, their old way of saying, "I love you."

Smiling back at him with a perfect set of fanged teeth, Callum followed Jacob inside after Sarah turned and headed to her living room to find a seat.

Sarah took Jacob's hand and connected with him, saying, "So, what brings you two handsome men to my home?"

Heat flooded his cheeks, and he basked in the compliment.

Hiding his fluster the best he could and failing, Jacob said, "August asked me to stop by and let you know that he, Mercy, and Amelia are headed to the mountain town. Their mission is to implement the nanotech, find the source of the fungal infection, and spread Jael's gift of language and knowledge."

"Good. The traveling avocado salesman said the people I sent with him were having trouble getting anyone to connect with them. They've been wary of outsiders. That was the town on the other side of the mountain. He won't go near the mountain town because of the fungal infection."

"That's a shame. Maybe since the group we're sending will be bringing a cure, they will be more effective at spreading the gift," Jacob said as he released the hand holding Callum's to scratch the back of his neck nervously.

"Sending Mercy is what will be effective. That woman could move a mountain with her will alone. Never doubt her. That mind of hers is like Oz's, Callum's, *and* yours. She just moves to a beat that no one else can hear but her. My August is more like his father and needs a bit of direction. If it wasn't for Mercy, I would worry about August constantly," Sarah explained, with a look in her eye that left the fruit between Jacob's legs pruning in his pants.

He wouldn't tell a soul what Sarah just revealed about August, not after that look. He sincerely wondered if he would have to pry his balls from their hiding place or if they would eventually fall back into place on their own.

Trying to regulate his breathing, Jacob said into the connection, "I think you're right. I will get her on more projects when they return. She hasn't shown a desire to do any of the more technical jobs."

"She doesn't like it, but she has a brilliant mind that you should utilize. The same goes for the sweet man standing next to us. He is exceptionally gifted, and I suspect he has been less than forthcoming about that fact."

Rolling his tan eyes, Jacob said, "More than anyone knows. I think he just hates being told what to do by Oz. Honestly? He just despises Oz altogether. I think Oz hooked up with him, and then ditched him so I can't blame Callum."

Sarah hid a smile and said, "Just wait until Oz and the team are headed up north. Callum will shine, and I'm sure he will put us all to shame."

Nodding and smiling as he quickly peeked at Callum, who was busy studying August's dad's abstract art hanging on the wall. Jacob asked, "Why didn't you want to run for President?"

"Jacob, besides August and his father, I've lived through everyone I have loved being taken, killed, or dying naturally. I can't handle any more death or loss. My well of emotion is tapped. There's nothing inside of me left to give."

Sinking his head with the sharp reminder of their place in the galaxy, Jacob said, "I shouldn't have asked. I'm sorry."

"It was not anything I was hiding. Oz is a good leader, as are you and my son. I'm sure you'll have a change of command happening eventually. Who do you have in mind?" Sarah asked sincerely.

"Are you really going to do your Sarah thing and affect the integrity of the election again?"

Throwing her head back and laughing, Sarah said into Jacob's mind, "See? I'm just too unethical to be anyone's leader anymore. If you must know, I think both Amelia and Luna would make influential government leaders. Both are ideal candidates for our next President. You finding Luna while you were buying avocados was just pure luck. I know you said you simply had a strong feeling she was important. You were more than right on that account."

Jacob mused, "Mercy has raved to me about how brilliant Amelia is. Her fearless ability to selflessly leap head-first into her work is something I deeply respect.

"I don't know much about her personally, but I think August wants to support Zoe as his pick for General. Before we take the human's base, we need to pick our second in command in case anything happens."

"Jacob, you know Oz can try and run from all of this, but his responsibility to his people will always find him," Sarah said while looking at him pointedly.

"How do you know that? If he and Jael took off right now, we would still take our planet," Jacob explained, evident confusion written on his face.

"But would we keep it? Once you make it out into the bustle of the inhabited solar systems, will you be savvy enough to get through every situation? Will you be able to spot a manipulation or something missing from a pattern? Oz, you, and Mercy all have that particular gift, but Oz is the only one who *knows* he can do it. The only one *confident* in it."

Looking defeated, Jacob sighed as he admitted, "OK, you've made your point. How do you do it Sarah? Sort all this *nonsense* out and make sense of it?"

Clearly not wanting to answer, Sarah just said, "Listen. Once you figure out that if you shit where you sleep, you're not going to sleep very well, the rest is pretty simple."

Absolutely confused at Sarah's words, Jacob said, "Um, OK. That's about it for the updates. Did you have anything I need to pass along?"

"No, things are slow and easy again up here since Amelia made the vaccine. Tiny robots, correct?" Sarah asked, with a wide grin gracing her full lips.

Chuckling, Jacob nodded and said, "Yes, Amelia and Carter's tiny robots."

"Was it hard to knock out all of the elders to vaccinate them?" Sarah asked.

"No. We used a heavy sedative. They won't remember anything."

Smiling, Sarah pulled her hand away and broke the connection. She led Jacob and Callum to the door and hugged them both before shutting the door behind them.

Taking Callum by the hand, Jacob led him to the end of the row of homes, then toward the small pond and marsh outside of the village. As they walked through the woods, Callum was nearly skipping with excitement to see what Jacob was planning. They had spent so little time together recently, and Callum was nearly jumping out of his skin with anticipation.

They neared the pond and walked around the edge to the marshy area. Confused, Callum raised an eyebrow and pointed out to the marsh behind the pond. The reeds filled the edges of the shallow water, and tall grass grew from high points in the waterlogged soil.

He was clearly asking why Jacob was taking him to the edge of the swamp, but Jacob had carefully plotted the timing so it would be perfect. He had been waiting for this time of the year to roll around and for this day in particular, but he wouldn't tell Callum *why*. It had driven Callum mad for months. Jacob pulled a blanket from his bag and laid it down on the grass and soft ground before pulling out their meal. The massive willow tree they were seated under began rustling in the soft breeze. The humid air warmed their skin.

After devouring the delicious plates of roasted mixed

nuts and salted avocado with flatbread, Jacob tapped Callum on the shoulder and pointed toward the air above the marsh.

Suddenly a mass of buzzing began, and Callum leaned closer to Jacob while darting his light blue eyes around wildly.

The buzzing grew in intensity, then a mass of bright blue and green fireflies of all sizes emerged from the soggy ground. Swirling and dancing in the air, the beautiful glow of their lights twirled and twisted in the air all around them. The buzz and swirling colors became a colorful wind and spread out into the woods like a mist.

Jacob looked over at Callum and found his eyes glittering with fascination. He had seen glimpses of the firefly singing day at the pond in memories but had never seen it in person. No one understood why they only left the safety of the pond at the same moment in time within the span of a thousand moons. Jacob tried to connect, but Callum shook his head and brought his lips to Jacob's hand instead. Placing a kiss on Jacob's palm, Callum pulled him closer and took his face into his hands.

Closing his eyes and brushing his lips against Jacob's, Callum was filled with love for this man. His heart soared as Jacob deepened the kiss and slid his tongue along the inside of Callum's cheek, carefully avoiding those razor-sharp fangs. Kissing this way was a new adventure since Jael's arrival, and Callum loved it.

Leaning forward into Callum, Jacob laid him back and settled on top of him. A mess of hands and clothes resulted in the two being disrobed and rolling around on the blanket, unable to hold back their passion for one another.

Not wanting to wait any longer, Jacob thumbed his tip for that first bead, then wet his length with lube. He positioned his tip over Callum's entrance, eliciting a breathy moan from him in anticipation. Callum leaned his head up to meet Jacob's eyes as he entered him slowly. Tipping his head back and releasing a long slow breath, Jacob fully seated himself and trembled with the tight sensation.

Running his hand down Jacob's ribs, Callum's fingers softly rolled over the ridges of his sculpted abs. Callum was so in love with this man that he could hardly catch his breath. Jacob slowly began moving inside him, and he took Callum's length in his hand. Unable to resist and with pleasure beginning to crest, Jacob started rolling his hips into Callum faster until he saw Callum's lips part in a delicate moan. With the look on Callum's face and the wet heat spilling over his hand, Jacob tipped over, and his body shook as he emptied himself into Callum.

The two lay on the blanket and caught their breath before heading over to the pond to swim. They both needed a bath since their bodies were slick with sweat. Some of the blue and green fireflies buzzed around overhead. Jacob swam over to Callum and took his hand to connect.

Jacob said, "I love you. I don't know who I would be right now if you hadn't given me a chance all those years ago. That thought scares the venom out of me. I don't ever want to be without you. I've loved you since the moment I saw you."

"You would probably be sad and lonely, just like you were when I first met you. I know your parents had just been taken when I came into your life. It was apparent you cared about me, but I feared being hurt again. I know I probably could have picked a better time to show you how I felt, but I couldn't stand your sad face. It was killing me. I just knew if

I didn't have you right then, I would have gone insane," Callum admitted while he treaded water to stay afloat.

"I had never even so much as looked at a person before you and cared at all. No matter how many people I was with, they were all empty. That first kiss with you was a bit of a shock, but damn, it was *everything*. Looking back, I wouldn't change anything. I needed your affection at that moment more than you'll ever know."

"I've loved you for a long time, a really long time. Longer than you know." Callum said as he broke the connection and slid his lips to Jacob's.

The usual sounds of a vibrant village were missing. All August, Mercy, and Amelia heard was an eerie silence as they walked along the stone paths between the rows of homes and small shops.

No sounds came from inside any of the homes. All the front yards were overgrown. Some of the more extensive gardens had spilled over onto the path, the vines of gourdes and squash reaching out like long fingers from between the slats of the fence panels. Every window and door were sealed shut, and some of the larger cracks were stuffed with neutral-colored silk. The paths were littered with needles blown from the massive pine trees that were all around.

As they reached the center of town, August thought he could hear a knocking sound coming from the end of one of the stone pathways. He tipped his head, and they followed as he searched for the source of the only sound in the town. They continued down the long path, and when it split, August stopped to push a braid away from his ear and listened.

This time the knock was much louder.

He tipped his head in the direction of the sound again, and everyone followed him to the end of the path. From there, they could tell that the knocking sound was from a large wooden mallet. Seeing nothing, they kept going until August threw his hand up for them to stop. He carefully curled his index finger over his shoulder, so Amelia and Mercy approached each side slowly and quietly.

When they looked over the edge of the fence, what they witnessed caused searing bile to rise in their throats. More than twenty townspeople were bound by their hands and feet, and their ropes were nailed to various trees. All were gnashing their broken teeth and chittering. Some were growling.

All were fighting their bonds in the same direction. They were focused on a single person who was nailing the end of a rope to a tree. The other end of the rope was tied around the neck of a nude, deranged blue man with blue-black hair who was lying on the ground. He was bound and desperately trying to snap his teeth at the large person with tan skin and solid white hair, the person who was ultimately sealing his fate.

August softly whistled from behind his silk mask as he, Mercy, and Amelia all put their hands over their chest in solidarity. Hearing the whistle, the person's head snapped up and saw the trio standing there. The towering person held the hammer to chest and then tipped the head, conveying that the trio should wait a moment to connect.

As the person walked up the small hill, hammer in hand, all the mottled-grey infected people changed their angle and twisted their heads. The twenty or so lost people followed along as the person walked up the path like they were watching their dinner escape. Once they neared, their hulking frame was more pronounced, and August looked up into orange eyes as he stuck his hand out to connect.

After the connection was sealed, August began by showing them a few glimpses of his time with his family.

Then, with his heart in a self-inflicted vice to keep his emotion from spilling over into the connection, August showed his first love and then his loss.

They showed great emotion, and it overwhelmed August. He looked up at their face, and they had eyes wide with sorrow. Tears glittered as their loving nature was expressed. August was barely able to catch his breath as they released a hint of their anguish at August's loss through the connection.

August went on and passed them a hint of his own deep longing for change. Once the feeling was received, they nodded in understanding. Then, August allowed his grand emotions of hope to flood the connection before he showed the images of Oz finding Jael.

They grabbed August's arm with their right hand and squeezed it in shock. August then quickly shared his and Jael's eventual connection and again flooded them with feelings of hope and love. He desperately hoped that this person would accept these feelings, so that he would know they were ready.

The person sent August feelings of deep inquisitive desire, longing for more.

He was more than ready, August decided, as he looked into their focused orange eyes. It was a gift to be able to share the key to freedom in the midst of so much sorrow and death.

He *loved* this part.

Watching as their eyes widened, August passed the gift of language and Jael's knowledge to them.

Within a count of ten, their hands began shaking, and tears poured from their eyes as they received the last of the gift and threw their arms around August. August had made sure to include his own memories of Amelia working in her lab and the cheers which erupted all over the base at her cure.

Unable to help herself, Mercy wrapped herself around their slowly calming body. Within her and August's embrace, they finally regained a sense of peace and brought their head up.

They looked over to Amelia, and she smiled as she pulled her mask down while raising her medical kit. Jumping back from August and Mercy, they had a bewildered look and pointed to the writhing people below and then to the med kit.

Amelia just smiled and nodded, her mask lowered under her chin. August and Mercy both pulled their masks down and smiled at their expression of absolute relief.

They slammed their massive body to their knees, shaking and sobbing as they grasped the sides of their own head, white braids falling forward over their shoulders. They had a look of lightheadedness about them.

Amelia dropped to the ground next to them and pulled out the first of over a thousand thin, two-inch-long nanobot injectors. She placed the narrow cylinder against their forearm and pressed the trigger, injecting the nanobot serum into them. Pulling out her tablet, she activated the nanotech then nodded to them that it was done.

They immediately reached their hand out to connect with Amelia.

Shouting with urgency and with tears pouring like rivers from their eyes, "Son, sick! PLEASE!"

"Show me," is all Amelia said before they leaped to their feet and sprinted at top speeds all the way to a small house nearby.

They were sobbing and pleading with every pounding step.

They flew at the door and crashed through, running into the darkness of the home. The trio followed them into one of the bedrooms and saw the small, sweet face of a sick child wrapped in sheets and lying on top of a small silk mattress.

Amelia swung her head back with relief at the sight of the child being fully responsive, with big wide orange eyes and no grey patches on the bright golden skin. Grinning, with her eyes burning, Amelia let out a slow breath of relief through her pursed lips.

It wasn't too late.

Unable to do anything but act, Amelia fell to her knees on the wood floor in front of the boy with a crash. She pulled the next injection from her med bag, promptly injecting it into the five-year-old boy's searing hot arm. After the nanobots for the boy's immunity were injected, she filled a syringe with antifungal to kill off the existing infection.

The trio had arrived just in time to save this little life.

She pulled out her tablet and activated the nanotech. Moments later, the procedure was finished, and she smiled at his parent. They dropped down and smiled at their son, then hugged the small boy to their chest in relief.

Amelia raised her hand and tapped her index finger on their shoulder. They smiled at her and nodded as they rose to their feet, guiding her to the other end of the room to connect as they sat down on their padded bench.

"How many people are in your town?" Amelia asked slowly and carefully, hoping they had already sorted out at least some of the language.

"I don't know. Maybe a little over six hundred of us are left. We've lost hundreds of our people. I've marked the homes of the sick," they said slowly and deliberately.

"My name is Amelia. You met and connected with August first. Mercy is the brown-haired woman there. We need to find the source of the infection if you haven't found it yet."

"No. We have not found it. I marked all the sick homes with thick black mud smeared on the top of every door."

"That's perfect. That means August can look for the planted body while we cure the rest of the town."

"Planted? What does that mean?" they asked, confusion written on their face.

"Your town is being flushed out by the same people who have been abducting us for generations. They are trying to make the entire town move so they can take people more easily."

Horror spread on their face, and Amelia said, "Don't worry, we have a plan, and a base. Here, I'll show you a bit."

Amelia ran through a few memories of the base and her lab.

After showing them the memories, they simply asked, "Can my name be Choir? I think I will want to sing when we are free."

A mix of fear, hope, and sorrow slammed into Amelia at their words.

"Your name can be whatever you wish. Let's go heal your town, Choir. Take me to their back doors. We need to be sure that we stay under complete tree cover as we heal your people," Amelia said before breaking the connection and standing to collect her medical bag and tablet.

Mercy and August both waved to the boy and left out of the back door. Soon after, Amelia and Choir shuffled out of the back door of the home. Before closing the door, Choir simply held a hand up telling their son to stay home. He nodded with a wide grin, clearly already feeling better, and they shut the large wooden door with a soft scrape against the floor and a click.

Amelia nodded to Mercy and August, and she and Choir headed off toward the homes of the townspeople who were the closest to madness.

August and Mercy headed straight for their camp which had been set up upwind from the town. They needed to change into their armor before attempting to find the source of the fungal infection.

August wasn't risking anything when it came to Mercy.

August and Mercy finally reached their camp after a mile of walking. Mercy was ready to get this next task over with. She didn't want to tell August, but she was absolutely terrified of the infected people who had crossed over the line and lost their minds. On Jael's world, the media had been obsessed with zombies, and Mercy felt bile rise in her throat at the thought.

Here, those horrifying "zombies" were *real*.

Amelia had explained it all to her. Once the spores break through the blood-brain barrier, they settle inside the middle of the brain, around the central arteries, in order to take root. The spreading fungal fingers slither through the soft brain cells and dine, absorbing the broken-down tissues as they go.

The fungus uses the brain and body's tissues to feed its stem and cap.

Mercy couldn't think about that when she was heading to find the source of the infection. Unable to hold back her disgust and fear, Mercy vomited bile all over the ground.

Halting in his tracks, August turned and walked back toward Mercy. Rubbing her back with one hand, he just stood holding her hair back with the other and patiently waited for her to recover. Once she stood, he took her face in his hands and kissed her forehead.

She *could* get through this.

She knew she could.

She *had* to.

Releasing her pent-up breath, Mercy nodded, and they continued. The camp they had set up earlier in the day was just over the hill.

As soon as they saw the camp, Mercy put on her armor as August prepared a small meal. She hadn't eaten much since they had left the base, and she wasn't hungry, but she knew it could be a while before she would want to eat again. She needed to eat, that much was obvious.

So, she didn't protest his offer and sat down next to August in her solid black, intelligent armor. He handed her a small bowl with dried fruit and nuts, and she began forcing it down.

The way the armor hugged her body was a comfort, and it reminded her that they were on a mission. She needed to keep her emotions in check.

It wasn't the time to cry or get upset.

She didn't have time to get sick again.

It was time to *work*.

After finishing his roasted nuts and dried fruit, August

slipped into his armor. The suit's neck opened, and it slid over his bare skin easily. He couldn't find any buttons -- then he shook his head at himself as he remembered the suit was held together by magnetic fasteners along the seams.

The armor can only be removed if the wearer wishes it or if someone wearing the same type of armor takes it off. If the suit doesn't get the right signal upon removal the person tampering with it will receive a severe, deadly shock. The magnetic fasteners are locked together with an electric current that originates in front of the H-cell batteries and travels under the electromagnetic absorption panels.

August slipped on his helmet, and watched as Mercy slid hers over her head.

After she had bundled her hair and tucked into place under the back of the helmet, she turned back to look at August and said, "Are you ready to get this over with?"

She heard her helmet sealing around her neck and her ears popped with the change in pressure.

August answered, "Yes. Remember, it could take us days to find the planted body."

August could *feel* her narrow her eyes behind her darkened face shield, and she said flatly, "*Don't* remind me."

The two headed toward the house closest to their camp. August pointed to the gap in the trees at the side of the house, so Mercy walked around it and stayed under the tree cover. August reached the door first, and the door was unlocked. He went inside, and Mercy followed.

"I'll check the bedroom on the right. You look to the left," August instructed.

Mercy nodded and entered the room to the left. Looking around, she found cloth strewn about. It was partially used as a sewing room, and Mercy's heart caught as she thought of her own sewing room. She looked under the table and under the child's bed in the corner but saw nothing.

"This room is clean, August."

"This one is, too. Let's go to the next house," He replied.

Nodding, Mercy followed August out of the house, and he left a long, deep slash across the door with his knife before he closed it.

After a few homes on the same street came back empty and clean, August and Mercy went around their camp and up to a separate row of houses that August hadn't seen when they looked around the first time.

They inspected all those homes and found nothing. They had likely been vacant for many months.

Noticing the layers of dust in the second home, Mercy said, "August, I think these were the first homes that were hit. You said Oz and Jacob think they are trying to flush people out of this town. So, that would mean they find it inaccessible. Why would the humans put an infected corpse in a home? Wouldn't they put it somewhere they could reach?"

"I wish I could kiss you right now, Mercy. You're a fucking genius," August said as he headed over to and out of the open window.

The window had been their mode of entry, since both doors were exposed to open sky.

The two headed up the side of the ancient caldera's edge. The mountain they stood on, like all the mountains in the middle of their continent, mainly consisted of long-extinct volcanoes. Either they were dead and crumbling, or they were fully dormant. They knew the mountains had been volcanoes because of the distinct shape of the summits and the occasional wafting clouds of sulfuric gas seeping from the center of the highest peak's crumbling caldera.

Once he reached a high point in a tree, August said, "OK, how do I access the visual features on this helmet?"

As he said the words, the screen popped up at arm's length, and August quickly found the settings he needed.

"Oh, wow. Well, never mind then. The helmet heard me," August said as he flipped through the options.

Any other time, Mercy would be giggling at August, but she couldn't even muster up a small smile.

Peering around from his perch in the giant pine tree, August gasped when he finally spotted what he was looking for. The person was hung from a tree by their neck. After zooming in, August found a desiccated body with a single massive fungus stalk growing from its temple.

Cringing in disgust, August said, "Mercy, I spotted the corpse. Just go to camp, and I'll take care of it."

"Not a chance. I'm not leaving you to do it by yourself. I'm with you until this is finished," Mercy said, even as she cringed with every word.

Sighing at his beautiful, stubborn woman, August slid down the pine tree. Stopping only at wide branches, just to keep dropping down between them without delay.

Once he dropped onto his feet next to Mercy, they headed in the direction of the hanging body. Although they had found the body's location, August felt like something was off. The skin on his arms tingled, and his senses went on high alert.

Something wasn't right.

They continued walking, and August wanted to increase his auditory awareness, so he said, "I need to hear my surroundings better."

Listening to his request, the helmet amplified the sounds around them. That's when he heard it. Taps? It wasn't footsteps but more of a clicking sound.

Then scratching.

It was getting closer.

Looking at Mercy, August tried to focus on the increasing sounds. He heard a snap from up in the tree. Just as he raised his head to look, something large crashed onto them from high above. August was disoriented and shook his head, trying to clear his mind as he heard a blood-curdling shriek coming from Mercy's helmet. A red light at the corner of his visor blinked, showing him where the noise came from.

Whipping his head around, he found Mercy grappling with a deranged and snarling infected young man. His greying skin had a shining sheen of sweat. Leaping to his feet and still in a daze, August rushed the few feet to Mercy.

Mercy whipped the young man over and pressed her arm into his chest. In one motion, she retrieved her plasma sword from her belt, pressed the activation switch, and sliced the growing stream of plasma across his neck. His lanky body slumped as the remaining life left the young man's tan eyes. His matted brown hair was a sorrowful halo around his half-severed head.

Blue blood poured from his gaping neck, and Mercy rushed as she pulled his shirt up and around the wound to keep the blood contained. A collection of oozing bite marks and missing skin was evident on his chest. He had been attacked by an infected person. Mercy's heart broke for him and his family at the sight. As she looked at the dirt surrounding his head, she knew they would have to dig up the contaminated soil underneath and take it when they disposed of the body.

This was why they didn't just kill them when they went mad.

The fungus spores would seep into the ground with the blood and feed off the organic material in the soil to grow their stem and cap. It would only grow to a miniature size, but the spores that spread in the air from the tiny caps were just as deadly.

The bandage made of his torn clothes held, and Mercy cried out in relief, "Thank the creator for these plasma swords!"

August chuckled as he rubbed his sore neck and said, "I think you just passed the physical test for the next mission."

"I am so overjoyed to hear that," Mercy said without looking up, her tone flat.

Clearly, she was not interested in August's comment.

Chuckling again, August said, "OK, let's cut down this fungal-filled fuck and throw him down the mountain so we can go home."

Clearing her throat in astonishment, Mercy said, "Wow. Fungal-filled fuck is what we're going with?"

Shaking his head, he scaled a tree that he knew was close to the hanging body, and after a bit of searching, he found where the stiff, dried-out body hung.

"I can't get up there without being seen from the sky. I need some ideas," August said, wearily.

Throwing her hands up, Mercy said, "Just, um. Act like a big scorpion. A giant scorpion would pull it from the feet and work its way up, right? Just pull hard enough that the head pops off!"

Mercy beamed with pride at her quick plan and smiled

as she looked up toward August.

Pausing a moment in thought with his hand on his hip, August pointedly said, "Is this the plan were going with? Maybe let's come up with an idea that does not involve a dead person's *head* popping off?"

Mercy just deadpanned him as her visor went clear so he could see her face. She said flatly, "Not a thing, sorry. Just let me know when you yank the feet so I can, hopefully, catch the head."

"I didn't think you were going to make the plan even worse but, *here we are,*" August said flatly with his eyes closed and his head tipped up.

Quickly scaling further up the pine tree, he roughly exhaled a breath of frustration as he carefully approached under the feet of the dangling body.

"I heard that," Mercy said, hands on her hips and eyes narrowed.

"Thanks a lot, you damn helmet," August grumbled under his breath.

"I really don't think that's the helmet's fault, August," Mercy said with her arms held out and ready.

After she heard the sound of August pulling on the person's foot, he laughed as he yelled, "Heads up!"

Mercy shot her eyes up just in time for the severed head to fall directly into her arms, a large white fungus protruding from the temple and clusters of smaller ones beginning to grow out of both eye sockets. The teeth in the mouth were nothing but broken stumps, and it took everything Mercy had to not vomit into her helmet.

Twisting her head around to take her eyes off the grotesque sight in her grasp, Mercy yelled, "Oh venom! I take it back! This *was* a horrible idea!"

Laughing, August could hardly get his words out as he said, "His body is coming next! I'm *not* carrying fungal Fred all the way down."

Backing up, Mercy braced herself for the sight of the headless, dried out body.

With frustration in his tone, August asked, "Are you out of the way? I really wanna let go of decomp-dude's wrinkly ass ankle. He feels like a people-prune and it's really creeping me out."

Scoffing at all of August's grotesque comments, Mercy said, "Oh that's so fucking sick. Uh, yeah. I'm out of the way now."

Right as August released the body, Mercy asked, "Has anyone ever told you you're fucked in the head? Did you *really* just say people-prune? I think I'm going to be sick again."

Moments later, a large body plopped onto the ground. A thin rope from August's armor was cinched around its neck, over a piece of silk clothing, which sealed the open neck's stump. Mercy was thankful he had thought of that. She didn't want to carry the extra weight of contaminated dirt. Dragging the wrapped bodies to the steep part of the mountain side would be heavy enough without extra soil.

August slid down the pine tree and planted his booted feet next to the body with a graceful landing.

Taking the severed head from Mercy, August said, "You could have put it down. We have to go get the body bags before we toss them off the cliff. Plus, we need to sterilize and change into street clothes before we can be seen."

"Lead the way," Mercy said as she shook her head and held her hand out toward the campsite.

47

After she finished bundling the body and head in a sealed silk bag, Mercy said, "Is it just me, or was that body oddly light for its large size?"

"I think this person had their blood drained. I'm assuming he was male from his size. I'm sure some organs are probably missing too based on the caved in the stomach. If we did an autopsy, we would probably find plenty of evidence left from the humans," August said before he finally pulled off his helmet.

They had each dragged a body, and Mercy had the dried-out body from the tree. She suddenly felt guilty because her load had been much lighter than August's.

She shook her head after removing her helmet then set the helmet down out of sight next to August's load. They both pulled up their silk masks to keep up appearances. They had already stopped at the campsite and changed into inconspicuous tunics and loose pants.

The cliff was on the opposite side of the town from

where they had found the body in the tree. They had to pull the body bags all the way around the perimeter of the small town, leaving them both quite winded by the time they arrived. The journey was more than four miles according to the maps on the helmets' holoscreens. They cringed with every breath behind the masks and missed the filtered clean air of their helmets. Immune or not, they were still disturbed at the idea of inhaling any of the spores.

Mercy joined in and helped August pull the bags toward the cliff's edge. August turned to Mercy and wished he could speak aloud to her like he could with the helmet on, but instead he just met her eyes and smiled to reassure her it was all going to be OK. They pulled the bags to the edge and pushed them over. Mercy and August each peered over the edge to watch the bags fall. The bags hit the bottom of the cliff and rolled down into the valley directly below.

The sound of rustling leaves behind them sent August leaping in front of Mercy. Two masked people emerged from between the trees, dragging a body bag. They both turned and looked at Mercy and August.

Tipping their heads, August noticed how loose their masks were. They continued dragging the body toward the edge. August also noticed that their bag was the same as his and Mercy's, so he smiled to himself. They must have already met Amelia and were likely dumping some of the freshly deceased from the area where they first met Choir.

August followed the two masked people back into town with Mercy in tow. Once they reached the edge of town, August tipped his head to the two people with red skin and black hair, and they walked up to what looked to be their home. Mercy spotted Amelia's blue hair in the distance and tapped August so he would look where she was pointing. He nodded, and they headed toward Amelia, who was heading inside the shaded front door of a home with Choir.

They didn't hear much from outside, so August softly knocked on the door. Swinging it open, Choir, in one move, came outside while simultaneously shoving Mercy inside. With bewildered eyes, Choir looked over at August and seemed dazed. Then, a high-pitched scream erupted from inside the home. Choir's eyes widened.

They were surprised when the door swung open again. Mercy shoved the small med bag of nanobots into Choir's chest and shewed them away. She slammed the door behind her, and August caught a glimpse of excitement on her face before the door shut.

With the second scream, it finally dawned on August what was happening. He remembered the neighbor two doors down screaming for three days while having her baby. His mother had explained that the cream-skinned woman with brown hair had been pregnant with three babies, and that was why she was in so much pain. After a third scream erupted from the home, Choir couldn't take it anymore, and they took off to the next house.

August would just keep injecting the sick people with the nanobots and let Amelia and Mercy attend the pregnant person inside, he guessed. He hoped the program on the tablet was simple enough for him to work. He was suddenly relieved he didn't have any actual medical knowledge, or he would have been the one in there.

That thought scared the hell out of him.

Inside, Mercy and Amelia surrounded a young person who lay in a heap of blankets on the bedroom floor. They were at least a day or two into their childbirth. The home was sparse and had little furniture. With the person slick from sweat and panting, Amelia wondered how she was going to calm this person's fears. They were panicked by the newcomers who just stabbed them with the mini syringe loaded with high-tech nanobots.

Amelia took a risk and connected with them between their contractions.

Connecting with someone during birth could allow the pain of contractions to be felt by both people. Amelia decided to forego easing them into it and sent the new parent Jael's knowledge as well as a few glimpses of Amelia practicing medicine at the base.

Experiencing labor pains was on Amelia's *never ever* list, and she pulled her hand away to break the connection at the precise moment.

The young person looked eternally relieved and nodded but didn't respond. They grasped Amelia's hand to squeeze and scream as another hard contraction ripped through them. Amelia felt around on the person's round belly and found it was hard as a stone.

Amelia checked to see if they were nearing the end of labor, and she discovered that this person was mere minutes away from delivering. The baby's head was descending into the birth canal and visible, so Amelia needed to get this person into position for a smooth delivery.

Nodding to Mercy that it was time; Amelia eased the person up from their squatting position on the floor and helped them lean forward. They were positioned on their knees, with both of their thighs spread so that the baby could slide out. Amelia held her hands under their pelvis to grab the baby while Mercy stood in front and helped hold their shoulders up for support. Mercy slid her hands under their sweaty arms, and they immediately reached up and grabbed her by the biceps in an iron hold.

The person looked up to Mercy with terror in their brilliant yellow eyes, tears lining the rim. Mercy set her fear and emotions aside and smiled down at the young person, giving them the brightest grin she could muster.

Amelia whistled, and with a groaning grunt, the person pushed once, and the near-colorless, milky-skinned baby slid out into Amelia's waiting hands. It was a tiny baby. Too small, Amelia quickly realized as she passed the newborn to Mercy after cutting the thin cord with a small knife. When it sank in what this meant, Amelia got her hands ready under the person again and whistled once more.

A screamed filled the small room as they pushed, while Mercy held a baby in one hand and grasped the person under the arm for support with the other.

A second baby emerged with the same milky colorless skin as the last one. The tiny flexible tail curled up the moment the newborn hit the cool air. Amelia cut the cord and wondered how many more were coming.

Mercy had just enough time to find a place on the person's bed to nestle the newborn. Passing the second baby to Mercy, Amelia reached around and felt the pregnant belly of the person, still very round and hard as a rock. Amelia could feel two more distinct lumps and signaled to Mercy that they had a few more coming. Wide-eyed and unsure of where to put the second newborn, Mercy began wrapping it up in silks as she looked for a spot to put the child.

Mercy wrapped the baby up as fast as she could. The thought of being handed more was overwhelming. The person's bed was small, but she didn't want to lay the newborns on the floor.

Preparing her hands a third time, Amelia whistled, and the person pushed. Nothing happened. Amelia whistled once more, and again they pushed. Nothing happened.

Amelia gently pressed on the top of the person's ample belly. The person began nodding and groaning, then whistled as they pushed. Hands ready, Amelia barely caught baby number three, who slid out quickly.

Amelia looked up to find Mercy still wrapping baby two and balancing her left arm which was stretched out in support of the crouching young person. The newborn's head was held in Amelia's hand, and she prayed to the creator that she didn't drop the next one. Baby four followed immediately, and they didn't have time to whistle. In a near panic, Amelia shot her hand under the person and caught the newborn, laying it down on the silk below.

The young person fell on their face with their long black hair strewn about, but Mercy and Amelia could do nothing to help as they both had babies to attend. Amelia carefully set one of the newborns on a clean blanket, then followed by wrapping the other. Amelia wrapped the two babies together; she then did the same with the two Mercy had on the bed.

Next, she had Mercy sit down on the floor and hold all four babies in her lap so she could help their parent. The young parent's babies had come out quickly, and thankfully, she didn't require any stitching. Tearing happened with single pregnancies and not multiples because the individual size of the babies was much smaller. These babies might weigh three pounds each, at the most. The person held their arms out for Amelia to help and sat up to see all their new babies.

Laughter erupted from them, and Amelia looked at them, puzzled. She tapped her fingers together and the person nodded.

After connecting with them, Amelia asked, "Is everything alright?"

"More than alright! I am delighted. I was carrying a child for a couple who could not conceive. They're going to be overjoyed to learn they now have four children!" the person said while they chuckled.

Smiling, Amelia said, "You did great. Would you like me to get their new parents so you can rest?"

"Yes, they're next door. Thank you. For *everything*. The ability to put my thoughts into words is like a breath of fresh air that I didn't know I needed. How can it be passed through our connection?" they asked.

Amelia smiled as she responded, "Language and the muscle memory to speak are both learned, and the information is stored in the central nervous system. When we bridge our minds, they essentially become one for the short time our nerves are interconnected. I can pass over the muscle memory for their spoken sounds as well as the words themselves and their meaning. All three combine to give you the near-instant ability to speak. Usually, we keep this gate tightly shut because our connection is used strictly for communicating images. I must ask, how would you prefer to be addressed, and what name would you like?"

With a mesmerized look on their face, the person said, "I know my home is practically empty, but I need to know how I can help. I am a woman, and I want to be called Lark."

"Before you come to the base, please go, or find someone

else to go, to the village on the other side of the mountain and spread the gift and our mission. You've already received the activated nanobots, so you are immune to fungal infection, *and* you won't be put under as easily. Our enemy cannot knock you unconscious now."

"Done. I know which people to send to the east villages, but I'm not sure they will be received well. Those villages are highly superstitious, and they don't trust anyone. I've always wanted to travel to your village with the silk farms."

Looking over at Mercy, Amelia gave a small smile at the sight. She was admiring all the newborns with a twinkle in her eye and quickly falling in love.

"I'll go get their new parents now. Just lie down and rest until we return."

Moments after Amelia's exit, Mercy could hear her knocking on the neighbor's door and entering their home. She looked down at the babies and wondered if she would one day have children.

In Earth years, she was only in her mid-thirties, and her species could still have children well into their eighties. She had plenty of time to decide if being a parent was right for her.

Knowing what she did, she knew she wouldn't even consider having children until they gained their freedom.

Thankfully, the youngest children are never taken. At around ten years old, the odds of being taken go up considerably. Mercy felt her heart racing in her chest as she tried not to think about why they would want to take children as young as ten.

She embraced the four babies and thought back to their birth, and how Amelia knew precisely what to do. She had guided the room. It flowed out of Amelia like it was all a rehearsed dance. And the way she caught the last two newborns!

Mercy's eyes stung as she replayed it all in her mind. She loved watching Amelia work in her element. It had been a beautiful experience, and one thing was for sure, Mercy wanted Amelia to be there if she were ever having a baby.

48

"Are you *sure* it's not going to work?" Oz said, irritation in his tone.

"Oz. I already told you. The two-component arms are going to become tangled the moment the missiles are deployed. I have done the test simulation over two hundred times. They tangle at least seventy-one percent of the time," Jacob said as he pushed his black braids off his shoulders.

Oz tucked a piece of loose hair behind his ear as he asked, "How do you fix something like that?"

Leaning his head over to glare at Oz, Jacob said in annoyance, "If I *knew*, I wouldn't have asked."

Shaking his head and trying to hide his frustration, Oz grumbled, "Show me the parts and the problem."

Walking over to the enormous rocket, Oz saw the missiles neatly lined up in their deep channels, set flush along the outside of the core of the rocket. They each had their own docking bay and release arms. Oz wondered how the hell there could possibly be a problem but waited patiently as Jacob pulled up the simulation. He hoped it was a simple simulation error, but Jacob and Carter weren't known for mistakes.

The dread in the pit of his gut began churning as he watched.

Approaching the sizable 3D viewing screen, Oz watched as the small missiles became tangled and then impacted one another, resulting in a mass explosion. Sighing in defeat, he wondered what the hell could be done about this.

Not wasting any time, he pulled his glass tablet from under his arm and dialed Jael, asking, "Will you come down to the rocket construction area in Jacob's lab? Bring Carter and Zoe. Tell them it's important."

"Sure. See you in a few," Jael replied and hung up, her face dissolving instantly into nothing above Oz's tablet.

A short time later, Jael arrived with Carter and Zoe tagging along behind. They all reached the view screen that Oz was watching as the simulation continued its loop.

All three stood and stared at the scene on the holoscreen, and all three gasped in unison when the missiles tangled and exploded. The loop started over, and they all looked bewildered.

"How do we fix this without returning to the drawing board?" Jacob asked, defeated and with concern growing in his usually kind tan eyes.

Jael spoke first after noticing the collective anxiety growing in the room. She quickly said, "I don't know how to fix this, but I do know some of the most creative, hard-working people I've ever met are standing around me. If anyone is up for this challenge, it's all of you."

The room seemed to take a deep assuring breath at Jael's words. One thing was clear to Jael, this group of geniuses was riddled with anxiety, and that was something she could relate to. After a long consideration, they all began shifting where they stood, and Jael could tell they were finally focused.

"Can the arms be shortened? Does this also happen with the rocket that houses our satellites? Or just the missile-only rockets?" Zoe asked, her eyes narrowed on Jacob.

"Just the rockets with the missiles. They're packed too close, but we don't have enough time to build a fourth rocket. Plus, our resources are too meager. We wouldn't be able to pull it off for several months, if at all. These three rockets are finished, aside from this one major glitch, so we need to try and correct this. I don't know how I missed such a significant problem during the design phase."

Jacob leaned his head to the side toward Jael and said, "By the way, thank you for doing so much research on space propulsion back on Earth. Your knowledge has been invaluable to my process. I basically copied the design from a magazine article you read about some smelly fellow."

Smelly fellow? She wondered who he was talking about but didn't dare ask. Jael wasn't sure if she should tell him what she had been thinking for a while, that her recall wasn't even close to what his was. She couldn't use the information nearly as well as he could.

Through the connection, Oz had shown her how to pick apart her memories and pull out the information she needed. Her memories had become thousands of hours of visual records, where she could isolate the things she had seen but never processed. She wondered if she had even read the magazine article, or if it had been one of the times she had pretended to read so no one would talk to her. Those memories were much harder to recall.

"Thank you," was all she could mutter through her racing thoughts.

Zoe tapped her boot against the stone floor while staring at the holoscreen and asked, "What if you changed the angle of the arms after release? Does it allow enough room? Or what if we deployed them in two different batches? I feel like this can be solved with logical strategy alone, and then no physical changes will need to be made."

"Are you suggesting a think tank?" Oz asked Zoe, one black eyebrow raised in her direction.

"Exactly. We need to bring some food and drinks down here. We might be in Jacob's hidey hole for a while," Zoe teased as she shot Jacob a sly grin and bounced her brown eyebrows a few times.

Rolling his eyes at Zoe's cheesy attempt at a joke, Jacob said, "It's not my *hidey hole*. It's called an engineering lab and fine, I'll go to the mess hall and grab food and drinks."

"The *alcoholic* kind, Jacob. If you show up with just juice, I'm gonna be pissed," Zoe said over her shoulder with a flare of authority.

Stopping to listen, Jacob then continued to walk. He didn't even so much as acknowledge Zoe's request.

Taking her eyes to her tablet, she called the kitchen and said, "Risk, Jacob is coming down there to pick up dinner for us. We *need* alcohol. He didn't seem too excited about that."

After Risk let out a howling laugh, he chuckled as he said, "Got it. Grab the red mangoes first, hot stuff."

The holoscreen abruptly shut off, and Oz leaned over toward Zoe and said, "Thanks. I must agree. Any mechanical problem *Jacob* can't fix calls for alcohol."

Carter looked puzzled for some time after the holo-graphic loop had stopped. No one dared bother him, as he clearly had some intense mental processing happening. Several minutes of silence passed while they all followed suit, staring at the empty space where the holoscreen simulation had been running.

"I wonder if we could create a different flight pattern for when they are first ejected from the docking bay? Maybe we could make them dance to prevent the collisions?" Jael suggested quietly, more to herself, but fully aware everyone around her had superior hearing.

The entire group slowly turned to look at her, and after a few moments, Oz smirked as he finally said what the group had been thinking, "And all this time, you thought you couldn't contribute ideas. But here you are, giving us our first realistic option."

Jael looked over at Oz inquisitively with her brown eyes wide and said, "Oh. I didn't think anyone would even listen to my idea. I kind of pulled that from nowhere."

Carter's deep laugh filled the enormous room, and he looked over at Jael as he said, "Your mind is how you ended up here in the first place, don't forget that. Jacob designed our missiles' engines to operate in zero-G at above light speed. It was based entirely on *your* design of the electromagnetic drive. We simply increased the frequency of the electromagnetic waves filling the central chamber. Theoretically, the science is sound. We have crunched the data in simulations endlessly, and we have more than ninety-nine percent confidence in the design."

Jael whipped her head around to Oz and squeaked, "You didn't tell me Jacob based the missiles' engines on my EmDrive experiment."

"I'm not sure why, but I thought you knew?" Oz asked as he took a step toward Jael.

"No. I didn't," Jael abruptly sat on the padded bench behind them by the wall, stars growing in her vision from her heart pounding. Why did she feel so odd to find out something wonderful?

Oz quickly sat next to her and said, "I'm sorry, I really should have said something."

"I'm just a little overwhelmed, that's all," Jael explained as she gently patted Oz's strong thigh.

After walking over to Jael and sitting on the long bench, Zoe asked, "Carter, how long would it take to re-write the program to include a trigger command that would change the trajectory and position of the missiles."

"We could use proximity sensors. If we mounted them on the arms, maybe we could get the arms to fold inward and hold flush against the missile until they're needed. We aren't sure if the human's satellites have any defensive capability. If they do, we need to be able to attach the missile with the arms to ensure its total destruction. The last thing we need is to partially cripple the satellite and not entirely destroy it," Carter suggested as he slipped his hands into his pockets.

"That might actually work," Zoe said, with her hands on her hips.

The door to the cavern flew open, slamming against the wall, and Jacob grimaced at the sound as he walked through it. The bags of food from the kitchen went swinging in his grip as he whipped back around to head inside.

"Carter, can you help me set out the food?" Jacob asked, and Carter headed over to assist him.

"If half of the missiles are being guided by people here at the base, then should we just focus on the other half that spread automatically from the rocket? Maybe we should have a set program for the missile release and not start the manual controls until all of them are at a safe distance?" Zoe explained, as she inconspicuously tried to locate the bag with the red mangoes.

"I think we need to develop a program that incorporates all these elements. Sensors that help the arms avoid tangling are necessary, without question. So, after we design the missiles' dance, we can use a program to keep the initial missiles' trajectories separated," Oz said while they all headed toward the table and food that Jacob and Carter were setting out.

Jacob nodded with a blooming smile of relief and asked, "I agree. Carter, can you head up to your office and get a team together to work on the framework for the program? We can work on the missiles' dance design and the arm proximity sensors down here."

"Sounds great. I'll eat and then head down. I haven't eaten in days," Carter said as he began slowly nibbling at his food.

"*Days?*" Zoe asked incredulously as she stared at Carter.

Carter looked at Zoe as though she was the one who was confused and asked, "You are aware we don't need to consume food every day, right?"

Rolling her green eyes so hard that they disappeared behind her eyelids, Zoe said with a concerned tone, "You *never* forego eating. Is something going on with you? Are you OK?"

"Now that you mention it, I have felt rather strange the last few days. It's unpleasant. It's almost as if a storm is brewing in the atmosphere, but nothing ever comes," Carter explained with his brow furrowed in thought as he stared at his plate of food.

Clearing his throat, Oz turned and suggested, "Maybe you should see Amelia and have her run some tests."

"Yes, I think that's something I will do right after we finish eating," Carter said while rubbing the top of his stomach with worry marring his usually calm face.

Carter refocused on his food while Zoe looked up at the view screen. She took a sharp breath and yelled, "That's it!"

As she stood, Zoe dumped the rest of her meal on the floor, the plate clattering against the stone.

Zoe grabbed her tablet from the table and pulled up a three-dimensional model of the missiles' deployment. She paused the loop then moved the rows of missiles so that they would tip on their side perpendicular to the rocket upon release from their holding channel. Then, she moved every second missile in the row so that they would slide over and create a new row in the middle. The second set of missiles would remain in their own row. They would create a diamond grid hovering at a ninety-degree angle from the rocket and thus avoid tangling because the arms of the missiles would be far enough apart.

"A dance to prepare the missiles before ground control takes over," Zoe said proudly as she threw the altered simulation onto the enormous holoscreen from her tablet with a swipe of her hand.

Everyone watched as the program played without showing an explosion, then restarted and simply halted after the missiles had all found their place.

Oz nodded and said, "Well done, Zoe. Now, where are those *red mangoes*?"

Zoe grinned and opened the half-emptied bag that was

next to Carter. Jacob glared at everyone around the room as Zoe pulled out the large bottle of pre-mixed alcohol from underneath the mangoes.

With an accusatory stare and his mouth open, Jacob asked, "Who the hell called Risk after I left?"

Laughter erupted in the room, and they all cheered as Zoe passed around the bottle.

49

After training the healers in the mountain town, Amelia spent some time ensuring they would continue spreading the nanobots by giving instructions on how to use the tablets. The antifungal would kill the spores, but they needed immunity, so the nanobots were essential.

The villagers would have open communication with the base now that they had the transparent holoscreen tablets. Jacob messaged their leader, Choir, and said that he would send a tech team with some additional equipment in a few weeks that would help locate the microphones in the trees surrounding the town. By this time, the field teams had reached nearly halfway up the mountain with signal towers that were hidden inside trees and massive tree trunks.

August handed the signal booster that they had brought with them to Choir right before he raised his hand to signal to Mercy and Amelia that he was ready to head off toward the base. The three stopped right outside of town to put on their armor and helmets. They collected their gear and bags after they packed everything up. The pine trees provided thick cover, and August looked up at the gargantuan trees with respect, feeling thankful for their protection.

Once their helmets were on and they could speak, Mercy said, "I can't wait for a hot shower. I don't think I've ever gone this long without a real bath. I'm honestly scared our body odor is going to attract a red-belly spider! or worse!"

They all chuckled in agreement as they headed down the steep slope. Following the zig-zagging path down the mountainside was somewhat uneventful, and the group slowly increased their pace. After becoming accustomed to their daily hot showers, not one of them could stand the unwashed feeling on their bodies, and all were trying to discreetly scratch, but it didn't work so well in the armor. They made it down the rough terrain by the end of the day.

As they all began preparing for a rest at the base of the mountain, Amelia and Mercy dropped their bags and walked off together to take care of their personal business behind a tree. They both pulled their attached equipment off and sat it on the ground while they relieved themselves. The two had just pulled their armor back up and were slipping their arms in when they heard August let out a blood-curdling scream.

His scream came blasting inside the helmets' speakers.

Amelia and Mercy's helmets muffled the sound, but they both got the message loud and clear and they took off in his direction.

"August!" Mercy yelled into her helmet speaker as she pulled the armor up and around her neck.

Coming around a large tree, they saw August pinned under the legs of a giant red wasp, face down and lifeless. Mercy screamed at the top of her lungs as her eyes fell on the massive, winged creature, and it struck her what was about to occur. The wasp's long thick body was a glossy black, and her fire-orange wings shimmered in the glow of the colorful auras in the sky that were peeking through the trees.

The iridescence of her wings sparkled as she began to spread them out.

She was preparing to carry him off...

So that she could bury his paralyzed body along with her egg.

The larvae that hatched would slowly eat him alive over weeks.

Crippling fear ripped through Mercy as she went far beyond her limits sprinting toward August.

"Amelia! What the fuck do we do?!" Mercy screamed in the helmet as her feet hardly contacted the ground.

She had never seen a giant red wasp, but she knew exactly what sinister plans this monster had in store for August.

Amelia just stood there stunned and fell to her knees. Mercy didn't give Amelia another thought as she launched herself in a running leap, landing on top of the massive beast's head with a thud. The wasp began shaking her head and tried to snap at Mercy's dangling legs, which hung in her face. Grasping onto her antennae, Mercy hoisted herself on the beast's head and pleaded to the creator that her plasma sword was not on the ground by the tree she had just squatted behind. Mercy wrapped her legs around the wasp's neck and locked her feet under her head.

August continued to lie lifeless on the ground as the creature seemed to be rocking over him. Mercy slapped her hips, trying to find her plasma sword, but it wasn't there.

Mercy had to fight the bile rising in her throat as she desperately tried to think of something.

Anything.

In her fear, rage, and uncertainty, she screamed, "Fuck!"

Mercy franticly began beating the creature's dense carapace to no avail. Her stinger was not going to be able to break through the hard exoskeleton, and terror filled her eyes as she realized she was running out of options. If she couldn't figure out what to do, this wasp would fly off with both of them. She likely had a nest, and Mercy would become the next victim.

Screaming into the helmet, Mercy screeched, "Please! I can't lose you! I can't fucking lose you!"

The fluorescence of the beast's wings hit her eyes as the deadly wasp slowly began to climb into the sky.

Out of nowhere, an idea struck her, and she screamed into the helmet, "Charge the suit! I need a charge! Fucking helmet, I need you to shock this bitch with everything you've got! NOW!"

A buzz in her ear was the only warning as a bright white, crackling electric current rolled down her limbs, growing in intensity as it headed toward her outstretched hands. The bright light from the white, sparkling electricity was so intense it sent flailing tendrils sparking and spreading up her arms.

Two balls of lightning formed around Mercy's hands before she leaned forward and screamed as she slammed her fists against the base of the wasp's buzzing wings. The monstrous wasp thrashed violently as Mercy forced her crackling fists to burn through the thin membrane of the glittering wings.

Her legs firmly gripped the wasp around its slender neck. In one motion, Mercy spread her hands out as wide as she could and forced her arms up to rip down the center of the vibrating wings. They hit the ground in a rolling heap, and Mercy gripped her legs around the wasp as the beast thrashed. Mercy prayed that August wasn't crushed when they hit the ground.

Or dropped from a height too high to survive.

Crying out in anger, Mercy shook the confusion from her mind as she kept burning and shredding the wasp's delicate wings with her electrified hands. She saw stars as her body was slammed into the base of a tree, and she screamed again as she burned all the way through one of the wings. Relief blossomed deep inside of her as she watched the wing hit the ground. The wasp was bucking, and Mercy frantically scanned the ground for August.

"Where is August?!" She cried out into the helmet.

The view screen popped into existence, and a red dot blinked a few yards away. Mercy fell from the beast's back as her legs finally gave out. It flung her away onto the ground, slamming her hard enough to knock the air from her lungs. Watching as the one-winged black wasp scurried off into the darkness of the woods, Mercy wheezed as she pulled her body up against the tree she had landed by and desperately tried to fill her lungs with air.

After she caught her breath, she asked the helmet, "Can you show me where August and Amelia are?"

Two red dots popped up on her holoscreen, and she scanned the woods to ensure they were all still alone before she stood up and walked toward the first red dot.

As she approached August, she looked at his legs closely. Mercy found a single, small, tough white sack of viscous liquid and several puncture holes in his armor. He had been stung several times.

"What is this?" Mercy said to herself as strings of goop stuck to her fingers after puncturing the membrane of the sticky sack.

It struck her what it was, and she panicked. She tried to scrape the wasp egg off the back of August's leg with a small stick that she found next to him. After she removed the grotesque white egg sac, she flung the stick as far as she could.

Mercy whipped her head around in all directions and found Amelia doubled over on the ground, one hand bracing herself in the dirt and the other over the faceplate of the helmet.

Concern growing with her approach, Mercy asked softly, "Amelia, are you OK?"

When she neared her friend, Amelia seemed to be heaving, so Mercy pulled off her helmet and crouched down next to her. Amelia wrenched her helmet off her head to catch her breath, and her cheeks were fire hot with rivers of tears streaming down them. A powerful sob left her lips, and Mercy threw her arms around her.

After a few breaths, she hardly managed to say, "My mother, my mother."

Tears flowed as she continued, whispering into the crook of Mercy's neck, "Please don't let it take my mother. Please."

Mercy held her friend tight as she sobbed.

She didn't dare ask as Amelia leaned into her. She just sat down next to Amelia and pulled her friend's head into her lap as she lay down.

Mercy stroked her friend's shoulders as tears continued to pour from her blue eyes.

Slowly turning her head to August, Mercy took a deep breath of relief as she watched his head move slightly and one of his arms twitch. She wondered if the wasp was able to inject him with a full dose of her venom or if she had interrupted her plans.

She didn't dare ask Amelia.

After about an hour, August rolled over and groaned. The wasp must not have injected him with a full dose of her venom. Mercy could hear the groan from the speaker in her helmet next to her. Amelia shot her head up and looked at Mercy bewildered.

Mercy just smiled and said, "It's OK. I burned her fucking wing off Amelia. She's gone now. She can't take anyone else, ever again. August is safe. We are all safe."

With pain in her eyes Amelia started to speak, "Merc, I, I'm so."

With glittering eyes, Mercy grabbed Amelia's face to stop her words and then softly said, "Shh, none of that. We are all OK. I love you, my sweet friend. I had this one. You can help fight the next monster."

Amelia squeezed her eyes shut and grasped Mercy in a crushing embrace.

After they had both gathered their wits and their tears had dried, Amelia and Mercy put their helmets back on and decided to forego their rest and walk for another day. August had finally woken but stayed silent, even after they lifted him to his feet. Most of the rest of the journey was spent in silence, with August being half dragged between Amelia and Mercy, his arms over their shoulders for support.

They only stopped for one rest and, once August was

walking on his own, they walked another two days through the dense woods to reach the cave's entrance. None of them said a word to one another during the journey.

Mercy took off her helmet after jumping down into the lava tube then leaned over to Amelia and said, "Finally! A hot shower!"

Amelia just stared at her and said, "Yeah, uh, I need one too."

Clearly still groggy, August shut the base door behind him after he went inside and didn't wait for Mercy and Amelia.

They both looked at the closed door for several moments in silence before finally opening it and going inside.

Once they stumbled inside, they walked toward the hallway that crossed Amelia's apartment. Amelia said, "I guess, I'll see you later?"

"Yeah, I'll see you tomorrow. The venom will wear off in another day or so. Have him come see me after work tomorrow for a checkup either way," Mercy said as she walked away toward her apartment.

"I'm so sorry, Amelia," Mercy whispered to herself as her blue-haired friend slowly made her way down the hallway.

50

The first group of volunteers from the mountain town arrived the day after Mercy, August, and Amelia reached the base, and Jael was there to greet them with Callum.

Opening the door, Jael said, "Welcome to the base! My name is Jael."

The group of people waiting in the sealed entry area looked at one another and began smiling before they filed into the brightly lit, broad main hallway of the base. Looking around in awe, they all seemed speechless.

Jael said, "Would you like to see your assigned rooms first, or would you like a tour now?"

A young person in the front with brown skin and light-tan hair spoke first. The person cleared their throat and slowly said, "We would like to see our rooms first."

A smile appeared as they realized how easily their words flowed.

A few of the others nodded, and Jael said, "No problem, follow us."

After a short walk, they arrived at the multi-room apartments where Amelia lived. She opened the door of the vacant apartment that contained rooms for all of them, and they followed her through the open door. Callum was being extraordinarily quiet, and Jael wondered if something was going on with him.

"This apartment has five rooms. I take it you will probably want to stay together?" Callum asked right after he caught Jael staring at him like he had something on his face.

"We don't really know one another. All of us are young, and we don't have many ties back home. Our new town leader, Choir, spread the request for a specific type of person to head to the base and fight for our freedom."

A young man in the group with brick-red skin and brown hair spoke up and said, "After the fungus had kept us hiding in our homes for so long... we all wanted to do something to help. Only a few of us weren't essential to getting the town back up and running like it used to be."

A young woman with tan skin and black hair spoke up and said, "My name is Lark. Amelia and Mercy delivered my surrogate babies while they were in town with the cure. I found a volunteer to nurse the babies so that I could leave with the first group and come help, especially after what they did for me."

"You walked for several days right after giving birth? How? I haven't spoken with Amelia and Mercy yet, and I had no idea. I don't think they rested much on the journey, and I didn't get many messages from them either. I'm so glad they were there for you, and we are lucky to have you with us. We need as many strong people as we can get," Jael said as she shook her head in surprise at what Lark had just revealed.

Smiling at a gob-smacked Jael, Lark said, "I take pride in being a strong woman. Thank you."

They all started looking around and Lark found the bathroom. Jael said, "Once you're all clean and dressed, the kitchen and mess hall are to the left as you head back toward the front door. Just follow the loud talking and smell of fresh flatbread. Uniforms in multiple sizes are in the drawers. Let Mercy know what size you are, and she will get you all the clothes you will need."

With a smile, Lark said, "Thank you."

Nodding to Lark, Jael shut the door behind her and headed to find Oz. Pulling his name up on her messenger, she typed:

Jael: Should we have some music sent down to the mess hall as a warm welcome for the newbies who just showed up?

Oz: That's a brilliant idea, my love. I knew you and Callum were the perfect people to greet the new volunteers. Music will help inspire them to give their all.

She loved it when he said, my love. Something deep inside of her leaped with joy every single time. She wondered if it would always be this way.

"I can always tell when you're chatting with him," Callum said, with a smirk on his face.

Jael released a breathy laugh as she said, "You too, slick. You look like you're going to take a bite out of your tablet when you're talking to Jacob."

"What's that saying you Earthlings have? Touché?" Callum said while raising his blue eyebrows a few times.

They shared a laugh, and before he walked away, Callum said in a more serious tone, "I'm going to go look for Mercy. She said she needed to talk to me about something, and by her tone, I have a feeling it's not something *good*. Wish me luck."

Stopping by Carter's office, Jael saw the back of Zoe's brown hair in the tech lab, so she went in to talk to her.

Jael walked around a table covered in circuit boards and tools and asked, "Zoe? Do you think we could have some music playing in the mess hall for the new people? Um, did you talk to Mercy or Amelia yet?"

"Yes! Amelia said she delivered *four* babies with Mercy. Can you believe it was four?" Zoe asked, her khaki eyes blazing with interest and surprise.

"Four? Holy *hell*. Well, the young woman is here. Apparently, she was a surrogate. She walked all the way from the mountain town just days after having quadruplets," Jael said with a similar look of surprise.

"Are you going to tell Amelia now? I'll go on break and come too if you are," Zoe stated as she set down her tiny soldering tool and began rising from her stool.

The stool made a loud scraping sound on the stone floor as she pushed it back with her legs, and she finally stood at her full height.

Zoe turned to look around the room and said, "Hey, Pike. Take the speakers to the mess hall and connect them to Jael's tablet remotely. *Please*."

"Sure thing," Pike said from across the room with no emotion and without so much as looking up from his programming.

Zoe took off toward the door and muttered, "Let's go!"

Taking off after her, Jael had to jog to keep up with Zoe's long legs. Halfway to Amelia's office, Jael had to start running because she fell so far behind.

They reached the clinic, and Zoe busted into Amelia's

office, saying, "You are *not* going to believe who just showed up at the base!"

Laughing and catching her breath, Jael said, "Way to wait for short-legs back here!"

Zoe turned around and widened her eyes, and chuckled as she said, "Whoops! Sorry."

Whipping her head back to Amelia, she said, "I guess I was supposed to wait for snail-girl back there."

"Hey now! Just because I'm the slow alien does not mean I deserve to be referred to as a snail. On my world, I was referred to as a sloth, not a snail. A snail is just insulting," Jael said, still catching her breath and trying to hold back a giggle.

"Is there a reason you both interrupted my research time?" Amelia asked as she sharpened her eyes on Jael and Zoe.

"Lark. She's here," Jael managed to get out between breaths.

Amelia turned her head to the side in confusion and asked, "Who?"

Zoe answered saying, "The young woman with the four babies that you said you delivered. She's showed up with a group of five people."

Jael continued where Zoe left off, saying, "She said she found someone to nurse the babies and wanted to come with the first group sent to the base to volunteer. They should all be heading to the mess hall soon. I'm going to go tell Mercy. If you two want to go to the mess hall, we will meet you there."

Amelia turned her holoscreen off and tossed her lab coat over her stool as she stood up, "Sure. Let's go. I'm hungry anyway."

Jael took off in a brisk walk toward Mercy's office, realizing halfway there that she really needed to start running with August and Luna's training teams. She had gotten out of shape since her several months-long journey to the north and back down to the base.

After reaching the office, Jael walked in, and without even looking for Mercy, she blurted out, "Lark is here."

"Who?" Mercy mumbled as she whipped around to look at Jael.

Jael scrunched her nose and said, "The pregnant woman that you and Amelia helped! Did you two really not catch her name at some point?"

"What? Are you serious? Where? Wait, why the venom didn't Callum tell me?" Mercy asked with a digital pencil hanging out of her mouth while an image of boots rotated on the 3D holoscreen's projection.

Jael wondered if she was drafting some new tactical boots to go with the armor Mercy had designed with Callum. Everyone at the base was still wearing the original boots, which Mercy had painstakingly made by hand at her home in the village.

"They all said they would be going to the mess hall. They should be there soon. Lark showed up with a group of five from the mountain town. They're all cleaning up, then heading down to eat," Jael said as she watched Mercy get up from her seat and put her digital pencil on the table next to her tablet.

Quickly shutting off her holoscreen, Mercy followed Jael out of the office and into the hallway.

"I thought I would never see her again. She was already two days into her labor when we got to her house to give her the nanobot injection. Amelia was incredible," Mercy said and then trailed off with glassed-over eyes.

"Four babies? How does your kind handle that many babies at once? I'm not sure humans can do that successfully without modern medicine," Jael cringed thinking of all the horrible things that could go wrong during human childbirth.

This was just one of the many reasons she was relieved that she and Oz would never be able to conceive. She wanted kids. She just didn't want to *have* them herself. The sheer thought of being pregnant made her see stars.

"Sometimes multiple births come with extra, deformed, limp arms made of skin and fat. Plus, it doesn't always go so well. We have stillbirths, miscarriages, and sometimes even severe congenital disabilities. If it's known the pregnancy is not viable, or if the person didn't wish to become pregnant, most will choose to have a healer help start the process of expelling the fetus. From your memories, we have the same struggles that humans seem to have. We don't have as many people die in childbirth, though. I think it's our flexible hips."

Jael had some steaming hot memories of those flexible hips, and she was flooded with heat.

"Yeah, I know *all* about those flexible hips," Jael couldn't help but say as her cheeks burned.

With a burst of laughter, Mercy replied, "I think all of our dirty minds are finally rubbing off on you."

"I would say *something* was rubbed off on me," Jael said with her eyes suddenly wide with shock at her own words.

Mercy roared with laughter as they strolled into the mess hall. Walking toward the kitchen to fill a plate, Jael looked over and saw Oz sitting at a table reading something on his tablet.

He was completely unaware she was there.

After making her heaping plate of fruit and roasted nuts, she made her way over to Oz and sat down next to him with a plop.

He whipped his head around to look at her, then he scanned the room, and his yellow eyes went wide, "When did you get here?"

"While I waited to fill my plate, I've been in line staring at you like a creep. Mercy and Amelia helped deliver *four* babies and the surrogate mother is already here to volunteer," Jael explained with a wide grin.

"Being present for the birth of a child creates an intimate bond. I was there for the birth of my sister, but I was very young and didn't appreciate it for what it really was. Beautiful," Oz said with a far off look in his eye.

Jael knew he must be visiting the memory of his sister's birth because his eyes glossed over. She rested her hand on his thigh and rubbed along his leg a few times in comfort.

"Lark!" Mercy hollered, as Lark walked into the mess hall, her arriving group still together and following behind her.

Amelia began walking toward them, but Mercy couldn't contain her excitement and ran to Lark and the rest of the group. Oz and Jael turned around and watched as Mercy, Amelia, and Lark hugged and squealed in excitement. The laughter continued and Jael watched as they began chatting with wide grins on their faces. The happy moment was a bit surreal and so genuine that it made Jael's throat catch. Her emotions were a storm and she reached over and gripped the table for support as she watched the three women find a table to sit at and talk.

Leaning over to Jael, but not taking his eyes off the scene unveiling in front of them, Oz said softly, "*This* is why we have to win. *This* is why we fight, and *this* is why we win."

51

"We are off shift at the same time? And you're sure neither of us has something we're supposed to be working on?" Mercy asked, a tiny crease forming between her eyes as she nervously rubbed her hands along her sides and down to her rounded hips.

The nervous hand-rubbing was something that Mercy had done since she was just the little girl living next door. August closed his eyes briefly, then opened his bright russet eyes, rimmed in thick, dark crimson lashes, deep enough to look black. He took a step forward.

August exhaled roughly as he narrowed his gaze at Mercy, softly saying, "I told you we are going somewhere. Will you get ready and stop trying to *ruin* the surprise."

Mercy froze suddenly and gasped before she said, "Are you taking me on a *real* date?"

Rolling his eyes for the tenth time that day, August said, "Yes. Now you've ruined it. Thank you for that."

Giggling and slapping her previously nervous hands over

her mouth. She slowly slid her hands down her chin and said, "It's still a surprise! I don't know where we're going."

"Please just get your hot ass dressed so we can go," August said as he leaned his head back, feigning annoyance.

Skipping off to the shelves in the bathroom, she pulled out a light cream dress that she had wanted to wear, but never had a reason. She had made it from cream silk she got from one of her old neighbors by trading some of Rew's tan silk. She was careful when she slipped her tail through the hole in the back as she pulled it up. The long flowing dress had thin straps that went over her soft shoulders and a billowy floor-length skirt. She walked out and found a stunned August.

After a long moment, August finally released his held breath and softly said, "You look like Jael's memories of sunshine."

Filling with warmth, Mercy only replied, "Thank you," and put her hand out to follow August.

August led her out the door and down the stairs of their apartment toward the command room door. Mercy wracked her brain, trying to figure out where August was taking her. Their last outing, which she guessed could be considered a date, had just been a run through the woods. He wore some perfectly fitted dress pants and a button-down shirt. Now dressed in some of the modern clothes that Mercy had made for him, she didn't think it was going to be the same as last time.

She hoped anyway.

As they navigated the long narrow hall toward the main hallway, Mercy slid her thoughts to her new friend Lark. She hoped that Lark would try out and make the team that was going on the mission.

"Has Lark signed up to try out?" Mercy blurted out, causing August to slow down a bit.

Picking back up his pace, August didn't turn his head around all the way as he asked, "Who is Lark?"

Mercy answered, "The young woman who just showed up a few days ago with the group of five from the mountain town. Amelia and I helped deliver her four babies. I know I told you about her. Her house looked just like yours, completely bare. It hardly looked like she even lived there."

Looking back at Mercy quickly as he kept walking, August said, "I remember now. Sorry I've been so busy lately. I *promise* I'll try to make more time."

Mercy couldn't believe he had forgotten. She had teased him about how much their houses looked alike. She squeezed his hand and didn't say anything else as they headed to the main door of the base. August opened it up, and a whoosh of air blasted by them. They were walking toward the hole in the ceiling of the lava tube when Mercy noticed a slight chill.

"Do you think it's going to rain?" Mercy asked as she wrapped her arm around her waist.

As he looked up at the sky through the large hole, August answered, "It's not supposed to. One of the members of Carter's tech team has taken an interest in weather, and they said it won't rain until tomorrow sometime."

Mercy hiked her dress up over her wide muscular thighs and crawled on August's back. He knelt, and she made sure to brush her hand along the underside of his tail as she climbed on, eliciting a shiver then a low growl from August. He turned his head around and narrowed his eyes at her before he crouched down in preparation to jump.

Mercy couldn't get the rain prediction off her mind and said, "I want to know everything about the weather. How did they predict it without radar or satellite?"

"Do you really think I know the answer to that? I'm just Jacob's work bitch. I think most of the time, he doesn't want me to work on anything important, anything I might accidentally break anyway," August grumbled. He leaped out of the lava tube and onto the ground with Mercy on his back so she didn't tear her dress.

"I mean, you *are* sort of a brute. I've seen you break a log in half with just your hands. You also broke through a wall once, by accident, but you still did it," Mercy said while smirking.

August scoffed and replied, "I was hoping you didn't remember that."

Chuckling as she climbed off August's back, she was careful not to catch her nice shoe on his tail. Mercy said, "Of course, I remember. There was a massive crash next door. I bet the whole street heard it. Then your dad went out right afterward and chopped a tree down. You had a huge dark mark on the side of your face, and your whole shoulder was solid black for a few weeks. I put the pieces together."

August narrowed his eyes at Mercy before saying, "I was startled! I was resting, and I thought my mother was gone. It turns out she was just in her room, and when she shut her door too hard, I panicked, leaped from my bed and crashed through the wall into the living room. I had those bruises for over a month. My father still teases me about it all the time. Even though I've been busy at the base, he finds a way. He got ahold of my mother's tablet and messaged me about it just a few days ago. '*Hey son, break through any walls today?*'"

Rolling his eyes, August adjusted the small pack hanging

on his shoulder, and he shook his head as he walked ahead of Mercy.

After walking through the heavily wooded area around the base, August headed away from the village and deeper into the woods.

Turning his head around, August smirked at Mercy and said, "You only get one hint. I'm not taking you near anyone else or near any of those damn microphones."

A thrill went through Mercy at his words, heat gathering deep inside. She was almost done with all the walking in her new shoes, when she finally saw all the colors. A small area of wildflowers glimmered with bright reds, oranges, and yellows, with soft, delicate textures.

"How did you know about this place? Did you find it yourself?" Mercy asked as she scanned the beauty of the hidden spot.

August cleared his throat and said, "I saw it when we were on our way back from collecting sand at the coast for Jacob. I didn't point it out to anyone else so I could take you here first when I had time. Thankfully the guys didn't notice it at all. I think they were too busy trying to get home so they could escape from one another."

Ignoring most of his rambling, a rush of heat flooded inside of Mercy, and she flung her arms around August.

Mercy leaned into his ear and whispered, "It's perfect."

August slipped his bag off his shoulder and dipped Mercy for a kiss before standing her back up and saying, "Let's eat first. I brought something you love."

Beaming, Mercy stood and waited while August laid the blanket out on the ground in the middle of the field, so that all the colorful flowers surrounded them. Mercy sat down and inhaled the perfume from the flowers spinning in the breeze. The scent was intoxicating, and she quickly decided she was in love with this place.

"I thought you would love it here," August said as they both sat down on the double-layered, silk blanket.

As she admired all the colors, she felt eyes on her. Mercy brought her gaze to meet August's and found him looking right at her. Admiration and affection were in his eyes as a smile spread on his handsome face.

"I like the dark red and bright orange flowers the best, I think. Do you know what the yellow flowers are? I've never seen them before. They're gorgeous. I'll have to bring some back to the girls," Mercy said as she held a red flower with long, thin petals and a bright yellow, fuzzy center.

Pulling out two covered plates, August set them down and then pulled out two bottles.

With a smile still on his face August handed Mercy a plate and bottle, and said, "The bottle has juice and alcohol. I made sure that Risk mixed it. I know how you love his mixed drinks."

"Oh, you do know me so well. This is my favorite!" Mercy looked down at her oversized strawberry pastry and grinned before she picked it up with both hands and began devouring it.

Chuckling, August began eating his own pastry and then downed his bottle of mango-orange juice with alcohol. The alcohol burned as it went down, and August had to try not to choke as his eyes watered.

Whistling and looking at the bottle with his brow furrowed, August said, "Damn, that was *a lot* stronger than I was expecting. I maybe should have drunk that slower."

He peered with one eye into the bottle and then shrugged before capping it and placing it in his bag.

Mercy finished her pastry and followed suit, downing her mixed drink. She was used to Risk's strong drinks, and the alcohol was hardly noticeable to her.

After replacing the cap of her bottle, Mercy smirked and said, "What are you talking about, strong? That was perfect."

Licking her lips, Mercy looked over at August, who was clearly not listening. His eyes were flooded with desire, and he was creeping forward. Mercy met him halfway; her lips meeting his in a flurry of heat as they lay back on the soft blanket.

"Take this fucking dress off before I rip it off," August growled as he hooked a finger and pulled gently on the little straps.

Grinning, Mercy slipped her arms out of the straps and slid the dress down over her generous curves. August took over and pulled it the rest of the way off, finding Mercy bare underneath. A cool breeze slid past her nude body, causing her nipples to tighten.

August couldn't take his eyes away from her.

Growling deep in his throat, August said, "You didn't have a damn thing on under that dress? Fucking venom, you're so hot." His lips descended onto her full chest.

Slowly concentrating on one brown peak and then the other, he nipped at the tip before sliding his tongue down her side, eliciting a shiver from her. Laying her down on the blanket, August settled over her and kissed a trail down her soft body.

Grabbing her leg, he swung it over his head and slid his long tongue from the top of her rear right down the middle and ending at her throbbing bud. Mercy clamped her legs together and let out a delicious moan. August chuckled as he wedged his arm between her thick thighs.

He looked up and grinned at her as he said, "I would die a happy man suffocating between these thighs."

He shoved them apart as he continued swirling her bud with his tongue. Throwing her head back, Mercy rocked her hips. Her breaths became short as he reached up and held her hips in his iron grip to still them.

Continuing the twirls with his tongue, Mercy writhed and grasped at the blankets all around, desperate for anything to hold onto. Deep clicks sounded in her throat as she threw her head back in ecstasy. With the pressure building, Mercy began crying out as her release slammed into her, his rough tongue still rounding her most sensitive place.

With her whole body shaking with the waves of pleasure, Mercy grabbed August's hands on her hips and shrieked, "August!"

Finally pulling away, August smiled at her and said, "I've been thinking about that all week."

He licked her one more time down the center, causing her to yelp. As he settled on the blanket, Mercy crawled on top of him and began kissing his neck.

Tilting his head, August saw that one of the little yellow flowers had a slight bulge at the base. Noticing his sudden change in focus, Mercy stopped and looked up.

Just as Mercy slid her eyes to August's, the flower made a popping noise and blasted August in the face with bright yellow pollen. She shot her upper body up and away from the cloud of pollen to avoid inhaling any of it.

The last thing she wanted was to sneeze, especially after what he had just done to her. She could feel the wet heat begin slipping down her leg.

After sneezing a few times while Mercy stared at him, August finally looked at her like he had never seen her before and said, "Oh, hello. I think I like where this is going."

"What in the fuck?" Mercy said, with absolute confusion in her golden eyes.

Climbing off August's still-clothed body, she slowly reached over to her bag and grabbed her tablet, completely nude but uncaring at the moment.

August sat up and was staring at her with a strange hungry look, yellow powder spread out on the side of his face.

After dialing the number, Amelia's tall form materialized in its entirety on the holoscreen.

Amelia coughed a few times, then with wide eyes said, "Mercy, *why* are you calling me naked?"

Mercy looked down and waved her hand at Amelia's oddly intense shock and said, "Oh, don't worry about my tits. That's not why I'm calling. August doesn't know who I am after being sprayed with the pollen from a yellow flower. I need help. He looks like he wants to bite me."

"I won't bite too hard, I promise," August winked as he held a rather creepy grin on his face.

"Amelia, please hurry," Mercy pleaded to Amelia's holoform before hanging up and dropping her tablet to grab her dress.

August began looking around and getting uncomfortably close to the red flowers. He reached up and grabbed one of the taller stems and bit into it.

"August! Spit that out! Don't eat the flowers!" Mercy demanded, panic growing as she thought he might be getting worse.

Looking narrowly at Mercy because of her sharp words,

August chewed and swallowed the red flower petals in defiance.

"*Shit*. Amelia, please hurry," Mercy said in a whisper to herself as she finally got her dress straightened so she could put it on.

After slipping it over her head, she shimmied into the dress and pulled it down over her curves. Once she was dressed, she looked down to see what August was doing.

He was curled in a ball on the blanket with his face down.

What the hell was he doing?

Mercy looked around him and saw he had the end of the blanket in his mouth, and he was chewing on it!

"Oh, fuck me with a stinger! That's *not* food, August!" Mercy said with a panicked tone.

Dropping the soggy bite of the blanket out of his mouth, he said with a heavy slur, "I don't know who August is, but I sure do want to know who *you* are."

"Fuck, oh fuck. OK? Um, I am Mercy, and we are *friends*. We were having a picnic. Our other friend Amelia is coming, and she's going to bring you some medicine to help you."

"Oh, I don't need any medicine. I feel great." Just after August spoke, he reached over to the tree ripped off a piece of bark and put it in his mouth.

"August, please stop eating bark. If you're hungry, I can get some food out of my bag," Mercy offered, backing up as he slowly approached her with his eyes ablaze. The bark he had been chewing on fell out of his mouth in a slobbery heap on the blanket.

"Oh, oh, venom's tits! Just, um? Stay right there. Just sit

down right there," Mercy said as she pointed down at the blanket.

August complied, with glossed-over eyes and a strange smile on his face.

"Mercy?" Amelia said from behind her, causing her to leap in fright.

Exhaling roughly, Mercy ground out, "Scorpion balls! What took you so long?! He keeps getting worse!"

"I had to get Oz, and we grabbed Callum on the way. They're hiding. Stay calm and just wait."

Out of the corner of her left eye, Mercy saw something green and black drop from the foliage above and land on top of August.

With a yelp, she leaped backward. Amelia caught her but lost her balance, and they both tumbled back, falling in a heap. Mercy did her best to sit up to see what was happening and found Oz holding an empty syringe while standing over a knocked-out August.

"I'm glad that worked. Callum. He's out. Come help me carry his heavy ass," Oz said over his shoulder.

"Why didn't we get a cart?" Callum asked in an irritated tone while he glared at Oz.

"I'm not explaining it again. Just lift his legs so we can get him to the clinic and restrain him," Oz said in an exasperated tone.

"What the hell was in that flower?" Mercy asked Amelia, who was now standing up and brushing the crushed bits of leaves off her lab coat.

After fixing her hair, Amelia looked down at the yellow flowers and said, "I have never seen these before. I hope it's not another attack from the humans. Let's pick some and get back to the lab right away."

She handed Mercy a few large test tubes, and they crouched down to pick the flowers.

"Get one with a lump under the base of the petals," Mercy said before handing Amelia a flower in a tube then picking up the blanket along with their picnic.

After they had the flowers picked and the area cleaned up, they headed inside the base and to Amelia's lab.

Once they arrived, Amelia pulled out her smaller microscope, then made an odd face, "This pollen is like none I have ever seen. It's a strange, crystal formation."

Putting away her microscope, Amelia opened the sliding door to her backlit counter and began placing the pollen samples in various liquid solutions to find the chemical structures.

Mercy looked over at August, sedated, and strapped to the bed, with drool running down his face. She wondered if the effects would be permanent, and fear laced through her at the thought.

"Is he going to be, OK?" Mercy asked quietly.

Amelia peered over from her lab work and said, "I suspect the chemical in the pollen has hallucinogenic properties. Maybe the flowers use it to make other flowers look tastier, sparing the yellow flowers?"

Mercy slid her eyes from her friend and back to August and gasped before she said, "Oh, um, Amelia. August is awake."

Amelia looked up from her work and leaped off her stool. She found August fully awake and staring at her from the glass wall of the locked exam room.

The stool clattered to the floor behind Amelia.

August smiled and then licked the glass all the way across the wall while giggling to himself.

"He can't see us. I'm going to have to find a gene to trigger and get him to go back under. Maybe I can find a sleep gene that I can turn on? I have no idea how he is awake right now. We used three times the standard dose of the anesthesia we just formulated." Mercy looked to Amelia and found her wide-eyed and reaching for her tablet without taking her eyes off August.

Once she grabbed her tablet, she shifted her eyes to the holoscreen and scrolled for some time while August sat on the floor. He searched all over the bed then began gnawing on the end of an exam bed's strap.

A few moments after Amelia found what she was looking for, August's head began to sway, and he fell over, hitting the floor with a thud.

Amelia sighed and said, "Damn. I'm so glad that worked. I induced a dormant sleeping gene from our infant stage of development. Grab that silk strip in the drawer over there and tie it around his eyes, so he doesn't open them and wake up. Then, help me get him back on the table."

Grabbing the silk strip, Mercy tied it around August's eyes then grabbed him under his knees to hoist him up. Amelia held him under his arms, and they heaved as they slid him back onto the table.

Amelia walked over to the communication panel and said, "Hey, Luna, can you send someone down to fix the table? August woke up and broke free. Also, I need some August-proof straps this time, please."

"He got loose?! How is that possible?" Luna asked with confusion marring her gentle face.

Amelia stepped to the side, and on the communication's panel, Luna saw the table with August sprawled on it, an arm flopped off the side. All the tan-colored straps were hanging, shredded and frayed at the ends where he had fought them and won.

"Oh, venom. That's *wild*. Alright, I'll send someone down with some much stronger straps," Luna said before ending the holo-call.

52

After resting for several hours, Mercy got sick of lying down and went to the clinic to check on August. As she walked down the bright hallways of the base, still bustling with people that were working, she wondered where they would be a year from now. Would they be free? Or would they be entrenched in an all-out war? She hadn't honestly stopped to think about the future now that they actually had one.

What would their world look like?

Would they still be the same people?

Would they all be alive?

Mercy placed her hand on the glass wall and watched August's slow breaths. His eyes moved back and forth under his eyelids, and she wondered what he was thinking about, or dreaming about, she guessed. She hoped they were good dreams.

She had always cared about him and wanted him, but she never thought she would fall in love with him. It had always been such a faraway wish to be with August. He was all she had ever dreamed of. While it was strange for her to think that there was only one person for her, there wasn't exactly a large selection of people to pick from.

Even if there was, she would still have picked him, she thought as she watched his hand twitch under the bindings.

Being unable to tell him how she felt after their date made her feel incomplete and like a hole was forming inside. She needed to tell him. The deep desire for him to know her feelings right away harkened back to the constant fear of being taken. Sometimes your loved ones were just gone.

She couldn't delay expressing her feelings, not ever, she decided.

She recognized her pounding heart was driving her to tell him she loved him, and so she decided to go to work early instead of going back home. The chance of something happening to him was almost impossible since they were safe in the base. As the door clicked behind her and her holo-screen came to life, she did her best to pretend she didn't feel the hole inside of her growing.

She walked over toward her armor that was hanging up on the rack and ran her hand over her plasma sword. Angst stirred through her, but she brushed it off as she put on her helmet to test the new visual programming that Carter had installed.

Down the hall, Carter was in his office, unable to rest as well. Staring at his holoscreen with all his perfect test results, he was wondering why he felt so wrong inside.

He felt a rush of dread, and at that moment, a massive blast rocked the base.

In a panic, Carter bound out of his office just in time to see human soldiers in solid black uniforms come pouring through the base's front door. Slamming into the door as he backed into his office, Carter ignored it as it came back and hit him a second time while he slammed his fist down on the base's alarm.

As sirens blared in the base, chaos ensued outside Carter's office.

Carter sprinted to Mercy's office next door and flew in the door just as she finished slipping on her armor.

"Humans are in the base!" Carter yelled as he ran toward the hanging suits of armor to get some of the charged plasma swords.

Mercy nodded as she sprinted past him, her plasma sword buzzing to life in her hand.

Oz's face popped up on the holoscreen communicator next to the door, and he said, "What the hell is happening?!"

Carter yelled, "The humans found us!"

The screen blinked out, and Carter could hear Mercy outside in the hall yelling, "Fuck!"

Mercy, clad head to toe in her solid black armor, silently leaped from her place in the hallway as she pulled a second plasma sword from her belt. She landed directly into the middle of the running soldiers. The soldiers leaped back in fright as her second plasma sword buzzed to life and she didn't hesitate as she charged for them.

Mercy jabbed one of her plasma swords forward and skewered one soldier in the gut as she cut the arm off another.

Spinning and slicing, Mercy cut down soldier after soldier, crimson blood spilling onto the floor. Arms and heads rolled from their former owners as she danced through the screaming soldiers, leaving nothing but death in her wake. Her enraged voice echoed inside her helmet, and Mercy saw nothing but red in her vision. The new programming provided a three-hundred-and-sixty-degree view of her surroundings and gave her a massive edge against the attacks coming from every angle.

This was for her parents, her neighbors, her people.

She would kill them all.

Darts filled with the sedative pelted her armor.

She prayed she could hold off the humans and give Carter and his team enough time to prepare themselves to defend his office and lab.

Carter knew he had to hurry. His hands shook as he grabbed a handful of plasma swords and checked that each one had a charge. He turned around and grabbed August's helmet as he sprinted to the door.

As he ran to distribute the swords, he watched as Oz came running from the end of the hall with two plasma swords and no armor. With his eyes focused, he whistled at Oz and tossed him the helmet. Oz dropped one of his plasma swords and caught it. He secured the helmet on his head and dropped to his knee grabbing his sword from the ground. With his second sword back in hand, he continued running, then descended like a bolt of lightning on the soldiers heading toward Jacob's lab.

He spun with his plasma swords extended. Blood sprayed, and screams erupted as he cut a path through the charging soldiers. Oz said a silent thank you to Carter as some type of gas was released deep in the cavern.

Some soldiers at the front had electric ropes, and the soldiers at the back were all equipped with dart guns. All the humans had masks over their noses and mouths, but their eyes were visible.

Their eyes were filled with anger, terror, and awe.

After six darts hit Oz with no effect, the soldiers in the

front began screaming, "*Nōn descendent!*" They're not going down!

Dripping with the blood of his enemies, Oz cleared his mind and became the humans' worst nightmare. Sparing no one and standing barefoot in a lake of red blood, he stood his ground at the door to Jacob's lab. When the crowd of human soldiers began to pull back and push against the people behind them, Oz had no intention of turning off his rage.

"*Inferficendus omnes!*" They're killing us all! Cried a soldier right before Oz stuck his sword through the man's gut, his entrails spilling on the ground as he fell.

With his tail primed for a strike and both plasma swords crackling with power, Oz leaped forward and spun with his swords outstretched. Blood-curdling screams were muted by the helmet, and Oz was unfazed.

They could scream all they wanted.

He had no intention of stopping.

One soldier yelled out as he was slashed across the chest, "*Exercetē! Nōn descendent!*" Run! They're not going down!

By the time Carter's team was assembled around his door to join the fight, some of the soldiers closest to Oz were trying to kneel in surrender. The remainder were a bustle of chaos and screams. Those in charge were at the back of the crowd and were barking orders that they were not going to surrender. Carter stood guard at his office door, knowing that what was behind him was priceless to their mission.

He would die before he let the humans get ahold of his tech.

Mercy was headed toward the base's front door, not waiting for backup. She screamed with rage as she continued to cut into the human soldiers who were shoving themselves in the door.

As she passed his office, Carter grabbed Mercy's arm and pulled her from the fight. Yanking her into his office, he looked both ways to make sure it was clear before he turned his focus to her. She slid her visor up to hear him better.

"Where is everyone?! Where are Amelia and Luna?" Carter asked frantically.

"I don't know!" Mercy screamed out.

She ran from Carter's office, terrified for Amelia and Luna, who were supposed to be in their apartment. The entire hallway was filled with the human soldiers, still pouring in from the base's door. They were so thick she couldn't see anything through the chaos. Only a handful of her people had plasma swords, and many were injured, using their stingers and fists as their only weapons. Mercy's vision blurred as she ran through the madness and death.

A soldier came running toward her with an electrified rope. She pulled her plasma sword from her belt as she spun around to meet the soldier face to face. She turned it on at the perfect moment for the soldier to impale herself.

After the spray of red blood from the soldier's gut, Mercy slid her visor up and spat in the soldier's face as she fell. Mercy didn't wait to see if she had inflicted a killing blow and turned off her plasma sword, slipping it back into place on her belt. She slid her visor back down as a cloud of gas exploded around her.

Running as fast as her legs would carry her down the hall and past the med room, she crashed into the apartment door, which slammed open with a bang. Mercy found Amelia and Luna frantically putting on their armor. Both of their hair was wet and down, fresh out of the shower. From the look of it, they had been preparing for their shift.

"Face shield!" Mercy yelled as the visor slid up in an instant.

Taking a deep breath, Mercy cried out, "It's the fucking humans! They found us!"

Outranking both, Luna yelled, "Shit! I'll go find Jael and make sure she is OK. Amelia, your armor is charged so you go help protect the rockets with Oz! Mercy, you too! Both of you run!"

Not sparing a moment, Mercy and Amelia ran toward Jacob's lab. Amelia slipped her helmet over her head and pulled her plasma sword from her back.

Mercy jumped at a soldier that was running toward Jacob's lab. Her plasma sword buzzed to life. Landing on her feet in front of the soldier, Mercy decapitated her in one twist of her wrist, causing a spray of blood across Jacob's lab door as the soldier's head hit the ground.

Amelia followed right behind and jumped to the other side of a red, blood-slicked Oz. The three made a circle to defend their only chance at freedom. Their rockets filled with satellites and missiles could not be discovered.

Cursing at herself that she had not charged her new armor, Luna watched as Mercy and Amelia did as she ordered. Looking down at her plasma sword with full batteries, she said a prayer of thanks and slipped it into her belt. At least she had her sword. She looked up and took off sprinting past the open door of the med room across from Jacob's lab and headed toward the command area's door. Swinging it open, she found human soldiers at the end with the door open.

Heart slamming through her body, Luna screamed

inside her lifeless helmet and ran with everything inside of her toward the humans at the other end of the long hallway. They saw her and began running as fast as they could, but Luna, in her rage, was much quicker. She pulled her plasma sword from her belt and the shimmering bright weapon of pure energy sprung to life.

She leaped in the air and barreled into the last soldier, knocking him to the ground. as he tried to shut the large door on her. She cut the head off the man to the right of the door and then twisted around to gut the woman to her left. She then plunged her plasma sword into the face of the man between her bare feet on the ground. Her heart pounded in her body as she pulled her sword from between his eyes. Hot red blood poured into a puddle around her bare feet as she scanned the room in a panic.

When she looked up, Luna found a group of soldiers at Jael's door. She took off in a sprint toward Jael's apartment, leaving bloody footprints in her path.

Searing hot anger shot through her, and she pulled her helmet off as fast as she could. The face shield had become foggy because the battery was completely dead.

With every fiber of her being, her voice filled the cavern as she screamed, "JAEL!"

Lava filled her veins as she threw her helmet to the ground and sprinted toward her defenseless friend.

As she ran the last few yards toward the five remaining soldiers that were heading inside Jael's door, Luna whispered to herself, "My friend, my friend, my friend, please be OK. I'll do anything for you to be OK."

Plasma sword already spinning above her head, she came down on the soldiers like a bomb with a thunderous scream on her lips.

Their cries of pain were deafening without her helmet, and their crimson blood sprayed her face. She desperately hoped Jael was hiding.

With four soldiers down, Luna leaped over their blood-spewing bodies to land at Jael's open doorway, fear eating her alive.

She walked into silence.

Turning her head to check all directions, she found that the apartment appeared empty.

It was too quiet.

Slowly turning the corner to the kitchen, Luna found Jael with a soldier holding her mouth and arms. His mask was down, and he had a sneer on his pale face. One soldier was on the ground in a pool of blood with a long kitchen knife sticking out of his neck. Luna smirked at her friend's handiwork and looked up to glare at the man holding onto Jael.

The soldier said, "*Blatta confunda, quid audēre surripis et abdis haec mulierem innocentiam humana. Cogitābāmus virī rubrī tuī interficerat eam! Quomodo ea est hic et vira? Quid id est vos cimices sordidae facēns hic? Cogitabās inciperās rebellionem parvum? Quid? Respondēte mihi si intellegis verba blatta confunda obsita.*" You fucking cockroach, how dare you steal and hide this innocent human woman. We thought your red male had killed her! How is she here and alive? What is it that you filthy bugs are doing here? Did you think you could start a little rebellion? Huh? Answer me if you can understand words, you fucking overgrown roach.

Luna looked into Jael's eyes and saw her fear.

She saw her love and her friendship.

She was not letting this sick fuck take her friend.

Meeting the man's green eyes, Luna said with a deadly

calm, "*Nōs capēbas. Mors eius simulābāmus abdere eam ab tē. Eam cogēbāmus docere nōs loqui et nunc planetam nōs recipēmus.*" You caught us. We faked her death to hide her from you. We forced her to teach us to speak, and now we will take back our planet.

Spitting on Luna's foot, the man smiled as he said, "*Facēbāmus tē et tenēmus tē! Tū legitime bonōrum est sub UTC lege. Dedete nunc aut interficam docentem linguam tuī.*" We made you, and we own you! You are legally our property under UTC law. Surrender now, or I *will* kill your language teacher.

Luna complied, falling to her knees and raising her hands. She dropped her plasma sword and curled her tail behind her. She calmed herself as she peered into Jael's eyes and gave her friend a hint of a smile.

Jael began shaking her head furiously at Luna.

Her frantic eyes were pleading with her friend not to surrender.

The moment her plasma sword rolled away, and Luna's hands were raised, the man let go of Jael's arm and pulled something from his belt with a faint click.

Jael saw the gleam of the railgun from the corner of her eye, but it was already too late. She screamed into the man's hand over her mouth as he brought the gun level to Luna's chest and fired.

The sizzling and cracking of the railgun as the round slammed into Luna's chest brought time to a standstill. He had aimed right above her chest plate, and the armor sizzled as the direct hit pierced the lifeless armor.

Something changed in Jael at that moment.

The final string had been shredded.

The last thread to the meek person Jael was before, *broke*.

Luna's eyes widened in shock. She looked down at the hole in her chest and slowly slumped backward onto her ankles before falling and landing on her back.

A presence fell over Jael, stronger than a raging storm but calmer than a breeze.

The angle of her open mouth gave Jael the perfect opportunity to take a bite of the attacker before she finished him.

He was going to die, but first, he would suffer.

A blood-curdling scream hit her right ear as she bit through flesh and ripped through tendons with her teeth. She heard his gun hit the floor and knew this was her chance.

Ripping her head away, Jael took his finger with her.

Blood dripping down her face, Jael spat the man's finger at her feet before diving for Luna's plasma sword. The moment her fingers grazed the handle, she slid her hand around the grip and rolled over. Jael surged to her feet right as the man regained his bearings and reached for his gun on the floor.

Jael was just far enough away.

She took one wide step and landed with one knee on the ground and one leg outstretched toward the dark-haired man.

Pressing the button on the handle, she pointed the sword toward his head. The sword buzzed to life with a blinding light, and the end pierced through the man's face within an instant. He hadn't even had a chance to hold up the railgun.

Holding him in place, Jael held her outstretched arm and the sword steady.

She fully intended to watch the life leave his eyes.

The man gurgled and shook as she watched his bright red blood spill from his lips as he died on Luna's plasma sword.

Turning off the sword, Jael dropped the handle to the floor and crawled to Luna. The man fell on his face as blood poured from his wound.

Luna's eyes were open, and she was still there. Barely.

Blinking her eyes and sliding them to Jael, Luna tried to speak, but only blue blood trickled from her shaking lips.

Tears slid down Jael's face and she reached for Luna's hand. She whispered, "Shhh, it's OK. I'm here. I got him, Luna. We're safe. You saved me. You came for me."

"Luna, I love you. You didn't get enough time. Wait for me on the other side." Jael stooped down and kissed her on her forehead as Luna's eyes fluttered shut.

A single tear slipped free from Luna's eye as Jael stroked her blood-soaked white hair.

Jael squeezed Luna's hand and whispered into her ear, "One day, we will meet again. I know there is more after this life. Luna, I promise I'll see you again someday. I love you so much."

Opening her eyes one last time, Luna released a final gurgling breath before her lungs filled with her own blue blood.

Tears poured from Jael's eyes like rivers of sorrow.

Luna was gone.

Luna died for *her*.

Lying on the floor next to her friend's still body, Jael

looked up only when Oz arrived, covered in blood with darts still sticking out of his shoulder and neck.

Mercy was next, then Amelia, but Jael didn't take her tear-filled eyes away from her lifeless friend. Jael held Luna's hand to her chest and finally took a full breath as they lay together in the pool of red and blue blood on the floor.

Everyone in the room made a circle around Luna and Jael. No one spoke a word, but they all knew what had happened. Callum and Jacob ran inside the apartment in their street clothes, with not a scratch or drop of blood on them.

Carter and Zoe were not far behind.

Everyone silently stood around Luna and Jael as Oz took in the scene, the blood on Jael's face and mouth, the bullet wound in Luna's chest with her feet both angled back under her bent knees. The dark-haired man, face down, missing a finger, with a plasma sword hole through his face, steam still wafting from the wound. Another man with blonde hair had a kitchen knife through his neck, and a mix of pride and sorrow swelled in Oz.

Oz bent down to Jael and put his hand on her shoulder, then quietly said, "You killed them, Spots."

Slowly, Jael slid her gaze to Oz and, with tears of fury in her eyes, softly said, "I bit his God-damned finger off, then I skewered him through the face. It wasn't enough, but it will do. *For now.*"

Oz just nodded and stood up, heading toward the door of his apartment and walking toward the middle of the command room. Everyone followed, one by one, and gathered around the table with Oz.

Staying behind a moment, Jael kicked the man who killed Luna in the face twice before being the last to head down to the command area. Everyone watched her as she made her way to the table to stand next to Oz.

Oz waited for Jael to stand next to him to begin.

He stood tall at the head of the table and said, "Many are wounded, but Luna is our only casualty so far. We took forty-one prisoners. The humans have over one hundred and twenty-four dead. According to one of the first humans to surrender, they came with one hundred and seventy. We are missing six. The base is being combed. They did not enter Jacob or Carter's labs, but they did ransack Mercy's office. There wasn't anything in there that we can't swiftly replace. I don't know about the apartments or any of the other offices. The trip line in the lava tube worked perfectly and took out ten soldiers. The spring-loaded darts laced with our venom were effective, and we have Jacob to thank for that brilliant idea.

We need to do a head count of our people and ensure no one is missing. Zoe, please conduct the count, and I will connect with some of the prisoners to find out what happened. I want to know how the fuck they knew about us. Tomorrow, we will have a meeting to figure out what we're doing next. Everyone that had armor and a helmet issued to them needs to charge the batteries *immediately*."

Before walking away from the table, Oz leaned toward Jael and wrapped his arms around her, and said, "We are starting your training tomorrow, my love."

"How about now?" Jael said as she looked up into Oz's eyes, blood still drying on her face.

After kissing her head, he softly said, "I have a lot to do right now. Just go to Mercy's apartment."

Jael narrowed her eyes at Oz and said, "No, I am going to

go to our apartment. I'll help with the bodies and start trying to get the blood on the floor cleaned up."

Oz stood silent for a moment before he shook his head once and quietly said, "You don't have to do that. I'll have a team come up and clear the bodies and clean the blood."

Jael looked into his bright yellow eyes and said sharply, "Oz, I *need* to clean the blood."

53

Walking from the impromptu meeting with Oz, Mercy stopped in her tracks. The thought of August sedated and restrained in the exam room slid across her mind.

She said, "No," softly as her vision blurred and her heart pounded.

Fear ripped through her as she turned and bolted to the clinic, slamming through the doors of the hallway. Mercy ran to the right and then went sailing through the open clinic doors to find the thick straps cut and August missing from the exam room.

"No! Please, no!" Mercy cried out into the empty clinic.

She grabbed her head to try to stop her spinning vision, then ran back toward the command hall's doorway. Watching Amelia as she was coming through the door, she grabbed her friend's shoulders. Mercy could hardly say the words.

"Did you, did you wake August? Please tell me he is

awake," Mercy pleaded to Amelia, tears sparkling in her eyes and heat searing her skin.

Tilting her head to the side, Amelia softly said, "Mercy? No. I was defending Jacob's lab. Why? Mercy, what is wrong?"

Falling to her knees, Mercy saw stars cross her vision and felt the blood rush from her head.

August was gone.

They would go searching, but she knew they wouldn't find him. The restraints on the table had been cut clean through. She would have already found him. He was gone.

Amelia rushed to hold her up and gripped her arms frantically, saying, "We don't know that he's missing. Mercy, can you hear me? Mercy? Someone get my med kit. Now!"

In a dense fog of pain and shock, Mercy just sat there on her knees and stared into a vast nothingness.

After *everything*, August was gone.

He was *gone*.

What was she going to do?

Amelia tried again to rouse Mercy's attention and softly said, "Mercy, breathe. Just breathe. I've got you. We will find him. Mercy. I swear to you, we will find him."

Amelia leaned up from crouching by Mercy and grabbed a woman while she was passing by. In a seething tone she said, "Get Oz. Get him and tell him to find August. Now!"

"He's gone," Mercy said while kneeling on the blood-splattered stone floor with her eyes vacant.

Quickly tilting her head to the side to look down at Mercy, Amelia raised her hand and signaled to the dark brown-haired woman to run and do what she asked. After she ran off toward the command room, Amelia sat down on the cold floor next to Mercy and slowly slipped her arms around her.

After over an hour, Oz and Jacob carefully walked up to Amelia and Mercy. Oz knelt and sat next to Mercy, and Jacob did the same. Both silent.

All she whispered was, "He's gone."

Slowly rising from the floor, she got to her feet and softly padded straight to her apartment without saying another word.

Oz watched her with sadness in his gaze. She could barely lift her feet. She walked at a painfully slow pace toward the command room's hallway and disappeared behind the door. No one uttered a word or moved until the door shut behind her.

Turning to face Amelia as he rose from the floor, Oz softly said, "August is the only one of us missing. He and six soldiers. They must have slipped by in the chaos. I thought we guarded the door better than that, but I guess we didn't."

"I'll go tell Zoe she's just been promoted. She was his pick for second in command," Jacob said softly with tears in his eyes as he got to his feet and walked away.

Oz was torn over the loss, but he knew Jacob and Mercy would both be *broken* over it for some time, if not permanently. It all depended on whether or not they would eventually find him. He began wondering if Mercy would be able to cope well enough to be able to go on the upcoming mission. He knew she loved August, even as a child. They had to find him once this fight was over on their planet. They *had* to find him. He couldn't imagine a life where he never saw his best friend again. Shaking his head and trying to get a grip on his own mind, Oz tucked some loose hair behind his ear.

He looked around and everyone had done their part. All the dead bodies had been hauled off and the pools of blood were soaked up from the hallways, with only red stains left on the stones. Oz knew there was only one more task left before he could return to Jael.

He had to get information out of the soldiers they had captured.

Once he reached the group of bound human soldiers by the base's entrance, Oz cringed inwardly about what he was going to have to do. It was bad enough to have done it twice before, but this would be in front of everyone, and he would have to maintain his composure. He no longer had any intention of hiding the lengths he would go to from his people or theirs. It was the act alone he dreaded, potentially force feeding himself more first-hand memories from the humans who had harmed his people. As he approached, he heard footsteps behind him and slid his eyes around to find Zoe walking up with a stoic look in her eye.

After Zoe reached his side, Oz spoke to the soldiers, "*Quis hic ordonem altissimum tenēt?*" Who holds the highest rank here?

Eight soldiers pointed to one man, and he cowered before meeting Oz's eyes.

Shuddering out a breath, the man said, "*Vero.*" I do.

Zoe's stepped forward, grabbed the man by the collar, and dragged him in front of Oz.

Speaking to the man, Oz said, "*Aut facēmus modum facilem aut modum durum. Narrās mē quid inferi tu et amici praecipuī tuī hic irrumpentem in castra nōs. Vel beatus sum terebrāre in calvariam tibi et reperio ad mē.*" We can do this the easy way, or the hard way. You can tell me what the fuck you and your special friends here are doing breaking into our base. Or I am happy to drill into your skull and find out for myself.

With a look of disdain and disbelief, the man said, "*Tū rogans mē cur nōs hic sunt? Cur homina nōs interfices in silvās? Quid habent blattae stupidae facēbant omnes hōs?*" You're asking me why we are here? Why did you kill our people in the woods? How have you stupid cockroaches done all of this?

Filled with fury, Oz nodded once, and Zoe pounced on the man, flipping him over and holding his body face down.

Oz knelt, put his hand on the man's head, and placed his finger at the base of his neck.

Leaning down, Oz smirked as he whispered, "*Hic dolitūrus est parvum.* This is going to hurt a little.

Without further warning, Oz shot the spine at the end of his finger into the man's neck, and the man released a high-pitched, blood-curdling scream. His body shook from the pain while he urinated on himself. Zoe scowled at the pool of urine forming and scooted one of her boots over to avoid it.

Oz made sure to make the connection as painful as possible. Ethics be damned. This fool *deserved* to suffer.

The soldiers began pressing their bodies into the corner of the hallway, some gasping and others stoic, but all doing anything they could to get away from Oz and the others of his kind. One of the guards took notice and snapped their teeth at the humans, eliciting several gasps, and one male soldier in the front began to shed tears.

Oz continued to burrow into the man's neck until the

human stilled. Zoe let go as Oz took the information he wanted.

Zoe looked around at the soldiers and set her eyes on the one crying as she asked, "*Quis proximus est? Vel narrātūrus es mē cur inferī tū hic est?*" Who's next? Or are you going to tell me why the fuck you are here?

A small human woman in the front row with dark brown hair and green eyes spoke up saying, "*Opinarī reaffere tē omnes, quisque fundāvimus in specibus. Illa iussuī nobis sunt. Nōn cogitāvimus fundaverimus.*" We were supposed to bring you all back, everyone we found in the caves. Those were our orders. We just didn't know we would find, the woman trailed off.

"Oh. *Ille fundaveris meī homines nōn blattae stupidae cogitās sunt? Ille non sumus stupida et tacita amplius sunt? Ille docueramus linguam tuī in praesens?*" Oh. That you would find out my people are not the dumb cockroaches you thought we were? That we weren't stupid and silent anymore? That we have learned your language in an instant? Zoe asked, curling her lip in disgust.

With a crease forming between her eyebrows, the woman slowly nodded yes and then said, "*Narrābo omnes cogito. Noluī esse hīc in loco primō.*" I'll tell you everything I know. I never wanted to be here in the first place."

A scowling man beside her leaned in and screamed in her face, "*Tū proditor confundus! Tū admittēnes perduellionem adversus Imperatricem!*" You fucking traitor! You're committing treason against the Empress!

Zoe casually walked over to the yelling man, reared back and swung her fist, connecting squarely with his temple with a crack. The blonde-haired man promptly fell to his side and didn't move again.

Looking over to the woman, Zoe said, "*Si libet habēre locum secretum loquī nobis?* Would you like a private place to speak to us?

Turning to one of the armored guards, Oz said, loud enough for all to hear, "*Si ullum eīs movent antequam movēreunt ad cellam carcerem, arbitrium plenum habēs vel exhauriunt eīs vel detruncant. Nihil interest ad mē.*" If any of them move before they're relocated to the holding cell, you have complete discretion to either drain them or cut their heads off. Doesn't matter to me.

A few of the humans turned and looked around frantically at their fellow captives, and all were on edge.

Upon receiving a nod from the light brown-haired guard, Oz turned to Zoe, held his hand out and said, "*Post tē.*" After you.

With the human woman in Zoe's iron grip, they walked to the command room, and Zoe sat her at a table. Oz walked to Jacob's apartment to let him know he was needed, then went upstairs and asked Jael to join them with his tablet.

Jacob came walking down the stairs with some brand-new black headphones in his hand. He handed them to the woman before finding his seat at the table.

Once everyone was seated, Oz said, "Jael, please pull up the translation program and sync her headphones so I can use English and she will hear everything in Latin. The app will also translate her words for those of us who don't know Latin."

After a few short taps, Jael nodded to Oz and said, "Done. You can go ahead."

Oz nodded at Jael, then said, "This one soldier has decided to be cooperative and answer our questions. First, what is your name, soldier?"

She spoke in Latin, and the tablet translated, "Aurelia is my name. My family is impoverished, and I have an elderly father at home. I had no choice but to enlist in the great legion, like many of the others. I don't want to die just because the UTC's science experiment evolved and fought back. I don't blame you, especially now that I know the truth. I'm never going home. They would kill me after what I've seen here, anyway. I'll tell you anything you want to know."

"What do you mean you didn't have a choice?" Oz asked with his brow furrowed and lowered over his piercing yellow eyes.

"Humans need to eat three times a day, don't you?" Aurelia in Latin asked Jael sincerely.

Jael nodded to Aurelia after the translation, and then Oz asked, "So, you found us because of the three we killed in the woods? How did you find the base?"

"Yes, they had made a call to the UTC-S7 command center, and someone heard the screams. They sent someone to investigate and must have found some kind of evidence that it had been your kind. They sent over one hundred search teams out to the area, and someone finally saw numbers of people going in and out of the cave in timed groups. The Empress herself put out an order to bring back all of those in the caves who showed signs of evolving. We were supposed to take over and then prepare to capture all who entered until no more came," Aurelia said in Latin, and then the tablet translated it into English.

"How many of you are up north at the UTC-S7 command center?" Oz asked as he tucked a tuft of hair behind his ear.

"Including the one hundred and seventy that were sent

here, there are one thousand and sixty-seven humans at the UTC-S7 command center," Aurelia spoke slowly in Latin so that the tablet could catch every word.

Trying to hold back his shock and dread at the sheer number of soldiers, Oz asked, "Where are they located exactly? Could you draw me a map?"

"I will map out the entire command center floor plan, plus map out where all the soldier's camps are located around the S7 command center. I'll do anything you ask," Aurelia said in Latin with her eyes wide and hopeful.

"Why are you helping us? And why do you seem to know more than the soldier Oz connected with?" Zoe asked, confusion marring her face.

Clearing her throat, Aurelia said in Latin, "I had two choices before I joined the legion. To sell my body, or, well, to sell my body. I think I got fucked a lot worse by choosing the path I did, but it had its benefits. If I go missing in action or die, my father gets my pension until he dies."

"Look, I'm not going to lie. The brain drilling is something I'll have nightmares about forever, but I've been treated far better as your prisoner than they would have ever treated you as a servant. I have a chance to survive here. As for why I know so much, I am simply a collector of valuable information. Most of my people just don't care as much as I do. We've become complacent as a whole. That's the way the UTC and the first humans prefer it."

Becoming visibly uncomfortable, Jael shifted in her seat, and a frown bloomed on her mouth. Oz slid his hand over to her knee, and Jael whipped her head to him. He smiled at her in reassurance.

After a moment, Oz tilted his head to the side in thought and said, "Someone get Aurelia a drink, please.

Preferably from Risk. Do you like mango and orange juice mixed with alcohol?"

Snorting, Aurelia couldn't help but laugh until she realized Oz was not laughing. He was sincerely offering her a fruity alcoholic drink. Her eyes darted around the room, and she cleared her throat as her pale face turned a deep shade of pink.

When Aurelia finally spoke, she said in Latin, "I've never tasted a mango. So yes, I would love that. I've only had an orange once. Why are you being so nice to me? This is some kind of setup and I'll be let down in a bad way. I'm about to die, aren't I?"

Aurelia whipped her head around to everyone at the table, while they looked at her with absolute concern.

With a scowl, Zoe sharply asked, "What kind of fucked up world do you come from?"

"A ravenous one," Aurelia said in Latin as she slid her hands up to wipe her weary eyes.

Getting up from her seat, Zoe said, "I'll get you a mango and a drink, extra strong."

Nodding, Aurelia looked as though she was losing color. Jael reached over, touched her shoulder and said, "No one is going to hurt you as long as you keep your word."

She didn't believe Jael. Oz squeezed Jael's knee and said, "Yes. As long as you show us where the entire legion is located, you will be well fed and cared for, in custody, of course."

She nodded and said in Latin, "I don't know where the great legion is located, but I can make a map for the UTC-S7 Command Center and the training facility on my planet. It's called Emendo."

"How many are in the great legion?" Oz asked.

"Humans? There are over fifteen million. There are only around a hundred thousand non-humans enlisted. Humans live in extreme poverty on multiple worlds across several systems. We turn to military enlistment as a means to feed ourselves and sometimes our families. We are also offered free education, and some eventually can earn a free home. Some families have all their children enlisted and sometimes one or both parent.," Aurelia said in Latin as she adjusted herself on her stool.

Clearing his throat and holding back the terror of what he had just learned, Oz asked, "Why are humans so impoverished?"

Scoffing, Aurelia looked up at Oz and answered in Latin, "Because, the rich own the lush and beautiful worlds, and we got stuck on the terraformed and ruined planets. The rich from my world built paradise on a beautiful moon circling a gas giant while the rest of us choked to death on a planet they poisoned with industrial waste. My sister died of cancer when she was a baby. My mom worked in the sweltering plant down the street from our house, and she didn't know she was bringing home radioactive breast milk to my baby sister every night. They didn't give her a lead shield, and her breasts stuck out farther than the force field. She had no idea. After we lost my sister, my mom died of breast cancer. When I eventually left for the great legion, my father was relieved because he finally had only himself to feed. Now he's too old to work, and I have to give him all of my pay so that he can survive."

Once the drink and a whole mango were in front of a wide-eyed Aurelia, Zoe walked up to Oz and whispered in his ear. Aurelia's mouth dropped open as she reached up and grasped the cup. She sniffed it and took a sip, her face lighting up and a smile growing on her lips.

"We will finish this tomorrow, Aurelia. Zoe, can you take her to the spare apartment and allow her to change? Then post a guard at the door, please," Oz said, as he stood and looked down with disgust at the uniform she was wearing.

Zoe nodded solemnly. Oz turned to the table, bracing his hands on the hardwood as he said, "We just received a message from this *Empress*. Zoe said it popped up on her view screen, and she saved it. We need to be prepared."

Zoe continued walking away with Aurelia, and as soon as they disappeared into the apartment, Oz reached over and took the tablet from Jael's lap.

Placing the transparent glass tablet on the table, Oz pulled up the message from Zoe and sent the video to play on the larger holoscreen on the wall. It began playing, and a short blonde woman with her hair in a bun at the nape of her neck stood in a seemingly empty glass room with a clear glass balcony railing around it. She wore a grey military jacket with a red sash around one arm that was crossed and tied under her other arm. A black pencil skirt and tall heels that were a shade of grey that matched her military jacket flawlessly completed her outfit. She exuded power and had a cruel presence.

The woman's smile was enough to make Jael's stomach drop to her feet.

Under her breath, Jael scoffed and said, "No way."

In an enthusiastic tone, she said, *"Fundo tuum rebellionem improbulum parvum! Cēperis aliquot militēs, sed noli sollicitari. Habēo mulit plus venitus est ad tē."* I have found your naughty little rebellion! You may have taken a few soldiers, but don't you worry. I have many more coming for you.

Turning her head, she reached her arm out and wiggled her finger in a beckoning motion at someone off the screen. First, two shadows crossed the room, then a beautiful, bright blue woman with a curled tail and a grey band around her neck came into view. She was wearing a loose grey button-up shirt and loose pants. Her hair was pulled in a tight ponytail, and she had a human soldier at her back.

As Jael turned, the look on Oz's face was pure terror.

Jael didn't have to ask who the woman on the screen was.

It was Mazarin.

His *sister*.

She stood to the right of the blonde woman, who looked suspiciously like someone Jael knew on Earth, and glared into the camera. Mazarin's bright blue eyes seemed to glow with fury and strength.

Sliding her gaze back to the screen, they all watched as the blonde woman spoke again, "*Ut vidēre habēam aliquis praecipissimus tibi hic. Debuī solvere fortunam parvam recuperāre. Non credis quid facēns ad eam! Despicatus. Ii ibi tempore meā sententiā. Fortasse vir viridis tū et ego faceris commercia pauca. Tū et rebellēs tibi deponitis, et non demitto omnem amas ad infera planetam eadem ut misi tuum amicum rubrum.*" As you can see, I have someone very special to you here. I had to pay a small fortune to get her back. You wouldn't *believe* what they were doing to her! Despicable. I got there just in time, it seems. Maybe, green man, you and I could make a few trades. You and your rebels give up, and I won't send all of those you love to the same hell planet that I shipped your red friend to.

As if Mazarin could understand every one of the blonde woman's words, as well as the words she didn't say, she closed her eyes for a moment and then looked directly at the camera and gave it a smirk. Mazarin turned her head, and in an instant, she ran and leaped from the glass balcony head-first with her left arm tucked at her side. Her right fist was closed, and it was positioned over the middle of her chest.

Jael grabbed Oz's arm and slapped a hand over her gaping mouth.

Mazarin landed off the screen with a crash and a sickening crunch.

The soldier casually walked to the balcony edge and peered over, turning back to the blonde woman and shaking his head.

Mazarin was gone.

The blonde woman smirked and said, "*Licet, ibi habēs. Conicio respondit tibi. Mī peditēs vidēbund tē mox. Exspecto cessionem plenam.*" Well, there you have it. I guess she answered for you. My infantry will see you soon. I expect a full surrender.

Oz slowly brought his hand up to cover his parted mouth, and Jael kept ahold of his arm. The video shut off, and Oz swiftly sat down on his stool, Jael followed, and the rest of the group sat down in a rush. Everyone was staring at the table, attempting to understand what they had all just witnessed.

After several beats of silence, Oz spoke first and cleared his throat before saying quietly, "My sister was trying to tell us something. She was always finding ways to drive our mother crazy. She would bend the rules *so precisely*. No one ever did anything without her getting in a win for herself."

Pulling the video up again on the tablet, Oz zoomed in

on Mazarin as she came on the screen. Instead of looking at the blonde woman like he did the first time, he watched his sister.

His clever and competitive little sister.

He watched her closely.

He rewound and watched three more times before cracking a sad smile and sending the video back up on the screen.

"Watch her left hand. Count the taps," Oz said, with stars rimming his eyes and a smirk on his face.

Everyone watched intently, and at the end, each wrote how many taps she made against her leg with breaks in between.

Scoffing and furrowing his brow, Oz said, "It's a numerical code. I don't know what the code is for. But I'm sure my sister just gave us something we can use. She just sacrificed her life to give us intel."

54

At the table in the command room, Oz stood in front of the base's leaders and wondered what the hell they were going to do now that they had been discovered. He had thought about it for hours with no profound moment of clarity.

In his mind, there was only one choice, but it wasn't necessarily a good one.

After releasing a deep breath, Oz said, "I think we should continue with our plans. We just need to speed things up. We need to move the launch up to next week."

With his tan eyes wild, Jacob sat up straight in his seat and said sharply, "What! Are you out of your mind? I haven't finished all the simulations yet!"

"They could be here in a few weeks, Jacob. You *heard* Aurelia. She said they have a great legion that numbers in the millions. Nearly one thousand of them are just a few weeks walk north of us. They outnumber us significantly. Who knows what additional vehicles they have and what other weapons," Oz said, hoping he was making the right decision.

Jacob just scowled at Oz's response. He crossed his arms in irritation and glared, unable to come up with a rebuttal.

Clearing her throat, Zoe spoke up and confidently said, "They probably won't kill us, Oz. I think that is obvious. They might kill *you*, but they probably won't kill the rest of us. We are worth too much."

"Did anyone notice that she gave us a lead on where August was sent? Aurelia said, 'hell planet.' That could just mean somewhere hot. We should ask her more about it," Jael said with in a bolder than usual voice. She couldn't stand the tension in the air and wanted to change the subject.

She wasn't sure where this bout of confidence came from, but she would take what she could get.

Noticing the change in Jael, Oz raised an eyebrow and said, "You're right. Let's have her join us."

Sliding his eyes over to the bottom right apartment, he nodded to the guard, who opened the door and brought the timid Aurelia out to the table.

They handed her the headphones while Jael prepped the tablet with the translation software. When it was ready, Jael nodded to Oz.

Aurelia was sat next to Oz, and he said, "What can you tell us about this?"

Oz pulled up the video of the blonde woman and played it for Aurelia. When Oz's sister jumped from the balcony, she grabbed her shirt over her heart and closed her eyes.

After recovering from the initial shock caused by the end of the video, Aurelia in Latin said, "Who was the blue woman? Do you know her?"

"She was my sister," Oz said, pain laced in every word.

With her mouth agape and a hand still over her heart, Aurelia said in Latin, "What all do you need to know? I'll just tell you everything. That's the Empress herself, and they're on the bridge of her imperial ship. It has a beautiful flower garden under the balcony."

Aurelia closed her eyes tight, trying to remove the image of the flowers crushed by Oz's sister's broken body.

"Can you tell us anything about the planet where they sent our friend? The hell planet she referred to?" Oz said as he gripped the edge of the table hard enough that Jael noticed and put her hand over his.

Aurelia grimaced and spoke in Latin softly, "It's a harsh place named Aduro. The planet is a former terraformed world in a human-controlled system. It was made thousands of years ago. It is hot and dry. It's only used for its monazite mines that produce significant amounts of helium, uranium, erbium, thorium, lanthanum, and cerium. The monazite is highly radioactive, so they only use your kind for the mines because you don't get cancer or radiation poisoning. There are probably thousands of your people on the planet being used as slave labor for a royal family. They own the planet and sell all their supplies to the UTC by contract. They buy the slaves at a discount for a lower price on the product."

With growing suspicion about how much Aurelia seemed to know about this hell planet, Oz asked, "How do you know so much about Aduro? We need to know *everything.*"

"Aduro is the planet closest to the planet where I am from, Emendo. Aduro is positioned closer to the star in our system, which makes it much hotter. Melior is the name of the planet-size moon that the wealthiest people moved to, and it's directly behind Emendo. It circles a gas giant which produces its own heat. Melior is a beautiful paradise.

"Aduro is where our worst prisoners go to work alongside your kind until they die from the radiation or cancer. The only other people on Aduro are the royal family, but they are all rich enough to afford to be genetically altered so that they are immune to the radiation. They've built a lush oasis under a massive dome. The dome is positioned over the north pole of the planet, and the royals who live there are all recluses."

"Everyone on my world hates the rich. We hate the UTC. If you win your planet back, I'll take you to my planet. I'll show you exactly who knows how to get to Aduro and rescue your friend," Aurelia said in Latin, her eyes sincere and concerned.

Sitting up and looking right at Aurelia, Oz said, "*When* we win. We have no plan to stop after finding August. We plan on freeing all our people. *Everywhere*."

With her mouth agape once again, Aurelia looked around the table at all the straight and serious faces.

Aurelia's expression fell, and she said in Latin, "There are so many worlds where your people are enslaved. The UTC has other slave planets besides this one. This one is just their big secret."

"What do you mean this planet is their big secret?" Oz asked sharply.

His eyes narrowed on Aurelia.

Taking in a slow breath, Aurelia answered and in Latin said, "They paid us substantially more when we took this assignment just to remain silent about everything we saw and learned. If we don't, we must willfully submit to execution, or they will wipe out your entire family, including children. They are thorough and use DNA, so any unknown relatives are also slain. They drag them into the street and electrocute them until their bodies begin to smoke and char. The bodies are not allowed to be moved until they rot, and their bones are picked clean by urban scavengers."

With her eyes distant, Aurelia in Latin quietly said, "That was my assigned post before this one."

Sliding her eyes over to Jael, Aurelia asked in Latin, "May I ask you what system you're from?"

Visibly uncomfortable, Jael had no idea what to say and blurted out, "Um, planet Earth?"

Furrowing her brow, Aurelia asked in Latin, "Where is Earth? I've never heard of that planet."

Speaking up and interrupting Jael, Oz cleared his throat and said, "She doesn't know where her planet is, only that the UTC had been there at some point in its history. They had your language on her planet over a thousand years ago. Her language, English, is based on it. We are speaking English, and the translator changes it so you can understand."

"I have heard people speak that language before. Would your Earth be called anything else? You're not talking about one of the planets that is sacred to humans, are you? One of the planets where humans evolved independently?" Aurelia said in Latin with wide eyes and her mouth hanging open.

Nodding slowly, Jael confirmed this.

Shifting on her stool, Aurelia blew out a breath from between her pursed lips and then said in Latin, "We were told it was a myth and that the people who speak your language are lying about their origins. Some of them are homeless and wander, rambling in a language that sounds like yours. Most of them just learn our language and go on with their lives. If they don't stay silent and keep claiming they're from a sacred planet, we were ordered to execute them, publicly."

"You're saying there are other people who speak my language on your world?" Jael asked.

Aurelia nodded and said in Latin, "Yes, there is another language with a strange dialect that is like my language but nothing like yours. I wonder if it originates from the second planet that humans came from. It is said that it exists in a different system. The rumor is, the UTC is hiding hundreds of worlds that they've surveyed over the hundreds of thousands of years they've been exploring the galaxy. No one has ever successfully resisted them. So, this is all hearsay. I can't confirm anything, but I know people from home who could answer these questions with proof."

"We are taught that humans are superior because we evolved independently on multiple worlds. Some are still undeveloped technologically but have early civilizations, and some are primitive. That's all I have heard from people who are part of a secret underground resistance on Emendo. I wish I knew more, but I know places on my planet where you can get all the information you could possibly need. It comes at a cost, but you will find the answers you want, or at least where to go to find them. Only the rich have the money to know all the big secrets."

Nodding at the posted guard, Oz said, "You can take her back to the apartment now. Thank you, Aurelia. Your information is invaluable."

"Sure. If there's anything else I can help with, please let me know. I'm almost finished with the maps," Aurelia said as she walked toward the guard, reaching up to pull the headphones off.

Oz nodded and said, "Thank you."

"Carter, how much longer until the room is prepared?" Oz asked as he rose from his stool and stood next to the table.

Carter looked up at him with weary eyes and said, "We only have a few more things to prepare, then we can start moving all the holoscreens and equipment in here. I want to run a few practice rounds with simulations after we get set up."

Nodding, Oz turned to Jacob and said, "How much longer until we can launch?"

"I need at least six more days. I eliminated all the unnecessary testing, but it will be impossible if we encounter another problem," Jacob said, scowling and clearly upset about moving up the launch date.

"We need to send scouts to see how close the humans are," Zoe suggested quietly as she was typing on her tablet.

"Callum, how is Mercy?" Oz asked quietly, his eyes narrowed.

He nodded and gave a hint of a smile as he said, "She has eaten, and she has rested. She is quiet, but if I know my friend, she is going on the mission, and I don't think any of us could stop her even if we wanted to."

Oz released a deep breath and said, "Understandable. Zoe, how is plasma sword training going? Have you selected the group that will be going on the mission? How is the boat construction going?"

Popping her head up from her tablet, Zoe answered, "Yes, the group has been selected. If you are sure you only want fifteen, anyway. The boat was just completed earlier today. I'm glad we didn't wait to start building it. It's small enough for us to pull behind two of the hoverbikes. We just need to complete the integration of the new H-cell batteries on the boat's hovercart. Carter designed it so that the cart and the hoverbikes to return to the base after we use them to get to the coast."

Oz leaned on the table, bracing his hands as he said, "Great news, and yes, I only want fifteen. The majority of the volunteers will remain at the base and defend what we've built. We will need to maintain communication with them. They will be running the satellites and keeping us informed on enemy movements. Things at the base are not going to stop when we leave. Jacob will remain here and see to it. Carter, unfortunately, you are now necessary for the journey. I know we discussed you staying. Without Luna, we can't go without you. I think we need to bring Aurelia, so please brief everyone that we will all need to take turns guarding her until we build trust."

Carter nodded and said, "I understand."

Oz looked at Carter and then Zoe and said, "Carter and Zoe, please choose replacements for your positions right away."

"We launch the rockets in six days. We leave in seven."

55

Vigorous exercise was what Jael desperately needed to loosen her nerves after the base attack, and vigorous exercise was what she got. Hardly able to catch her breath, she watched as her tailed man became vengeance.

Oz resembled an olive-green God of death with his glowing plasma sword as he flipped and spun around the room, cutting down every target in seconds. The crackle of the sword echoed against the walls. Jael didn't look as graceful as Oz, or any of his kind for that matter, but she got the job done. They were both dripping with sweat, and Jael's eyes burned from the salt.

After learning the basics of the cold plasma swords, she and Oz had been practicing until she felt confident.

The handle held tight in her hand, Jael spun it in an arc and said, "I feel like a *superhero* with this thing."

Chuckling at the awe in Jael's eyes, Oz said, "It's just an oversized, dimmer version of a plasma cutter. It has the same tech in the helmets that converts carbon dioxide into oxygen, then it sends an electric current into the stream of oxygen. It also feeds the stream with oxygen pulled from the air. It's really pretty simple. It's only unique because you don't need eye protection, and it's cordless. Only drawback is it doesn't work in the vacuum of space."

"Oh, that's all?" Jael said sarcastically while panting, her clothes clinging to her damp body.

Grabbing her water, Jael chugged it and wearily said, "We are finished for today, right?"

"Yes, we're finished. Eager to get back home?" Oz asked with a growing grin.

Giving Oz an exaggerated nod, Jael said, "Of course, I'm eager to get back home. We have a hot shower there!"

Laughing, Oz led Jael from Mercy's old office and work-space back to their apartment. The office was converted to an additional training area since the humans had wrecked the training room.

They walked by Amelia's clinic, where she was conducting the last of the physicals for the fifteen people going on the mission. Waving to her friend as she walked by, Jael wondered how they would all make it through the mountain's harsh conditions. None of them were used to the cold, and Jael knew they were all dreading it.

Once they entered the command room, they walked toward their apartment. Jael wondered what Oz would do with the prisoners. Climbing the stairs, she couldn't help but look into Aurelia's window and wonder if she would have an opportunity to talk more with the human while they were traveling.

She forgot all about the prisoners when Oz pulled his shirt off and tossed it in the laundry bin in the corner of the bathroom. The defined muscles in his back alone were enough to get Jael hot. Not to mention that curled tail of his was really growing on her.

Oz whipped around and sharply said, "Why the hell do you still have your clothes on?"

Quickly stripping off her clothes as Oz approached, Jael was overwhelmed by him. He always seemed to know exactly what she wanted.

It was intoxicating.

He was intoxicating.

She peeled off her tactical pants and shoes, then removed her sports bra.

Once her clothes were removed, and she was bare to him, he slowly walked around her and said, "When was the last time you saw yourself in a mirror?"

Racking her brain over his question, Jael tried to remember the last time she saw her own reflection.

When the memory finally popped into her head, she said, "It was in the bathroom at the junior college's physics' lab. An eyelash was caught in my eye, and I had to go dig it out. That was only a few hours before I accidentally transported myself to this planet."

Oz took a few steps backward and reached over to pull a sheet off a full-length mirror propped up on the wall behind them.

Jael gasped at her own reflection. She was glowing. Her body had changed entirely, and it was so drastic she was speechless. Her arms were toned, and her stomach had lines of muscle. Her legs were thick, and she had toned curves that she had never seen on herself. Even her breasts were finally more than just a pair of perky nipples. She had *actual* breasts for the first time in her life.

Walking around her, Oz leaned over her shoulder and

whispered in her ear, "You should see the view from the back."

The heat in his eyes was burning her from the inside out.

With her instant rush of confidence, Jael asked, "What? The other side of the mirror?"

Narrowing his eyes and with authority in his voice, Oz said, "Get on your knees, Jael."

Gladly sliding to her knees, Jael looked up at him from the floor, and he pulled his length from his pants, gripping it with one hand.

"Open up," Oz said while grabbing Jael by her braid.

Complying, with her heart pounding in her chest, she opened her full lips, ready to take him.

Taking her braid firmly, Oz slid his length into her waiting mouth, and she accepted him as far as she could.

"That's good, Spots," Oz said between breaths as he angled his head back.

Jael grasped his hips with one hand and began to take his length in and out of her mouth. His pants slid down to his thighs, and she grasped him around his rear and slid a finger into his back entrance. He released a soft yelp and swiftly looked down at her with wide eyes that were filled with fire. He stopped and pulled himself free of her mouth then took them both to the floor.

Jael wanted to find out more about that little yelp of his, but quickly forgot all about it when he grabbed her under her knees.

Shoving her thighs apart he slipped his soaked length inside of her in one deliciously rough thrust. Crying out, Jael grasped Oz by his shoulders as he slammed into her over and over.

Continuously and quietly chanting, "Oz," Jael tipped over with a soft cry.

Oz leaned his head back and made deep clicks in his throat. With the sound of his clicks, her inner walls tightened around him and caused him to follow. He grasped her hips in a bruising hold as he spilled into her.

Leaning over her and trying to catch his breath, Oz had a strange look of confusion and began poking at something inside of the top of his mouth. He dug around for a moment, and then his eyes went wide with surprise.

With a plop, Oz's tooth fell out of his mouth and onto Jael's chest.

"Is that your tooth?!" Jael screeched as she looked down at one of his front teeth sitting between her breasts.

Oz snatched it from her chest, and she scolded, "You never went to see Amelia, you lying sack of shit!"

Smiling with a tooth missing on the front top left, right in front of his sharp fangs, Oz shrugged as he said, "I got busy."

He finally slid out of her, and he grabbed a towel to wet and clean her up.

Jael leaned up on her elbows and said, "What is more important than seeing a doctor about your tooth, Oz?"

"You," he replied without looking over.

He leaned over her and cleaned her gently, so she lifted her rear from the floor to give him better access.

Rolling her eyes, Jael huffed and said, "Get off me. We have to shower and then go see Amelia. We cannot go out into the bustling galaxy with a toothless President. You look like a redneck from West Texas, except green. All you need is a cowboy hat and some rock-hard, starched jeans, and you would be set."

Rising off the floor, Oz chuckled as he helped Jael to her feet and slapped her rear before saying, "We will have a quick rinse and then head to the clinic. I'm sure Amelia has some techie nanobot solution."

Once they were showered and changed, they headed to Amelia's clinic and sat down to wait for her.

Her patient turned out to be Pike, and when he finally left the clinic, Amelia emerged from the exam room and said, "So, how can I help the two of you?"

Holding the broken tooth between his finger and thumb, Oz said, "This fell out."

"It just fell out?" Amelia asked, looking at him incredulously with one eyebrow raised.

Oz lifted one side of his lip in an odd smile and said, "Yes. It just fell out."

Amelia looked at Oz pointedly and then at Jael and asked, "It just fell out?"

Bursting with laughter, Jael couldn't hide anything from her friend.

Still chuckling, Jael managed to say, "No, we were having sex, and it fell out on my chest."

Throwing her head back with laughter, Amelia braced herself on the wall beside her for balance.

"I needed that laugh. Today has been rough. Come on back, and I'll glue it in," Amelia said as she headed into the exam room.

"Glue it?" Oz asked with confusion marring his face.

"What? Do I look like a dentist to you? I'm not growing you a new tooth, Oz. I have some excellent glue. We are immune to cancer and radiation. A little glue is not going to hurt you. Stop giving me that look," Amelia said as she turned around and opened a cabinet door.

"Sorry, I just assumed you would have some medical miracle with the nanobots. I'm a little shocked at the simplicity," Oz said as he tried not to chuckle.

"It's just a broken tooth. Our teeth are solid and have small roots, but they aren't alive like human teeth. They don't require a blood supply. Open up for the glue."

Leaning his head back, Oz opened his mouth, and Amelia squirted glue in the hole where his tooth had been, then simply shoved it back in. She held it and counted to ten in her head before she let go and looked at it closely.

Amelia stood back with a smile and said, "There. Good as new!"

56

A knock on the apartment door brought Oz to his feet, and as he padded across the cold floor, he desperately hoped it was good news that he would find on the other side. The overall mood in the base had been dismal in the days since the attack.

After cracking open the thick wooden door with a creek, Oz found Jacob on the other side. His big tan eyes were full of hope for once, and Oz released a heavy breath.

Jacob cracked a rare smile and said, "The rockets are ready to launch. You told me to come to get you the moment we were ready. All the simulations point to a successful launch and deployment of satellites and missiles. We are finally showing an over ninety-eight percent success rates."

Slowly turning his head to Jael, Oz knew this was it. Everything was about to change, and his and Jael's life would be upended again. Were they ready? He honestly had no idea. All he wanted was to free his people. On top of that, he knew Jael wanted to avenge Luna's death with a passion.

"Let's go," Oz said to Jael, a smile growing on his previously solemn face.

Rising from her spot on the bench, Jael set her empty plate on the small kitchen table and nodded. She followed close behind Jacob and Oz as they walked down the stairs to the command area. In the center of the command room, Carter's team had set up holoscreens for all the teams that would control the missiles. There were over one hundred people in the command area, and all were silent. After all the years of forced silence, many still found comfort in the quiet.

Becoming unnerved by the absolute silence, Jael leaned over to Jacob and asked, "Did everyone who lives in the apartments get their belongings out? And are the rest of the helmets out of Mercy's old office closet?"

Jacob nodded as he said, "Yes, everything is out. All the prisoners have been moved to cages in the woods and are under video surveillance. They have no idea they're alone up there."

Jael chuckled. Carter clapped his hands twice and spoke loudly to the room, "Now that I have everyone's attention, I need all the teams that will be guiding the missiles to find a seat. We are launching in twenty minutes. If you've left anything in the main cavern that you cannot live without, this is your last warning to get it. There is no guarantee the blast doors in Jacob's lab are going to hold, and the rest of our base may end up in cinders."

Only murmurs were heard among the people finding seats, and no one ran off to retrieve anything. Jael was slightly surprised to see not one person had forgotten anything. She knew for sure that she would have been that one person who had to run back and get something she forgot. She watched where Oz was headed, and she decided quickly she wanted to stay close.

Oz found his position in the front, and Jael chose a seat in the front row right behind him and close enough to talk if she needed. This was all nerve-wracking, and she said a little prayer for strength. The creator knew she would need it. Fifteen minutes had crawled by, and Jael's screen finally lit up with new readings from the missile she was set to guide and then detonate.

This was really happening, and it was happening now. Memories of their preparations flooded her mind as she hoped the blast doors on Jacob's lab would hold during the launch. The possibility of one of the rockets exploding and killing them all was real, but she knew the chance was low, so she swallowed down her fears and focused on the present. It was a risk they had to take. She took deep breaths to calm her racing heart as she looked around her then up toward Oz.

Standing at the front of the room, Oz, Jacob, and Zoe watched a large screen while Carter was behind them, running the program to launch the rockets. Jael could see a large blinking red box that simply had the word "LAUNCH" written on it.

The team in charge of securing the new massive metal door at the end of the hall closed and locked it. When they returned, Carter nodded to them.

Carter pressed various options on his tablet during the few minutes they had left, and then when the timer was up, he said, "One minute until launch."

Carter passed the countdown across all the holoscreens, and Jael could see the red numbers decreasing. Meanwhile, her heartbeat was steadily increasing. No matter how deeply she breathed, she could not calm her wildly beating heart.

This was it. Everything they had done came down to this. She decided they were either about to blow themselves up or embark on one hell of a journey across this wild world. Then, they would travel the galaxy, something she had only dreamed was possible.

Whatever happens, she thought, this ride had been worth it.

It had all been worth it, she thought as she looked up at the man she loved.

The clock hit fifteen seconds, and she waited for Oz to begin the countdown.

"Five, four, three, two, one," Oz said in a slow count. Carter looked down at his tablet and pressed the blinking red box.

A second later, the cavern began to shake.

Leaning over to Oz, who had a concerned look in his eyes, Carter whispered, "That's just the door's opening."

Oz's eyebrows shot up, and he said, "Do we need to take cover?"

Chuckling, Carter said, "No, my friend. We will not feel the engines lift the rockets. Given our allotted time, they are radically sophisticated and ingenious."

Mercy felt the ground stop shaking, and she looked out of her apartment window for first time since she had come home without August. She saw everyone she loved up front and realized she was missing the best part. Nothing would stop her from witnessing this, not even her own agony. She hurried downstairs and found Amelia in the crowd to the side of the missiles' guidance teams.

Throwing her arms around Mercy, Amelia held her tight and said, "I'm glad you're here for this."

Amelia grabbed Mercy's hand and held it tight. Callum

came up behind them and took Mercy's other hand. Mercy's eyes burned as she looked up at the large holoscreen. She watched as the massive rockets slowly emerged from their home in Jacob's lab, one by one, and shot into the sky.

The three rockets had separate cameras mounted on them, and they each popped up on the main holoscreen, showing their ascent into the sky. Looking around the room, Oz didn't think anyone was breathing except Jael. Only a few short moments later, the rockets broke the edge of the atmosphere. Oz couldn't tear his eyes away as the rockets began maneuvering into position to open their bay doors and release the missiles.

Time began to slow for Oz as he held his eyes on the doors. The massive metal doors slid open, and the missiles danced into formation. It all looked exactly like the simulations. Half of them began to move forward, driven by the people sitting at the holoscreens behind him.

His brilliant people, along with his incredible human woman.

Within seconds, each missile had its targets set and was soaring toward the enemy satellites. Jael's engine design was powering them, and pride swelled in Oz as he watched them flash in and out of existence, then materialize in front of their targets. They were much quicker than the simulations had predicted.

They were instantaneous.

Were the little armed missiles *jumping* to their target points?

A thrill went through Oz, one that he had never experienced before. True bliss coursed through his veins as he watched the surreal scene unfold before his eyes.

The main view-screen had a map of the satellites and a

live camera feed of the action. Taking in a deep, slow breath to calm himself. Oz couldn't help it and he flinched inside as the first missile struck its target. Someone behind him stood up and shouted.

Soon shouts filled the cavern as, one by one, every missile found its mark. Jael's missile hit its target and she leaped from her seat, unable to hold back her delight.

Watching from the back, tears poured down Mercy's cheeks as the enemy satellites erupted in flames and scattered into space. Within three minutes, every enemy satellite was down, and the remaining missiles were being spread out over the top of the atmosphere of the planet while their own satellites were finding their positions. The auras in the sky could be seen in all their glory, spread out across the center of their sky.

Once the live satellite feeds popped up, a view of their world sprang to life on the massive holoscreen and screams and cries of joy erupted in the cavern. A large group of UTC soldiers could be seen, halfway to the village from their command center in the north. The soldiers were already turning around and heading back north when the feed lit up the screen.

Turning to face Carter, Oz smiled as he said, "Let's show these humans who they messed with. Drop a missile in their path, just north of their front line. Make them walk around the steaming hole in the ground."

Turning his head to look at Oz, Carter grinned as he said, "It would be my pleasure, Mr. President."

For the first time, Oz felt something other than disdain for his title.

This time he felt pride.

Looking at his view screen after a few simple selections,

Carter turned back to Oz and said, "Just a few seconds, and they will have quite an obstacle in their path. Our message will be clear."

Nodding, Oz turned back to the view screen and noticed Jael hugging the person next to her while they were both jumping. Jael's eyes met Oz, and she leaned down to crawl under the table. She popped up next to him, and to her surprise, he threw his arm around her and turned her to face the screen.

Just as the three missiles hit the ground north of the soldiers, Oz pointed to the screen, and Jael threw her head back and laughed. She turned around and threw her arms around Oz as the rest of the people in the cave screamed in celebration.

Jacob walked up to Carter, Oz, and Jael and smiled as he said, "The blast doors in my lab held, the base is intact, and the sliding cavern doors are now sealed. Since we now have eyes on their command center up north, I verified that Aurelia's maps of the soldiers' camps are accurate. We did it."

Delighted with the news, Carter looked over and could see Aurelia in the window of the spare apartment, a broad smile on her face, both hands pressed against the glass.

Callum walked past Carter's line of sight, and he turned back to his holoscreen to run some tests.

Callum reached over and grabbed Jacob's face for a celebratory kiss he had been patiently waiting for. Jacob threw his arms around him, and they tangled themselves in one another's arms as their lips met.

Clearing his throat as he stood at the head of the room, Oz whistled, and the sound filled the command room. Silence fell in the cavern and all eyes moved to look at Oz.

Speaking with an authority he finally felt honored to

hold, Oz said, "The blast doors held, and the base is intact. You can begin moving everything back tomorrow. Today and tonight, we are celebrating."

A voice from the crowd yelled, "Someone find Risk!"

And the whole room erupted in raucous laughter.

With the first smile on her face since the raid, Mercy turned and found Lark standing behind her.

Lark threw her arms around Mercy and said, "You were there for me when I needed help. Whatever you need, I'm here for you. We already got our tablets, so if you need anything, send me a message. We should get some drinks together since we can celebrate tonight. Are you up for it?"

Smiling at Lark and Amelia, Mercy realized August would want her to be happy. He would want her to live, not just survive.

"Sure. Let's find Risk," she said as she looked around for the eccentric cook.

Amelia was beaming and, with her tall stature, she was able to spot Risk laughing with some people in the corner.

"I found him. He's over in the corner!" Amelia said, pointing in his direction.

Lark pulled Mercy behind her, and Amelia followed. They found Risk, and when they walked up, he looked at Mercy and nodded as he got up from his chair.

"I was going to ignore the demands for alcohol, but since it's you, golden eyes, I'll go open the bar," Risk said with his usual drawl.

Mercy loved his attempt at a Texas accent. She knew they all had a little bit of an accent because of Jael, but Risk embellished it, and it was thoroughly entertaining.

With a bright smile, Amelia said, "Thank you, I think we need something extra strong tonight."

"Sure thing, doc. I'll be right back," Risk said as he walked toward the door.

Right after Risk walked out, Oz whistled again and when silence fell, he said, "It's time our people had a name. Our ancestors, the scorpions, have a name in Latin, Nepa. I think it should be part of our scientific name, but I believe our people should be called the Iungo. Iungo means to join or connect."

Nods of agreement began across the room, and Oz said, "Then it's settled. We are the Iungo people."

When Risk returned with the alcohol, anyone who wanted one took a drink. Laughter and delighted smiles spread through the room.

Callum jumped on a table, held his drink in the air and yelled, "I think our humble leaders deserve a round of cheers from all of us."

Callum turned around and smiled at Oz before he said, "Thanks to them, we *will* be free."

The cavern erupted in cheers and shouts as Callum downed his drink, then hollered at the top of his lungs as he leaped off the table.

57

Walking through Oz's village and being out in the open were not things that Jael thought she would ever be able to do. The tiny houses had lush fenced-in gardens and barrels positioned under rain traps on the rooftops. They looked so like the home she had lived in back on Earth. Aside from a few minor differences, the resemblance to the homes from her old neighborhood back in Texas was astonishing. The only significant difference was that this neighborhood had gardens in lieu of yards with crunchy dead grass.

"Your village is lovely. I wish we could stay and watch the changes," Jael said with her eyes glittering under the light of the swirling auras.

"I wish this was it, and we could just go back to the tree-house. I would want to come to visit my village, but I miss our home," Oz admitted as his eyes focused on something far in the distance.

They were mere minutes away from departing for the coast, but they had one more stop beforehand.

Knocking on the door, Oz was not looking forward to this goodbye, but he wouldn't leave without seeing her.

Swinging the door open, Oz's mother stood before him, tears not yet dried from the news about Mazarin. The back and forth of emotions from both of her children being taken or cast off were draining. One returned from certain death, and another sacrificed herself for intel to win their freedom. Her heart was in shambles, but an immeasurable pride kept her grounded and grasping onto hope.

"We can finally speak, in the open at that, and you're off on another adventure. Why am I not surprised, my son?" Faye said, a sweet smile of love blooming on her face.

Laughing at his mother's words, Oz said, "We promise to be careful. I just hope we can pull it off."

Faye reached out, grabbed her son's warm hand and said, "I know you can. Look at what you've already accomplished, what you've survived. It kills me to think of what you will face out there, but just know that I am honored to be your mother. See it through. One day, I want to see other worlds with you."

Reaching out to embrace his mother, Oz softly said, "I will. I promise."

Just then Rew came walking up behind them and Oz knelt to pet the sweet spider. Jael joined him briefly before they stood up again.

"I have my tablet, and I'll message you if anything interesting happens around here," she said with a sparkling wink.

"OK. We will see you soon," Oz said before his mother slowly shut the door, her tears silently flowing before the wooden handle clicked shut.

Oz looked back at Jael and quietly said, "Are you ready, Spots?"

"Yes. I'm ready," Jael said softly, trying to hold back tears as she followed behind Oz.

Once they reached the rendez-vous point with the rest of the people that had been selected for the mission, Jael hoped she could ride with Oz and didn't have to steer her own hoverbike. They terrified her, and she had no understanding of how they stayed afloat over the ground. She remembered driving her old tuna can, and how she always wanted a futuristic car. She was now fully regretting it.

"I see that look. Do you not want to pilot one of the bikes?" Oz asked as he grinned at Jael.

"Nope. Can I ride on the front of yours?" Jael asked, a concerned look still fresh on her face.

Chuckling, Oz nodded and said, "Of course."

"How are they getting back to the base? I assume you're not leaving them on the coast when we get on the boat, right?" Jael asked as she walked over to the bike and poked it, causing it to rock back and forth slightly.

Looking back at her while preparing his pack, Oz said, "They can reverse their course, retrace their journey and find their way home. They have some of Carter's most intelligent programming in them. I wish we could take them, but they were designed after the boat, so the boat is not equipped to transport them. We will be on foot through the mountains."

"Oh, joy," Jael said, and she sighed at the thought of future exhaustion and sore feet.

Chuckling again, Oz said, "You will probably do a lot better in the cold than the rest of us. We are not built for the cold at all. I'm getting nervous just thinking about it."

The rest of the team showed up one by one and prepped their hoverbikes with their gear and the armor they would each put on before getting on the boat.

Jael was not surprised to see Carter show up with Aurelia in tow and no guard accompanying her. Carter held a jar close to his chest as he packed up his hoverbike. Jael knew exactly what, or rather who, was in that jar. Tears stung her eyes as she turned and refocused on organizing her things.

When Mercy arrived with Amelia and Lark, Jael's heart started beating at a much faster rhythm, and she tried to think about it as if it was an extended camping trip, the camping trip with Oz that never happened. They were hiking through the mountains, then heading off to sabotage the enemy command center as well as release the captive Iungo people. Jael liked that name a lot more than the Latin *Blattae* that the UTC used.

Other worlds?

Space travel?

These things would be real very soon if everything went according to plan. They just needed to get through the several hard weeks that it would take to complete the mission.

Carter nodded to her with his arm still tightly around the grey glass jar. Grief shot through her as she couldn't help thinking about Luna. They were bringing her ashes to spread over the water when they reached the ocean. She thought about all the laughs they'd had, everything they had been through. Luna should be here, and so should August, Jael thought to herself as she watched Amelia and Mercy climb onto their sleek, long, hoverbikes.

Oz looked behind him at Jael and said, "Are you ready?"

Taking a moment to look around, Jael sighed and nodded before climbing on in front of Oz. There was no way she would fit behind him. He wrapped his long arms around her, and she leaned forward to stay out of his way. The bike hardly moved when she got on, and the experience of being suspended in the air was something she wasn't prepared for.

The hoverbike was incredible, and Jael had to ask, "How does this work?"

"I have no idea. Something about the planet's mild radiation coming from the core? And there was a part about electromagnetic waves? The rest I didn't pay attention to," Oz said.

Laughing, Jael said, "You didn't pay attention? Since when do you not pay attention?"

"I couldn't stop thinking of my tooth falling out onto your chest after we had sex the other day. Please don't move much. It's not easy for me to drive with that ass of yours between my legs," Oz whispered into her ear from behind her, causing a shiver to slide down her spine.

Before Jael could respond, Oz took off into the woods weaving the hoverbike between trees. Daring a look back, Jael found a line of hoverbikes behind them and wondered how the hell the boat would make it through some of the narrower areas between the trees.

As she looked back to the left, she saw a broader path that had thin divots from wooden wheels running along the ground. Just as she thought maybe the boat was on its own hovercraft next to them, it glistened in the light of the auras behind them on the wide path. It must have been too far behind them for her to have noticed before.

Once the entire team arrived at the beach, Jael was so windblown she wondered if she would be able to salvage her braids.

Patting her wild hair, Oz said, "I'll braid your hair again on the boat if you want."

Whipping her head around, Jael gave Oz a look that reminded him of what usually happened after he braided her hair.

Narrowing his eyes at Jael, he walked closer and whispered, "Does that look mean you want to wait until we stop to rest, after we make camp on the other side?"

Shaking her head at Oz's comment, Jael said, "That's not fair."

"It's not fair, but I do think it's funny," Oz said as he slapped Jael on the rear.

With a teasing scowl, Amelia said, "Will you two get a room? The rest of us have things to do."

Mercy, Zoe, Lark, and Amelia all laughed, and Jael felt her skin light on fire. Turning around, Jael grabbed her armor and put it on as fast as she could, hoping to hide her searing face.

Amelia looked around at everyone wearing the armor Mercy had designed, and she beamed with pride at her friend's work.

"This armor is badass, Mercy," Amelia said, looking down at her own tall figure, clad in the black high-tech armor.

Smiling at Amelia, Mercy said, "Thank you. Carter did all the hard work. I just had the idea."

Mercy looked over at Carter. He was busy calling Jacob and saying, "We are loading the boat and changing into our armor now. We will contact you again when we make camp on the other side."

Nodding, Jacob ended the video, and Carter dropped his tablet into the self-sealing bag along with his tactical clothing, then slung it into the boat. He returned to his hoverbike and pressed a button on the panel. The holoscreen disappeared, and the bike reversed course.

After everyone suited up, they gathered around Carter, who held the precious jar with the remains of their beautiful friend. Tears began pouring from Carter's eyes as he silently opened the lid. They all stood in a circle around him, and one by one, they put their closed fists over their hearts.

Jael did her best to fight a sob as Carter leaned down and poured the soft grey ashes into the water at the shore. He remained crouched for some time as he allowed his emotions to spill over before setting the jar on the sand and standing up. Aurelia stood next to him, and her tears of solidarity moved something in Jael. Maybe there was hope that these humans could change, could grow.

Jael's heart was in tatters over how broken Carter was. She had no idea he and Luna had been so close. She would make a point to speak to him about it during their trip. He was so quiet, and Jael's stomach twisted at the thought of him grieving alone. Aurelia put a hand on Carter's shoulder, and he gave her a kind nod before he silently put his hand out toward the boat, inviting everyone to board.

As they all approached the boat, Oz lowered it into the water, then he sent the small, rounded hovercraft back to the base. They all climbed in, and Zoe found her way to the controls near the front. Oz plopped down next to Jael while everyone else found a seat on the long benches on either side of the small deck.

Jael looked down at the handles along the boat's edge and said, "Do we need to put our helmets on for this?"

Oz looked back and smiled before he said, "No, you

won't even get wet." He winked at her then nodded at Zoe. The boat took off with no sound and flew over the waves.

Jael struggled to take a full breath as a sense of peace fell over her while they floated across the water without a single wave rocking the boat.

They were *untouchable*.

A holoscreen with sonar popped up, and Jael watched as a massive sea creature passed under their suspended speedboat. The waves slapped the sides of the boat and crashed over it, but not a drop fell on them.

There was a clear shield around the boat.

Watching the shore grow smaller, Jael saw the sky in its glorious entirety, and she was speechless. The gorgeous mass of twirling colors which made up the auras stretched the entire equator and reached almost to the edge of the planet. They gave the vast sky a pale indigo glow.

The view of the sky was breathtaking, and she felt Oz lean in next to her, his arm sliding around her and gripping her tight.

Smiling, Oz whispered in her ear, "This is just the beginning."

Wheeling the large, bright red and bronze man down the hall to the clinic was the last thing on Cinis' list of things to do, but after the UTC sent half the command center's clinical staff to stamp out the rebellion, they were painfully short staffed. Shifts were now more than half a day, and they were desperate for some kind of rest. The man twitched, and Cinis almost screamed, only stifling it with their sweating palm.

Running down the hall with the gurney, Cinis reached the clinic and asked, "*Nōn ago hunc. Estne hic ubi it?*" I don't do this. Is this where he goes?

Nodding her head, the woman in the reception area looked back down at her monitor before she said, "*Ad locum retro, vidēbis.*" To the back room, you'll see it.

Wheeling him to the back, Cinis became ill as they thought about what the doctors were going to do to this being. Shaking their head, they nearly left the dark-red haired man in the hall and ran, but they knew they would just end up in a collar next to the slaves if they failed at their duties -- or worse, they thought as they rubbed their neck.

The UTC would come after their sister and grandmother.

"*Ego miser. Ego miserior. Placē ignosce mē.*" I'm sorry. I'm so sorry. Please forgive me, Cinis whispered in the red-haired man's ear as they wheeled him into the door at the end of the hallway.

Walking out and shutting the door behind them, they watched with bile churning in their gut as the nurse walked over and finished strapping the large man's head down onto the spinning gurney. The nurse grabbed one of the devices used to cauterize fingernails and toenails.

Cinis thought for sure she would give him some anesthetic first.

To their horror, she didn't hesitate as she clamped his hand in the device and set the machine's settings before turning it on.

The red haired man's eyes shot open, and he screamed as the nurse just stood there with a smirk on her face. Cinis banged on the door to the clinic, and the nurse pointed to the exit, shaking her head at Cinis.

This was inhumane, and Cinis was disgusted with all of it. These creatures were not Blattae. They were intelligent beings.

They had to walk away this time, but given the proper chance, they wouldn't walk away again. They would wait for the right time, they decided. No more standing by and doing nothing. Right before leaving, they turned around and looked back at the man with the dark-red hair. The nurse was putting the device on his right hand, and he was thrashing against his bindings.

Cinis knew who that orange-eyed man was.

He was the green man's friend.

This was *fucked.*

They couldn't believe it when they heard the green one was still alive. It had all been a trick.

Walking back to their office and their observation monitors, they stopped at the main viewing room and watched a moment. Something unexplainable was holding them there to watch.

Three large objects began growing on one of the monitors, and everyone in the room seemed to be entranced by them. Not understanding what was happening, Cinis walked toward the open door of the room and kept watching. They looked down at one of the other screens and couldn't help but rack their brain to figure out what they were seeing. The large, rounded cylinders were flying directly toward the UTC's monitoring satellites.

A realization swept over Cinis, and they sealed their lips together as silence took a hold over them.

They were not saying a word.

Those were rockets, and they came from the ground between the trees. Backing out of the room, Cinis slowly met the wall on the other side of the hallway as the rockets passed right by one of the satellites' cameras.

Through the emergency coms, someone in confusion asked the base Commanders, "*Quis coniēcit missile ab solo? Quid missiles eārum constitŭerunt deducerī in orbitam hodie? Salvete? Aliquis respondēte mē!"* Who shot a rocket from the ground? Were there rockets scheduled to be launched into orbit today? Hello? Someone answer me!

Shaking their heads, several of the people watching the screens stood and began backing away. They gathered together and watched on one single screen. The rockets opened and released projectiles that blinked in and out of existence. The projectiles popped back into view next to each of the satellites, seeming to re-materialize out of nothing.

One after another, the screens began to go black.

Cinis was filled with an indescribable joy as the reality of what was happening sunk in. They were fighting back.

Cinis ran to their office and watched as their screens went black, one after the other. Smiling into their darkened screens, Cinis simply stood in awe as the sirens sounded for the first time in thousands of years at the ancient UTC command center.

It was music to their ears.

NEXT IN THE RETICERE SERIES…

Reticere Series Book Three, Janus, follows Jael, Oz, and their team as they journey north toward the enemy base.

Back at the Iungo base, Jacob and Callum travel through the remote villages on the other side of the mountains to recruit soldiers for their mission.

On a hot, terraformed planet, August struggles as he works in the radioactive mines deep beneath the surface.

ACKNOWLEDGMENTS

The difference between writing this book, and my first, was the sheer amount of research that was needed. When I was in college, I studied astronomy, which touched on astrophysics. Revisiting that school of thought has been a delight. I had a blast developing the technology and space propulsion systems discussed in the book.

As far as the biology, genetics and nanobots, I have my father, Dr. Jack Maxwell, to thank for assisting in my learning and developing realistic nano technology for my characters. He was instrumental in forming the larger series genetic plot, as well as this books specific mycology related plot. (By the way, if you are an entomologist, I do know the difference between an orb spider and a black widow.) My husband, Brandon, has an aversion to spiders, so it has been interesting writing the story and not discussing it with him. My children, however, are begging for a G rated version. We will work on that edit later.

Thank you to the rest of my family for their support, especially my mom, Sherri Maxwell, who listens to me talk constantly about these books. My friends, specifically Alejandra Toledo, have been with me on this journey, and my love for each of them is heartfelt. Writing has made many dark days brighter. Thank you and know I appreciate each reader as we travel the cosmos.

Additionally, I would like to thank Amanda Fox for the Latin translations and Bridgette Nevarez for last minute edits.

ABOUT THE AUTHOR

Lauren Logan is a neurodivergent, disabled science fiction romance author from North Texas. After high school and junior college, she attended the University of North Texas and studied Psychology and History. She met her husband in 2008, married in 2010, and they now have two little boys. They all enjoy watching science programs about astronomy as well as staying caught up on the latest Star Trek episodes.

In 2015 Lauren developed a passion for hair and began a journey that would lead her to hair school in her thirties. She specialized in vivid color and within a year and a half she had been nominated as a top 100 pastel colorist in the Behind The Chair global hair awards. Unfortunately, the ultimate hair honor had come too late. A few months before her nomination was announced, Lauren had been forced to quit her dream career as a vivid hair colorist. The loss was devastating and she fell into a dark place.

November of 2020, Lauren was formally diagnosed with an autoimmune disease, Rheumatoid Arthritis. The disease course is aggressive and effects nearly all of her major joints, as well as both hands and feet. She has developed mild deformities in her fingers, making any chance of regaining her former hair career impossible. On rainy days you can often see her walking with a cane because the changing weather can bring on a flare. Since her diagnosis, she spends much of her time unable to leave her bed due to the constant pain and fatigue. The medication she is prescribed leaves her immunocompromised as well as having many difficult side effects.

Refusing to let her disability steal her ambition and kill her determination, Lauren began writing at the beginning of April 2022. Over the course of one year, she completed two full length Sci-fi novels, and she is now well into editing the third with many more to come. Writing gives her hope and being an author gives her a future. She pours everything she is into her stories and she hopes you love them as much as she does.